Knights:
The Eye of Divinity
Book 1 of the Knights Series

Robert E. Keller

ISBN: 978-1490369310
ISBN-10: 1490369317

DEDICATION

This book is dedicated to my wonderful wife Tracy.

CONTENTS

ACKNOWLEDGMENTS

Those phantoms from the subconscious mind, emerging in the deep hours of the night and bearing random bits of knowledge of a tale left for me to piece together alone. Without their constant nagging, this novel would have remained lost in the fog.

Also, all the great fantasy writers who have inspired me.

And my talented cover artist, Carolina Mylius.

Chapter 1: The Sacred Text

Lannon Sunshield's father seemed worse than ever on this day, an aura of gloom and despair engulfing him like a poisonous fog. Lannon shrank back from that aura, but it seemed to reach from his father like dreary fingers that gripped the boy's heart and kept him from fleeing from the house. Lannon's mother didn't seem to notice, as she was lost in her usual evening rage.

"You're utterly useless," Lannon's mother snarled at her husband. "I work all day until I'm so tired I can hardly move, while empty ale jugs pile up around your feet. The least you could do is clean up after yourself."

"You know I'm sick," her husband muttered. For a moment the darkness thoroughly infested his gaze, a writhing shadow that hinted at the madness in his soul. "I can't handle things like I used to. Otherwise, you'd never have to lift a finger to do any work. I'd do it all with a smile on my face."

She threw back her head and laughed mockingly (which was one of her favorite gestures). "You say some truly funny things, husband. But I know better. You were lazy before you got sick. No, the burden of work around here is mine to bear alone."

Lannon cringed. He hated it when his parents acted like he was useless. Even though his mother's words weren't directed specifically at Lannon, they made him want to sink through the floor. Unlike his father, Lannon was ashamed of his laziness, but he did nothing to remedy it. He would stand by and watch his stick-thin mother labor to carry in firewood, and then he would warm himself before the stove. He thought dishes somehow washed themselves, and he would kick something out of his way before bothering to pick it up. Tory, however, worked hard every day, gutting fish until her hands went numb at her job in town while the men stayed home and made messes.

Lannon's parents waged their war amid an ugly battlefield that came in the form of a shoddy cabin in the middle of nowhere, complete with a leaky roof, bug-infested logs, and a yard full of decaying junk. It was the home of a man who bore a dark illness of the spirit for which no cure seemed to exist. Lannon's father spent hours glaring at bugs on the wall and making threats. He'd been arrested twice in town for splitting barrels open with an axe and insisting scheming dwarves were hiding within them.

Meanwhile, Lannon spent his days wondering when the madness would end. He had no friends, and every day was the same old thing. He wandered the forested valley that surrounded his home and then wandered it some more. He caught fish and then put them back so he might catch them again. He battled trees with sword-sticks and waited. And waited some more. He never knew for sure what he was waiting for, but he guessed it was adulthood and escape.

Lannon's father was named Doanan, and his mother was Tory. The fact that they both had names was all they seemed to have in common. They fought so much that almost nothing in the home wasn't cracked or broken. Yet their rage was seldom directed toward Lannon. Instead, the boy was treated with an odd sort of pity that was worse than being the target of rage (when he wasn't being completely ignored).

"I can do some stuff around here," said Lannon, already knowing what the result would be. "I'm fifteen years old and not a child anymore."

"Do you want me to get up and work?" Doanan said to Tory, not even glancing at Lannon. "What tasks shall I perform, your majesty?"

"Just drink your ale and be silent," Tory said, "like you always do. I don't expect you to do any work, Doanan. I gave up on that years ago. But the least you can do is keep your toothless mouth shut while I slave away."

On this warm summer afternoon, Tory had just returned from the fishery. As usual, her clothes were covered in scales. She continued bellowing at Doanan while she scrubbed her gnarled hands in a bucket of cold stream water. "I do all the work," she spat. "All of it." She looked like a spindly preying mantis rubbing its legs together. "And what do I get for my troubles? I get to come home to you, Doanan--the sorriest sod in Silverland."

Lannon's father sat slumped in a battered chair. His hairy legs poked out from beneath a filthy robe, and ale jugs surrounded his bony feet. What remained of his grey hair pointed skyward in dirty tufts. His skeletal face was covered in a map of lines, his brown eyes resting above dark spots. His mouth held shadowy gaps where teeth should have been. That mouth hung open in a huge, delighted (scary, certainly) grin. A dastardly twinkle shone in his eye, as he glanced from his wife to where Lannon stood by the door ready to escape.

"Oh, is that right?" Doanan said, still grinning. "So I'm the evil man here. This is truly funny. Isn't it, Lannon?"

Lannon knew better than to reply.

Undaunted, Doanan went on. "Look at your mother, Lannon. Just look at her. She's the big queen bee of this royal hive."

Tory raised an eyebrow and stuck her scrawny neck out toward him. Her short black hair was cut in a bowl shape with uneven edges, boyish like her gaunt face. Her left eye was open wide with bulging mockery. "That's right. I am the queen bee. And don't you forget it, husband. You know why? Because I'm the only one that does any work. If it wasn't for me, this home would fall apart."

Doanan's huge grin twisted into some kind of humorless leer. "Maybe so. But don't forget that I saved you from working yourself to death on that farm. Your father would have had you slave away until your knees were ground into meal and your back was brittle like cornstalks from a frost. If I hadn't come along to save you, your father would have--"

"Leave my father out of this!" Tory shouted. "He was ten times the man you'll ever be. And if you speak ill of him again, I'll tear your eyeballs out!"

Doanan spat on the floor. "So this is what I get for a life of sacrifice? This is what the gods have rewarded me with?"

"Be quiet, you crazy fool," Tory said, turning back to her task of scrubbing her gnarled hands. "Why don't you drink yourself to sleep? It's all you're good for these days. Goodness knows I spend enough on your ale. You might as well use it up so I can go waste more money."

"Ale is all I have, woman!" Doanan growled, kicking a jug across the room and sending a frightened rat scampering for cover. "You know it helps fight my illness. Without my ale, I would decline swiftly."

Tory threw back her head and cackled until tears actually streamed down her face. "Oh, tell me another lie, husband. You're not fooling me, and Lannon knows how you are. The boy is not blind."

"Yes, he is blind," Doanan whispered, "and so are you." He hung his head. "So is everyone in this world."

The gloom seemed to squeeze Lannon tighter, radiating from his father in nauseating waves. The sickness was soon to start making Doanan rant about things that had given Lannon countless nightmares. Lannon glanced at the door but could not bring himself to flee just yet. He felt paralyzed by his father's gaze.

"Don't start your foolish talk," Tory said, turning away quickly (but not so quickly Lannon couldn't see that her face had paled a bit). "You know that nonsense scares the boy."

"Maybe he should be scared," Doanan said. "Why not? The gods know I am. I told you, Lannon, that the shadow is the blood. Remember? It is too deep for you to see--*the Deep Shadow*. The dark beneath the dark. It is the blood, flowing beneath the skin of our world. I can feel it in my dreams. It chokes me." He gazed at Lannon crookedly. "Do you think you comprehend what fear is, my son? The Deep Shadow is fear itself. Larger than the heavens. It could eat our world just like that!" Doanan snapped his fingers. "Strip away our flesh, enslave our souls."

"I said stop that talk," Tory said, with her back to him. "I mean it, Doanan." Her hands were shaking.

"It wants to devour everything, Lannon," Doanan went on. "Whatever it touches, it undoes. Our world gets dissolved, along with our skin and bones. Then our souls are captured by sorcerers who use us in their ongoing wars. We suffer in unimaginable ways. And we can never find peace."

"I said that's enough!" Tory slammed the washbasin aside, splashing soapy water everywhere. She turned and lunged toward

Doanan, her hands raised in a choking gesture. She was so appallingly thin that Lannon looked away in helpless disgust. "One more word," she said, and you won't have to worry about your crazy dreams any longer!"

Doanan nodded, his face grim. "I'll keep quiet for now. But Lannon knows I say these things to warn him. It's for his own good. Right, my son? You understand, don't you?"

Lannon shrugged helplessly, and the paralysis that gripped him seemed to diminish. As the boy gazed at his father, he could only feel deep pity for an old man who was fighting a losing battle against some terrible, unseen foe.

Lannon's father gazed into infinity. "It's all for nothing," he whispered. "Struggle and struggle some more, and in the end, a bit of dust for our troubles. That's what's left. Just a bit of dust to mark the end of all things."

Tory flew at him.

They continued their little war, and Lannon wandered out into the yard, slamming the door behind him in frustration.

"Are you trying to break my door?" his father bellowed after him. "Sure, go on and wreck everything, you sorry little..."

Lannon sighed loudly, blocking out his father's muffled rants. "What a fine day!" he shouted, raising his arms dramatically. But as he looked around, he found that he liked what he saw. Mist swirled through the ancient oak forest, rolling across the grassy clearing where the cabin sat. The sky was purple with thunderclouds, the air charged with electricity, making Lannon's hair stand on end. A storm could hammer down at any time, and Lannon welcomed it. A storm symbolized change. Rain and mist could conceal and inspire. Mystery was interwoven into the wet earth and mossy tree trunks, in the creeping mist and the angry frown of the clouds. The dim, unhappy cabin suddenly seemed a world away.

Fresh air, heavily scented with damp forest, filled Lannon's lungs. He gazed skyward, hoping the rain would come and soak him to the skin, hoping it would awaken change within him somehow. On this day, the forest he usually despised had become powerful in some sense he couldn't comprehend, and he would walk in it gladly and give himself completely to its embrace.

Their old horse, Grazzal, stood near the edge of the field

inside the split-rail fence Lannon's father had built years ago when he was healthy. The horse raised his head, watching Lannon with his dark eyes. The coming storm sent shivers down his mane, and he stomped nervously. The roof of Grazzal's tiny stable was caving in, offering little shelter against the weather. Lannon had tried halfheartedly to repair it, but he wasn't good at fixing anything, and in the end he'd thrown an old quilt over the hole. His mother had promised to bring someone from the town of Knights Welcome to repair it, but she never seemed to get around to it (though she used Grazzal to take her to the fishery every day). Lannon suspected his mother had no intention of repairing it, considering how old the horse was. When Grazzal died, she would get another horse, and then maybe she would have the roof fixed.

Lannon stroked Grazzal's mane. "I'll fix your roof soon enough," he said. "At least before winter." He sighed. Maybe the quilt would hold.

Then, with the dismal cabin at his back, Lannon set off into the maze of mist and shadowy tree trunks, following a narrow path crisscrossed by gnarled roots. He picked up a stick and swung it absently. The fresh, earthy scents and ethereal fog helped soothe his mood, and he imagined himself as a warrior on a quest, ready to club some nasty Goblin hiding behind some huge oak. Of course, no real monsters existed this far from the Bloodlands, but that didn't stop Lannon from imagining one might have somehow made the journey. He swung his club against a rotten stump, scattering pieces here and there like Goblin bone and brain. "Die, wretch!" he growled. "And die swiftly! Ha!"

Lannon struck the stump again, and this time his stick broke. He moved on, still carrying half of his weapon. Mossy boulders, little streams, and ancient trees sprung from the mist here and there to greet him. The humidity made his forehead drip. As always, his mind crept back to his family situation. How could he persuade his parents to get along with each other and create a happy home? And as always, he could find no answer. Once he reached adulthood, he could escape the situation by moving out, but for them he saw only a dark and miserable future.

To battle the oppressive monotony of his life, Lannon had

explored this wooded valley many times over, until finally reaching the conclusion that there was only one remotely interesting place here, and it was small. Lannon called it *the Quiet Spot*. Sometimes when he needed to escape, he went there, and he could feel it calling to him on this day.

Lannon left the trail, pushing branches aside and stepping over rotten logs. A day like this was a blessing, for everything seemed to have a different look and feel. With all the fog, Lannon felt like he walked in a strange land rather than woods he'd grown up in. The same old trees, stumps, and boulders that Lannon was so familiar with took on odd shapes in the mist. Visibility was so poor that he nearly wandered past the Quiet Spot without realizing it.

The Quiet Spot was a circle of mossy boulders that stood amongst the giant oaks, with a little stream running through the middle. Lannon knelt by the stream and splashed water in his face, washing away the sweat from the humid day. He ran his fingers through his tangled blond hair, pushing it from his eyes, and gazed at his reflection in the stream. He was not a shining example of a healthy fifteen-year old boy. The flesh of his thin face looked startlingly pale, his bright green eyes staring out in stark contrast. He was a bit on the skinny side and short for his age.

His parents' harsh words to each other still echoed in his head, and their bitterness was something he could never seem to get used to. Someday (probably all too soon) his father would die from his disease, and then all of their arguments would mean nothing. Why couldn't they see that?

Lannon stared gloomily into the stream, wondering why his home had to be so remote. The isolation seemed to make all of the problems so much worse. But Lannon's father had always preferred the solitude and the quiet, claiming it helped ease his burdens somehow, and all of the wholesome plants and trees here seemed to give him greater resistance against the growing sickness.

Lannon scooped up cool water in his hands and drank deeply, splashing most of it down the front of his tunic, and his troubles were momentarily forgotten. He could feel the strength of the Quiet Spot reaching into his heart and soothing it. It was in the smell of the trees, the soil, and the moss. Lannon had found the words *Knights Valley* engraved in one of the boulders, and whenever he came here, he often imagined he was a Knight resting after a long day of combat and adventure. This area left him feeling peaceful and quiet inside like no other place could.

Lannon heard a hissing noise and looked up. A Tree Goblin was hanging from an oak limb in the fog, watching him with its huge eyes. The scrawny pale-skinned Goblin, which was only a little bigger than a rabbit, made no immediate move, but its eyes gleamed with contempt. Its mouth split open to reveal rows of sharp little teeth, and again it hissed at Lannon, before uttering a low snarl.

Lannon chuckled. "You don't scare me, little Tree Goblin."

The Tree Goblin's eyes narrowed, the evil gleam shining deeper and more menacing, while its mouth opened wider. Its face became a grimace of doom. Slowly it lowered one hand, and the black claws contracted and opened several times, as if desiring to be fastened upon Lannon's neck.

Lannon leapt up and growled. With a screech, the creature shot up into the treetops and was lost from sight. Lannon smiled and called out "Some kind of monster you are!" Being the only Goblins capable of reproducing outside of the breeding grounds known as the Bloodlands, Tree Goblins were common in these woods, and Lannon was grateful for that. He was fascinated by Goblins in general, and these timid branch dwellers could sometimes provide playful amusement for him, which he sorely needed.

Lannon sat around for a while, watching frogs leap about by the stream, and then he stood up and sighed, suddenly realizing how hungry he was. It was nearing dinnertime, and he'd slept through the lunch of fried mushrooms (he hated mushrooms prepared in any fashion) his father had cooked. If he wanted to eat, he would have to return home.

***

When Lannon reached the clearing where his house sat, three horses with finely crafted saddles and packs stood at the edge of the grass, looking like grey statues in the mist, their huge, muscular bodies seemingly carved from stone. Only their dark eyes moved, cautiously watching Lannon as he stepped from the forest. These horses were free to move about, yet they simply stood and waited patiently for their masters to return. Displayed on the black saddle blanket of each horse was the Crest of Dremlock Kingdom--a bizarre image of a cluster of three purple crystals set on a white background. Below each crest was a name and title in green letters: Cordus Landsaver, Lord Knight; Taris Warhawk, East Tower Master; Furlus Goblincrusher, West Tower Master.

Lannon's breath caught in his throat, so shocked was he that Knights had come to his little valley. But there was no mistaking it. The names and titles were very familiar even to someone as isolated as Lannon, and the breed of the horses alone was a giveaway, for these great beasts--called Greywinds--were bred exclusively in the stables of Dremlock Kingdom. No one but a Knight was permitted to ride one. Without a doubt, these horses belonged to the Knights of the Divine Order--and to the three most respected of all, the Lord Knight and his Tower Masters.

Lannon couldn't fathom why such famous Knights would venture into his remote valley. He peered in through a window. The three Knights were indeed in his home, seated around a table in the dining room and eating heartily. His father sat at the table also, looking pale yet not greatly concerned, while his mother, her hands trembling, served milk from a pitcher. Tory's face was bright red with embarrassment, undoubtedly due to the messiness of the house.

"The Knights are just visiting," Lannon whispered nervously. "Probably just passing through." Perhaps they were on their way somewhere important and had simply stopped in for a meal and a rest.

Gathering his courage, Lannon hurried inside. He'd seen these Knights before, but not this close, and for a moment he could only stare in awe at them. Taris Warhawk, the Birlote (or *Tree Dweller*, as some called them), wore a grey, hooded cloak. His bright green eyes, which were set in a pointy-chinned face, reflected wisdom and power and contrasted his bronze-colored skin. Furlus Goblincrusher, despite being a bit short in height--he was, after all, an Olrog (or *Grey Dwarf*, as some called them)--was reputed to be one of the strongest Knights ever. His plate armor and battle axe looked to weigh a ton, yet the muscles that bulged beneath that armor were more than up to the task. His beard, which was a darker shade of grey than his flesh, was as broad as his chest, while his small eyes were set beneath drooping brows. Cordus Landsaver, the Lord Knight of Dremlock, was taller than the other two, and he wore a shining silver breastplate, engraved with an image of three towers, that Lannon's gaze kept straying to as if drawn there by some unseen force. His dark hair and beard were somewhat unkempt, his blue eyes fierce.

"Greetings, Lannon," Cordus Landsaver said. "We've been waiting for you."

Lannon struggled to find his voice. Then he blurted out, "Good to meet you." He bowed somewhat shakily. He strove to calm his nerves, wanting only to make a good impression on the Divine Knights.

Cordus and Furlus exchanged an amused glance. But Taris Warhawk's gleaming eyes regarded Lannon coldly from under his hood.

"Your father tells me you were named after his brother," said Cordus. "Yet you bear the last name of *Sunshield*. A Knightly name, from the sound of it."

Lannon nodded. "My father gave me that name."

"And it's a fine name," grunted Furlus Goblincrusher. "He bears a shield of light. Not just any light, but the greatest of all found in nature--that of the sun itself. Darkness cannot exist in the presence of such a light. Yes, it's a fine name indeed."

"I disagree," said Taris Warhawk, a sneer on his lips. "The sun knows nothing of good or evil. His shield then is neutral. It serves neither justice nor corruption. It simply exists like the sun--a soulless object without Knightly stature."

"The sun gives life and warms the world," said Cordus, smiling. "Without it, all would die. What you do think, boy?"

Lannon shrugged, unsure of how to reply. Heroic last names were a tradition with the Knights, but *Sunshield* was a name Lannon had always felt was stupid. Why couldn't his father have picked something bold sounding like *Dragonslayer* or *Axemaster*? For some reason, his father had always hoped he would become a Knight of the Divine Order. Lannon had never believed there was even a slight chance his wish would be granted and he'd passed it off as more of his father's insanity. But his father had taken it very seriously. Back when Doanan was still able to work, he'd paid a woman in Knights Welcome to teach Lannon how to read and write, and he'd taken the boy to that town every year for Admittance Day (which was a day when the Knights recruited Squires) until Doanan became too ill to travel. The Knights had never even glanced at Lannon until now.

"Answer him, Lannon," his father commanded.

"It's a good name, I guess," said Lannon, avoiding looking at Taris. When Furlus and Cordus nodded in agreement, Lannon gained a little confidence. "I don't think my father could have chosen a better one." Doanan beamed with pride, having no clue how much his son actually detested the name.

"I like it," said Cordus. "But a name is still just a name-- amusing and worth some friendly debate, but certainly not very important. So can you fight?"

"I'm not too bad at it," said Lannon, stretching the truth to the breaking point. He gazed at the floor, unable to look the Lord Knight in the eye. He didn't know if he could fight, since he'd never tried it before (unless one considered swinging sticks at rotten logs to be fighting).

"The boy doesn't look very strong," said Furlus.

"I can use a club," said Lannon. "I've practiced in the woods." This, at least, was true. He'd begun to realize the Knights might be considering making him a Squire, which Lannon had always dreamt of, and he struggled furiously to think of ways he could impress them despite the fact that he didn't consider himself very impressive.

"Might be handy with a mace," said Cordus, nodding to Taris. "But are you stout in spirit? For that is even more important."

"Maybe," said Lannon. "I'm not really sure about that." He was certainly more stouthearted than a Tree Goblin, if that meant anything. "Is there a way to test me?" Lannon knew there was, for he'd seen other lads tested in Knights Welcome on Admittance Day.

"Come over here," said Cordus. "I'm going to find out for myself what you're made of."

Lannon glanced at his father. Doanan nodded to his son. A desperate hope was in his father's eyes. This was the most important test Lannon would face. It would probably determine whether or not he would become a Squire.

Lannon shuffled over to Cordus. He knew he wasn't very powerful, being a bit on the skinny side, but in the back of his mind he hoped Cordus would find something of value in him. Maybe Cordus would see something in Lannon that was hidden even from the boy. Perhaps the Lord Knight had already glimpsed something and that was why he was testing him. Did Lannon dare even hope?

"Kneel," Cordus commanded.

His knees feeling a bit weak, Lannon knelt before the great Knight. He didn't look at his father and mother, but he knew their faces were tense with anxiety. Cordus placed a hand on Lannon's forehead and held it there for a few moments. Warmth spread through the boy, reaching deep into his being and drawing forth his secrets. Feeling exposed and vulnerable, Lannon squirmed beneath that touch.

"Hold still, lad!"

Finally the Lord Knight withdrew his hand. Disappointment was in his eyes. "Enough," he said. "You've done well."

But Lannon knew he'd not done well at all. Glancing toward his father and mother--especially his father--he saw that they knew, too. Doanan's greatest wish was for him to be a Knight. If Lannon failed now, after coming this close, it might push Doanan the rest of the way into the grave. But Lannon could do nothing about it. It was up to the Knights.

"It's my turn," said Taris. "Come here, Lannon."

Feeling a spark of hope, Lannon went to Taris and knelt. Though Taris seemed at odds with Lannon, the boy hoped the Birlote would see something Cordus had missed. This time a wave of energy seemed to flood through Lannon. It left him paralyzed yet it was not as discomforting as Cordus' touch. It lasted only a moment.

"That is all," said Taris, removing his hand. His expression beneath his hood was rigid, leaving no indication of success or failure.

Next it was Furlus' turn. His touch was more like that of Cordus--a probing of Lannon's secrets. Furlus took a bit more time than the others. When he pulled his meaty hand away, he frowned and shook his head. "Not much there."

"We shall talk," said Cordus, to the Tower Masters.

The three Knights went into the living room, standing amid heaps of junk. They spoke quietly, yet Lannon had sharp ears and could hear much of what was said. He leaned against the table, watching them anxiously. He avoided looking directly at his mother and father, yet from the corner of his eye he saw they were holding hands, their eyes closed as if in prayer. This was the first time Lannon had seen them show any sort of affection for each other in many years.

Cordus paced about, while Taris and Furlus stood with their eyes fixed on their leader. "I truly thought the Signs were pointing to this boy," the Lord Knight mumbled. "Yet his Knightly Essence felt very weak, almost nothing. I doubt he could ever amount to anything. Yet he bears the name of *Sunshield*, and during the Communication, the Divine Essence said to watch for the mark of the sun, which would be found just beyond the Four Lakes. How can I ignore this? Yet I sensed no special power within him."

"I like the boy," said Furlus, "but his will is certainly not forged of steel. And I also sensed no hidden power."

"Lannon has no exceptional talent for sorcery," said Taris. "And he seems to lack any other special abilities. Yet I feel, instinctively perhaps, there is something different about him. We need to test him further somehow. Remember, we know little about the Eye of Divinity. Yet one thing we do know is that it is highly unpredictable. I feel we should talk with Lannon alone, and learn more about him."

The Lord Knight glanced sternly toward Lannon, and the boy took to gazing at the floor, pretending not to be eavesdropping. After that, the Knights whispered amongst themselves, and Lannon couldn't make out any of it. Meanwhile, their previous words tumbled through his mind, and the only thing he could gather from it was that they had yet to make their decision regarding him.

Doanan placed a trembling hand on the boy's shoulder. "I know the Knights are deciding your fate, but whatever happens, I'll be proud of you until the end of my days. Take heart in that, if no other good comes of this."

Lannon forced a smile, knowing his father might indeed be

proud of him but that it would in no way curb Doanan's deep disappointment if Lannon failed to become a Squire. Yet at least for once his parents weren't fighting about anything. The little house seemed strangely quiet.

As the Knights entered the dining room, Doanan sighed deeply, as if the will and strength had been sapped from him. He glanced back and forth from the Knights to his son. He looked as if he wanted to say something but was holding himself in check. Doanan's lifelong dream--as crazy as it had always seemed to Lannon--now hung in the balance, and Lannon's father could do nothing but wait. His words would make no difference to the Knights.

"We would like to talk to you outside, Lannon," said Cordus, "and learn more about you. There are questions that still need answering, but we need to speak to you alone."

"We could go to the Quiet Spot," said Lannon. "It's the best place in the woods, with lots of old stones. I go there all the time. "

"It's not necessary," said Cordus. "We only need to step outside for a moment and ask you a few questions, while your parents remain in here."

"I would like to see this Quiet Spot for myself," said Taris.

Cordus nodded. "If you must."

"I would be very much honored," Tory said, "if you would all return for dinner later. We are poor, but I offer you the best we have."

Cordus bowed. "Thank you for your kindness, but we probably won't be staying that long. Once our business with Lannon is finished, we must move on. The affairs of our kingdom cannot be kept waiting."

"Cordus may change his mind," said Furlus. "We could use a good meal, and he may yet come to his senses. You'll want to set the table just in case."

"That won't be necessary," said Cordus, nodding to Tory and moving toward the door. "But again I thank you for your kindness."

Furlus motioned to the table and winked at Tory. "Red meat, my lady, if you've got it. And ale, of course." Furlus nudged a jug with his toe. "I see you have plenty of that, at least." Furlus laid a few silver coins on the table. "For your troubles, of course."

"I wouldn't think of it," said Tory, though her eyes strayed longingly to the coins, which were worth more than she made in a month at the fishery. "You are a guest here, and this is not an inn."

"Consider it a gift for your hospitality," said Furlus. When she still made no move to pick up the coins, he frowned. "Will you not accept a gift from a Knight of Dremlock Kingdom?"

Tory's face reddened, and she swiped up the coins. "Of course we will! And we thank you most sincerely. I shall prepare a meal at once."

Doanan stepped toward Lannon and seemed eager to speak to his son, but then he hung his head and said nothing.

* * *

As they strode through the woods on foot, Lannon's heart raced as he led them onward. He was overflowing with the hope that he would be made a Squire, that he would at last be free of his miserable existence in this remote valley. He felt there had to be some way he could convince the Knights he was worth choosing (even if he actually wasn't). Lost in his ponderings and anxieties, Lannon wandered past the Quiet Spot in the misty woods for a fair distance before realizing where he was. But the Knights knew nothing of this forest, and so Lannon simply acted as if he knew exactly where he was going, circling back until they reached the stream surrounded by the ring of mossy boulders.

Taris Warhawk kept his distance from the others, leaning against an oak by the water. He'd almost faded into the mist, with only a vague outline of his cloak visible next to the huge, knotted tree trunk. Furlus stood next to Cordus, his arms folded across his barrel chest, frowning as he gazed at the ground.

Cordus glanced about and breathed deeply, taking in the scent of the moss and twisted oaks. "This spot feels like some areas of Knightwood, a forest which surrounds my kingdom, and the trees here are of equal stature."

Lannon nodded. His apprehension was strong, but he tried to look to the positive side of things. Even if he didn't end up a Squire, why not just enjoy spending time with these great Knights while the time still existed?

"Tell me a few things about yourself, lad," said Cordus.

Lannon gulped, struggling to think of anything even slightly interesting about his life. But there was nothing, and so finally he just told the truth. "I mostly just live here in the valley," he stammered.

"Have you ever had any strange experiences?" Cordus asked. "Dreams getting confused with reality? Or knowing things you should not be able to know? Strive to remember anything out of the ordinary."

Lannon tried, but could only remember a few odd and senseless dreams. He related them to Cordus.

"Nothing exceptional there," muttered Furlus.

Taris pulled moss off some of the boulders and knelt to study the exposed rock. "These stones were placed here deliberately," he called out. "Many have fallen, but once they formed a precise and partial circle. Quite unusual."

"Try harder, Lannon," Cordus said, apparently ignoring Taris. "There is no need to hurry. Just think carefully back over the years."

For a moment, Lannon considered making something up. It wouldn't be hard to invent one or two incidents to gain the Lord Knight's interest, provided they weren't too fantastic in nature. Lannon felt he was smart enough to make himself sound believable. Yet before he put his imagination to work, he struggled briefly with his conscience and his fears over lying to the leader of what was widely considered to be a sacred kingdom. Finally he realized his desire to escape this valley and become a Knight was too strong. He would lie if he had to and deal with the consequences later.

But Lannon never got the chance.

How long have you lived here?" asked Cordus.

"In Knights Valley?" said Lannon. "All my life."

"What did you call this place?" said Cordus, raising his eyebrows.

"*Knights Valley*," said Lannon. "I found the name on a rock."

"Show me this rock," said Cordus.

Taris Warhawk seemed to take sudden interest in the conversation. He moved over by them, a silent shadow in the mist.

"It's right over here," said Lannon. He brushed some twigs and leaves off a boulder. I found the name under some moss."

The three Knights stared at the engraving with their brows knitted in confusion. They glanced at each other and then at Lannon.

"It's just three runes," said Furlus. "This is not Olrog, Birlote, or Norack writing. Are you trying to trick us, boy?"

"I don't think he is attempting deception," said Taris. "I believe these runes are engraved in the Sacred Text. This must have been a meeting place of the Dark Watchmen. The circle of boulders reveals that. Only someone with the Eye of Divinity could read this. Lannon must have the gift."

"Then Lannon is the one we've sought," Cordus said, grinning. "Our journey here has paid off." Then, glancing at Lannon, he became stern again. "Unless he is lying to us."

"It says *Knights Valley*," said Lannon, baffled.

"The Sacred Text cannot be read by anyone but a Dark Watchman," said Taris, "which is one who possesses the Eye of Divinity. To all others it is meaningless--a code that cannot be solved. I doubt the boy is lying to us, Cordus. It seems he would lack the knowledge to invent such a scheme."

"But his Knightly Essence is weak," Cordus said, turning to the sorcerer. "This is very strange. What do you make of it?"

Taris shook his head. "I don't know yet."

"Maybe when strong enough," said Furlus, "the Essence is hidden. One cannot judge a man's strengths by appearance alone. Often the greatest power is also the most deeply concealed. By looking at me, you'd swear I could crush any man in Silverland with my bare hands. Yet once I was hurled to the ground by an old Knight who knew how to move his body so that my own weight was turned against me. So you see that it is possible to keep amazing powers concealed."

"Regardless," said Cordus, "we must surely make him a Squire. There can be no doubt."

"Yes," said Taris. "Lannon Sunshield shall become a Squire."

Lannon stared in disbelief. "Me? A Squire?"

"I shall give you a brief explanation, Lannon," said Cordus, "and it will have to do. We came here in search of one who possesses the Eye of Divinity, which is a rare magical ability. The

Divine Essence--our god and the true King of Dremlock who dwells beneath our kingdom--pointed the way to this valley, and we found you. Because you have use of the Eye, as your ability to read the Sacred Text proves, you will indeed be made a Squire, and you shall learn to master your power so that it may serve Dremlock. That is all you need know for now."

"The door is open, Lannon," said Furlus, "and someday, perhaps, a new Book shall be crafted in the Deep Forge bearing your name in silver."

"The bearer of the Sunshield Book, " said Taris, "may offer hope to all of Silverland. At last the tables may have turned in our favor!"

Cordus frowned. "Do not speak of such things, Taris, until the time is right. And as for you, Lannon Sunshield--are you ready for what lies ahead?"

"I feel ready," said Lannon, which was not stretching the truth, but mutilating it. Lannon couldn't fathom what he'd done to deserve this, and he had no idea what to expect in the days ahead (or just as importantly, what the Knights would expect of him). It was a mystery that would only be solved in its own time.

"Well, you are not ready," said Cordus. "So don't go talking nonsense. I can see that it's going to take a lot of work to mold you into a Knight. There is a difficult road ahead of you. Do you have any idea what it means to be a Divine Knight?"

"I know a little bit," said Lannon, "mainly from a book I have. I know it's your duty to defend Silverland against the Goblins, mostly."

"Then you know that is it not always fun or pleasant," said Cordus. "Many die fighting for Dremlock, and those who survive must always work hard and have little time for rest. Squires have to work just as hard as Knights. And simply because the Divine Essence pointed you out to us, and you appear to possess the Eye of Divinity, does not mean you bear any special protection other than that granted by your own abilities. Death could take you without warning. There are many grim paths that can be walked, leading to many terrible ends. Don't ever allow yourself to feel arrogant or secure."

"I understand," said Lannon, lowering his gaze.

Cordus patted him on the shoulder. "I just want you to keep a clear head about things, so you're better prepared for your new life."

"Then it's time to move on to Knights Welcome," Furlus said eagerly. "After all, there are other prospects that should be tested, and truthfully, the Lord Knight and his Tower Masters should not be roaming around without a company of guards. If the High Council discovered this, it would mean trouble for us."

"We no longer need to go to Knights Welcome," said Cordus. "We've found what we came for. Now we must hurry back to Dremlock. I'm not concerned about us traveling alone. We can fend for ourselves."

"Yet it is very risky," said Furlus. "If we were ambushed and killed, Dremlock would be empty of its three most prominent leaders."

"We're not kings," said Cordus, grimacing. "We're Knights. We can look after ourselves. And right now, we need to ride swiftly to Dremlock, and so we shall!"

"But what about a good meal?" said Furlus. "We should at least linger on a bit and have dinner with the boy and his folks. What harm could come of that, Cordus? We would lose an hour of travel at the most."

"So the real issue arises," said Taris, grinning. "Furlus' fat belly."

"We have plenty of food in our packs," said Cordus. "We can eat when we make camp later. As soon as Lannon says his goodbyes, we shall leave immediately for Dremlock. I don't want to stay in this valley any longer than we have to, for there is still much daylight left for traveling." Cordus whispered something in Furlus' ear. The Grey Dwarf nodded, but he still did not look happy.

***

When they got back to Lannon's house, the Lord Knight confronted the boy's parents. "Will you allow your son to be made a Squire of my kingdom? If so, he will be bound by the Sacred Laws of Dremlock henceforth."

"This is what we always wanted," said Doanan, his face crinkling into lines of relief and joy. "This is the greatest gift anyone could grant us!"

Tory pushed past the Knights and hugged her son fiercely. Lannon noticed how terribly thin his mother's arms felt, like bones with just a layer of skin stretched over them, and he hoped this turn of events would help her regain her appetite.

"I knew they would choose you," Tory whispered, her tears leaving his cheek wet. "Your crazy father always believed."

"Our fortunes have changed," said Doanan, hugging Tory for the first time in years. "Lannon is going to be a Knight!"

"Not a *Knight*, necessarily," Cordus cautioned them. "He is a Squire at the moment, and he may never actually reach Knighthood. That depends on many factors."

"But he's been given his chance!" Doanan howled, swinging Tory around as if all of his strength had suddenly returned. He seized Lannon's arm and yanked him close. "You have a future now, Lannon. You're going to be a great Knight."

Once the celebrating had died down, Tory asked the Knights, "Will you at least stay for dinner? If only to give us more time to say goodbye to Lannon. We won't be seeing him again for a long time."

"She has a point," said Furlus, nudging Cordus. The Grey Dwarf had caught scent of meat boiling on the stove.

Cordus nodded reluctantly.

Doanan uncorked some ale, and the four men sat in the living room and talked until dinner was ready, while Lannon eagerly helped his mother with the preparations. Lannon was having the best time of his life, overflowing with excitement, while his mother seemed conflicted. One moment tears were in her eyes and the next she was laughing at Lannon's poor cooking skills. Lannon's father seemed back to his old health, and he talked sensibly, lacking his usual grim tone. When in his right mind, Doanan was as practical and likable a man as one could meet, laughing and joking with the Knights while he smoked a pipe. They chatted about issues concerning Silverland and Dremlock Kingdom.

At last the table was set. It was not a great feast as far as quality went, but there was plenty of it. Everyone--including Tory--ate until they were stuffed. Halfway through the meal, Lannon's father grew silent, his face darkened by a frown. Tory watched him with a pained, knowing look.

Cordus whispered something to Taris, and then said, "Again, I thank you both for your kindness, but we have stayed too long."

Doanan's eyes narrowed. "I would like a moment alone with my son before he departs with you, Lord Knight. Or is that asking too much?"

"Have your talk," said Cordus, exchanging a quick glance with Taris. "But then Lannon must pack his things. We wish to get in at least a little traveling before dark. Dremlock awaits our return."

Doanan took Lannon out into the clearing, while the Knights tended to their horses. "My son," he said, as he leaned heavily on a cane, "don't worry about me or your mother in the days ahead. We'll make do one way or another. But I've always felt you were destined to be a Knight of the Divine Order."

Lannon searched his father's eyes. He saw the same old fears, but gleaming amongst them was a new light of hope. "Why did you think that, Father?"

Doanan shook his head. "Some things are better left unmentioned for now. This world lies in peril. A great darkness reaches out to take us all. But you can defeat it. As a Knight of Dremlock, you will do many great deeds. I'm certain of it. Once, many years ago, I was shown the truth of things, and it was good in some ways--yet it also changed me for the worse. My mind grew richer, but my will weakened. Then the illness overcame my body and left me a ruined man."

Lannon sighed. "I don't understand. What truth were you shown?" He always hated it when his father spoke cryptically.

"Someday you'll know," said Doanan. "This world is ancient, Lannon--far older than either of us can imagine. A struggle has existed here since the dawn of life, a struggle for food. Things eat other things to survive and grow. The darkness would devour us as well, to fill its belly and become greater. That's the only way I know how to put it."

Doanan's eyes held a crazed, distant look that scared Lannon. The sickness was in his mind again. "The things I feel, Lannon, I hope you never know. It makes my flesh frail and my blood cold to think of it. The horror that awaits us..."

Suddenly Lannon wasn't sure of anything. Did he even want to go forth and be a Knight? Would he have to face the things his father feared so deeply?

Doanan turned away for a moment, and the two stood in silence. When he turned back, a shadow seemed to have fallen over him. "Are you just a selfish boy?" his father said, his face twisting into a bitter expression. "Was I wrong about you? Maybe you're not who I always believed you were, and you should never leave this valley!"

"What are you saying?" Lannon whispered.

"Who will take care of us when you're gone?" said Doanan. "Your mother and I have nothing, Lannon. Look at you--agreeing to abandon us so easily. Where is the deep reluctance I expected? You'll eat off the fat of the land while we go hungry."

"It's not like that, Father," said Lannon, reaching toward Doanan's arm. Doanan flinched away from that touch. "I thought you wanted..." Lannon let his words taper off and swallowed. He lowered his gaze.

"Yes, I wanted you to be a Knight," said Doanan. "Because I believed in you, Lannon. But now you have given me great reason to doubt."

At that moment, Cordus started toward them, leading his horse. "We must hurry, Lannon," the Lord Knight called out sternly. "Pack up what you will, yet try to take only what you need. Food and drink are not necessary, as we have plenty of that. Yet you should bring a blanket. Now be quick about it!"

Lannon hesitated, gazing at his father again. Lannon knew Doanan was not in his right mind, but his father's words still made him feel guilty for leaving.

But Doanan seemed to have regained his senses to some degree, and he gave Lannon a pained smile. "Do as he says, my son. You must listen to Cordus and the other Knights, and not to my pathetic words. The Knights will teach you wisdom. I didn't mean to sound grim or angry. I'm just tired, and my stomach is unsettled. You will have many good things come to you in life. Now go and fulfill your destiny."

Chapter 2: The Bloodlands

Lannon packed quickly. Among the things he took with him were a couple of shabby books he'd read many times throughout his childhood called *Tales of Kuran Darkender* and *The Truth about Goblins* (both by an author named Jace Lancelord). Because books were rare, Lannon's father had paid a considerable sum of money for them back when he was able to work. Neither novel was in good condition, and *The Truth about Goblins* was so old it was on the verge of falling apart, with some of it unreadable. But those two books were Lannon's most prized possessions.

Lannon exchanged goodbyes several times with his parents before he actually got going, and just before he rode off with the Knights, he made his mother promise she would have Grazzal's stable fixed in the near future. Then he went to the old horse and stroked his fur, telling him the good news. Grazzal nibbled at Lannon's fingers, his dark eyes full of whatever wisdom a horse was able to acquire during its lifetime.

All things considered, Lannon parted ways with his parents feeling happier than he'd ever felt in his life. The Knights promised Lannon they would send a White Knight (a specialist in the healing arts) to try to cure his father's illness, which they said was an evil, deadly, and potentially infectious disease of magical origin that would grow more dangerous as time passed. There was no guarantee of success, since Doanan was thoroughly infested with the illness, and even if he was cured, he could suffer a relapse at some point. But it was still a better situation than Lannon had hoped for. And even if Doanan remained ill, his greatest wish had already been granted.

As they rode from the valley, the afternoon sky was grey and featureless, the mist lingering in the lowlands. The Four Lakes, which lay just beyond the northern rim of the valley, were not visible in the fog. Lannon rode with Taris, for the sorcerer was the most slender of the three and had the most room on his horse. As they passed over the hills, the Knights took to arguing about various issues, and Lannon listened with amusement as they went back and forth with their debates. It was different than when his parents argued. It was a jolly sort of bickering between men who seemed to have everything. (This was Lannon's first assumption, but it didn't take him long to realize these Knights faced problems that ran deeper than he could have imagined.)

Riding with the Knights of the Divine Order on his way to a new life of training as a Squire made Lannon almost giddy with delight. He couldn't wait to reach Dremlock Kingdom. Lannon was burning with curiosity to learn more about the skill that had made him a Squire. The thought that he was gifted somehow sent excited shivers down his spine. But he said nothing, figuring the Knights would tell him about his gift when they were ready.

As the afternoon slipped toward evening, they met many travelers on the road. Most were excited to see the famous Knights and stopped to chat, which made Lannon sit tall and proud in the saddle. The Knights always spoke politely, but Cordus made it clear he had no time for small talk--sometimes simply giving a nod and saying "May the Divine Essence warm you, traveler," before galloping on past.

Finally they came to an oaken bridge that crossed the Grey River, beyond which another road branched off leading westward. Lannon had never heard of this river until the Knights mentioned it, and he asked how it had earned such a name.

"It's as grey as Furlus' skin in some spots," Taris answered. "This river flows down from the Goblin Sea, where Foul Brothers go to drown themselves when they're old. Their bodies pile up, and the rotting grey matter is washed down this river."

"Foul Brothers?" said Lannon. "You mean the Goblins that look like us but are actually stupid? I read about them in my book *The Truth About Goblins*."

Taris nodded. "No one knows why they end their lives that way, but it makes parts of this river very unclean."

As they left the bridge behind, keeping to the North Road, the hills began to give way to flatland and farms. Corn and wheat fields were everywhere, and trees were sparse. Overhead, hawks, crows, and vultures wheeled about, sometimes swooping low for a look at them. Once a Goblin Vulture passed over, probably having strayed out of the Bloodlands in search of sheep. It shrieked at them in contempt. Lannon caught a glimpse of its humanoid face, which had bulbous black eyes and a mouth like a bloody gash. He pressed close to Taris. The only Goblins he had ever seen before in real life were Tree Goblins that were too timid to attack anyone but infants (and then only if they had absolutely no chance of being discovered). However, the Knights barely bothered to glance at the winged monster, and with another contemptuous shriek it soared off.

When evening had descended, and the road was becoming lost in the gloom, the Knights finally made camp. They chose a spot next to a cornfield, dug a fire pit, and settled in for the night. Despite the thick clouds, it was a warm and pleasant summer evening for camping in the open. Coyotes howled amid the corn, and bats darted in and out of the firelight. Furlus and Cordus smoked pipes and drank some ale, while Taris seemed to require nothing beyond a few sips of water.

As usual, Taris' face was partially lost in shadows beneath his hood. Lannon kept staring at the sorcerer, pondering his mysteries.

Taris took notice of Lannon's scrutiny. "Why do you gaze at me, lad?"

Lannon was caught off guard and could only shrug.

Taris continued to peer at Lannon from beneath his hood, and the boy began to squirm. The shadows hung about Taris' bright green eyes, contrasting their gleam, and some unseen power seemed to radiate from there. The Birlote's face, framed by flowing silver hair, was strange and sinister to Lannon. Taris had a hook nose and a pointed chin. He looked somewhat devilish. Lannon couldn't see Taris' ears, but he had a feeling they were pointy like his chin.

Taris, who had slipped his boots off to reveal large, muscular feet with sharp toenails, kicked Lannon lightly in the chest and knocked him over. "Enough with your staring, boy!" he hissed.

Trembling, Lannon sat up and apologized.

"The lad is just curious," Furlus muttered, laying down to

sleep, "that's all."

"I'm sorry," Lannon said again. "I meant no offense."

"You are forgiven," said Taris. "You have a curious mind, which is typically a good thing. We three are easy going, and you need not be afraid to speak or act freely in our presence." He cleared his throat. "Well, aside from receiving an occasional kick, that is. Yet some Knights of Dremlock--especially those of the High Council--would take great offense if you gazed at them like that. At Dremlock, you must watch your manners at all times, Lannon, or the consequences could be dire."

"I'll be careful," said Lannon. Being a Squire was already sounding much different than he'd always imagined, and part of him wondered just what he was getting himself into. He began to picture rigid Knights glaring at him as he walked the halls, and trials and meetings, and many long days and nights ahead. But he felt surely it had to be fun in some ways too. Just learning swordplay and sorcery alone would be worth putting up with strict Knights and hard work.

Lannon moved back farther from the flames. "Why do we need a fire? It seems warm enough tonight."

"It's a watch fire," said Cordus. "We're not that far from the Middle Bloodlands. Goblins sometimes creep forth in search of victims. They usually avoid towns and farms, but they will sometimes attack travelers camped out in the open. A fire usually keeps them away."

"I thought Goblins never attacked anyone outside the Bloodlands," said Lannon. "I thought they lacked the courage."

"Who told you such nonsense?" said Cordus. "At one time that may have been true. But today Goblins attack people anywhere they choose."

"It's in my book," said Lannon. "*The Truth about Goblins,* by Jace Lancelord." His voice was full of pride.

"Jace Lancelord?" said Taris. "That name is familiar. I remember a Knight named Jace Lancelord, back when I was a young Squire, who was booted out of the order for dabbling with forbidden magic. He had a talent for writing, too. He must be long dead by now--as that was well over a hundred years ago and you

Noracks have such short life spans."

Lannon shrugged, unsure of what to say.

"Let me see that book," said Cordus, frowning. "Jace Lancelord," he mumbled. That was followed by muttered words Lannon couldn't quite hear.

With a trembling hand, Lannon pulled the book from his pack and handed it to Cordus. The Lord Knight flipped through some of the pages, sneering at the crude drawings and simple paragraphs within.

"Undoubtedly the ramblings of a failed Knight," said Cordus. "This book was probably written strictly for profit and not for the good of humanity. Don't believe a word of this, for it could get you killed. Goblins are not to be fooled with. At Dremlock you'll be taught the *real* truth about them."

Shaking his head in disgust, Cordus handed the book back to Lannon. "You would be wise to just toss that in the fire." The Lord Knight curled up in his blanket and turned his back to Lannon. He soon began to snore.

Lannon gazed gloomily at the flames. His father had been proud of those books, and that one was Lannon's favorite. Yet Cordus had acted as if it were less than worthless. He suddenly found himself missing his home and his folks. It was easy to forget the constant arguments that went on between his parents, now that he was no longer at home, and he remembered them in a more pleasant light.

"Don't worry about it, Lannon," said Taris. "Cordus meant no harm. He was simply trying to look after your best interests. May I see the book?"

Lannon handed it over.

Taris flipped through the pages and chuckled. "Though showing no date, I can tell it is very old. Who knows, there could be something worthwhile here--especially if it was written by Jace Lancelord, rest his soul. I remember him as a wise and unpredictable man that sometimes looked too deeply into things he might better have ignored. It's a fine book, Lannon." He handed it back to the lad. "Just keep it out of Cordus' sight."

Smiling, Lannon tucked the book away.

"I'd like to be a sorcerer," said Lannon, speaking on impulse. Taris looked so strange and powerful sitting there in the firelight and shadows. He wondered if Squires got to practice sorcery very often, or if one needed some sort of special qualifications to be taught the ways of magic.

"There are many who would," said Taris, "but it's not for everyone. You have a different skill than mine. That's what you need to remember. No matter what trials you face ahead, stay focused on the one talent that made you a Squire. For that talent--called the Eye of Divinity--is as great as any."

"What does the power do?" said Lannon.

"The answer to that question is shrouded in mystery," said Taris. "As far as I know, it works in three stages--*Sight*, *Body*, and something called *Dark Wave*. *Sight* allows you to gain knowledge of things--even secret or guarded knowledge. *Body* creates physical changes upon a person and their surroundings, which can vary greatly depending upon the user. *Dark Wave*, however, is a mysterious force that few have ever gained use of. Little is written about it in the records of Dremlock Kingdom."

"What's the difference between all that and sorcery?" said Lannon.

"There is a key difference," said Taris. "A sorcerer like myself gains power from a source that Birlotes--or *Tree Dwellers* as some call us--refer to as the Webbing. It is the magical barrier that protects our world from the Deep Shadow, or the dark realm of Tharnin. We mold this Webbing--which is neither evil or good--to fit our needs. But the Eye of Divinity unlocks abilities that do not come from the Webbing. In ancient times, sorcerers wielded tremendous powers that came from within--like the Eye of Divinity. But their knowledge vanished with the ages, their secrets buried perhaps forever, and now the definition of a sorcerer is one who either gains neutral power from the Webbing, or evil power from the Deep Shadow."

They did not speak for a time, while Taris tended to the fire. Then the sorcerer sat down closer to Lannon and spoke in a whisper. "I will tell you something, while we have a chance to talk alone, but the others must not know I mentioned it. Dremlock Kingdom lies in peril from within. Certain members of the High Council have been infested with the Deep Shadow--like your father's illness, only even more sinister in nature. That is why we are in such a hurry to get back. Though there are still some on the Council who can be trusted, Dremlock is at greater risk while the three of us are away."

"Then why did you leave the kingdom?" said Lannon. "Why didn't you send someone else?" He was shocked by Taris' words. He would never have imagined that Dremlock--which he'd always believed was the noblest place in the world--could be tainted by evil.

"Only the three of us," said Taris, "have the ability to identify the Eye of Divinity in a subject--or so we thought. You proved us wrong, for had you not read the Sacred Text on that boulder, we would have believed you were just an ordinary lad and might have chosen to look elsewhere. Regardless, we left our kingdom during a time when it gravely needed us there, and we can only hope that disaster has not befallen it. I'm telling you this so you'll understand that not everyone at Dremlock can be trusted. Take care, Lannon."

"But why do you need the Eye of Divinity?" asked Lannon.

"Be patient, and eventually you will know," said Taris. "For now, you should get some sleep. We have a full day of riding ahead of us."

Lannon lay down and pulled his blanket up to his chin, wondering what forces existed inside him. Could he be like the sorcerers of old that Taris spoke of? Would he ever master the Eye of Divinity and become a powerful Knight, or would he even make it to Knighthood? He didn't like that last question, so he forced it from his mind and dwelt on the other ones until he slipped off to sleep.

***

They started out in the grey light of dawn. As the day passed, the farms and cornfields gave way to soggy lowlands. No one seemed to live out there. Save for a few crows and vultures, even animals were scarce. They met no travelers, which added to the eerie feeling building in Lannon's mind. Boulders and stunted trees dotted the lowlands, and the road became mushy, making the horses snort and stamp with displeasure as their hoofs sank in. Adding to the gloomy atmosphere, the sky remained a dull block of grey. The travelers could only see a short distance ahead in the fog, and the boulders and twisted trees briefly took on sinister shapes as they materialized into view.

Lannon wanted to know if these were the Bloodlands. But a somber mood had overtaken him, and he just sat in silence like the others. They kept a steady pace all day, interrupted only by a couple of brief meals. The air grew damp and chill. A light rain began to fall. Lannon huddled under his shabby brown cloak, feeling miserable and uneasy. Something wasn't right here. The Knights had barely spoken to each other the entire day, and whenever one did speak--usually concerning something brief and necessary--the response was a grunt, nod, or shake of the head.

"Why haven't we met anyone?" Lannon finally asked. "It seems like we're the only people on this road."

"We're nearing the Middle Bloodlands," said Cordus. "Most travelers don't follow the North Road at this point, because the Bloodlands are the breeding grounds of Goblins. The Goblins are spawned by Iracus Trees, which nurse them on blood. There is another road, back at the Grey River Bridge, which splits off and leads west. It does not pass through the Bloodlands."

"Why didn't we take it then?" said Lannon. Truthfully, he wanted to see the infamous Bloodlands and glimpse some of its strange inhabitants. Maybe he would even see a Mother Nest, which was a giant Iracus Tree with a swarm of Goblins nursing on it. The dangers didn't concern him much, for he rode with the three greatest Knights in Dremlock Kingdom and felt that surely nothing could harm him.

"Because the West Road would lead us far out of our way," said Cordus. "We would have to travel all the way to the Mountains and then cut back. And if we were to go around the Bloodlands the other way--that would take us through the Guardian Mountains, which are full of dangers I won't even speak of. The North Road, however, will more or less take us straight to Dremlock. We will save many days of travel. But fear not, lad. We're more than a match for any fish-eyed Goblin that dares try its luck. And there are Rangers who spend their days wandering the road, making sure travelers are protected and keeping the monsters at bay. In fact we probably won't even come across any of the filthy beasts, save for a few Tree Goblins and Vultures."

Lannon breathed a quiet sigh that certainly wasn't one of relief. To Lannon's way of thinking--the more Goblins, the merrier the trip would be.

"If you ask me," said Furlus, "the worst thing about the Bloodlands is not the danger of Goblin attacks or quick pools--it's the stench. At times it becomes almost unbearable, even for an Olrog like myself to handle."

"The Bloodlands have grown more dangerous recently," said Taris. "This road was used frequently by travelers only a couple years ago. Rangers were plentiful back then. Now many of them have given up on this stretch. They just don't earn enough in tips anymore to make it worth the effort."

"Now Knights are the only ones who use it," said Furlus, "save for the truly brave and truly stupid--if there's much difference between the two."

"Enough," said Cordus. "We don't want to scare the boy."

"I'm not scared," said Lannon, and then quickly added, "or stupid, either." That sent the three Knights into booming laughter.

That night they camped in a tent. Lannon fell asleep pondering what the Bloodlands were going to be like. Occasionally Taris would rise and go tend the small watch fire he somehow kept burning outside despite the rain. Later that night, Furlus took to snoring so loud the tent seemed to shake, and the others had to keep elbowing him in the ribs to shut him up, which made him mutter curses at them.

The rain continued the next day. They didn't ride far before a weathered sign came into view from the fog by the roadside. It announced:

BEWARE! MIDDLE BLOODLANDS AHEAD
GOBLIN BREEDING GROUNDS!
STAY ON THE NORTH ROAD AT ALL TIMES!

"Cover your noses," grumbled Furlus.

At first Lannon thought the Knights were exaggerating about the stench. But it crept up on him, building bit by bit, until he seemed to be choking on it. The rain grew heavier, the mist thicker. The trail became treacherous, with deep, muddy pools and great black roots that made the horses stumble. The trees that reached forth from the fog grew larger and more twisted, and shadows seemed to hang like doom amid their branches. These were obviously Iracus Trees, but Lannon no longer cared. He hung his head low against the steady drizzle, and he kept shifting about in the saddle trying to find new positions that would ease the soreness from riding. Once in awhile he looked up, imagining that the Firepit Mountains and Dremlock Kingdom would meet his gaze, but always there was only more fog, mud, and the evil-looking trees.

Lannon's thoughts dwelt more and more on home. Were his father and mother at peace now, or were they still ranting at each over every petty thing imaginable? He was nagged by guilt for leaving them to their fate, and he had to keep reminding himself that this was something they had wanted for him.

The rain fell harder. The roots that crisscrossed the road became larger and more tangled, forcing the travelers to ride at half their normal speed. The Iracus Trees grew closer together, almost as a forest in places. No sign of animal life existed here--not even Goblins, from what Lannon could see, on the rare occasions when he bothered to lift his head for a glance.

Furlus pointed at a particularly vicious tangle of roots, shaking his head. "What's wrong with the Rangers these days? They've grown lazy, if you ask me. This road used to be decent for traveling, aside from the smell. Now look at it."

"Would you want to spend weeks or months here," said Taris, "doing little but killing Goblins and chopping at roots and trees?"

"If that's how I made my living, yes," said Furlus. "And I'd do a better job than these lazy Rangers, who don't know what hard work is."

The sorcerer laughed. "What we do is not, at the worst of times, any more miserable than what these Rangers put up with. If some grow weary of it and seek their fortune elsewhere, who are we to question it?"

The Grey Dwarf glowered at Taris. "You say I know nothing of hard work? Who spends the most time with the Squires, seeing to their training? Who runs the Deep Forge and keeps the other Olrogs in line? And who hides away in his tower practicing his witchcraft, day in and day out? I do most of the work around Dremlock!"

"Enough," said Cordus. "I know we're all miserable, but I don't want to hear this nonsense from my Tower Masters. The stench is bad enough. Do my ears need assaulting as well?"

As they rounded a curve, from out of the mist rode a woman on a great white horse that was heavily laden with packs. She wore battered chain mail and dirty clothes. A dagger and sword hung from her belt, and slung across her back was a bow and a quiver of arrows. Her long auburn hair was pulled back in a ponytail. Her green eyes were stern, her face hard yet beautiful. Crouched next to her was a black wolf, watching them intently, ready to spring if the need should arise.

The rider raised her hand and the Knights halted. For a moment she sat in silence, studying the Knights and Lannon with a piercing gaze that seemed to leave no detail hidden. Then she spoke in an amused voice. "Cordus, Furlus, and Taris. Are you three on an important mission? Is this boy a spy of the Blood Legion, or a Goblin in disguise?"

"Is this any way to greet Divine Knights, Saranna?" Cordus said.

Saranna smiled. "Maybe you're not as *divine* as you think, Lord Knight. Right now you look as wet and muddy as any tree-hacking Ranger."

Lannon tensed up, wondering if a fight was brewing. Surely this Ranger had to be a fool to speak that way to the Knights.

But the Knights only chuckled.

"It's good to see you again, old friend," said Cordus. "But we must make haste and have no time for idle talk."

"I have more on my mind than idle talk," said Saranna. "There has been trouble up ahead. A wagon was hit and a rich merchant slain. His money and goods were stolen."

"And have the ones responsible been brought to justice?" said Cordus.

"They have not," said Saranna. "They've gone deep into the swamps, where even Rangers dare not travel."

"Then the thieves are good as dead," said Cordus. "The swamps will devour them. We need not concern ourselves with this matter."

"The thieves live," said Saranna. "For they are Goblins."

"Are you saying lowly Goblins stole a merchant's goods?" said Cordus. "Everyone knows Goblins lack such intelligence."

"It was done by Goblins," said Saranna. "The tracks are unmistakable. And the money chests were ripped open. I found claw marks in the wood. This isn't the first time Goblins in this region have done things like this."

The Knights exchanged knowing glances. Then Cordus leaned forward and frowned. "The merchant should not have been allowed to travel this road. Only Knights must be granted permission to pass here henceforth."

Saranna shrugged. "I lack such authority, Cordus. I'm simply here to protect travelers and earn my tips."

"I see," said Cordus. "Regardless, I have a favor to ask of you--that you refrain from mentioning this incident to anyone. We wouldn't want to stir up panic all over Silverland. That could cause trade to slow or even stop, and could possibly lead to hunger or other ills. I know that as a Ranger--and the best of your lot as far as I'm concerned--you might feel obligated to inform the people of danger, but in this case silence is the wiser path. And I now grant you authority to close this road to all who lack written permission signed by my own hand. It seems the North Road has become too dangerous to be kept open to public use."

Saranna sighed thoughtfully. "I'll discuss it with the other Rangers. Together, we can close this road to the public. Yet folks should be warned of this danger. If Goblins are becoming intelligent enough to steal money... Well, I've never heard of such a thing. This is huge news, and strange beyond imagining!"

Lannon's gaze passed back and forth from the Ranger to the Knights, and chills crept over his flesh. Goblins, growing as intelligent as humans? Lannon had always imagined Goblins as being nothing more than fierce, yet mindless, monsters--simple animals. If they actually were gaining human-like intelligence, it would make them vastly more dangerous, and he suddenly lost all desire to encounter any.

"We are doing everything possible," said Cordus, "to solve this mystery. You have to trust me, and give us time."

She nodded. "For now, I'll wait and do as you wish. Yet if the road is closed to the public, how will we make our living? We cannot survive on nothing, Lord Knight."

"From this point on," said Cordus, "you will be paid by Dremlock. You will keep the road maintained for Knightly use. In exchange you'll receive more silver than you ever made from tips, and superior weapons and armor." He took a leather pouch from one of his packs and tossed it to her. "And now here's a tip for your dedication to defending this road, Saranna."

Furlus and Taris also tossed pouches to her.

The Ranger sat like stone for several moments, while rain drizzled down. Her green eyes gazed unblinking into Cordus' blue ones. Lannon watched her in fascination. There was something very compelling about Saranna--something rugged and unyielding, yet deeply feminine.

Finally Saranna nodded. "I agree to your terms for now. But this means nothing, really. As the whole, the Rangers shall decide what must be done. There's more to this tale than I have time to tell you here."

Cordus nodded. "The message the Rangers sent us was received, so we know what has been taking place out here. But we can spare no Knights at this time. We are scattered all over Silverland right now."

"A desperate situation?" said Saranna.

"As desperate," said Cordus, "as any ever encountered by Dremlock. Now if there is nothing else, we must move on."

"Farewell," said Saranna, "and ride with caution, for the North Road has become black with peril. Four Rangers were killed in the last month alone. The West Drop and East Bloat trails are both overrun by Goblins. There's going to be a meeting at the Dead Goblin Inn tomorrow night, and then we'll learn the fate of the North Road. No one is safe here anymore."

Furlus eyed Saranna with a smug look. He pointed a thick finger at her. "Save your warnings, Ranger, for those who need it. We can look after ourselves."

The Ranger's black wolf snarled, eyeing Furlus distrustfully.

Saranna bowed. "Whatever you say, Tower Master. Good luck to you all. By the way, don't think we are ignorant about the so-called Goblin Puzzle, for it's no great secret!" With that, she galloped on past them and was swallowed up by the fog. The wolf looked them over once more, and then trotted after her.

"The Goblin Puzzle?" said Lannon.

"Don't concern yourself with such talk, Lannon" said Cordus, his eyes narrowing in irritation. "You're going to Dremlock as a Squire. You will train as the other Squires do and receive no special favors. The first thing you need to learn is that some knowledge is forbidden to you at this time. The Goblin Puzzle is something that falls into that category. If you hear someone mention something you don't understand, push it out of your mind for now. We'll teach you all you need to learn, when the time is right."

"You'll learn about the Goblin Puzzle soon enough," said Taris.

Cordus shot the sorcerer a warning glance, which Taris blatantly ignored. "Probably sooner than you'll want to," Taris finished.

Lannon fidgeted about restlessly, tormented with the need to ask about the Ranger's statements, hoping the Knights would discuss it with each other. But they maintained a staunch silence and instead concentrated upon navigating the Greywinds through the rain, mist, and mud.

At one point they passed the remains of the wagon. It lay on its side in pieces. Even to Lannon's untrained eye, there was no mistaking the claw marks in the wood. Lannon shuddered, pressing close to Taris. For an instant he felt exposed and vulnerable. Goblins had torn apart the wagon and killed the merchant. Who knew what they might be planning? Maybe they were watching right now from the mist and tree branches.

Not far beyond the wagon, they came across the first great Iracus Trees--the Mothers. Bloated and twisted, with reddish needles on their low-hanging branches, these Goblin-spawning trees had now almost completely taken the place of the others. Their bark was grey and sickly looking, and their roots were huge, rising up in arches and disappearing again beneath the mud. The Rangers had hacked down any of the trees that dared grow too close to the road, and they lay like giant, pale skeletons in the fog.

The stench clung to the travelers' lungs and throats with the thickness of molasses, fixing their faces in tense masks as they struggled to breathe.

"Where will we sleep tonight?" asked Lannon.

"At the Dead Goblin Inn," said Furlus, with a touch of pride in his voice. "We can rest the Greywinds, take a break from the stench, and get good food. It's for Rangers, mostly. Yet the inn actually does well for business, since it's the only one along this stretch. It's run by an Olrog."

"The Mother Trees are thinning out," said Cordus. "The Dead Goblin lies just ahead. I can almost smell the incense from here." Even as he finished speaking, the Mothers gave way to the lesser Iracus Trees again, with the road becoming mostly free of roots. The rain suddenly burst into a downpour, and the Knights drove their horses into a gallop. As they passed down a long, straight stretch of the trail, a sign faded into view from the fog that said:

DEAD GOBLIN INN
CLEAN ROOMS, GOOD FOOD,
AND BEST OF ALL,
NO STENCH!

The inn was set back a bit from the road, almost obscured by the mist. It was three stories high and made mostly of huge logs. The Knights took the Greywinds behind to a stable, where they surrendered them to a young Ranger whom they tipped generously, and then entered the inn.

The Dead Goblin was an appropriate name for it. Behind the bar was mounted the boulder-sized head of a Cave Troll, which was the main attraction. But there were also many smaller dead, stuffed Goblins within--such as Vultures, Tree Goblins, and a Foul Brother standing in one corner, its sad, dumb eyes gazing into nothingness and its hands raised as if to ward off the attack that had felled it. Thick stalks of incense burned in every corner, filling the inn with a sweet aroma that almost, but not quite, blocked out the stench of the Bloodlands.

Lannon stared in fascination at the trophies. Every corner he glanced at seemed to contain something interesting, and his eyes could not take in all the sights with just one pass, or even ten.

Mingled with the Goblins were wooden carvings, twisted Iracus Roots that had sinister shapes, and paintings of famous Rangers of the past.

Several Rangers sat at tables, talking over dinner and drinks. None of them greeted the Knights. Their faces were grim, and they muttered quiet words to each other. A dark tension hung about the place. The Olrog innkeeper, whom one of the Knights addressed as Sambar, was a bit shorter than Furlus, and his huge beard and flowing hair were a darker shade of grey--almost black. Ale was poured for Furlus and Cordus, and milk for Lannon. Taris drank water.

"There was some trouble earlier this day," Sambar said grimly.

"We've heard," said Cordus, sighing.

"More and more attacks!" said Sambar. "Goblins showing intelligence--even organizing into groups. What in Tharnin is going on, Cordus?"

"I wish I could say for sure," said Cordus.

"I fear the legends of old," said Sambar. "The Deep Shadow was not destroyed in the ancient war. All the Crimson Flamestone did was drive the Barloak demons back to Tharnin. The Shadow itself still exists. Could it be that another great assault is soon to be waged upon our world?"

Lannon wasn't sure what Sambar was referring to, since he didn't know much about the history of the land. But he wanted to hear more, for he felt a sudden, overpowering anxiety grip him at Sambar's words.

Cordus shook his head slowly. "There are many mysteries. But real history is fused with myth. I think the greatest peril to our world lies right here in Silverland, as it has for centuries. Beyond that, who knows?"

Sambar sighed. "Yet as far as Silverland goes, I fear the North Road is soon to fall. There are barely enough Rangers left to maintain it. I don't know if I can keep the inn open much longer. If the Dead Goblin closes, that's pretty much the end of the North Road. The Rangers need a place to sleep, to escape the stench, and so do travelers."

"It's a matter of money, then?" said Cordus.

Sambar stroked his beard. "It certainly is."

Cordus nodded. "Dremlock Kingdom will make a contribution to the Dead Goblin Inn--money and supplies as needed."

"That solves half the problem," said Sambar. "But what about the attacks? Rangers are getting killed defending a road few use anymore."

"You need better weapons and armor," said Cordus, "which will be supplied. And as soon as any Knights can be spared, I will send them down this way."

Sambar nodded. "But we need help in a hurry, Cordus, or it's going to be too late. Only the most rugged Rangers remain, and they're growing bitter toward Dremlock Kingdom." Sambar added in a whisper, "Look at their faces."

The travelers turned. The Rangers were staring hard at Cordus, anger in their eyes. A couple of them shook their heads in disgust.

"As soon as I reach Dremlock," said Cordus, turning back to Sambar, "assistance, with the exception of Knights, will be sent immediately. The North Road is vital to Dremlock Kingdom, as it gives us a direct route to the southern cities."

"But not so vital you can spare a few Knights?" questioned Sambar.

"We have none to spare," Cordus repeated wearily. "Do not doubt my words, innkeeper. If I could spare even a single one to help defend the road, I would do so. But right now it's just not possible. Now we would like some dinner."

Furlus licked his lips. "You know what I want, Sambar."

Sambar nodded. "Red meat, of course. If you weren't so ugly, Furlus, I'd mistake you for an Olrog."

Furlus chuckled. "Furlus Goblincrusher is everything an Olrog should be, Sambar. I've got blood like the fire pools of the deep, and skin like mountain rock."

"And the face of a mountain *goat*," said Sambar.

That statement brought on laughter from everyone but the Rangers, who continued to glare at Cordus with deep contempt.

Lannon kept staring a sword that was made of some type of animal bones that hung behind the bar. The sword was elaborately constructed, the bones fitted neatly together to form an elegant and fierce-looking weapon.

"That is a real Dragon-bone sword, my young friend," said

Sambar, nodding to Lannon. "It's for sale, at thirty silver pieces. *Kingdom* pieces, that is."

Furlus Goblincrusher chuckled. "Thirty kingdom pieces, for a sword made of bones? Waste of good coin, if you ask me."

"Dragon bone is quite rare," said Sambar. "And stronger and sharper than steel. And much lighter too."

"I didn't think real Dragons existed," said Lannon. "I read in my book, *The Truth about Goblins*, that Dragons are just winged Goblins, like the Vultures."

"Your book spoke true," said Sambar. "Dragons are a type of rare winged Goblin. The ones spoken of in legend probably never existed. But modern Dragons are a very special sort of Goblin, possessing great power. No man has ever slain one, or even seen one die, but their bones can be found in the cliffs beyond the West Drop. They're not easy to obtain, and very difficult to forge into bladed weapons."

"And those bones are better left to rot," said Furlus. "The best weapons and armor are made from Glaetherin, the strongest metal in existence."

Sambar nodded. "That may be true, but Dragon bone is stout stuff nonetheless, and only Divine Knights are permitted to wield Glaetherin. Even you must admit, Furlus, that Dragon bone is a worthy material."

Lannon's eyes were fixed on the magnificent sword. "I wish I had enough silver. I would definitely buy it."

"You're better off with weapons and armor forged in our kingdom," said Cordus, waving in a dismissive gesture. "That sword is no doubt a fine weapon, but it is vastly over priced. Sambar has been trying to sell that thing for years."

"The boy clearly wants the sword," mumbled Sambar. "And goodness knows I could use the money. This is a chance to help me out and help keep the Dead Goblin Inn open for business."

"But it looks exactly like the Kingdom Sword of Dremlock," said Cordus, frowning. "Some might mistake it for that and believe Lannon has been given special permission to wield it. This could cause resentment."

"It is better than the Kingdom Sword," said Sambar, "which

everyone knows is a fake. Your Kingdom Sword is actually made of Cave Troll bones rather than Dragon bones."

Furlus chuckled. "Yes, it's true. Our legendary Kingdom Sword is nothing but old Troll bones carved to look like those of a Dragon. It's the worst kept secret in Dremlock, yet always a topic for debate."

"But my sword is the real thing," said Sambar. "I can prove it." He took down the sword and handed it to Furlus. "See if you can break it."

Furlus grunted as he sought to snap it two, his huge muscles bulging from the strain. Finally he handed it back to Sambar. "Yes, innkeeper, it is Dragon bone. But it is still second rate compared to Glaetherin."

"It is slightly different than the Kingdom Sword," said Taris. "As you can see, this sword has a red sash tied to it, whereas the Kingdom Sword is adorned with a green sash. A minor difference, but still a difference."

"And there you have it," said Sambar. "The sashes are a different color and no one could possibly confuse them. The boy should have this sword."

"Do you really want the sword, Lannon?" said Taris. "You would not be allowed to carry it until you pass the Color Trials and become a true Squire. And you must never try to claim that it's the Kingdom Sword. You'll have to leave the red sash fastened to it at all times."

"Yes!" Lannon said excitedly. "I would love to have it."

"I'll purchase it for you," said Taris. "You can carry it until we reach Dremlock, and then you must leave it my care until after the Color Trials." He nodded to Sambar. "Consider this an additional contribution for your dedication to keeping the Dead Goblin Inn open."

Furlus shook his head. "It's a fine enough weapon, but not worth nearly that many kingdom pieces."

Cordus shrugged. "It's Taris' money, and he may do what he chooses with it. And if it helps Sambar out, it's for a good cause."

Taris paid the innkeeper, and Sambar sheathed the sword and handed it to the sorcerer. Taris then presented the sword to Lannon. "May this serve you well," he said, eyeing Lannon sternly from beneath his hood. "Over time, a Dragon-bone sword--just as with any sword made of Goblin bone--will bond with its owner, and in spite of what Furlus believes, it will serve you well enough. This is my gift to the savior of Dremlock Kingdom."

Cordus slammed his fist down on the bar. "Taris! That's enough of that talk. The boy hasn't even passed the Color Trials yet."

"Lannon may fail the Trials," said Furlus. "What then of the sword?"

"I will speak no more of it," said Taris, turning away.

Cordus patted Lannon on the back. "It's a good sword, and I'm sure you'll do fine in the Color Trials."

The sword felt light and perfectly balanced in Lannon's grasp. He could barely bring himself to believe that Taris had just given it to him.

Sambar started to open his mouth as if to say something, but then he closed it again and shrugged. "More ale?"

That night the travelers bathed themselves and slept in clean rooms. Lannon's belly was full of good food and drink, he had a new sword, and Dremlock Kingdom was growing ever closer. He should have been content. Yet even upstairs, behind locked doors, he could feel the anger of the men and women below. It seemed to fill the air, contrasting the sweet aroma of the incense and merging with the faint stench of the Bloodlands, which could never be completely concealed here. And deep uncertainty weighed down on him, making him restless. Just what was expected of him in the days ahead? How much were Knights concealing from him, and ultimately, what was the risk? His deepest fears whispered to him in his father's voice that death wasn't the worst fate one could encounter.

Chapter 3: Goblins, Hills, and Elder Lands

After a quick yet delicious breakfast, they set out from the Dead Goblin. The rain had slacked off, but the mist remained heavy. The Iracus Trees thickened, and the Mothers appeared again, their arching roots crisscrossing the road. The Knights drove the Greywinds as fast as they dared.

At one point Furlus' horse stumbled and went down, dumping him headfirst into the mud. Lannon started to laugh, but when he saw the look on Furlus' face, he strangled it. Bellowing curses, Furlus lunged up, his beard dripping filth and his dark eyes blazing with fury. He wiped his beard with his sleeve, grabbed the root that had felled his horse, and tore it two. Dark blood poured out from the severed ends. The angry Tower Master cast the ends aside.

"I've had enough of this, Cordus!" Furlus' brow was knotted with rage. "We leave a comfortable inn and ride like Tharnin through this slop--for no good reason! We could have stayed another night and waited for better weather."

Cordus sighed. "Do you want to go back? You saw the way the Rangers regarded us. I don't know about you, but I have no wish to spend another night at that inn. And, considering what we're facing, we dare not waste even a single day. Now get on your horse and ride with us, or go stay with the Rangers. But I'll move on and tonight sleep amongst the Northern Hills where I won't have a bunch of contemptuous people breathing down my neck."

Furlus nodded, his face red with embarrassment. "Since you put it that way, I'll keep quiet." He patted his horse and then swung up into the saddle.

"Where's the Scribe," Taris said, smiling. "We need to record this wondrous moment. Furlus Goblincrusher admitting he is wrong!"

"I admitted nothing, oh dark one," said Furlus, wringing out his beard. "I simply said I'd keep quiet for now. Let's just concentrate on getting through this giant dung pit. I've had too much open sky above me on this journey, and now these filthy Bloodlands are getting to me. I guess I just need to get back to the silver mines and the Deep Forge."

"Of course," said Taris. "We all know how lovely the mines are."

"A Tree Dweller like you wouldn't understand," mumbled Furlus.

The stench and misery continued throughout the day. The riders became distracted, paying little heed to their surroundings. They simply pushed onward as the hours slipped by. They ate a quick lunch of dry foods, without dismounting, and rode without pause until dinner. At dinner, they seated themselves on a log and forced down some leftovers from the inn.

When they set off again, the Iracus Trees formed a forest, while the mist became almost like a solid wall. They were forced to go slower than ever. Twice, Taris stopped his horse and sat still, gazing off into the fog as if straining to see or hear something. But when asked about it by Cordus, he simply shook his head and they continued on. Because the sun was lost from view, it was difficult to tell what time of day it was, but they felt it was nearing evening.

When Taris stopped for the third time, the sorcerer spoke. "I think Goblins are watching us. I can't tell how many, or their kind."

"How long have they been following?" Cordus asked.

"I'm not sure."

Furlus readied his axe. "Something to interrupt the boredom, I guess."

"Let us hope they're not Goblin Lords," said Cordus, drawing his broadsword. "That's the last thing we need right now."

"Not likely," said Taris. "No Goblin Lord has ever been spotted near the Middle Bloodlands. But anything is possible, I suppose."

Cordus shook his head. "Before breakfast, Sambar described, for me alone, Goblins that resembled Lords. A Ranger spotted them on the road. I fear they might be planning to finish us off before we reach Dremlock."

"I'll bet they're waiting for us to pass through the North Gate," said Furlus. "Then they will try to ambush us."

"You should have told us earlier," said Taris, shooting Cordus an angry glance. "Why did you wait?"

"I didn't want to scare the boy," said Cordus.

"But if these are indeed Goblin Lords we're dealing with," said Taris, "then we should have been watching for them."

"We were staying alert, regardless," said Cordus. "I intended to tell you, but the hours slipped past quickly."

Lannon glanced about, but all he could see was mist. His hands clenched Taris' cloak so hard his fingers ached. He thought he could feel yellow eyes peering out at him, teeth and claws ready to rip the flesh from his bones like they had done to the merchant. He began to tremble, suddenly wishing he were safely back in Knights Valley or at Dremlock Kingdom--anywhere but in the Bloodlands.

"Calm yourself, Lannon," Taris said to him. "We will protect you."

"Draw your sword, Lannon," Cordus commanded.

"What?" said Lannon. "You mean...?"

"You ride with Knights," said Cordus. "You are expected to fight with us if need be. You wanted the sword, and now it is yours. Thus, we no longer protect an unarmed lad. Now, draw your sword!"

With a trembling hand, Lannon drew the bone sword from the sheath at his belt. It felt cumbersome and useless in his grasp. He had no desire to test his skill against the Goblins.

Cordus nodded to him. "You will fight only when ordered to, however. Is that understood?"

"It is definitely understood," said Lannon, breathing a sigh of relief.

The Knights stared off into the mist, and exchanged concerned glances. Grim tension hung between them. Even the horses seemed to feel it, for they whinnied nervously.

The land crept upward and then flattened. The mist thinned, revealing two huge boulders on either side of the road. Smaller boulders lay just beyond them, barely visible in the fog. Thick Iracus roots clung to the two big rocks, hanging off them like ragged spider webs, their strands disappearing into the mist.

"The North Gate," Cordus said quietly. "The Hills lie not far beyond. This is where the Goblins will probably make their attack."

Taris rode up alongside him. "I sense the Goblins are close." The sorcerer pulled a stone dagger from his cloak, and it erupted into greenish flames.

Just then, a tall figure walked from the mist. It was a Foul Brother--yet certainly not one of normal intelligence (which for a Foul Brother was virtually no intelligence at all). It wore a black cloak and carried a twisted wooden staff. It was powerfully built, with hands and feet that were slightly larger than those of a human, and its head was bald, with deep lines in its forehead. Its dark eyes--usually sad and dumb on these creatures--were narrowed with focus. A single red rune was painted on its forehead.

Lurking behind it were two dark, wolf-like Goblins with tails and claws, their green eyes shining wickedly. They held back, standing on their crooked hind legs, just barely visible in the fog. The humanoid Goblin walked between the two great boulders and stood facing them in the road. It raised the staff menacingly.

"A Lord!" Taris whispered.

Cordus held forth his broadsword. The blade gleamed brightly--almost white--as if charged with pale energy.

"Stand aside," Cordus ordered the Goblin Lord. "You dare block the path of Divine Knights? We are on important business."

The Goblin snorted with laughter. A whisper curled out from it like icy fingers that seemed to creep over their flesh, causing chills. The horses shifted about uneasily, but held their ground. Lannon pressed closer to Taris. His heartbeat was pounding hard in his ears.

"I am simply a messenger sent to warn you," the Goblin Lord said. "Soon Dremlock Kingdom will fall. The ways of the past will no longer prevail against us. Leave Silverland while you still can."

Furlus drove his horse forward, scowling, but Cordus stopped him with a motion of his hand. "What is this nonsense you talk?" said Cordus. "Do you really think your words make any difference? Your fate is sealed in steel and blood. Silverland will soon be free of your evil."

"I do not fear you," the Goblin Lord hissed. "You cannot slay me. I alone seal your fate and that of Dremlock Kingdom. Give up, Lord Knight, while you still have the chance. There is no shame in it."

"Give up?" Cordus' blue eyes burned with fury. "Defend yourself, Goblin, for I now take your filthy head!" With that, Cordus' slapped his horse on the neck. The Greywind steadied itself, snorting, and then charged.

The two wolf-like creatures slipped away into the mist.

The Goblin Lord hurled its staff at Cordus. The twisted piece of wood smoldered with dark flames as it tumbled towards the Lord Knight.

Cordus cleaved the staff in two, causing it to explode in a shower of purple sparks and burning fragments, most of which glanced off Cordus' magnificent silver breastplate. Unharmed, Cordus calmly brushed coals from his beard. The Goblin turned to flee.

Cordus' gleaming blade lashed out and sliced off the Goblin Lord's head. The body slumped to the ground, the head rolling off into the mist.

"Let us ride swiftly from this place," said Cordus. "Do not look back, Lannon."

But as they started off, Lannon's curiosity got the best of him. He and Taris rode at the rear, with Cordus in the lead, and so he chanced a look behind him. Sprouting from the neck of the dead Goblin were dark tendrils. They slithered across the ground towards something in the fog. Quickly Lannon turned away, his face pale.

From out of the mist behind them came evil laughter.

***

"Why didn't they try to finish us off?" Taris asked, as the horses again slowed to a trot. "That entire affair seemed pointless."

"The Goblin Lord and his Wolves were sent to intimidate me," said Cordus. "If I falter, so will Dremlock Kingdom. That is what our enemies believe. We were expecting an attack, so they surprised us with a warning." He nodded toward Lannon. "If they knew the true nature of this mission, they would surely have thrown all their might against us. Obviously, some secrets remain hidden to our foes."

"But how did they know we were on the North Road?" said Taris.

"They watch us," said Cordus, "with methods we cannot yet imagine. From the moment we left Dremlock, they must have planned that encounter at the North Gate. They suspect we're on a vital mission, the three Tower Masters riding alone from Dremlock when our kingdom is in peril. Yet what have they learned? Only that we ride with a boy."

Gazing into the fog, Taris said nothing

"We should not speak of this," said Cordus, "when the lad is with us. Lannon, you shall not mention a word of this to anyone. If you do, there may be grim consequences that even I cannot foresee. Being exiled from the kingdom would certainly be one of those consequences." The Lord Knight stared hard at Lannon, his eyes burning deep into the boy, demanding total obedience.

"I won't tell anyone," said Lannon, and he meant it with all his heart. Emotions swirled through his mind--terror over the future, awe of the Knightly power he had just witnessed, and a lingering gloom from the Goblin Lord's aura. He felt he could understand his father's illness better now, after what he had encountered in the Bloodlands. The darkness was real, and it was hungry--just like his father had said. He had felt the very surface of it, and underneath lay things he dared not try to imagine.

Lannon realized his father wasn't weak willed at all. He was a strong man to have stared into the very heart of darkness and still kept some measure of his sanity. Even after many years of existing inside him, clawing at his father's body and mind, the shadows had not yet consumed him.

As evening settled in, the Middle Bloodlands began to give way to hill country. The hills were huge, the road winding between them and sometimes creeping over them. The Iracus Trees surrendered to towering pines, which grew sparsely and were straight, tall, and noble compared to the twisted Goblin trees. The roots vanished from the trail (save for an occasional knotty pine root), and the stench slipped away, leaving only fresh air. The weather had cleared some, and from the hilltops they could see the Firepit Mountains beyond the forests, hills, and misty valleys.

Crumbling stone ruins stood on some of the hills. Most resembled the remains of keeps and fortresses, while others were little more than shapeless masses of rubble. "These are the Elder Lands," Cordus told Lannon. "Some of the most ancient kingdoms on our continent of Gallamerth existed here. The names and origins of many have been forgotten, for they were here before the Birlotes came--before the White Guardian itself came from the Great Light above Stormy Mountain to teach the races the ways of peace." Cordus pointed to ruins on a particularly tall hill. "Serenlock Castle lies there, Lannon. That is where we'll camp this night."

Lannon studied the ruins closely. They didn't look like they formed a castle--just a bunch of boulders in a big heap on the hilltop.

"Doesn't look like much from here, does it?" said Cordus. "But that castle was once the main rival of Dremlock Kingdom. King Ordamer Kessing of Bellis constructed it for the sole purpose of bringing down Dremlock. Obviously, it failed."

"A poor location compared to Dremlock," grunted Furlus.

"Yes," said Cordus, "But Serenlock was defended on all sides by a massive wall. When the castle fell, the wall was torn apart and the blocks moved to Dremlock to form parts of the West and North towers."

"Why did Dremlock allow Serenlock Castle to be built?" asked Lannon. "Why didn't the Knights just come over here and stop it?"

"A good question, Lannon," said Taris. "But we weren't at war with Bellis during that time. We knew why Serenlock was being built, but Dremlock refused to strike the first blow. Our nobility would not permit it."

They guided their horses up the great hill and into the ruins. The Greywinds, despite being sure-footed animals, slipped now and then and panted from the effort of climbing such a steep slope. Lannon clung tight to Taris, feeling like they were in danger of tumbling back down. Much of Serenlock Castle had collapsed on itself and sank into the hill, but some of it was still well preserved.

As they passed upward between the boulders, Lannon made out familiar shapes like parts of stairs, floors, and walls. Cordus seemed to know exactly where he was going, leading them around and even underneath great obstacles, until at last they emerged onto a wide slab on the hilltop. The slab must have been a courtroom floor or something of the like. Here, between four towering statues of Knights, they stopped to make camp, with open sky above them.

Cordus built a fire inside a circle of small stones between the four statues. The Knights gave their horses feed bags and then gathered around, unfolding blankets. Furlus had stashed away a leg of lamb from the Dead Goblin, and now he brought it forth to gnaw on, while Cordus smoked a pipe. As usual, Taris seemed to crave little beyond his required meals, which he had already eaten, and he sat motionless.

Cordus nodded towards the statues. "These represent the Four Lords of Serenlock Castle, Lannon."

The towering statues were made of marble, and depicted men bearing swords, axes, and heavy armor. They were crumbling and mossy, yet still vivid. One stood out from the others due to the insane look in his eyes. His wild hair flowed long, and in one hand he held an Olrog head, which he grasped by its beard. Somehow this was the most lifelike of the statues, and the sight of it made Lannon's heart race. The crazed eyes seemed to burn into his soul. Lannon could not look upon this statue for long. He turned away, wishing he had never set eyes on it but needing to know more about it.

Cordus smiled at him. "Each of these great Knights has a magnificent tale behind him. But the most intriguing of all-- certainly the most tragic--is the story of Tenneth Bard, the Black Knight. You will learn much of the history of Dremlock, Silverland, and even our continent of Gallamerth as you advance into Knighthood."

"I want to know about Tenneth Bard right now," said Lannon. A deep sadness wrenched at his heart, underneath which lay a darkness spawned by something he dared not peer into.

Cordus frowned and shook his head. "Some things are better left untold, for the time being. I don't wish to burden you with too much knowledge until you are ready for it. This tale can wait until another time."

"Okay," said Lannon, getting under his quilt. He pulled it over his head, trying to block the statue from both eye and mind. For some reason, he needed to hear the story of Tenneth Bard, though he doubted it would offer him any comfort. Yet sometimes *not knowing* was the worst feeling of all.

An hour passed by. Cordus lay down to sleep, and soon started to snore. Furlus finished gnawing the meat from the bone and also lay down. Taris alone sat by the fire, and he beckoned Lannon over. "Come, I will tell a bit of the tale you've been waiting to hear. No harm will come of it."

Lannon eagerly left his blanket and sat down across from Taris.

"Tenneth Bard was once an exceptionally talented Knight of Dremlock," said Taris. "But he was expelled from the Order for violating the Sacred Laws. He became a pathetic drunkard, wasting his life away, until King Ordamer of Bellis called upon his services. He joined with the Knights of Serenlock in their attempt to destroy the Divine Order. But his former failure had changed him. He was no longer sane or stable. The darkness was in his heart, and drove him deeper and deeper into madness. When Serenlock was defeated, Tenneth Bard escaped and became a Black Knight--sworn to topple Dremlock."

"Why was Tenneth Bard expelled from Dremlock?" asked Lannon, hoping to avoid the same fate. The *Sacred Laws* sounded quite rigid.

"The sad thing is that it was all quite needless," said Taris. "Tenneth Bard made a mistake that he probably should not have been banished over. Yet time and again, great Knights have been cast from the Divine Order for petty violations of the Sacred Laws. And time and again, it has come back to haunt Dremlock."

"Was Tenneth Bard ever killed by anyone?" said Lannon.

"After Serenlock was defeated," said Taris, "Tenneth Bard formed a band of Black Knights called the Blood Legion. When the Divine Knights finally hunted down and broke up his clan--temporarily, mind you, for the Blood Legion exists to this day--he escaped into the Northern Bloodlands and was never seen again. Those are the most dangerous Bloodlands of all, filled with horrors that defy the imagination, and it has always been assumed that he perished out there."

"Why were these statues left standing?" said Lannon.

"As a tribute to our victory," said Taris, "and a warning to future plotters against Dremlock."

"I feel like the statue of Tenneth Bard is watching me," said Lannon. "He certainly does look insane." He folded his arms across his chest and shivered.

"I think there was something evil about Tenneth Bard," Taris said, "that went beyond his insanity. I believe he was in league with dark and powerful forces--perhaps the Deep Shadow itself, which is where all foul sorcery comes from. Even to this day, we may not fully realize what damage he did to Dremlock Kingdom."

Suddenly Lannon felt guilty. He glanced at Cordus, who was still snoring peacefully under his quilt. "Maybe I shouldn't know these things," he whispered. "Cordus thought I should wait to hear of it."

"These are histories you would learn regardless," said Taris. "You're not just a lad who happens to be traveling with us, Lannon. You are soon to be--officially--a Squire of Dremlock Kingdom, and as such, you will learn many things about the past. Now try to get some rest. We still have much traveling to do."

Lannon curled up in his blanket and tried to sleep. For half the night he lay awake, his heart troubled by things he could not understand, feeling Tenneth Bard's crazed eyes upon his soul. Finally he slipped into dark dreams of warfare and bloodlust. He felt the weight of centuries bearing down on him, a shifting tide of glorious victories and renowned men and women--but also of crushed dreams, failed honor, and fallen Knights. Shadows clashed amid the hills and mountains, while Goblins crept out from the gloom of the bloated Mothers to make war on life itself. The dreams lasted the entire night, and Lannon could not escape them until the grey dawn touched his eyelids.

***

The Knights seemed in good spirits the next day. As they rode through the Northern Hills, they talked of jolly things that Lannon listened to with interest for a while and then grew bored with. They spoke of battles past and humorous affairs, of failed Knights and talented ones, the state of the land (with no references to Goblins), and the relationships of the Birlotes, Noracks, and Olrogs. They also talked of things Lannon found boring, like trade and taxation and the value of money. Soon Lannon's mind began to stray from their conversations to thoughts of his folks, the journey, and what awaited him at Dremlock.

By afternoon they had reached the forest lands of Hethos, where trees stood reaching heights of two hundred feet or more and had trunks as wide as cabins. The clouds had broken this day, and the sun streamed down amid the furry pine branches, scattering mottled patches of light across the forest floor. The mist was clearing up. Hethos consisted of vast stretches of woodlands interrupted briefly now and then by farms, hill country, and grasslands.

They stayed the night in a little town called Fargun's Vale that was full of hunters and trappers. It was a rough place, but had a fancy inn called the Divine Alehouse, which was built exclusively for Knights and Rangers. Yet even in this thick-walled inn, which lay on the very edge of town, the travelers could hear brawls and shouts throughout the night.

The next morning, they set off with the shadows still thick about the forest. The wooded hills and valleys continued on, and the ride there was pleasant, the day's warmth held in check by cool breezes. The air was fresh and sweet in their lungs, and the forest was rich with animal life--a welcome change from Bloodlands. They took long breaks for lunch and dinner, resting on soft pine needles, and their spirits were high.

By late afternoon they had reached the muddy banks of the Sorgrot River, which flowed down from the Firepit Mountains. The Firepit range towered above them, stretching from east to west as far as they could see. The forest climbed high into the peaks, a carpet of green clinging to the mountainsides.

Lannon got his first glimpse of the great stone wall that protected Dremlock Kingdom, which sat on a plateau about a quarter of the way up Darkender Mountain (as the Knights called the great peak). Lannon could see a few buildings here and there on plateaus leading up to where Dremlock sat.

The travelers followed the road, winding upward alongside the river. The shadows of evening descended swiftly amid the pines and boulders, with blazing stars visible in the open spaces between the boughs. Wolves howled amongst the forests and rocky ledges, drawing threateningly close at times. The Greywinds snorted contemptuously at the wolf howls and trotted with their heads held high. These warhorses, seldom afraid of anything, were used to the wolves and did not fear them.

The Knights lit lanterns, and soon the shadows around their sphere of light became too thick to peer into. Yet still they followed the road on its steady climb upward into the mountains. Gradually the river curved away, the roar of rushing water growing ever fainter.

At last they reached a wooded plateau where a town called Hollow Deep sat, which consisted of several shops and a place called Knights Lore Inn. "We shall sleep here tonight," Cordus said. "And early tomorrow ride on to Dremlock."

Unlike the Dead Goblin Inn or the Alehouse in Fargun's Vale, the stay at Knights Lore Inn was a jolly affair. The folks inside greeted the travelers with laughter and cheers. They were given delicious food, baths, and the best rooms in the place. Immediately after Lannon's meal and bath, Cordus told him to go to bed while the Knights engaged in a bit of merrymaking downstairs. The lad was disappointed, for many strange characters inhabited this place--some who looked Knightly, as well as some Ranger types, and a few mysterious fellows who preferred to sit in the shadowy corners. The atmosphere was warm, pleasant, and exciting. A richly dressed Bard sang songs of Knightly battles and victories.

As Lannon lay down to sleep, he listened to the sounds below, wishing he were part of the merriment. Yet soon his thoughts turned to other matters. Dremlock Kingdom was close--somewhere up above him on the mountainside--and in the morning he would climb to that legendary place to begin his new life. He kept shifting about restlessly, certain he would stay awake all night and end up dead tired come morning. But the feather bed was agreeable with slumber, and the Bard's signing, faint and unintelligible though it was from there, helped him relax until he slipped into a deep sleep.

Chapter 4: The Tower of Arms

When Lannon awoke, he opened the window shutters to see bright sunlight pouring down amid the trees, and he realized he had slept until midday. His pack and his sword were missing, and he concluded the Knights must have moved the items for some reason. He hurried downstairs and found no sign of them. He asked the innkeeper--a thin man with pasty skin and a long beard--if his companions were still in bed.

The innkeeper chuckled. "Seldom do the Tower Masters sleep past the first rays of dawn, my young friend. They decided to let you sleep late, though, because they felt you had a rough go of it on the trip." He pointed to a fellow enjoying a drink at a table. "That's the Knight you need to see."

The Knight at the table wore silver chain mail and a sheathed sword. A brown sash was slung across his armor. His hair was short and curly, his face young and smooth. He took notice of Lannon and smiled, his blue eyes twinkling with amusement.

Lannon hurried over and sat down. "I'm looking for the three Knights. We were supposed to go to Dremlock Kingdom this morning."

The man laughed. "Well, you've found me instead. The Tower Masters went on ahead earlier, but they sent me to guide you. You won't be seeing much of them now, for they are very busy. My name is Cartlan Nobleblood. I'm a Knight and the Squire Master of Dremlock, which means you answer to me at all times. Is that understood?"

Lannon nodded halfheartedly, overcome with disappointment. He had wanted to ride into Dremlock in the company of the three great Knights. They had made him feel important, whereas this Cartlan fellow instantly shrank his ego.

"We have to get going," said Cartlan. "The Color Trials begin this afternoon, and all the new Squires must participate in them."

Cartlan and Lannon set off from Hollow Deep on horseback. Knights, merchants, Rangers, and common folk wandered up and down the mountain road. Dwellings were plentiful along the steeply climbing trail, ranging from log cabins to mansions. Inns and taverns were also abundant, with many bearing colorful names such as the Black Dragon Ale Den, the Golden Feasting House of the Knights, and even the Divine Inn of Unending Merrymaking! There were many colorful shops, some alleging to contain weapons and armor fit for the Knights themselves, and even a small Fortuneteller's den called the Eye of Divinity. Lannon took a long look at this last building. The Knights said he possessed a talent bearing the same name. Did he, then, have a Fortuneteller's gifts?

As the road ran higher and steeper, the shops, inns, and houses vanished, leaving only the massive Knightwood pines and rocky outcroppings. Once in a while Lannon would glance up and catch glimpses of the mountain's dizzying heights, but he couldn't see Dremlock or the wall that protected it.

"Where are my things?" asked Lannon, remembering his missing pack.

"Your stuff got thrown away," said Cartlan. "No Squires are allowed to bring their goods into Dremlock. It's not necessary." He turned and smirked.

Lannon sat in stunned silence for a while, while Cartlan took to humming a cheerful tune. Lannon began to question what kind of men these Knights were, to just dispose of his personal items so ruthlessly. Would the Tower Masters have allowed that to happen? It didn't seem likely, considering Taris had paid good money for the Dragon sword, but maybe they didn't know of it.

"I was merely joking about your things," Cartlan finally said. "They were carried off by Taris Warhawk to Dremlock. It's possible the sorcerer put a dark spell on them, though, so be careful. Sometimes he can get irritated and do things like that. If you break out in boils, you'll know why."

Lannon smiled, thinking this Cartlan was really a fool. Lannon knew Taris better than Cartlan suspected. If anything, Taris had taken Lannon's items out of concern for them.

"I'll be careful," Lannon said. "I wouldn't want boils, especially with the Color Trials coming up today. I'll need to be at my best."

Cartlan chuckled. "You might just want to save yourself the trouble and pass on the Trials. You don't look like Knightly material. You'll probably end up wearing an orange sash anyways. But Orange is okay. We always need servants in Dremlock."

"What's so bad about Orange?" asked Lannon.

"Nothing," said Cartlan, "if you don't mind belonging to the lowest, most disrespected class of Squire in Dremlock. Everyone knows Orange Squires get the weakest training and worst assignments. It's kind of a sympathy class--you know, a little something for the failures. They can never become Knights, and just stay on to make a living serving food, tending the courtyards-- that sort of stuff. It's downright humiliating, if you ask me. If I were Orange, I'd rather just leave the kingdom. Yet many of the lads swallow their pride and remain for the money and comfortable living."

"Well, maybe I'll do better than that." The confidence in Lannon's words surprised him. "Maybe I'll beat all the trials."

Cartlan shook his head in amusement. "Don't get your hopes up."

Like Hollow Deep, Dremlock Kingdom sat upon a flat, wooded plateau. However, this plateau was much wider, nestled against the mountainside, covered in a pine forest. The mountainside acted as half of the wall that defended the kingdom, and the other half was protected by a natural barrier of stone, like a lip, that ran along the plateau's outer edge that faced away from the mountain. The lip formed a sheer wall over thirty feet high. Guard towers had been placed atop the wall, and any openings in the lip had been filled in with stone blocks. Yet the ridge itself was nearly flawless, making it difficult to believe this was a natural formation- -until one studied it up close and realized it was mostly a solid wall of uncut stone.

A huge tunnel mouth stood before Lannon and Cartlan, leading into the wall. Two thick pillars had been hewn from the stone on either side of the tunnel entrance, and a gate between the pillars blocked the way. The gate was silver in hue and made of bars as thick as Lannon's legs, and it had no keyhole or recognizable lock, instead bearing a wheel on both sides. A small stone guardhouse stood just inside the gate.

"Did the Knights carve this tunnel?" asked Lannon, amazed at the size of it. He wondered how they could have accomplished such a feat.

"Don't they have temples where you come from?" said Cartlan. "You should know how Darkender Tunnel was made. You should know all about the Divine Essence, and the White Guardian, and the Father of the White Guardian. You should know about Dremlock from start to...well, to where we are now. You should know all that!"

"I've never gone to a temple," said Lannon. "But I do know about the Divine Essence and some about Dremlock. It's in my book *Tales of Kuran Darkender.*"

"That's a stupid book," said Cartlan. "I've read it. So you mean to tell me you've never, ever, gone to a temple?"

"Never," said Lannon.

Cartlan turned, his mouth gaping open in disgust. "Just where are you from? Some sorry little valley off in the middle of nowhere? Did you grow up worshipping some pagan forest gods or something?"

"No," Lannon said, unable to come up with a better reply. His face was flushed red with embarrassment, and he lowered his gaze.

"Regardless," said Cartlan, "I don't have the patience to explain things you should already know. You'll learn all about Dremlock in due time."

Guard towers stood atop the wall on either side of the gate, each manned by two Knights armed with crossbows. As they caught sight of Lannon and Cartlan, a bell chimed out. A huge Knight, adorned in tarnished plate mail and a two-handed battle axe, stepped out of the guardhouse in the tunnel. He was at least seven feet tall, and most of his bearded face was concealed with a horned helm. He wore a red sash across his plate mail.

"Brought us another, Cartlan?" the Gatekeeper said gruffly.

Cartlan nodded. "Just a little fellow. Goes to show you the Tower Masters will take anything these days, Gellick."

Gellick chuckled. "Come now, Cartlan. Give the lad the benefit of the doubt. There could be more to him than meets the eye."

Lannon glanced at the two, his stomach growing heavy with tension. He wished more than ever that Cordus, Taris, and Furlus were with him. He felt alone and suddenly exposed for the weakling he was. He put his hands in his pockets and shrank down in the saddle. The Color Trials--whatever they were--could end up being dreadful.

Gellick strode over and gave the wheel a spin that looked totally random. But when the wheel stopped, a click arose. He shoved the gate open. "Have a good afternoon, Cartlan. And you, little fellow, hang tough. Size means nothing, all in all."

Easy for you to say, Lannon thought.

The floor of Darkender Tunnel was flawlessly smooth. Birlote torches shone on the walls--glowing crimson gems mounted on silver rods, hanging between paintings of the first Knights of Dremlock. At the tunnel's midpoint stood a silver statue of Kuran Darkender, the first Lord Knight, which was twenty feet tall and without blemish. A shield displaying the Crest of Dremlock was strapped to his arm, and his great sword was thrust towards the mouth of the cavern. His face was grim with a warning to all who dared enter here.

As Lannon gazed up at this statue, chills flooded his spine and he was suddenly swept away in glory. The strength and power of the Divine Knights swelled within him, challenging him to find honor and do great deeds.

As they passed around the statue, Cartlan gave it a slap and chuckled. "What's going on there, Big Pointy?"

The spell broken, Lannon glared at Cartlan. How could this cocky Squire Master refer to the greatest Knight ever as *Big Pointy?* That nickname made Kuran's giant, thrust-out sword seem somehow ridiculous rather than magnificent, and Lannon could not recapture the mood of before.

Farther along the tunnel stood another gate and another guardhouse, and beyond it was the tunnel's end. This Gatekeeper-- a much smaller Knight than the last--sat in the building eating lunch. He came out and greeted Cartlan. He wore chain mail and had a sheathed short sword at his waist. Like the other Gatekeeper, a red sash was slung across his armor. His bearded face was weathered, his eyes kindly. He smiled at Lannon, showing badly yellowed teeth, and the boy took an instant liking to him.

"I guess I can let you two pass."

"Got a small one here, huh Findel?" said Cartlan, motioning towards Lannon. "The Tower Masters aren't too picky lately."

Findel shrugged. "Oh, I don't know. Maybe he's a little on the skinny side, but who says all Knights need be muscle bound? To be honest, you aren't much in the way of strength yourself, Cartlan."

Cartlan's lips tightened, his voice becoming a bit shrill. "Whatever, Findel! I'm plenty strong and you know it!" His face burned crimson and he didn't look at Lannon. "So open the gate, because we're in a hurry."

"Patience, boy," said Findel, grinning. He casually strolled over and spun the wheel, which stopped with a click. Findel shoved the gate open and nodded, still grinning. He winked at Lannon and the lad smiled back.

Maybe it wouldn't be so bad here after all.

Lannon's heart pounded in anticipation of actually seeing Dremlock with his own eyes. Even now, he could scarcely believe he was riding into the kingdom built by Kuran Darkender. How had this all come about?

The ground of the plateau was rocky in places, mainly at the edges, yet it was mostly able to support plant life throughout. A well-worn road led away from the tunnel mouth into a forest of colossal pines. The sun hung in the open sky, though soon it would creep beyond the stone ridge, leaving the plateau in shadows. The three mighty Towers of Dremlock were not visible here due to the trees.

"This plateau is amazing, don't you think?" said Cartlan. "This is the perfect place for a kingdom, if you ask me, because it's so well protected. It's as if the mountain is reaching out to enclose Dremlock Kingdom. And yet a forest grows here within these stone walls. Some believe this plateau isn't a natural part of the mountain at all, that the White Guardian made it."

As they rode into Knightwood--as Cartlan called it--the Great

Stable was the first building they encountered, a massive rectangular structure surrounded by bare earth and fences. The pines had been cleared away around the Stable. Standing within a fenced area were rails for jumping, targets for bow practice, and straw dummies for lancing and swordplay. Several Squires were engaged in training in this area, their weapons flashing in the sunlight. Lannon found the smell of the Stable less than appealing, but nothing compared to the stench of the Bloodlands. Cartlan took his horse inside and they continued from there on foot.

Just beyond the Stable, to the left of the road, stood Dremlock Cemetery, surrounded by a tall iron fence with a locked gate. Small stone crypts and weathered statues stood amongst the pines, leading back into the forest. Sunlight poured down from between the furry boughs onto the tombs, highlighting some in gold and leaving others in shadow--as if these sunlit tombs were somehow special. Goosebumps crept along Lannon's flesh.

"Lord Knights of the past are buried here," said Cartlan. He pointed to the largest crypt of all, which stood at off to one side and was nearly hidden by the pines. "That's Kuran Darkender's tomb--minus his body, of course, which was never found. I've always wanted to get a peek in that crypt."

"Can we go in there?" Lannon asked.

"This Cemetery is haunted," said Cartlan, ignoring his question. "I know all cemeteries are supposed to be haunted--but this one *really* is. There are Knightly spirits within that have not found rest. Don't ever come creeping around here at night, if you know what's good for you!"

"I won't," said Lannon, feeling another wave of goose bumps. "It looks closed, anyways." As he gazed into the cemetery, a strange image popped into his mind--that of a huge black hand swiping out at him from amid the tombs. He quickly turned his gaze elsewhere.

"The Cemetery is only open to the likes of us once per year," said Cartlan. "And then only in daylight. The caretaker alone goes in there the rest of the time. Yet Taris Warhawk has been known to venture in now and then, come to think of it. He's into that sort of thing, I guess." And then he added in a whisper, "Goodness knows what he does out here, amongst all those corpses. I don't think you or I would want to know."

Lannon was tempted to defend Taris, but fought off the desire. It would just irritate Cartlan to think that Lannon knew the sorcerer better than he did, and since Cartlan was the Squire Master, Lannon had no desire to anger him.

Just beyond the Cemetery, the road split into three. They took the road farthest to their left. "We're going to the West Tower," Cartlan said.

"Why are the Towers in different places?" Lannon asked.

"This is Dremlock *Kingdom*," said Cartlan. "Not Dremlock *Castle*. And I'm not sure why it's broken up like that. I know the Towers were built on Olrog mines, so maybe the stability of the ground was taken into account. But there could be other reasons for them being separate. But I've heard they are linked by underground tunnels, which are only used in times of emergency."

"Will I get to see all of Dremlock?" said Lannon.

"You'll see more of the kingdom later," said Cartlan. "But for now, I'm taking you to the Squire's Quarters, where you'll stay until the feast begins. And truthfully, you'll probably never actually see *all* of Dremlock. There are places, I'm sure, that even Cordus Landsaver has never visited. I'd bet my life on it."

Now and then they passed small museums and monuments dedicated to various Knights and battles. Lannon wanted to stop and examine them, but Cartlan practically dragged him along, reminding him they were in a hurry.

At last they came to a clearing in the woods where the West Tower sat. Lannon drew in a deep breath at the sight of it. Made mostly of stone blocks taller than Lannon, the Tower was much larger than he had imagined it would be. It tapered up to a height even greater than the Knightwood trees at the clearing's edge. Many windows, doors, and balconies decorated its sides.

"Well, here it is," said Cartlan. "Quite a sight, huh?"

"Yes, it is," Lannon whispered, overwhelmed.

"The Training Grounds lie on the north side," said Cartlan. "That's where the Color Trials will take place."

Lannon studied the carefully cut grass, the small and colorful trees, and the stone walkways that made up the Tower courtyard. This keep was a thing of beauty the likes of which he had never dreamed of--all enclosed by the protective Knightwood trees that stood like quiet guardians at the clearing's edge.

"It's beautiful," he said, and then he realized that sounded less than manly. "I mean...it's amazing. I can't believe how big it is."

Cartlan nodded. "Just wait until we get inside."

"Where are all the people?" said Lannon, looking around. All he could see were two guards by the front door and one cloaked, hooded man trimming the little trees. "I always imagined Dremlock would be a busy place."

"It usually is," said Cartlan. "But today, with the Color Trials and all, a lot of people are at the Training Grounds. Also, many of our Knights are off fighting Goblins. And Dremlock only does business with the outside world two days a week. The rest of the time the gates of Darkender Tunnel are locked and no one is usually allowed in or out. Only kings, noblemen, or highly respected guests, if they've notified us in advance, can sometimes get in."

"Why is that?" asked Lannon

Cartlan stared at him with wide eyes. "Have you been living in a cave? We are practically at war, Lannon! Ever heard of Goblins? Ever heard of the Blood Legion?"

"Oh," said Lannon, blushing. "I guess I wasn't thinking."

"I guess not," said Cartlan. "To explain it better, these are dangerous times, and spies are everywhere. That's why we've been so closed off from the outside world lately. The Blood Legion has grown stronger and more active recently, and Goblins are getting smarter. The Knights have to keep an eye on everyone who comes through Darkender Tunnel and make sure they're not here on shady business. It takes a lot of work and manpower to weed out spies, you know."

The Tower's front door was twelve feet tall--a stone slab with an iron handle. Two muscular, bearded Knights stood on either side of it. Both wore red sashes over their thick armor. Their faces were stern and grim beneath their horned helms, and each Knight held a battle axe and had a large shield slung over his arm. As Lannon and Cartlan approached, the guards made no move and their faces did not change expression.

"Stern lot, aren't they?" whispered Cartlan. "I think they're pretty bored with their job, which makes them grumpy. But it's not as if they have a difficult task, if you think about it. They never have to face any real danger. All they have to do is stand there and look tough for a few hours each day."

Cartlan nodded to the guards. "Keld, Ramos. How's everything going today? I hope you're not having too much fun."

The Guards said nothing and slowly, grunting with effort, they pulled the door open. They stood sullen and silent as Lannon and Cartlan entered. The door was pushed shut behind them.

Lannon stared in silent wonder.

A huge hall stretched away before him, full of oaken tables and chairs resting upon a green-and-gold carpet. Life-sized paintings of Knights lined the walls. The only painting Lannon recognized was of Kuran Darkender, which hung above a stone fireplace at the opposite end of the hall. A door stood on each side of the fireplace--one labeled Kitchen and one labeled Armory Entrance. The right wall held a door marked Squires' Quarters. Two of the tables in there were larger than the others and adorned with silver tablecloths bearing gold trim. A stack of thick, leather-bound books lay on these two special tables, as well as tobacco, pipes, and writing utensils. Two men and a Birlote woman, all cloaked in green, sat at the fancy tables, studying books and papers. They didn't glance at the newcomers. Two Squires wearing Orange sashes stood nearby.

Towering suits of armor lined the hall, and ridiculously large swords, shields, spears, and axes decorated the walls, hanging between the paintings. The weapons and armor--though obviously too big to be wielded by anyone but a giant--had been crafted with extraordinary care. They gleamed brightly in the light of the many Birlote torches that lit the chamber, exquisitely detailed runes and pictures engraved into them.

"The Armory Hall," said Cartlan.

Lannon could only nod in response.

"See those Green Knights?" Cartlan whispered, pinching Lannon to get his attention. "Let me give you some great advice-- stay well clear of them at all times. They're second in power only to the Tower Masters. If you anger them, you'll be out on your ear. If you're lucky."

"What do you mean?" said Lannon.

"You know what's below here?" whispered Cartlan. "That happy little place called Dremlock Dungeons. Trust me, you don't want to visit there."

As they walked quickly towards the door marked Squires' Quarters, one of the Green Knights glanced up and caught Lannon's eye. He was a clean-shaven, silver-haired Knight whose age was hard to guess, though the rugged lines on his face indicated he was a bit on the elderly side. Lannon gulped, frozen for a moment in the Knight's stare. The Knight frowned at him, his eyes narrowing. He took a puff of his pipe.

"Come on!" whispered Cartlan, tugging Lannon along. "That's Trenton Shadowbane, the Investigator of Dremlock. You don't want to try staring him down!"

They passed beyond the door and climbed a staircase that led up to a hallway lined by six more doors. They entered one labeled New Squires. It turned out to be a round chamber filled with many beds and small nightstands, a very plain and boring room with bare oaken walls. Young men near Lannon's age occupied all but a few of the beds. The youths were busy chatting with each other, or playing card and dice games.

Cartlan led Lannon to an empty bed numbered forty-seven. "Your things are under here, minus that fancy sword. Taris said to let you know you could have the sword when you finish the Color Trials. When I see you again, don't expect any special favors."

Lannon ignored him and dragged his pack out from under the bed. He sat down on the hard mattress and looked around. He noticed that many of the lads were Norack (or pale skinned) like him--though there were several Birlotes and Olrogs amongst them. (The Olrog boys already had short beards.) A few of the youths bothered to glance his way, but the rest took no notice of him. His eyes passed over them quickly, and his heart began to pound anxiously. He began to long for the solitude of Knights Valley.

Hurriedly he pulled *The Truth about Goblins* from his pack and lay down to read. He opened to the middle and found himself staring, ironically enough, at a drawing of a Foul Brother--which, after the encounter at the North Gate--now seemed like a menacing creature rather than a sad, dumb one. He started reading, and soon became wrapped up in the book, unaware of the passage of time.

Suddenly he realized someone was trying to get his attention. "Hey, you there!" a voice called out. "Why don't you answer me? Get your nose out of that book for a second."

Startled, Lannon glanced up. A boy sat on a bed next to him. His hair was black and neat, his eyes were large and dark, and he wore black clothing. He was bigger than Lannon as many of the boys were, and solidly built.

"What's your name? I'm Vorden Flameblade."

Lannon introduced himself.

"Lannon is a weird name," said Vorden. "I've never heard of a *Lannon* before."

And Vorden isn't a weird name? Lannon thought.

"I can't wait for the Color Trials to begin," said Vorden. "I know I'm going to be picked Brown, at least. Maybe even Red. What about you?"

Lannon shrugged. "I'm kind of worried I might not do so well. What types of colors are there? I already know about Orange."

"You could be picked Orange, Brown, White, Blue, Red, or Grey," said Vorden. "Orange is the bottom, of course, which means you've failed. Brown is where most of the talented Squires end up, and it lies just below Blue in rank, I think. I don't know much about Blue, and only rarely does anyone get picked for that. It's some kind of a secret, special class. Grey is for sorcerers-- another rare class that's mostly for Birlotes. And then there's Red, which is what I'm hoping for. Red is second only to Green."

"Why not go for Green, then?" said Lannon.

"I can't," said Vorden. "You can only be Green if you've done great deeds and get promoted by a Lord Knight. Only High Council members are Green."

"What about White?" asked Lannon.

"It's kind of like Blue," said Vorden, "but not so mysterious. White is the Healing Class. White Knights seldom get to fight-- they usually just heal people."

"How boring," said Lannon.

Vorden raised his eyebrows. "Sure, but somebody has to do it. Who else is going to care for the sick and wounded?"

Lannon nodded guiltily, thinking of his father, who

desperately needed a White Knight to cure him. "I just hope *I* don't end up being White."

"You probably won't," said Vorden. "It's rare, and you don't seem compassionate enough for it. Of course, you don't look like a fighter, either. Truthfully, you kind of look like Orange material."

"When do we start the Trials?" Lannon asked nervously.

Vorden shrugged. "Hopefully soon. I just can't wait to go out and prove myself to the Knights!"

"Have you met some of the others?" Lannon asked.

"Yeah, I know most of the new Squires," said Vorden, "and some of the Knights. We've been waiting two weeks for the Color Trials to begin. But Cordus Landsaver said he didn't have enough of us yet, and went off in search of more. So where are you from, by the way?"

"Knights Welcome," said Lannon. "Just outside of it, actually."

"I'm from Gravendar," said Vorden, "the City of the Dead. It's much bigger than Knights Welcome."

"Why is it called that?" said Lannon.

"City of the Dead?" Vorden shrugged. "I guess because of all the Olrog tombs there. A lot of Squires here come from Gravendar, but even more come from Kalamede, the western city. There are others here from Knights Welcome, too. You might know some of them."

"Maybe," said Lannon, knowing he probably wouldn't.

"Let me tell you some things about this place," said Vorden. "First of all, avoid the Green Knights, because some are downright mean. The other Knights are more easy going, but you still have to mind your manners around them. The Squires are okay, with the exception of a few, and you should get along with them. We get good food here--three meals a day, which we eat in the Armory Hall. We turn in early, and get up early, but so far we haven't gotten any training. I guess we have to wait for the Color Trials before the Knights decide how to train us."

"How long before we can be Knights?" asked Lannon.

"That's an individual thing," said Vorden. "But usually it takes about four to eight years, from what I've heard. It all depends on how fast you learn, how talented you are, and how hard you work."

"So if you end up being Orange," said Lannon, "you get no

training and can never become a Knight?"

"Right," said Vorden. "Of course, you could always leave. That's probably what I'd do. If I couldn't be a Knight, I'd be too humiliated to stay. I guess I could go live as a Ranger or something."

Lannon thought of the Rangers who looked after the North Road, and wondered if Vorden knew anything about their hardships.

"Come on," said Vorden. "I'll introduce you to some of the others."

Just then, the door banged open and Cartlan entered. The room fell silent. "Okay, Squires, you've got just a few moments to get ready and head into the Hall. We're going to have lunch and then a meeting. After that, the Color Trials shall begin. Now follow along, please. And hurry up. We don't want to keep the Masters waiting."

"This is it!" said Vorden, grinning. "Now we're going to find out who is Knightly material and who isn't!" He straightened his black clothes and smoothed his hair (as if that would help him somehow), and jumped up.

Lannon put away his book and rose unsteadily to his feet. His stomach felt ready to sink to the floor. He couldn't fathom how Vorden could show such confidence (anticipation, even) over something Lannon found terrifying. But glancing around, he saw mixed expressions. Not many of the Squires showed the confidence Vorden seemed to feel. Most looked tense and hurried as they put on boots and belts and stashed away games and such. One lad seemed even worse off than Lannon, as his face had gone deathly pale and he was sitting on his bed holding his stomach.

"Poor sod," Vorden whispered, nodding toward the anxious lad. "That's Timlin Woodmaster, from Kalamede. I don't know why he was ever picked as a Squire. The boy has the courage of a Tree Goblin."

Lannon said nothing, understanding Timlin's fear. Less than a week before, Lannon had been a lonely lad living a secluded life in the woods, and now he was suddenly surrounded by boys his own age. Soon he would have to go before them and prove his worth in the Color Trials. But despite the special power the Knights believed he had, he didn't feel the Trials were going to be the least bit fun.

Chapter 5: The Color Trials

The boys gathered at tables in the Armory Hall. Eight girls, led by a grey-cloaked Birlote woman with short silver hair and soft green eyes, soon joined them. The Green Knights (there were five of them now) glanced up from their papers and gave stern looks whenever the chatter grew too loud. Vorden kept Lannon company, but they didn't talk much, except for a few comments on how anxious they were for the Color Trials to begin and how hungry Vorden was. Lannon didn't feel hungry at all.

Not long afterwards, the room fell silent as Cordus Landsaver entered the Hall, accompanied by two Knights. One of them had long white hair and beard, his face covered in many lines and wrinkles. He wore a plain, pale robe. He walked slowly, using a cane to help him along. The other, wearing a blue cloak, was bald and had a short black beard and stern eyes. The bald man and Cordus walked with deliberately slow steps to keep pace with the elderly man. Cordus positioned himself before the fireplace, and the other two took a seat with the Green Knights.

"I know everyone is hungry," Cordus said, "and so you'll be happy to learn that I haven't come to make a speech. However, we cannot begin the feast until my Tower Masters arrive. They should be along shortly." With that, he sat down with the High Council, in a special chair reserved in his honor.

A man dressed in a crimson robe and a feathered hat of the same color came in and stood before the fireplace. He was tall and broad-shouldered, with long black hair pulled back in a ponytail. His blue eyes twinkled with amusement, and his square jaw with bushy sideburns was set in a good-natured grin. "Greetings, new Squires of Dremlock Kingdom. I am Crestin Lightwielder-- magician and general entertainer of Dremlock. It appears we have time for a song or two, while we wait for the Tower Masters. I'm sure they'll be here very soon, my young friends!"

Everyone waited patiently while Crestin played a haunting melody, which he called *The Fall of Serenlock Castle*, on a flute. Lannon was reminded of the crumbling ruins in the Northern Hills, and for a moment a deep sadness washed over him that he didn't quite understand. Then he remembered the statue of Tenneth Bard--the Black Knight and the founder of the Blood Legion--and his sadness turned into a shudder as he envisioned the statue's insane eyes staring down upon him.

The song was rather long, and afterwards, when the Tower Masters still failed to appear, the Green Knights exchanged irritated looks. They kept glancing at a Dragon Clock on the wall, which indicated--with some of its scales changing from red to silver--that it was around 2:30 in the afternoon. They began muttering quietly to each other and shaking their heads.

Finally Crestin began a speech about Knightly virtues and how fortunate the Squires were to have been chosen. Then he rambled on about glory, honor, and the wonderful deeds of Kuran Darkender and some other great Knights. Lannon listened for a while and then his attention began to wander. Suddenly Crestin pulled a shining object from his cloak. He flicked his wrist and tossed a green fireball into the air, where it hung for a moment. Then, as the Squires watched in awe, it exploded into shafts of red and white flame that zigzagged around the room, just barely missing everyone and everything.

Chaos ensued for a moment, as Squires and Council members ducked their heads and shielded their faces. This was followed by laughter and cheers when they realized no one was being harmed. The flaming shafts fizzled out.

The Squires applauded loudly.

Crestin smiled. "Nothing to be amazed at, Squires. Just run-of-the-mill fireworks that any sorcerer worth his salt could produce." Unconvinced by Crestin's humble words, the Squires begged for more.

"Well," said Crestin. "It appears that I have time for a bit more entertainment. Let's see now...who can I make disappear? Feager Stoutheart? Gorain Gloryfinder? Zender Knightsblood? Let me think about this.... "

Before he got a chance to perform any more tricks, the tower's front door opened and in walked Taris and Furlus. Apparently they were arguing about something, as a few last insults were exchanged.

"And I won't see it done," growled Furlus, "because I've had enough of your idiotic ideas. And that's the end of it!"

"So then we're late for nothing," Taris grumbled back. "And in this case, I refuse to take the blame. Now be quiet and try to act respectable."

They spoke in low voices, but not low enough--as everyone in the Hall could hear what was said. Some of the Green Knights scowled with displeasure. Crestin Lightwielder struggled to contain his laughter.

Furlus straightened his armor and grinned, nodding. Taris bowed. Politely, the Green Knights rose and nodded back. The Tower Masters sat down, and the feast began. Orange Squires brought platters of food from the kitchen, and soon the tables were covered in them. Once Lannon caught scent of the food, his anxiety vanished and he ate heartily the juicy meats, soups, vegetables, puddings, and breads--all the while wondering if they would always feast this well. He washed it down with a mug of milk and then sat back, his belly hurting from too much food, which certainly was not the best way to head into the Color Trials.

After the meal, the two Tower Masters walked to the stone fireplace and stood with their backs to it. They greatly contrasted each other--one being tall, lean, and cloaked in shadow and the other being short, bearded, and enormously stocky. Furlus cleared his throat, then turned and whispered something to Taris. The sorcerer shook his head and motioned towards the Squires.

"Uh...hello, good Squires," Furlus said loudly, clearing his throat. "First let me say that you're a fine looking bunch and I hope you do well. Now to get right to the point, the Color Trials are made of five tests--the Blackstone, the Wall of Fire, the Wood, the Flaming Blade, and the Toadstool. I shall oversee the Blackstone, and Taris shall stage the Wall of Fire and the Flaming Blade. Vesselin Hopebringer, Lord of the White Knights, shall stage the Toadstool, and Carn Pureheart, Lord of the Blue Knights, shall stage the Wood."

"Remember," Taris said, "these tests alone will determine your class of Knight. Also bear in mind that sometimes success in a Trial is judged by effort and attitude. But regardless, just give everything you have and be satisfied with the results. These Color Trials are centuries old and have been perfected so there is little margin for error. We can determine precisely what class of Knight you should be, if any. You were chosen as Squires either because of Knightly Essence or natural talent, and in order to be picked for a class other than Orange, you must participate in each of the Trials. Boys and girls, weak and strong--there are no exceptions. When all is said and done, just accept your fate graciously and count your blessings. And may the Divine Essence warm you all. Now, if you'll follow us in an orderly fashion, we can get this task underway."

***

The Trial Grounds consisted of a round pavilion in a clearing behind the tower. The pavilion had a peaked roof, with a black and silver flag standing atop it that bore the Crest of Dremlock. Eight pillars held up that roof, and in between the pillars were rows of seats for spectators, except for one open space that marked the entrance. Most of the High Council was present. Cordus Landsaver sat with the Council members, cloaked in silver and sipping at a huge mug of something, with an Orange servant at his side. Three Brown Knights were also there, including Cartlan, along with several Orange Squires who stood ready to serve. Yet many of the seats were empty, adding to the eerie feeling that Dremlock Kingdom was practically deserted.

It was a bright and warm summer day, yet a strange feeling lurked in the air. The Knights' faces were tense and humorless. It was not the festive scene Lannon had always imagined, to say the least. It was quiet, rigid, and hurried. The Squires were brought close to the pavilion's edge, at the entrance, but were not allowed to go up the steps. They were expected to wait on the ground-- sixty-three Squires in all--until called upon to enter. The two Tower Masters stood off to one side in the pavilion, conversing with each other, while two Orange Squires carried forth a large black rock and a pair of silver gauntlets and laid them near the center of the floor.

Furlus stepped to edge of the pavilion, looking down upon the

Squires, and spoke. "You will be called upon one by one. You must try to lift the Blackstone off the floor. If you fail on your first attempt, you will be allowed to use the silver gauntlets, which possess magic that can increase your strength. Once you've made your second attempt, for better or worse, you must leave the pavilion and another Squire will be summoned to take your place."

The Blackstone was a small boulder with an iron ring embedded in it. It looked far too heavy for Lannon to budge.

The first lad called into action--a skinny one named Nathan Peacefinder--failed to lift the Blackstone on both attempts, and he left the Pavilion shaking his head in defeat. Using the silver gauntlets, the second Squire chosen managed to lift it about an inch before dropping it back to the floor. Results varied from there, with Vorden Flameblade doing the best of all. He managed to move the rock without the gauntlets (something no one else could do), and with them he was able to lift it up to his waist, where he held it for several moments before slowly setting it back down.

When Lannon's turn came, he struggled to stop the trembling in his limbs as he hurried up onto the platform. He walked over to the Blackstone, avoiding the Knights' gazes, feeling the other Squires' eyes upon him. He grasped the iron ring and pulled until his arms felt like they might stretch, but the weight remained stationary. With shaking hands, he slid on the silver gauntlets, which were too big for him, and he tried again to lift the dreaded Blackstone. He pulled furiously, hoping the power within the gauntlets would be enough. But the rock did not rise or even move. He wondered if the gauntlets actually possessed any magic at all.

Timlin, the scrawny lad from Kalamede who was still pale and scared-looking, did even worse than Lannon in a way. He displayed little effort as he made his attempts, as if he expected to fail. He kept shaking his head and shrugging helplessly, which made Lannon cringe yet took some of the sting out of his own defeat.

Now that the first Trial was done, Taris stepped forward and spoke. "During this next test, an illusionary ring of flames shall appear around a Squire. An hourglass will be turned, and the Squire has until the sands run out to pass through the flames. Once the sands run out, the illusion will have run its course."

When all the Squires had completed this test, Vorden again proved himself among the best, leaping forward courageously through the imaginary flames the moment the hourglass was turned. (None of the spectators could see the flames, since Taris placed the illusion--by touching his subject's forehead--only in the mind of the Squire being tested.) During Lannon's turn, he took several moments to summon enough will to throw himself through the searing wall of heat that threatened to burn him to ash, and by the time he made his escape, the hourglass had actually run out and the fire was vanishing from his sight. Timlin did the worst of all sixty-three Squires, however, for he huddled on the pavilion floor until time ran out completely, making no effort whatsoever.

The blue-cloaked Knight with the bald head and stern gaze came forward. "I am Carn Pureheart," he said, "of the Blue Knights. This next Trial is a simple one, Squires. There are no so-called magic items to aid you, and no sorcerer's tricks to fool your minds. You must break a wooden plank with the flat of your hand. You get one try at it, so focus long and hard before striking the blow. I will demonstrate the correct form."

Two Orange Squires held a thick plank. Carn studied it for a moment, and then slowly imitated the blow he would strike. He demonstrated a few times before breaking the plank with ease. "That's all there is to it."

Most of the Squires failed this test. The only two boys able to break the wood completely were Vorden and, amazingly, Timlin. Vorden gave only a slight smile after his victory, as if he had expected this result all along, but Timlin practically danced for joy as he left the pavilion.

When Lannon's turn came, Vorden whispered in his ear. "Take your time and focus. Then just relax and let go with all your might."

Lannon did as Vorden suggested, relaxing himself before unleashing the blow. He managed to crack the plank, hurting his hand in the process, but it did not break. He tried to hit it again but the Orange Squires tossed it aside. "Only one hit is allowed!" they cried.

Now the White Knight named Vesselin Hopebringer came forward. He was the ancient-looking man that had attended the feast in the Great Hall. An Orange servant brought him a pillow upon which lay a fat toadstool. His hands trembled as he held the pillow. "All I ask of you, Squires," he said in a shaky voice, "is to come forth one by one and touch the fungus until I tell you to take your hands away."

This Trial ran on for over two hours, as the Squires had to stand and touch the toadstool until Vesselin signaled them to stop, which sometimes took several minutes. And if the toadstool turned color, Vesselin would wait a few moments until it changed back again before the next Squire could proceed. Only four Squires passed this test, making the toadstool turn dark green beneath their touch.

As the shadows of afternoon grew long around the pavilion, and torches were lit, Taris made a dagger burn with blue flames. Each Squire had to grab the blade and try to banish the flames--which Taris insisted would not harm them--just by willing them to disappear. Several of the Squires passed this test, some more easily than others. A couple of Squires, including Timlin, were too afraid to even lay hands upon the fiery dagger. Lannon and Vorden were among these who courageously grabbed the dull blade but failed to banish the flames. The Squire who fared best at this was a Birlote girl named Aldreya Silverhawk, who banished the flames instantly.

Lannon was distraught. He had passed nothing, as far as he knew, and this might prove to Cordus that he lacked the Eye of Divinity after all (whatever that was). He might then be chosen Orange, and never be a Knight.

Now that the Color Trials had ended, Cordus came down from the seats and stood before the Squires. "You have all fared well," he said. "It is not our goal to keep you in suspense of the outcome, or cause speculation amongst you. And so before dinner you all shall receive your Color Sashes, and be sent to your appropriate towers to begin your training. Now go back to the West Tower and seat yourselves in the Hall."

***

The fireplace was ablaze in the Armory Hall. Lannon, Vorden, and a few other Squires sat at one table. Five wooden boxes stood near the fireplace. The Green Knights were back at their fancy table, joined by Cordus, Furlus, Taris, Vesselin, and Carn. Cartlan and two other Brown Knights sat at a table, while Orange Squires stood nearby. Crestin Lightwielder sang a gloomy song called *The Battle of Old Keep.*

The Knights talked quietly amongst themselves, and glanced through books and papers. Finally Cordus rose and stood facing the Squires. The Lord Knight regarded the Squires solemnly, making them squirm. The torchlight and shadows danced about the room, highlighting the glorious paintings on the walls. Cordus stood in the shadow of Kuran Darkender's huge portrait, and his silver cloak had been replaced by his gleaming breastplate and broadsword. His blue eyes seemed to burn like the Birlote torches that lit the chamber. The Squires sat in silent, humbled awe-- unable to gaze directly into his eyes, yet unable to look away.

"The time has come," Cordus said. "Remember to accept your fate graciously, and bear in mind that no class is permanent--save for Orange--and that one can always be promoted. Now let us begin. I now call upon Clayith Ironback from Gravendar. Come forth and receive your Color!"

One by one, the new Squires of Dremlock approached and were given a sash from the boxes. The sashes were narrow and bore golden trim to set them apart from the Knightly ones. The Squires showed mixed emotions as they were handed their Colors, with one boy shedding tears over an Orange sash and another leaping for joy over a rare Red one. When Vorden's turn came, he strode confidently up to the podium. He had, after all, easily passed three of the five tests and had clearly done the best of all the Squires. The look on his face said he expected no less than Red, but strangely enough he was presented with Blue. He stared at it like it was a thing from another realm. Then he bowed and hurried from the podium, his face troubled.

When Lannon's turn came, Cordus regarded him with a twinkle in his eye. "And for you, Lannon Sunshield, I give the Blue."

Lannon took the sash gratefully and bowed. He had no idea what it meant, but at least it wasn't Orange. He hurried back to where Vorden sat, eager to hear the lad's opinion on the matter.

Timlin was one of the last to be called upon, and the defeated look on his face said he was expecting Orange all the way. Yet he was wrong.

"To you, Timlin Woodmaster," said Cordus, "I present Blue." With a smile, Cordus held out the sash.

His mouth hanging open in disbelief, Timlin snatched the sash from Cordus, bowed shakily, and hurried away--as if he feared the Lord Knight might change his mind and give him the wretched Orange instead.

Now that the Colors had been handed out, the celebration feast began. The tables were laden with all manner of roasts, vegetables, breads, cakes, and puddings. Timlin joined Lannon and Vorden at their table.

"I can't believe I got Blue!" Timlin said, picking at a heap of food on his plate that was far bigger than he could handle.

Vorden sighed. "Do we even know what this means, Timlin? We were the only three picked for this Color. Why is that?"

Timlin shrugged. "Maybe we're special somehow. You did better than anyone else, and Lannon...well, he did okay."

"And what about you?" Vorden said, raising his eyebrows.

"I don't know," Timlin said, and for a moment he looked uncertain. Then he said excitedly, "I broke that board! Only you and I managed to do that. Maybe that Blue Knight, Carn Pureheart, saw something special in me."

"Obviously someone did," said Vorden. "And that's what I'm worried about. Nobody really knows what Blue is good for. They keep to themselves and won't say a word about their doings. A few days ago, I managed to get one of the older Blue Squires talking about Dremlock, and he spoke freely about anything except his Color class. It just seems like I gave my all in the Trials and that I deserved Red."

"Maybe you'll get it later," said Timlin.

"We'll see," said Vorden, with a shrug. "So what about you, Lannon?"

"I'm just happy I wasn't picked Orange," said Lannon. "I actually failed all the Trials."

"But you did okay in some of them," Vorden said. "And you managed to crack the board--which was more than most of the Squires could do."

"I still can't believe I broke it!" said Timlin.

"That was amazing," Vorden admitted. "I mean, for someone as small as you. It took all my strength to break that plank, and I hurt my wrist. It still aches." Vorden rubbed his wrist, as if to emphasize his point.

"My wrist is fine," said Timlin. "I feel great."

"You both did better than me," said Lannon.

"None of us are Knights yet," said Vorden. "And we may never be more than Squires. That will depend on how hard we work." He smoothed his black hair from his forehead and smiled. "But I guess I don't feel so bad, really. I'm sure the Knights wouldn't waste my skills on something stupid."

"I'm just happy I got picked for Blue!" Timlin said enthusiastically.

Vorden chuckled. "If you're happy, Timlin, I guess that's good."

Timlin nodded, picking at his mountain of food. (Vorden had already cleaned one plate and started on another, while Lannon was halfway through his.)

"Looks like we'll be training together," said Vorden. "At least for a while. Until I get what I deserve."

After dinner, Cordus Landsaver got up and spoke. "I have a task for you, Squires. Rub water upon your sashes, and watch closely."

Hurriedly the Squires plunged their hands into glasses and pitchers of water and rubbed it on their sashes. Like the others, Lannon watched in fascination as silver letters appeared seemingly out of nowhere.

Lannon Sunshield
Divine Squire of Dremlock Kingdom
1217 Year of the Wolf

Chapter 6: The Tower of Sorcery

Now that the Squires had received their sashes, they were organized into groups based on their Colors. The Orange (there were fourteen of these unhappy youths) were sent to Cordus' tower. The Brown and Red remained, for now, in the West Tower, while the White were sent to a place called the Hall of Healing. Lannon, Vorden, and Timlin--the only Blue of the entire lot--were to reside in the East Tower, along with twelve Grey.

The Grey were taken to the North Tower on secret business-- undoubtedly concerning their sorcery training--and Cartlan was chosen to guide the Blue Squires to their new home. He grinned at them, shaking his head. "Come on my merry lads. Into the Blue unknown we go." He chuckled, as if finding himself quite clever.

The three Squires gathered their things and followed. As they stepped out into the courtyard, Cartlan lit a torch, though pale light shone down from a full moon. Crickets chirped amid the grass and flowers, and wolves howled in the woods.

"Do you hear that?" said Cartlan. "We have wolves in Knightwood--huge white beasts. There are many rumors about them. Some even believe they're pets kept by sorcerers like Taris Warhawk. They only come out during the night hours. In the daytime they sleep in caves in the mountainside. At least that's what most folks around here believe."

"Have you ever explored the caves?" said Lannon.

Cartlan's eyes widened. "I'm not an idiot, Lannon, even if you are. I wouldn't go poking around in wolf lairs. Besides, the caves are forbidden to us." Suddenly, he pointed skyward. "Look at that."

A winged shadow soared overhead, blocking out the moonlight for an instant. The Squires caught sight of silvery feathers and huge wings.

"An Elder Hawk just passed over," said Cartlan. "Those things are big, and like the White Wolves are kept by some here as pets--according to rumor."

As they passed from the courtyard and entered the forest, only Cartlan's torch fire was left to guide them, for very little moonlight could penetrate between the Knightwood bows. Animal noises came from the woods all around, and at one point a heavy body was heard rustling through the underbrush next to the trail, before moving away. A wolf howl arose close by, causing all of them to jump and Timlin to let out a squeal. Cartlan's face had gone pale, which startled Lannon and the others. Seeing a Knight bear such a fearful expression did not fill them with confidence, to say the least.

"I don't usually wander the woods at night," said Cartlan. "Typically everyone is indoors by now, unless there's an outside feast or something."

Suddenly a figure stepped into the torchlight, causing Cartlan to jump and reach for his sword. But it turned out to be the green-cloaked Investigator, Trenton Shadowbane. His grey eyes were shiny and strange in the flickering light. He appeared to be unarmed.

"Hello, Cartlan," he said quietly.

Cartlan recovered his composure and bowed. "Greetings, Trenton. Just out for a walk tonight, now that the Trials are over?"

"Just out minding my own business," Trenton said coldly. "As you should be minding yours." He sighed deeply. "Very well, if you must know, sometimes I grow weary of the constant shifting of papers, the grinding of stone against flesh and senses. It is during these times that I seek solace in the embrace of the night."

"Of course," Cartlan said, glancing around nervously in an effort to avoid the Investigator's icy gaze. "I'm just taking these Squires to the East Tower."

"Mind the wolves, son," said Trenton, and the gleam in his eye grew brighter. "Knightwood knows nothing of the mortal flesh and its yearnings. To be brutally honest, the woods might swallow a man whole and not shed a tear."

Cartlan gulped. "I'll be careful."

Trenton adjusted his cloak. "I must be moving on now. Stay

on the path, lads, and make no trouble."

Cartlan bowed again. "We wouldn't dream of it."

Trenton nodded. Then he fixed his gaze on Lannon. "You really must think you're something special," he whispered.

"Huh?" said Lannon, not knowing what to say. The Investigator's piercing grey eyes sent goose bumps scampering all over his flesh.

"You heard me!" snapped Trenton. "My eyes are on you, Lannon. I know your heart, child, and if things start turning out badly, you'll pay dearly."

With that, Trenton strode on past them and was swallowed up by the shadows. A moment later another wolf howl arose, this one louder and closer--coming from the direction the Investigator had gone. It was followed by a crash as something big leapt away through the forest.

Cartlan and the Squires hurried away without looking back.

When they got a little further down the path, Cartlan wiped sweat from his brow. "That was really strange," he muttered. "That man is...well, what can I say? He's somewhat *different*. There are rumors about him."

"He seemed crazy to me," said Vorden. "What did he say about the woods?"

Cartlan shook his head. "Just forget what you saw and heard, Vorden. You'll be far better off for it. Remember, you're just a lowly Squire."

"I won't mention it to anyone," said Vorden. "But I won't forget it, either."

Lannon said nothing, still feeling the effects of Trenton's chilling stare. He couldn't fathom why the Investigator had singled him out--unless it had something to do with the Eye of Divinity. But why would that cause Trenton to be angry with him? Wasn't the Eye of Divinity supposed to be helpful to Dremlock somehow?

They came to where the road split into three, and they took the East Path. The land sloped downward some, and boulders began appearing amongst the trees. The pine trunks were gnarled and split, their roots clustered thick along the trail, and their boughs hung low like huge furry hands descending upon the travelers.

"This part of Knightwood has the most ancient feel to it," said Cartlan. "Ruins of Olrog dwellings stand here in the woods. Taris' tower is older than Furlus' keep, and it was built on some of those ruins, including the remains of the fortress built by Kuran Darkender before Dremlock existed as we know it today. Rumor has it that there are catacombs beneath the Old Keep, as the fortress is called--Olrog tombs filled with traps and riches, and even darker places that have been closed off with bars made of indestructible Glaetherin so that nothing can creep forth and enter the tower. But actually, who knows?"

"What do you know about the Blue Knights?" asked Vorden.

At first Cartlan looked irritated that Vorden had changed the subject, but then he stopped walking and stood in a silence for a moment. Then he sighed loudly. "I don't want to worry you or anything, but the few things I've heard about them were not very pleasant--to say the least!"

"What things?" Timlin asked fearfully, pressing close to Lannon and Vorden. The lad was shaking in his boots, his gaze darting this way and that into the surrounding shadows.

Cartlan turned and smirked, his cockiness and attitude of superiority resurfacing. "Very odd things, Squires. You'd probably rather not hear of them at this point. You'll find out for yourself soon enough."

"Fine by me," said Vorden, refusing to be drawn in.

"I'd like to know," said Lannon, wishing he were as strong-willed as Vorden.

"Tell us!" Timlin begged. "We should be warned."

Cartlan shrugged. "Very well, if you must know. I hear that they're actually assassins. They're throat cutters and backstabbers and spies. They sneak around in the shadows and kill people when they're sleeping."

Vorden shook his head in disbelief. "No way, Cartlan. The Divine Knights would never accept a class like that."

Cartlan laughed. "Think what you must, Vorden. But with the Blood Legion and all, and the recent troubles with smart Goblins, spies and assassins are badly needed. And Blue Knights aren't real Knights. They're just, well, assassins. Their Books never get put in the Round Library. No Lord Knight has ever been a part of that color class. Actually, I don't think any Greens have, either. I think

Blue Knights always stay that color."

"What?" said Vorden, his mouth hanging open. "You mean a Blue Knight can't get promoted? So I could never be Red, or Green, or a Lord Knight?" Vorden's body was shaking, so distraught was he all of a sudden.

Cartlan nodded. "From what I know, yes. Look at Carn Pureheart, the Lord of the Blue Knights. He was never made Green."

"I can't believe this!" said Vorden. "But I've worked so... No, I just can't believe it. You've got to be joking with me, Cartlan."

"Not at all," said Cartlan. "But calm down. I'm just telling of rumors. I suggest you relax and see for yourself before you get angry."

"I won't stab someone in the back," Vorden muttered. "That's not why I wanted to be a Knight."

Cartlan raised his hands helplessly. "You still get to train with the other new Squires every day. It's just that you'll receive your *special* training also--the training nobody talks about much because it's an embarrassment to Dremlock."

Lannon wished he could shut Cartlan up, and somehow permanently remove that smirk. Cartlan was probably just trying to get to them, and he was doing an exceptionally good job with Vorden--which irritated Lannon all the more because in the short time Lannon had known Vorden, he already seemed like a friend. And Lannon had never had a true friend near his own age.

Timlin just trotted along looking mystified yet hopeful, his hands in his cloak pockets. Once in a while he'd look at Lannon or Vorden, give a shrug, and then shake his head--as if the whole matter were beyond his comprehension.

Vorden mumbled quiet words now and then, his hands knotting into fists, while Cartlan strode ahead, whistling a merry tune.

***

Taris' tower looked much the same as the West Tower in size and shape, yet it seemed a bit taller and had a small river running through its courtyard. Crumbling boulders stood here and there, and the ground was sloped in a shallow valley of mossy stones. No flowers or carefully trimmed hedges existed here--just a natural landscape that needed no maintenance. The Knightwood pines grew close to the tower, their roots arching up from the ground in thick tangles. A stone bridge, webbed with vines, spanned the river.

An ancient scent arose from the soil here that reminded Lannon of Knights Valley, and for a moment he closed his eyes and breathed deeply, imagining he was back home. Oddly enough, the front door was not guarded.

"Where are the guards?" Lannon asked.

"The East Tower needs no guards," said Cartlan. "This is the Tower of Sorcery. It's protected by magic, and people are allowed to come and go as they please. Still, you can bet that even now we're being watched."

The Squires glanced up along the tower wall, their gaze passing over balconies and windows--some lit by lantern and torchlight--all the way up to the tapering peak. They shivered, their hearts pounding harder. This tower, for whatever reason, seemed somehow dark, sinister, and very ancient. Perhaps the feeling lurked in the mossy landscape and the vine-covered stone blocks at the tower's base, or perhaps it lurked in something else that only their subconscious minds could grasp. Regardless, as they gazed up at the moonlit keep, they were chilled to the bone.

"Don't stop now," said Cartlan gleefully. "This is your new home."

After exchanging nervous glances, they followed Cartlan to the front door, which bore a leering, demonic face forged of silver at the center. He grasped the door handle and pulled it partly open.

"Well, there you go," he said. "Good luck."

"What?" said Timlin. "You're just going to leave us here?"

Cartlan shrugged. "I was told to bring you here. I've done that, so my task is finished. I've got to get going now." Cartlan glanced nervously at the forest. "Of course I could wait a bit, I suppose. No, I better get going."

"Come on," said Vorden, pulling at Timlin and Lannon. "We'll be okay."

Reluctantly, the two boys followed Vorden into the keep. Cartlan slammed the door shut behind them and they were alone. Or so it appeared, anyway.

They stood in a round chamber with six oaken doors. Four of the doors were unlabeled, and one was marked Old Keep and one Dining Hall. A stone stairway led upwards and another led downwards. Five Birlote torches glowed here, yet the shining red gems were not enough to keep much of the chamber from being deep with shadow. The stairs rose and descended into darkness.

"Okay, what now?" said Vorden.

"Maybe we should wait," said Timlin.

"I'm with Timlin on this," said Lannon. "Let's wait for Taris, or somebody, to show us where to go. I don't want to get lost in this tower."

"I guess we wait, then," said Vorden, shrugging.

Not long afterwards, the door opened and a boy appeared. It was a Blue Squire named Fern Fairblade. Four silver ribbons had been stitched to one end of his sash. He was slight of build, with curly black hair and pale skin. He smiled at them.

"Hello," said Vorden. "You might be able to help us. We're looking for the Blue Knights." He pointed to his own sash.

"I'm afraid I can't help you," Fern said politely, squinting to read the name on Vorden's sash. "I'm just a Squire like you, Vorden, after all. And I'm late for bed. Goodnight!" He hurried up the stairs.

Vorden shook his head. "Some help he was."

They waited some more, and Vorden took to pacing about. Twice more Blue Squires entered (silver ribbons on their sashes), and each time could give no help and were "late for bed."

"Thanks a lot for nothing!" Vorden muttered at the last one.

Finally a Red Squire came in. He displayed five ribbons on his sash. He was bigger than Vorden and at least eighteen years old. His brown hair was shaggy, and he had a mustache and a bit of a beard. He nodded to them. "Hello. I'm Drethess Silverknight. I've not seen you three before."

"We're new," said Vorden. "We're not sure where to go."

Drethess read their names and smiled. "We have a Sunshield, a Flameblade, and a Woodmaster. Not too bad at all--maybe a little offbeat, but imaginative. I know a bit about this tower, though certainly not everything. I might be able to help you."

"Why are you here?" Vorden asked. "I thought only Grey and Blue Squires dwelt in this keep."

"All Knights of Dremlock," said Drethess, "must be able to wield magic to some extent, not just the Grey ones who specialize in it. That's what gives Dremlock an edge over the other kingdoms on Gallamerth. I'm soon to be made a Red Knight, and Taris has something special planned for me this evening! Anyways, the top floor is where you need to go--and then through the big wooden door. But you might as well just wait, because Taris was not far behind me. He should be here any--"

The door creaked open and Taris Warhawk stepped in. He nodded to Drethess. "I thought you would be here before dark, as I instructed. A bit late for wandering in the forest without good cause, don't you think?"

"I had to run a message to Moten," said Drethess. "A note from Kealin. I guess it was extremely urgent for some reason."

"Really?" Taris said. "How strange."

"Why is that strange?" asked Drethess.

"It is not important," said Taris. "Now go to the library. I will be there as soon as I get these Squires settled in."

Drethess nodded, bid the Blue Squires goodnight, and raced upstairs.

Taris turned to the others. "I see Cartlan left you in the lurch. Typical of him. Still, he is a good Squire Master, and his senses are sharp."

"He told us some things about the Blue Knights," Vorden blurted out. "Some things I didn't like."

"Is that so," said Taris, steeping closer. "And what were these things?"

"He said we'll be made assassins, that we'll backstab people and kill them in their sleep. And that we can never get promoted!"

Taris stood in silence for a few moments.

The others watched him nervously, wondering if Vorden's words had angered him. Was the sorcerer contemplating how to discipline them? Even Lannon wasn't sure what was going on in Taris' mind.

At last Taris spoke. "Not all of that is true, Vorden. You can indeed get promoted to another Color--if your talents allow it."

"What about the throat cutting and all?" said Vorden.

"It is a complicated matter," said Taris. "You may indeed be trained in some of those methods. But whether you do it or not is up to you. Only you can control your destiny, Vorden Flameblade, regardless of what training you receive."

"But why wasn't I given Red?" Vorden asked. "I did better than anyone!"

"You don't know that," said Taris. "The High Council alone judged how well you did. I must say, however, that you fared very well indeed and could easily have been given Red. But the Council felt your skills would be better served--at this time--as part of the Blue class. This could change in the future, and Red might then be yours."

"What about me?" Timlin said hopefully. "Do you think I did well?"

"In the test of focus," said Taris, "you did excellent, Timlin. That's why you were picked for Blue. Focus means everything to a Blue Knight."

"I won't even ask how I did," Lannon said, fishing for a complement.

"You did fine, Lannon," said Taris, "for one who's Knightly Essence is weak. In fact, you surpassed my expectations."

Lannon smiled. Taris seemed the sort to speak his mind, and Lannon was sure he spoke the truth and wasn't just trying to be nice.

"We've talked enough," said the sorcerer. "Follow me and I'll get you settled in for the night."

They followed Taris up the stone stairs, journeying past several floors. The tower had many halls and doors--some bearing labels such as Library, Grey and Blue Squires' Quarters for boys and girls, Guest Rooms, Storage Rooms, and some that were curiously labeled Dark Rooms. When they reached the tenth floor-- and by now Lannon's legs were growing wobbly beneath him from all the climbing, they came to a door marked Blue Squires--Boys. A huge oaken door at the end of the hall, covered in fancy Birlote runes, was labeled The High Council Chamber of Blue and Grey Knights.

"You're the only ones staying here right now," Taris said. "All the other Blue Squires have a fair amount of experience. We don't like to lump new Squires in with the decorated ones--those Squires who've mastered various aspects of their training and have received silver ribbons. It causes all manner of problems."

"What kind of problems?" asked Vorden.

"New Squires can feel overshadowed and pressed to learn too quickly," said Taris. "Their training can suffer as a result."

"You mean we'll train by ourselves?" said Vorden.

"Sometimes," said Taris. "Yet at other times you will train with the rest of the new Squires. You see, only during your special training--that which Blue Squires alone receive--will the three of you be isolated from the others. And you, Lannon, will engage in some of your training apart from even these two."

Lannon nodded, knowing such training would no doubt involve unlocking the Eye of Divinity. He kept his face expressionless, hiding the deep excitement he felt over Taris' words. Would the sorcerer train him one on one? Lannon could think of nothing more exciting than that prospect.

"What's so special about Lannon?" said Vorden.

"Lannon has a skill," said Taris, lowering his voice, "that only he possesses. That skill, called the Eye of Divinity, must be developed further. Meanwhile, none of you are allowed to speak of this to anyone."

"Who will help me with it?" asked Lannon, unable to contain himself any longer. "Are you going to be my trainer?"

Taris shook his head. "You won't actually require a trainer for this task, at first. You'll understand what I mean when the time comes. At some point I may have to give you guidance, but not until you've learned to summon the Eye of Divinity."

"I see," said Lannon, his heart sinking.

"We get this whole room to ourselves?" said Timlin, studying the door to their quarters with childish excitement shining in his eyes.

"Blue Squires are quite rare," said Taris. "Sometimes the Color Trials won't produce one for a year or more at a time. I find it extraordinary that three Squires were chosen Blue during these trials. As far as I know, that has never happened before. But we certainly have need of them."

"Who will train us?" said Vorden.

"Don't worry about such things tonight," said Taris. "For now I want you to get some sleep. Tomorrow you will be visited by Garrin Daggerblood of the Blue Knights. Garrin will get you started on your training, but there are others who will instruct you also."

Timlin opened the door and peered into the room. "Can you light a lantern? I don't like the shadows."

"The moon is bright tonight," said Taris. "You need no other light." He entered the room and opened the shutters on a round window.

"Now goodnight, Squires. And I wish you all pleasant dreams."

With that, the sorcerer motioned them inside and closed the door behind them. They could hear Taris whistling softly as he moved off down the hall.

The room was fairly small--compared to the other Squires' Quarters--containing only fifteen beds. The beds were all neatly made, with nightstands by them. Nothing else worth mentioning could be found in this chamber. The stone walls were bare, interrupted only by the window that let in a beam of moonlight.

Lannon's Dragon sword lay on his nightstand. He showed it off to his companions, but they didn't seem too excited by it so he sheathed it and put it back. "It's supposed to be real Dragon bone," he mumbled.

"It's a great sword," said Timlin. "I wonder what my weapon will be?"

The boys put their packs beneath their beds and lay down in a row across from each other, staring at the cobwebs on the ceiling beams. No one spoke for a while. Then Vorden voiced his frustration. "I can't believe this," he muttered. "What are we doing way up here?"

"At least we've got the whole room to ourselves," Timlin said.

Vorden turned and glared at him. "That's not a good thing, Timlin. I liked having lots of friends around me."

"I kind of like being in Taris' tower," said Lannon.

"This feels strange," said Vorden, "like we've just been cut off from the rest of the world--like we've been cast aside or something."

"It's not that bad, really," said Timlin. "It kind of feels right somehow."

Lannon and Vorden both glanced at the lad. Timlin lay on his side, his head propped up on his hand and his eyes shining thoughtfully in the moonlight--seeing something that only he could see.

"This is pathetic," Vorden grumbled again.

Lannon and Timlin said nothing. Neither was very outgoing, and they liked the solitude of this room. Lannon wanted to make friends with the other Squires--but not all at once, for that seemed overwhelming. This would give him a chance to get acquainted with them slowly. And he had already made two friends, which was more than he'd ever had in Knights Valley.

As one by one they drifted off into sleep, they were plunged into dark dreams. In those nightmares, screams came from catacombs below, while metal cages rattled and chains dragged across stone. Things moved in the darkness below the keep, twisted shadows filled with an insatiable hunger--always seeking to escape their forgotten chambers and taste the essence of the living once again.

Chapter 7: The Temple of the White Guardian

Early the next morning, the three Squires were awakened by a Blue Knight. He was young and average in size, with wavy black hair and a thin mustache and beard. He wore a cloak representing his color, with no weapons visible, and soft leather boots that made virtually no sound as he walked. He smiled and spoke in a quiet voice. "Greetings. I am Garrin Daggerblood. And I already know who you three are, so you need not introduce yourselves."

Lannon sat up hurriedly. By the look of the sunshine streaming in through the window, it was already late in the morning.

"I guess we slept past breakfast," Timlin said nervously.

Vorden yawned and stretched. "Nobody told us exactly when we should get up, Timlin, so what does it matter?"

Garrin chuckled. "Not to worry, Squires. I allowed you to sleep in, for there is little that needs doing this day. After lunch, we must attend a meeting at the Temple. And then I'll bring you back here where you'll be pretty much on your own until dinner, for I have obligations to attend to and your training does not truly begin until tomorrow morning. Now let us go eat. And don't forget to wear your sashes. You must always have them on whenever you leave your room."

They followed Garrin down to the Dining Hall. This room had one table that stretched nearly the entire length of it. A fireplace stood against one wall, containing only grey ash, next to the kitchen door. Drethess Silverknight--the Red Squire they had met on the previous evening--sat at the table eating lunch with another youth. A Blue Knight was seated there as well, sipping at a big wooden mug. He appeared to be in his twenties, yet was already balding on top. His face held a gloomy expression that brightened only slightly when Garrin came in.

Drethess greeted the Squires with a nod and went on talking to his companion. The Blue Knight nodded. "Greetings, Master Garrin."

Garrin smiled, and then his face grew somber. "It is good that you have returned, Kaelist, even if the others could not."

Kaelist shook his head. "My journey went very poorly. Trevek and Dolan were lost, as was Selenar, the Ranger who helped us once before. She was... She...died bravely. They all did. I barely escaped with my life, for whatever that's worth."

Instantly Lannon thought back to Saranna, the beautiful Ranger woman they had met on the North Road. He was glad it wasn't her who had been killed.

"This is sad news," said Garrin. "Yet I'd already heard about it--just before the Color Trials began. When will they be honored?"

"Three days from now," said Kaelist.

"I liked Trevek and Dolan very much," said Garrin. "I didn't know Selenar personally, but I'd heard of her courage. I will be there for the ceremony. Meanwhile, I would help ease your grief somehow, were it possible."

Kaelist shook his head. "It doesn't matter. My grief means nothing, for it cannot bring them back." His face suddenly held a wounded, haunted look--his eyes sinking in and his mouth hanging open. "It was all for nothing, and now I fear that no hope for us remains."

"We need not speak of this now," Garrin said quickly, glancing at his three Squires. "If you wish, we can go to my quarters and talk in private."

"Not now, Master," said Kaelist, staggering up from his chair. "For now I desire only to be alone." Kaelist left the Dining Hall, and that was the last Lannon and the other Squires ever saw of him.

Garrin sat down, his face troubled, while beckoning the others to do the same. When they had done so, an Orange Squire came out and took their orders. At Garrin's suggestion, the lads ordered stew and bread. Timlin tried to order two bowls, but Garrin gave a disapproving shake of the head. "Food is not endless here, Timlin. Scrape one bowl clean before you request another."

"I doubt he could handle even one bowl," mused Vorden. "Timlin has the eyes of a giant and the stomach of a mouse."

The stew was delicious, the bread baked to perfection. Lannon and Vorden ate quickly and heartily, while Timlin picked away at his soup, apparently finding many ingredients in it he didn't care for.

"That Knight seemed troubled," said Vorden, his mouth full of bread. "Looks like he had a rough time of it."

"Some of his close friends fell in battle," said Garrin, gazing at Vorden sternly. "These are dark times for Dremlock Kingdom. But you need to stay focused entirely on your training."

"What will our training be like?" asked Vorden.

"You'll train in the morning with the rest of the new Squires," said Garrin. "You will learn weapon skills and sorcery. But your special training as Blue Squires will be somewhat different. You will practice stealth, climbing, and picking locks. Yet do not think that you are becoming thieves or assassins, as some silly rumors suggest. Blue Knights serve a different purpose." He paused, smiling.

"What purpose?" said Vorden.

"When I feel you're ready, I'll answer that question," Garrin said. "But I assure you, Vorden, it will take nothing from your honor."

Vorden nodded. "That's good to hear. After what Cartlan said, I was afraid I'd be learning how to be a backstabber."

Garrin shook his head. "Foolish rumors, Vorden. But you will be trained to kill quickly and silently, without direct confrontation. This is not murder--especially when performed on Goblins, as is usually the case. It is simply another way of defeating an enemy. You're a smart lad. You should have guessed as much."

Vorden's face reddened and he said nothing.

"Why were we even chosen Blue?" said Timlin.

"Because of talent and necessity," said Garrin. "In these times, Blue Knights are badly needed, and you three have the rare talent that a Blue Knight requires. In the Color Trials, the Wood test alone determined that. It takes great focus and great Knightly essence to break that plank. Few Squires ever accomplish that feat."

"I didn't break it," said Lannon.

"No, you did not," said Garrin. "Nevertheless, you were chosen for Blue and you must not question it."

***

After breakfast they left the tower, stepping out into the sunlight that shone down upon the mossy stones of the shallow valley. A few enormous, puffy clouds hung in the sky, occasionally shadowing the sun as they drifted past. The air was warm, and birds whistled and chirped amid the pines that stood beyond the river. Garrin lit a pipe, and led them onward slowly, often pausing to take in the sights and sounds.

"We shall visit the Temple," said Garrin. "There we will see the Sacred Scriptures, which give the earliest history of Dremlock Kingdom."

Vorden sighed. "I'd rather just get to the training."

Garrin stopped and turned towards him. "So you care little about the histories of our kingdom. Yet how could you ever call yourself a Divine Knight of Dremlock without knowing why you are Divine? What makes Dremlock special, and the Knights who defend it?"

Vorden shrugged. "Talent, I guess."

Garrin shook his head. "If it were talent alone that made us, Dremlock would have fallen to Bellis or the Goblins or the Blood Legion long ago. Do you think Kuran Darkender was merely talented?"

"He was blessed by the Divine Essence," Lannon said. "I read that in my book *Tales of Kuran Darkender.*"

Garrin nodded. "The Divine Essence is our true god. It is the great enemy of the realm of Tharnin and of the Deep Shadow."

"I want to know about the Deep Shadow!" Vorden said eagerly.

A frown darkened Garrin's face. "Do not be so eager to hear of the scourge of our world, Vorden, lest its hand fall upon *you.*"

Vorden lowered his gaze. "I was just curious, Garrin."

"I understand," said Garrin. "It's just that we can never be too cautious when dealing with the Deep Shadow. Now first of all, I would prefer you address me as Master Garrin, since I am to be your trainer part of the time. And I suppose I will tell you the basic history of the Deep Shadow while we walk to the Temple, since it is something everyone should know.

"There was an age once, over twelve thousand years ago, when the only two races on our continent of Gallamerth were Olrogs and Noracks. The two races made bitter war upon each other, and hatred and bloodlust ruled the land. They worshipped pagan gods and such things as chivalry and honor were rare. But then one night, a Great Light appeared above a place known as Stormy Mountain--so called because storms rage endlessly above the peak--and from that light came a pale, glowing creature which would come to be known as the White Guardian. It journeyed down the mountainside and blessed the land, teaching Noracks and Olrogs the ways of peace and justice."

"What about the Birlotes?" Timlin asked. "Where were the Tree Dwellers?"

"Please do not interrupt me," said Garrin. "Now as I was saying--the White Guardian, which one might view as the *child* of the Great Light above Stormy Mountain, became the protector and teacher of the races, and Gallamerth seemed to have a very bright future indeed. The Guardian dwelt on our land for over five hundred years, and during that time the two races prospered.

"But then disaster struck. A massive rock fell from the heavens one night, landing in the ocean just off Gallamerth's shores. It devastated our land, destroying much life. But the Noracks and Olrogs survived, as well as most of the other species-- though some were lost forever. Our continent was plagued with a terrible winter that lasted four years and caused the destruction of even more life."

"What about the White Guardian?" said Timlin. "Oh, I'm sorry. I didn't mean to interrupt again."

"When the huge rock hit our land," Garrin went on, "the White Guardian was shattered from the shock waves, and the pieces of it were hurled far and wide across our continent. The rock's impact had a peculiar effect on the Guardian--causing it to explode violently into many pieces--almost like crystal being shattered by sound, if any of you Squires have ever witnessed that. These fragments, which still pulsed with life, were known simply as Flamestones--for they appear to be rocks that burn endlessly."

"Like the Birlote torches," Vorden said. "Are *they* actually Flamestones?"

"They are just imitations," said Garrin. "True Flamestones possess great power, and represent different parts of the Guardian's body--such as the Blood, the Flesh, the Heart, and the Mind."

"Did anyone find the Flamestones?" Lannon asked.

"Yes, many were found," said Garrin. "Entire wars were fought over them, and they have changed hands many times since those days. Right now most are owned by the Birlotes, who keep them locked away in the Hall of Sorcery in their tree city of Borenthia. Some have fallen into evil hands, while others still remain undiscovered. This may come as a great surprise to you, but the Divine Essence--our god--is nothing less than the *Mind* of the White Guardian. It is the greatest of all the Flamestones."

The Squires exchanged amazed looks.

"Will we get to see the Divine Essence?" Timlin asked excitedly.

"Unfortunately, no," said Garrin. "No one is allowed down there but the Lord Knight. Yet I can tell you a little bit about it. The Divine Essence exists in a crystal chamber somewhere below the Temple. Kuran Darkender--the first Lord Knight of Dremlock-- had a vision of it calling to him from the darkness of the Olrog mines beneath his fortress, and he and his Knights journeyed below, battling Cave Trolls and other Shadow spawn before finding the chamber containing the Essence. The Essence spoke to him, telling him he must forge a great kingdom--rather than the mere fortress that they had at the time--to battle the expanding Bloodlands. The Divine Essence gave us a purpose. And that is how Dremlock began."

"But what does this have to do with the Deep Shadow?" Vorden asked. They had stopped walking, and were standing in the forest.

"I'm getting to that," said Garrin, pausing to puff at his pipe. Then he continued. "When that great rock fell from the sky and devastated our land, it also ripped a hole right through the fabric of our world. Our world borders the dark realm of Tharnin, where the Deep Shadow exists--and so a portal between the two worlds was opened at the site of impact. The Deep Shadow is a force that endlessly seeks to expand and devour, changing everything into a phantom existence, corrupting the nature of reality itself. But it could not come through the portal into our world, because the life force of living things here repelled it. There was still enough life on Gallamerth to hold the Deep Shadow back. So it created the Barloaks--demons that could withstand the force of living things.

"These Barloak demons came through the portal and ravaged

our land, making war on the Olrogs and Noracks. Their goal was to destroy enough life so that the Deep Shadow could enter our world and devour the rest. You see, as the Deep Shadow expands it grows stronger, and if it could take Gallamerth, the rest of our world would fall easily to it. The entire world would be webbed in a sort of phantom darkness.

"Somehow, the Deep Shadow managed to trick the Olrogs into joining with it, and in return it gave them powers over weapon forging and other strange abilities that they still possess to this day. In fact, many of the Grey Dwarves still see Tharnin as the savior of their race--though they also hate and fear the Shadow Realm."

"So only us Noracks were left," Vorden said.

"Yes," said Garrin. "And you can imagine how that went. We were drastically outnumbered and swiftly losing ground. But then the Birlotes arrived in great wooden ships on our shores. They had abandoned their own land across the sea--a small island in comparison to our continent--for it had fallen to earthquakes and volcanoes and was in danger of sinking into the sea. The Tree Dwellers sought to make a new home on Gallamerth, and quickly joined with the Noracks in their fight against the Deep Shadow. The Birlotes possessed great magic, and forged enchanted weapons that were a match for the Olrog blades and hammers and could bring great harm to the demon Barloaks. Yet still the Noracks and Birlotes were losing the war.

"But then the Birlotes discovered one of the lost Flamestones of the shattered Guardian--a crimson one of tremendous power that was of its Blood--resting in the heart of a dead volcano. Their king, the great Olzet Ka, wielded this mighty weapon against the Deep Shadow. And with it, the Birlotes were able to triumph. Yet some areas remained corrupted by the Barloaks' evil. The Bloodlands grew out of that evil and spawned Goblins into our world. To the north lies the Desolation of the Deep Shadow--which is the worst of all the Dark Lands.

"Silverland started out as wealthy and prosperous, but the Goblins threatened to turn it into a stench-filled wilderness. Bellis, the largest kingdom on Gallamerth, sent a legion of Knights to defend Silverland and beat back the Goblins. And that is where

Dremlock and the Divine Knights enter my tale."

"Well, go on," said Vorden. "Tell the rest of it."

"Yes, tell us," said Timlin.

"We're not at the Temple yet," Lannon reminded him.

Garrin chuckled. "I would love to, since telling tales of the past is something I always enjoy. But you'll learn about the basic history of Dremlock Kingdom at the Temple, where Cordus Landsaver is expected to give a speech in just a short while."

"I'd rather hear it from you," said Timlin.

Garrin smiled. "Yet I don't want to take anything away from our Lord Knight, who is a magnificent speaker and certainly much better than I. Be patient, lads."

When they came to the intersection of the trails, Garrin led them down the middle road, and there they met many Knights and Squires in the woods, who all greeted Garrin warmly. As the forest gave way to the Main Courtyard, they found themselves walking on a stone pathway that led between rows of little red trees amidst which sang birds of varying sizes and colors. The Temple and the North Tower lay ahead in this huge clearing.

The Temple stood in the middle of the courtyard, while looming behind it was Cordus' tower--which was larger than the East and West Towers. The road split in two around the building as it led onward towards the keep. The Temple was made of stone, but had a copper roof weathered green. It was a round, two story building with a spectacular landscape surrounding it of little trees, flowers, and sparkling fountains. Atop the Temple was a bronze statue of Kuran Darkender. He was down on one knee, his face turned up towards the heavens.

The sweet scent of incense drifted from the Temple, mingling pleasantly with the summer day. Birds perched on the statue of Kuran Darkender and sang from the round windows in the Temple's walls. The beauty of the courtyard, mixed with the surreal scent of the incense, caused powerful feelings to arise within Lannon and the other Squires. They felt that they walked in a holy place--that beyond the crude fabric of their world existed the splendor of godly realms. The faith of the ones who had built this temple was strong, outlasting time and death.

Many of the new Squires were gathered outside the front entrance with their trainers. As the four approached, Vorden waved to some of the youths and hurried ahead to talk with them. Lannon and Timlin raced after Vorden.

Garrin and the other trainers gathered to talk amongst themselves. Vorden introduced Lannon to some of the lads, and one of them struck up a conversation. He was a Red Squire with bright blond hair, fair skin, and blue eyes, but his handsome face was corrupted by a sneer. "What happened at the Color Trials, Vorden?" he said. "I think you got cheated, my friend."

Vorden shrugged. "Blue isn't too bad, I guess. I can live with it--but I'd rather be Red like you, Jerret. I, too, think I deserve it."

"And what of this one?" Jerret said, motioning towards Lannon. "Most of the Squires feel he deserved Orange."

"It doesn't matter," said Vorden. "We should just be happy with what we have. The Knights have their ways. Who are we to question it?"

"I agree," said Jerret. "I don't care at all, because I know I got what I deserved. I'm just saying that some of the other Squires aren't happy about it."

"Then let them come and say it," said Vorden, looking around. None of the other Squires seemed to be paying attention. They were too busy talking, gesturing, and laughing--sixty-three youths who (with the exception of some of the Orange Squires amongst them) were having the greatest time of their lives.

"Derrick's the big complainer," said Jerret. "He passed two of the Trials, yet got stuck with Brown. He felt he deserved Blue at least."

Vorden sighed. "Look, Jerret. Blue is a special class. Not everyone can just be Blue. For whatever reason, it's a rare thing."

"Tell that to Derrick," said Jerret, as he moved off into the crowd.

Vorden went about socializing here and there, as the crowd split into groups, while Lannon and Timlin stood quietly beside each other. Lannon looked with envy upon Vorden. He seemed so confident in himself as he wandered about chatting with people, yet Lannon's stomach tightened at the thought of trying to initiate conversations with these strangers. He wanted to be like Vorden, he realized, more and more with each passing moment. Yet he had no idea where to begin.

Timlin seemed even worse off, standing with his gaze focused shyly on the ground and his hands in his tunic pockets. He was nervously humming a tune under his breath and shuffling his feet.

"I wonder when we can go in?" said Lannon, just for the sake of talking to someone--even if that someone had to be little Timlin.

Timlin shook his head and shrugged, a silent answer that did nothing to assist them in combating their isolation.

After that, Lannon just kept quiet and waited anxiously, his thoughts beginning to wander to more significant things. Here before him was the Temple, and beneath it was an actual god--the Divine Essence. The Mind of the White Guardian lay somewhere below his feet, still alive and full of wisdom. It had spoken to Kuran Darkender and told him of his destiny, and Dremlock had been forged. And now Lannon was a Squire in service of that god and the kingdom that it ruled over--and someday, if all went well, he would be a Divine Knight. How swiftly things had changed. Less than a week before, he had been playing in the Quiet Spot of Knights Valley, swinging a stick at the trees and rocks and imagining he was a Knight slaying Goblins. Now here he was--the dream made reality. But he was still having trouble accepting that reality.

At last the Squires and their trainers were called upon to go inside. They entered in an orderly fashion, with each group followed by its trainer. Just beyond the door was a short hallway of stone. Thick stalks of incense burned in brass holders in the corners, and Birlote torches lit the walls. The shadows and burning incense created an engulfing, pleasant atmosphere--one that demanded silence and respect. The boys instinctively said nothing above a whisper.

An iron door at the hall's end was engraved with the words:

WELCOME TO THE TEMPLE OF
THE DIVINE ESSENCE,
WHERE DWELLS HE WHO BREATHED LIFE INTO
THE COLD STONE OF THE MOUNTAIN.
THE TRUE LORD OF DREMLOCK KINGDOM

Beyond that door was the Temple's sanctuary--a large round

room with a domed ceiling. The ceiling bore painted artwork depicting Stormy Mountain, above which hovered the Great Light. Moving down the side of the mountain was the smaller light known as the White Guardian, shaped somewhat like a four-legged beast, with a head that looked too large for its body. The eight stained-glass windows in here told the story of Kuran Darkender's discovery of the Divine Essence and the fulfilling of his destiny. They depicted him having his vision of the god, relating that vision to the other Knights, the search in the catacombs beneath the keep, the evil that threatened them (represented by a shadowy form with fiery red eyes), the crystal chamber where the Divine Essence lay in wait, the god casting the light of truth and blessing upon Kuran, the constructing of Dremlock Kingdom, and finally--the Crest of the Three Towers.

Stone steps on four sides led up to an altar, where stood a silver sculpture of the three crystals that represented the Divine Essence. On the side of the altar were dozens of symbols written in the Sacred Text (which, among all the Squires, only Lannon could read but was too distracted to bother studying). Birlote torches glowed on the walls, and incense burned in every corner. A podium stood next to the altar, a huge leather-bound book resting atop it. Cordus Landsaver stood behind the podium, dressed in his flowing silver cloak, studying the book. Taris Warhawk and Furlus Goblincrusher flanked him. Five Orange Squires stood off to one side, each holding a scroll.

Wooden benches sat at the base of the steps, more than enough seats for all of the Squires and their trainers. Quietly they filed in and sat down, and then they waited in silence for Cordus to begin.

Finally Cordus cleared his throat and glanced up, his face solemn and his eyes stern. His piercing gaze swept the crowd, creating shivers and tense muscles. The Squires fidgeted nervously beneath that gaze.

"Greetings, Knights and new Squires of Dremlock," Cordus began at last. "I've called you here today to prepare you as best I can for what is to come. I chose the Temple, rather than the Meeting Hall in my tower, because herein lie the Sacred

Scriptures." He pointed to the symbols on the altar. "I don't expect anyone to be able to read this, for I myself cannot. But the translation dwells within this book."

He held up the book for all to see. "So as not to waste anyone's time, including my own, I shall do this in an orderly and swift fashion. I shall begin with the histories of Gallamerth and then Silverland--all the way up to the present day. After that, I shall read the Five Sacred Laws of Dremlock Kingdom."

Cordus began his tale the way Garrin Daggerblood had, but as he spoke, his eyes grew fiery and his voice thundered out. Extreme conviction lurked in every word, backed by the fierceness of his will. Sweat dripped from his brow, and his tangled hair was plastered to his forehead.

When Cordus at last reached the part where Garrin had left off, a Squire brought him his great wooden mug and he drank deeply before continuing. "Now I've come to the part of my tale," he went on, "that directly concerns our great heritage. The Knights of Bellis, led by Kuran Darkender, were sent here to Silverland to stop the Goblins from transforming it into a wasteland."

His eyes narrowed. "A wasteland, Squires! Here would exist nothing but bloated Iracus Trees and the foul beasts they spawned--and it would grow in strength like the very Deep Shadow itself, creeping beyond the mountains and devouring all that is decent. The Deep Shadow feeds on life--when such life lacks the strength to repel it--yet the dark creatures it spawns feed on wholesome and natural life regardless of its abundance. So in a sense, the children of the Deep Shadow are even stronger than their master, since the force of life cannot harm them. All that the Deep Shadow touches is corrupted and breeds further disease and despair.

"The Knights sought to destroy the Bloodlands completely, yet they needed a fortress secure enough to withstand any assault. They searched for many long and weary months, driven on by a need for a castle of peace and strength amidst the madness of a corrupted land. They found many potential sights for their keep, yet always Kuran Darkender was compelled to move on, until at last they climbed this very mountain. Discovering this hidden abode, they knew they had found the best possible location. They built a small fortress up here, amidst the abandoned Olrog mines. That fortress stands now below Taris' tower, and is referred to as the Old Keep. It is, mind you, a forbidden area, Squires!

"Well, one night Kuran Darkender had a vision that something magnificent lurked deep in the mines below their keep--something that beckoned to him like the music of dreams. The Knights set out to exploring the mines, and uncovered evils that I shall not name-- the very evils which brought doom to the Olrog miners. At the cost of many lives, the Knights beat back the evil and discovered our god in a chamber of crystal below. How it got there none can say-- but it came to be known as the Divine Essence, and was the final proof that the White Guardian yet lived!"

Cordus paused, studying the faces of his audience. Those faces--even amongst the Knights--were tense and excited, their gaze focused directly on him and nowhere else. He nodded in satisfaction before continuing.

"The Divine Essence consists of three crystals--as shown by this sculpture--that burn with a purple flame. It spoke to Kuran, and told him that his Knights must defect from Bellis and forge their own kingdom, which they eventually named *Dremlock* after a type of Dragon. This kingdom would make war on the Goblins until none remained. It taught Kuran Darkender and his Knights many great secrets--such as how to feel the Knightly Essence to determine a subject's talent level.

"Yet Bellis would have none of it, and demanded these great Knights remain part of their kingdom. In fact, Bellis was nearing war with the Grey Dwarves and was ready to abandon Silverland to the Goblins. When the Knights of Dremlock refused, Bellis sent all the Knights it could spare and they built Serenlock Castle, named after an even larger kind of Dragon, with the intention of destroying Dremlock.

I've been there, Lannon thought proudly.

"But Bellis was fighting on two fronts, and Dremlock proved very difficult to invade because of its location. Also, our Knights wielded weapons that burned with the flame of magic. We prevailed, and in so doing, we established ourselves as a kingdom to be reckoned with. Ours is, in fact, the only kingdom ever to defeat Bellis in warfare. Now you might be inclined to ask why Bellis would send Knights after us when they had the Olrogs to deal with. The answer is simple. The King of Bellis--Ordamer Kessing--did not always act in a logical manner. He was fiery and stubborn, and certainly less than wise, and he seldom heeded anyone else's opinion. And thus, as happens to most tyrants eventually, he was later assassinated, after Bellis' defeat at the hands of the Divine Knights. His son Belmore--a far more sensible ruler if not as iron-willed--then took his father's place as king and an age of prosperity and goodwill began. But I'm rambling on a bit now and I apologize."

Cordus cleared his throat, looking a bit sheepish. "So to get back to my tale, Kuran Darkender served as Lord Knight for thirty-seven years, and during that time Dremlock prospered. All three towers were completed, the Goblins were beaten back nearly to extinction, and business in Silverland was faring well. But then the evils that dwell in the Olrog mines rose against us, and a battle was fought below Dremlock Kingdom. As difficult as it is to believe, and as sorrowful, Kuran Darkender fell in combat with something of dastardly powers. His body, however, was never found--just his sword and his breastplate, left in a pool of blood. The sword was notched and the breastplate sheared through. Whatever killed him, Squires, was powerful enough to cleave magical Dwarven armor forged of Glaetherin--and it was powerful enough to take the life of the most talented and blessed Knight in our history.

"Now if this tale doesn't keep some of you Squires from trying to venture where you shouldn't go--you must certainly wish for death. For make no mistake, young ones, death lurks below Dremlock even as I speak!

"But that is enough talk of such things. I shall now read the Five Sacred Laws of Dremlock, as they apply to Squires." He motioned to the Orange Squires, and one by one, each came forward and handed him a scroll, which he read aloud.

"Squires shall never reveal the secrets of Dremlock to outsiders.

"Squires shall never enter a forbidden area.

"Squires shall not partake in relationships of any kind relating to marriage.

Squires shall never have dealings of any sort with the Deep Shadow or its children.

"Squires shall never use their powers for unjust purposes."

When finished, Cordus stood in silence for a time, as if giving the Squires a chance to think about what he had said. Then he continued. "Anyone who breaks one or more of the Five Sacred Laws can--and probably will--be instantly cast from the order. There are many other rules as well, which need no list. These are common-sense rules, such as never disobeying a Master without proper cause, and never sneaking out past bedtime or skipping training sessions. Take heart in knowing the Laws also apply to Knights and even myself--the Lord Knight.

"Some of you may wonder why you cannot marry when you get a little older. Well, the purity of Dremlock demands a sacrifice. We are Divine Knights--*Holy* Knights if you will. We cannot allow for distractions. However difficult it may seem at times, such thoughts and yearnings must be vanquished from our minds. Yet when we turn in our Books and retire, we are free of that one Law, and may then marry. The Sacred Laws were created by the Divine Essence and must be obeyed!

"That is all for now, Squires. You should now return to your quarters for the evening. Tomorrow you begin your training."

Garrin Daggerblood turned to the three Blue Squires. "Go to the East Tower for now. I have other business I must attend to. If you wish, you can visit the Library and read some books. There are lots of fascinating ones in there. Some even tell of Kuran Darkender's exploits."

"Can't we just wander around a bit?" asked Vorden.

"I'm afraid not," said Garrin. "New Squires are not allowed to just roam the kingdom at will. Always one of your trainers must know where you are."

"We'll see about that," Vorden whispered, believing only Lannon--who was standing closest to him--could make out what he'd said.

Garrin raised his eyebrows. "What did you say, Vorden?"

"I said that's probably for the better, Master Garrin."

Garrin frowned and nodded. "I'll see you a bit later then." With that, he left the Temple, giving a backwards glance at Vorden as he departed.

"That Garrin fellow has good hearing," said Vorden. "Still, we could linger a bit if we wanted to--you know, sneak around some. But I suppose it wouldn't be wise to risk getting in trouble before our training even begins. Come on, then. I guess we'll just head to the East Tower like the man said." He moved off towards the door, with Lannon and Timlin exchanging a relieved glance before following.

Chapter 8: The Passage of Days

The training was rigorous. The Squires were awakened at the first light of dawn by Garrin Daggerblood and sent to the Great Hall in Furlus' tower, where they were allowed a quick breakfast with the other Squires. Cartlan then led them out to where the pavilion stood, but their lessons took place under open sky. For the first three hours they did nothing but work on physical strength-- lifting heavy weights and wielding weapons some of them could barely even lift, such as hammers, axes, and broadswords.

Furlus Goblincrusher was on hand to give advice on technique, but Cartlan oversaw the actual exercises. Cartlan was in a serious mood (perhaps because Furlus was present), lacking his usual smirk and malicious attitude. Some of the Squires, like Vorden, excelled at this training, while others, like Lannon and Timlin, did poorly and grew sore and weary much sooner than the rest.

After that, for the next three hours they were taught battle skills like swordplay, shield use, and bow practice. Timlin mastered the bow more quickly than all the others, with Vorden and Lannon faring among the best as well. Vorden struggled fiercely to beat Timlin out, but Timlin effortlessly maintained an edge over him with the bow. Timlin grew ever more enthusiastic and delighted, while Vorden kept muttering, shaking his head, and cursing himself.

During the training, the Squires began to falter. They had been provided with light chain mail, but it seemed to grow very heavy as the hours wore on and it chafed their flesh. It was a hot day, and sweat poured off of them, burning their eyes. Lannon often found himself wondering how much more his body could take, yet surprisingly Timlin, in spite of his struggles with any task involving physical strength, never lost his eagerness and never once voiced a word of complaint. Lannon drew strength from Timlin's spirit.

Finally, following Cartlan's instructions, the Squires gathered in the pavilion's seats, wondering what was next and hoping it was nothing physically demanding. They sat with grim, weary faces-- some rubbing strained muscles and other sore spots. Taris Warhawk stood on the pavilion floor, a relaxed, shadowy form who seemed incapable of feeling their doubts and physical pains.

"Greetings, Squires," Taris began. "I know you have been pushed very hard this day. Even though it is not even lunchtime yet, many of you already stand at the breaking point and wonder how you can possibly go on. You may also wonder how you could ever get up tomorrow morning and do this again. Yet tomorrow you will be allowed to rest for the entire day."

Like all the Squires, Lannon's body grew used to such strenuous activities over time. He found his second training session a little easier than the first. After the battle training, they were sent to the Temple for two hours of history and educational lessons. Lannon was surprised to find that some of the Squires didn't even know how to read or write, and some knew virtually nothing of Goblins and were horrified to discover what they were truly like. Lannon loved these two hours of schooling. It gave him a chance to sit and relax after his rigid training, and he learned many things about the history of Dremlock and the surrounding lands.

After the educational lessons, the Squires retired to their quarters for rest and healing meditation, and they were given the following day off from training as well. This pattern of training, resting, and study lessons ran on for two months, and during that time, the Squires all got stronger and more skilled at weapons. But still they learned no sorcery and received no special training. They were provided with clothing and other basic necessities, but they were given no money--as only Knights and Orange Squires received payment for their services.

The three Blue Squires saw very little of Garrin Daggerblood during that span--only briefly on some days when he woke them in the early morning or when he ate dinner with them. Once Vorden asked him when their special training would occur, and Garrin simply told him to be patient.

Lannon got to know most of the other Squires by name, yet
seldom did time or circumstance allow him to interact much with
them (but he didn't try very hard, either). Vorden always seemed to
find time to converse with his friends, sometimes bending the rules
a bit in the process. When they weren't training, the Squires were
usually in the library or resting in their quarters after the brutal
training sessions.

They saw one girl quite often--Aldreya Silverhawk, the Birlote
Squire who had done well in the trials. She seemed extremely
snobbish, and never bothered to talk to the Blue Squires even if
one of them greeted her. She seemed to regard herself as very
important--and not without some justification, as she quickly
became one of Taris Warhawk's favored Squires. He took her
under his wing and trained her himself, and she had more freedom
than the other Squires. She wandered the halls at her leisure, and
was often found studying sorcery books in the Library. Lannon,
Vorden, and Timlin admired her beauty, but they were turned off
by her coldness and attitude of superiority. Vorden labeled her
Aldreya *Snootyhawk*, and he seemed convinced that all Birlotes
thought they were better than Noracks, secretly or otherwise.

Yet the three boys got to know each other quite well, and one
night they held an unexpected conversation about their lives. They
were sitting on two of the beds, with Vorden and Timlin facing
Lannon. It was a warm night, a pleasant breeze blowing in through
the open window, and they were in the mood for talking.

"What was it like living in Knights Welcome?" Vorden asked
Lannon.

"Actually," said Lannon, "I lived just outside of town."

"But you went there a lot, didn't you?"

Lannon thought hard about what he should say. Finally he
decided there was no harm in admitting the truth. "I lived in a little
valley," he said. "In the woods. I rarely went into town, and I don't
know much about cities."

"Were you a loner?" Vorden asked.

Lannon shrugged. "I guess you could say that."

"I was," Timlin said quietly. "I never had many friends. There
were a lot of cruel people where I lived, in Kalamede."

"Did they bully you?" said Vorden.

"Sometimes," said Timlin. "But sometimes I got back at them."

Lannon and Vorden exchanged questioning glances.

"What do you mean?" Vorden said.

A hint of a smile appeared at the corner of Timlin's mouth. "Well, you know...I just did little things. Sneaky things. Once I put a poisonous snake in a kid's pack." Timlin snorted laughter. "It bit his hand and wouldn't let go! He was sick for a few days and nearly died."

An uncomfortable silence followed.

"I guess that was some serious payback," Vorden said at last, glancing at Lannon and raising his eyebrows. "Anyways, I had it pretty good in Gravendar. I used to get in trouble a lot for exploring the Tombs, going into places I didn't belong. I had three friends with me who'd do anything I wanted them to."

Vorden sighed. "It didn't matter what I did. I could do anything I pleased back then, because my parents weren't around to do anything about it. So what about your folks, Lannon? Are they still living?"

"What?" said Lannon, his mind still focused on what Timlin had said. "Yeah, they're fine." He thought of his parents, and wondered how they actually were doing, if his father had been healed. He wondered if they had found peace or were still at each other's throats all the time. He made a mental note to ask Taris.

"My parents hated me," Timlin said, his face expressionless. "So I lived with my aunt. They used to beat me for most any reason. I've got lash scars to prove it." Timlin pulled up his shirt and turned, revealing thin, faint lines on his bony back. The lad was so skinny he looked half-starved.

"They're worthless," Timlin whispered. "I hope they die."

Vorden frowned. "You shouldn't say that, Timlin. My folks *are* dead. They caught an illness, and I got sick from it too. My little sister died also."

Lannon stared in shock at Vorden, trying to imagine such a horrific thing. "What did you do, Vorden? How did you survive?"

Vorden shrugged. "I lived in the streets of Gravendar. I'm not proud to say this, but I stole sometimes to survive. I got good at it-- picking pockets and such. But I always felt bad about it too, like something was wrong or missing in my life. Then, when Admittance Day came to Gravendar this last time, I decided to try my luck with the Knights. They picked me right away--before anyone else! From then on, I decided I would live an honorable life, like Kuran Darkender did."

"How did you get picked, Timlin?" said Lannon.

Timlin giggled. "It was kind of an accident. My aunt and me were visiting the market on Admittance Day, when I bumped into Taris Warhawk in the street. Before I could even apologize, he put his hand on my forehead. It felt really weird. Then he told me he would make me a Squire of Dremlock, if I desired it."

"What about you, Lannon?" said Vorden.

Lannon began telling his story, and once he got started, he couldn't seem to stop. He told everything (save for what Cordus had specifically asked him not to tell). He wanted badly to mention the Goblin incident in the North Road, but forced himself to keep silent concerning it.

"Is there more?" said Vorden, as if peering into Lannon's thoughts.

"Nothing more," said Lannon, looking away.

Vorden watched him for a moment, and Lannon could feel the lad's eyes boring into him. Then Vorden smiled. "Okay, then. If you say so."

***

At last, with two months gone by, the special training began. Their physical routine finished for the day, they were suddenly taken aside by Garrin Daggerblood. "Now is the time, Squires, for you to earn those Blue sashes you wear," he said sternly. "This training will be much different than what you're used to. As these lessons are not greatly physical in nature compared to the standard Knightly training, very little healing time will be required, and you should have no problem doing this after your usual routine. Your study lessons are now done with."

"Forever?" said Lannon, disappointed.

Garrin nodded. "However, we have a well-stocked library here in the East Tower. You're free to read any of the books within."

"Those study lessons were boring anyways," said Vorden.

"You shall learn the ways of stealth," Garrin told them. "You shall learn to pick locks, conceal yourself from an enemy, and climb up places you would never have dreamed of climbing before. And you shall speak of it to no one."

The special training took place mostly in the evening, and so the Blue Squires were allowed to sleep a bit later than the others. Garrin provided them with blue cloaks and soft boots, and taught them how to walk with silent footsteps on most any surface. He gave them lock picks and showed them how to open even the most complex locks. And he taught them how to climb ropes and rough surfaces.

The Squires came to love this phase of their training, and spent each day looking forward to it--for they were allowed at times to sneak around the kingdom (in carefully selected areas) and even to climb certain walls of Taris' keep.

Around the same time they began these extra lessons, Lannon was called upon by Garrin to unlock the Eye of Divinity.

"You need to learn to use your gift," Garrin told him. "I've waited this long to mention it because I felt you needed time to get used to your Knightly training routine. Summoning the Eye of Divinity will be difficult, and it will be easy for you to become discouraged. But if you work at it the same way you've done with your other lessons, you should be fine. Your friends can help you by giving encouragement and by keeping you focused.

"Each night, you must spend an hour before bedtime on the task of splitting your thoughts in two. You must learn to think of two different things at exactly the same time. This is not as simple as it sounds, for it takes more than just seeing the two things--they must be separated to different halves of your being. Only when you learn to do this will the Eye come forth. You will be allowed to leave your special training early to go practice this. This is a task you must do every night. When the Eye of Divinity is finally unlocked, you will know it without a doubt. And then you must inform me immediately."

Lannon didn't like the sound of this task from the start, and his frustration with it grew on a daily basis. For one hour (and sometimes longer) each night he would lay there struggling to think of two things--usually images such as colors--at exactly the same time. Yet nothing ever seemed to happen. And mixing the colors did not help. Black and white did indeed make grey in his mind, but that did nothing to bring forth the Eye of Divinity as far as he could tell. To do that, he realized, he would have to think of black and white simultaneously without blending them, in different parts of his being rather than just in his mind. But how was he supposed to do that? He felt that Garrin had been unfair to him by asking him to do something without really explaining how.

As the days passed by, the three Squires did little but train and rest, while summer and fall slipped away in a hurry, and the cold and rain crept into the mountain air. Then winter came, covering Dremlock in a blanket of white. One thing that continued to puzzle them was why they still had not been shown any sorcery. And try as they might, they could get no answer.

Lannon learned that his folks were doing well. His father had been cured of his illness, at least for the time being. A cheerful letter from them was brought to Lannon, and he wrote one back, though he knew it would not be promptly delivered, since letters from Knights and Squires were only carried to their destinations twice a year. Lannon was left feeling quite satisfied for a while.

The snow deepened, and massive shards of ice hung from the towers. Some of the Squires faltered and could not go on. These Squires had failed to properly learn the techniques or were too lazy or distracted to keep pace. Others violated the rules once too often and were banished from Dremlock. Vorden, who made time to mingle during and outside of training, usually kept Lannon and Timlin informed of what was going on around the Kingdom. New rumors spread daily among Squires and Knights alike. It was said that the Deep Shadow infested Dremlock, and that some Squires were possessed by it, like puppets controlled by unseen masters. Some claimed Corhen Whiteheart, a Green Knight of the High Council, had looked into these claims too deeply and been assassinated, while Trenton Shadowbane--the Investigator of Dremlock--did nothing. And indeed Corhen Whiteheart was not seen again.

It was also rumored that food and other supplies were running low, that trade had nearly ground to a halt, and that less than a third of Dremlock's Knights still lived, with the others having been killed by Goblins. There were even rumors that Goblins had taken over the entire forestlands of Hethos and were advancing on the city of Kalamede. Injured and half-crazed Knights returned to Dremlock weekly, and the Temple was busy honoring the recent dead. The Squires were never invited to these ceremonies, only learning of them through rumor.

Lannon grew a bit taller and more muscular, and could use his Dragon sword with decent skill. Even though he was behind the others in his skills, he had begun to feel like a Divine Squire of Dremlock. Yet the rumors worried him, and made him wonder constantly what kind of future he had here--what the Eye of Divinity would be used for and if it was even needed anymore. Vorden and Timlin could sneak around without being heard or seen, open locks without the need of a key, and climb walls fearlessly to deadly heights. But they had the Knightly Essence, and Lannon did not. So without the Eye of Divinity he guessed he would probably never be a Knight.

Lannon's task of summoning the Eye became almost an afterthought to his other training, and he usually gave just a halfhearted attempt at it before falling asleep. He began to resent missing some of his special training with Garrin, Vorden, and Timlin. No more had been mentioned about the Goblin Puzzle, and so it seemed something must have already been done about that.

Vorden and Timlin talked little about Lannon's quest to unlock his special power, apparently having given up on the idea that Lannon would ever develop that particular skill. Like Lannon, they actually knew nothing about the Eye of Divinity beyond the reading of the Sacred Text.

At one point Garrin asked about his progress, and when Lannon had nothing positive to report, the Blue Knight was grim. "You must try harder, Lannon. There is no other way, to my knowledge. It has to be done for one hour a night--no more and no less. If too little time is spent on it, the mind cannot properly warm up to the task, and if too much time is taken, the mind grows numb and confused. There is nothing that Taris Warhawk, myself, or anyone else can do to help you except to give encouragement. Always, throughout history, the Eye of Divinity has been unlocked in this fashion. No one really knows why or how. Keep focusing on two different thoughts, and sooner or later the Eye shall come forth. It has no choice."

"But I read the Sacred Text," Lannon said. "So isn't the Eye already unlocked? Otherwise how could I do that?"

Garrin shook his head sadly. "I wish it were that simple. Being able to read the Text is just a sign that one possesses the Eye. But it does not mean one can summon it or control it. Or can you? You should know, Lannon."

"I can't," said Lannon, with a sigh.

Growing desperate for help, Lannon appealed to Vorden and Timlin. Yet they seemed to take little interest in the matter. Their minds had apparently become melded with their training. It seemed that, to them, little existed beyond their daily lessons and accomplishments. Timlin had nothing to say, and Vorden simply shrugged and told him to keep trying.

The time seemed to pass swiftly, and before they knew it, eight months had gone by and had taken them into the heart of winter.

Vorden kept his true feelings well hidden over those months, until finally--for reasons known only to him--they suddenly surged forth. And the rigid schedule of training and resting was shattered.

Chapter 9: What Lay Beneath Old Keep

One night, while Lannon lay on his bed trying to unlock the Eye of Divinity (with his mind often straying from that frustrating task to more interesting things), Vorden and Timlin barged into the room, having completed their special training for the evening. In the flickering lantern light, Lannon could see by the excitement on their faces that something was up. He yawned and sat up, resting his bare feet on the cold floorboards. He wished, as he had many times, the East Tower were a warmer place.

"I have an idea," Vorden said, "about how you can summon the Eye of Divinity." He adjusted his sash, smoothed back his black hair, and smiled. "Since the Knights seem to think it's important for some reason, I feel like I should help. Maybe the fate of Dremlock depends on it somehow. I started thinking it over today and came up with something. It might not work, but it's worth a try."

"Okay," said Lannon, showing cautious optimism. "What should I do?" In the time that Lannon had known him, he had come to realize that Vorden almost always knew what he was talking about. If he had an idea, it was typically something brilliant.

"It's quite simple," Vorden said. "Timlin will stand on one side of you, and I'll stand on the other. I'll say something, and he'll say the opposite--like light and dark, for instance. And while we say it, we'll tap you on the shoulders. Maybe you just need a little help to get your mind focused."

"Okay," said Lannon, standing up. "I guess I have nothing to lose."

Vorden stood on one side of Lannon, and Timlin on the other. They agreed to use red and green as their words--Knightly colors.

"Get ready, Timlin," said Vorden. "When I signal you, say red, and I'll try to say green at the same time. And as you say it, tap Lannon's shoulder. Okay, here goes."

He signaled to Timlin and yelled "Red!"

"Green!" Vorden said an instant later, and Lannon's shoulders were tapped at exactly the same time.

For a moment Lannon felt dizzy and lightheaded. Then the feeling vanished and he was left wondering if it had actually existed at all.

"I think I felt something," he said. "But I'm not sure."

"We were way out of time on our words," said Vorden. "We need to keep trying until we get it right. Let's do it again, Timlin."

For nearly an hour, the boys tried to get their timing down. At first they were always just a little off on their words or else on their taps, but eventually they got it almost perfect. Each time the words or the taps were done at exactly the same time, Lannon felt lightheaded and dizzy, and he grew more excited with each attempt.

Then his mind suddenly split, and he became aware of two things at once. He was seeing a block of red in his mind and a block of green--not side-by-side or blended (as anyone might be able to view them), but as something else. They were solid entities that he could view carefully without distraction--and they existed in different halves of his being. He felt like he was divided in two. Then, from the gap that existed between his two selves, a force pushed its way out. Like a living extension of Lannon's will, it reached out and probed wherever he commanded it. It fell upon Vorden and Timlin, and he saw things that caused his throat to tighten.

Lannon saw that Vorden was dark in spirit and given to a strange road that could destroy him and all others who got too close. Timlin was innocent--cloaked in white--yet underneath lurked a sharp and deadly bite, waiting in surprise for those who could not glimpse it.

Horrified by what he saw, Lannon drew the Eye back inside him. His selves merged again into one, and the gateway was sealed.

"What happened?" Vorden asked him.

Unsure of what he should tell them, Lannon hesitated for a few moments. At last he said, "The Eye of Divinity came out, I think. But I didn't like what it showed me. It seemed like it was probing for secrets in both of you."

"Well, that's probably what it does!" Vorden said excitedly, clutching Lannon's shoulder so hard the boy winced. "It reveals hidden motives and strengths and weaknesses!"

"We should tell Master Garrin!" Timlin said.

"Right," said Vorden, walking over to the window and opening the shutters. The wind howled against the tower, and a puff of glittering snowflakes blew in on him. He seemed deep in thought for a time. At last he turned and spoke. "Not just yet, I think. We need to experiment some more--find out if it's truly the Eye and not something else."

"It has to be the Eye," said Lannon, sitting back down on the bed. "What else could it be?" Lannon shivered, and he drew his blanket around him. "Close the window, Vorden. I'm freezing." At last he had completed his elusive task, yet he felt little sense of accomplishment. He'd needed help from others, so had he truly succeeded? And the Eye had shown him things--whether true or not--that he had been ill prepared to witness.

Vorden shrugged. "It could be dark sorcery, or Knightly Essence. Who knows? I just think we should make sure. I've been doing some thinking...."

Vorden closed the thick shutters and turned to Lannon. He lowered his voice to a whisper. "You know that door down below-- the one marked Old Keep? I know it's forbidden and all, but I don't see what harm it would do to go down there and have a look around."

"I don't like that idea at all!" said Lannon, stunned that Vorden would even suggest such a thing. "If we were caught, we could be cast from the Order. And you heard what Cordus Landsaver said about creatures lurking down there."

"But the Divine Essence is down there as well," said Vorden. "And I've been having dreams about it. I think it's calling to me."

Timlin's mouth dropped open. "Vorden, why didn't you tell Master Garrin you were having such dreams?"

Vorden frowned "Why do we have to tell Master Garrin

everything, Timlin? This is something between the Divine Essence and me. I want to find out what my dreams truly mean, like Kuran Darkender did. Yet I'm afraid to go down there alone." He sighed, his dark eyes taking on a pleading look. "I need your help. The Knights would never allow me to venture down in the mines, dreams or not."

Lannon glanced at Timlin, and then back to Vorden. "I'm just worried we'll get caught, or worse--get killed down there."

"We'll take it slow and be extra careful," said Vorden. "If we see any signs of danger, we'll turn back. Besides, I honestly don't think there is any danger down there now. The Knights probably killed the creatures long ago, and they just say there's still some down there to keep people from seeing the Divine Essence. After all, why shouldn't everyone be allowed to see it? I think that's a rule based on pointless greed."

"But what if we're caught?" said Lannon.

"We'd certainly be in trouble," said Vorden. "But I think they'd forgive us. After all, you have the Eye of Divinity--which they seem to value greatly. And Timlin and me helped you summon it. Without us, you can't use it. They might punish us, but I doubt we'd be thrown out. Besides, we're Blue Squires. They won't catch us."

"I don't know," said Lannon, shaking his head slowly. He was thinking of what the Eye had shown him about Vorden and not liking any of this one bit. "I just don't think I can do it, Vorden."

For an instant, Vorden's face reddened with anger. "Very well, then. Be a coward. Maybe the other Squires are right about you, Lannon. Maybe you don't deserve to be Blue. Maybe you should've been picked for Orange. And some thanks I get for helping you use that stupid Eye thing. See if I ever help you again! "With that, Vorden yanked his boots off, lay down on his bed, and turned away.

Lannon stared helplessly at Timlin, feeling horrible inside and wondering what he could do. Vorden had been a true friend to him--someone he could look up to--and now it seemed he was going to lose that friendship forever. But the risks of what Vorden proposed were dastardly.

Timlin could only shrug in his meek, annoying way.

***

As Lannon lay in bed, staring up at the maze of wooden beams and cobwebs that crisscrossed the ceiling, he began to doubt his decision. Vorden had indeed helped him to unlock the Eye, and more importantly, Vorden had been a true friend to him from the start. How could Lannon just turn his back on him? But how could he ignore all his instincts and common sense and go along with Vorden's mad plan? Lannon certainly wanted to see the Divine Essence for himself--but not at such a risk.

Lannon thought he would not be able to sleep that night, which was not good--since training would resume again early in the morning. (Training now took place two days in a row with one day of rest afterwards.) His mind was in turmoil, yet beneath all the gloomy thoughts--buried deep but still very much alive--was a feeling of elation. He had called forth the Eye, and it was indeed powerful. Part of him wondered why he shouldn't just go along with Vorden's plan. If Lannon were truly blessed, the Divine Essence would surely help him make the right decision.

He prayed to it for an answer, and in the midst of that prayer he fell asleep. He dreamt of the Divine Essence in its crystal chamber. Its piercing light fell on him, beckoning him below.

"I will share my secrets," it whispered to him.

***

Even before Lannon awoke the next morning, he knew he had his answer. Neither the risk of losing his Knighthood nor even the risk of losing his very life could keep him from going in the dark and forbidden mines below. The Divine Essence had apparently commanded it, and Lannon could not refuse. A dream of the Essence was no ordinary dream. One only had to read the first chapter of *Tales of Kuran Darkender* to learn that. It had promised to share its secrets with Lannon. How could he ignore that?

When Lannon revealed his decision, Vorden was overcome with excitement, and seemed quite forgiving. He apologized several times for his attitude of the night before, swearing that Lannon would be his friend forever. The ease with which Vorden forgave him startled Lannon, yet he couldn't deny that a great burden had been lifted off his shoulders, leaving him feeling relieved but uncertain.

The day drifted by slowly. He could not seem to focus on his training and did poorly. All he wanted was for the day to end so they could get their plan moving before the anxiety wore his nerves down. Vorden, however, seemed to train with extra vigor and couldn't hide the delight he felt over something that terrified Lannon.

When at last all their training was done, the Blue Squires sat in their quarters talking it over. Vorden laid out a specific plan he had thought up during the day, and then Lannon knew beyond a doubt they were actually going to go through with this--something he hadn't quite believed until now.

"The plan is simple," said Vorden. "We'll all go down to the first floor together. While one of us picks the lock of the door to Old Keep, the other two will watch the stairs and listen at the front door for anyone approaching. Once it's unlocked, I'll swipe one of those Birlote torches off the wall and we'll head on in, closing the door behind us. No one will even know we went that way."

"What if someone notices the torch is missing?" said Lannon.

"Not likely," said Vorden. "And even if they do, how can they prove we took it? The fact is--they can't. Anyone could have stolen it for any reason."

"But what if someone sees us when we go down to the first floor?" said Lannon. "What should we tell them?"

"We say we heard a noise and came down to investigate," said Vorden. "And then we stick with that story no matter what. Look, don't worry about it. Most everyone's in bed by now, anyway."

"But what if someone checks on us?" said Lannon.

"We won't be gone that long," said Vorden. "But if someone checks on us and finds we're missing, we'll just tell them the noise story."

"It's not a strong plan," said Lannon. "There are a lot of holes in it, Vorden."

Vorden shrugged. "Well, then make up your mind. Do we go or not?"

Lannon nodded, remembering his dream. "I have to go."

"I think it's worth it," said Timlin. "To see the Divine Essence would be better than anything! Can I pick the lock? I'm good at that."

Vorden grinned, nodding. "You're the best at it, Timlin. Once we're past that door, you can also check the walls and floor for traps, while Lannon and me keep alert for danger. You'll act as Passage Man. I'll be Arms Man, and Lannon will be Scout Man. We go together as Blue Squires!"

"I wish I had more training," said Lannon. "But let's get on with it."

Suddenly there was a startled gasp. Shadows by the window took shape and a girl seemed to appear out of nowhere. It was Aldreya Silverhawk.

Her green eyes were wide. She wore a hooded grey cloak, and the hood had slid back to reveal her curly silver hair, pointed ears, and bronze-colored skin. In one hand she held a stone dagger, pulled tight against her chest.

"I can't believe what I've just heard," she whispered.

The boys jumped up, their hearts racing.

"What are you doing here?" Vorden said. "Were you spying on us?"

"No!" Aldreya insisted. "I wasn't spying. I was...just doing some of my training. I was hiding myself, blending in with the shadows."

"You were spying," Vorden said coldly.

"I heard everything," she said. "I know what you're planning, and you're not going to get away with it. I'm going to see Taris at once. I'll tell him what you're up to."

Lannon and Timlin glanced at each other, and then back at Vorden, waiting for him to find a way out of this situation. They had no clue what to do and were on the verge of panic, their faces pale.

But Vorden remained calm. "Go ahead," he said. "Tell on us-- and then I'll tell on you. You're not supposed to be in our room. It's forbidden for boys and girls to be in the same quarters together."

She hesitated for a moment, and then spoke. "Okay, if that's the way it must be. I'll just forget what I heard, and you forget I was ever here."

Lannon and Timlin breathed sighs of relief.

But Vorden wasn't finished. "It's not that easy," he said. "All we did was *talk* about breaking the rules. You actually *broke* them.

I think I should give a little yell and alert someone right now."

Aldreya glanced towards the door. "Wait--don't do that! I could be thrown out of Dremlock. I'm sorry I was spy...uh...training in here."

"Why don't you come with us?" said Vorden. "You're a good sorceress, from what I hear. We could use your help."

"Break the Sacred Laws?" the Birlote girl said. "Go beneath Old Keep?" She frowned. "Cordus said that monsters lurk down there."

Patiently, Vorden explained his theory about how the Knights were just trying to scare people away from the Divine Essence.

"At the first sign of trouble, we'll turn back," he said.

Lannon didn't believe even the slightest chance existed that Aldreya Silverhawk would agree to such a mad scheme. He was wrong.

"When should we go," she said, stepping forward eagerly. "I can't deny that I would love to see the Divine Essence. Who wouldn't? But when the task is done, no one must tell Taris anything. Understood?"

"Understood," said Vorden. "And *now* is the perfect time. We're all here, and we have tomorrow off from training."

"I don't have tomorrow off," she said. "I have to be... Actually, I'm not supposed to tell you that. Let's just say I need to be up fairly early. But I can handle it. I'm used to staying up late."

Aldreya smiled excitedly. "This is a good opportunity to test my skills. Truthfully, I've been doing a lot of sneaking around ever since I learned to blend with the shadows. I just haven't tried anything this daring yet. Besides, even if we get caught, I don't think Taris would let *me* be punished. I just can't imagine it!"

"Of course," Vorden agreed, with an amused, sideways glance at Lannon. "If anyone would be spared punishment, it would be you."

"Then I have your word on it?" Vorden said, stepping close to her. He extended his hand. "You'll go with us, and not tell anyone about this?"

"Yes, you have my word," she said. She glanced at his hand, and then gave it a quick shake. "I'll keep it secret, Vorden

Flameblade."

"I hope your word is good, Aldreya Snoot..." Vorden cleared his throat, his face reddening. "Aldreya Silverhawk."

She smiled again, and for the first time, the Blue Squires realized how truly beautiful she was. But it was a cold and dangerous sort of beauty--one that could not be trusted. Lannon pondered how quickly and easily she had agreed to this, and a warning flashed through his mind. Surely she was planning to betray them. Or maybe she was spying for Taris. Was Vorden blind to this? It seemed unlikely someone as intelligent as Vorden would fail to realize Aldreya cared little or nothing about them. She was a Birlote, and the Tree Dwellers were not known for their rule breaking. From what Lannon had seen, they obeyed even the smallest laws. She probably realized she lacked enough evidence to get them in trouble at this point, and was playing along with their plan in order gather a stronger case against them.

"I don't know about this," Lannon said. "Maybe we should talk things over first, Vorden, just between us three boys."

"Don't worry about it," said Vorden. "Aldreya's word is good."

"My word is *very* good!" said Aldreya, glaring at Lannon. "Why would you think otherwise? Birlotes do not lie."

Lannon stared back, unfazed. "I guess I don't trust you."

"I don't trust her at all!" said Timlin.

A hurt look appeared on Aldreya's face and she turned away for a moment. When she turned back, her face was impassive. "Think whatever you want, Lannon. If you don't want me to go with you, I'll leave."

"We want you to go," said Vorden. "Don't we, Lannon?"

Lannon shrugged. "I guess so."

"Then let's get going!" Aldreya snapped. "We don't have all night."

The boys grabbed their weapons and donned light armor (which had been specially crafted for stealth and ease of movement), blue cloaks (of the thick winter variety), and soft leather boots. Vorden peered out into the hall, and then motioned to the others to follow. As they made their way down from floor to floor, they stayed in the shadows as much as possible. The Blue Squires knew how to move stealthily through the dimly lit areas, but they could not hide themselves nearly as well as Aldreya, who seemed to all but vanish completely at times.

Chills crept along Lannon's flesh. This was Taris Warhawk's tower, and he was a great sorcerer. Would he somehow know what they were up to? Lannon felt like he was betraying Taris, and for a moment he hesitated, until Vorden turned and gave him a hard, questioning stare that got him moving again.

They met no one, and at last they reached the tower's first floor. Timlin moved towards the door marked Old Keep, and then turned back to Vorden with a puzzled look on his face. "What do I use to pick the lock?" he whispered. "Master Garrin keeps all our tools and stuff."

Vorden smiled and removed a set of lock picks from his cloak. He tossed them to Timlin. "Don't ask where I got them," he said.

Aldreya gave Vorden a cold stare.

Timlin grinned, gazing triumphantly at Aldreya--daring her to speak in protest of Vorden's thievery. Then he hurried over to work on the door.

Vorden listened at the front entrance, while Lannon--his body trembling and his heart pounding--kept watch at the stairs.

Several moments passed by in silence. "Hurry up, Timlin!" Vorden whispered. "You're taking way too long."

Finally Timlin turned and nodded. Vorden grabbed a Birlote torch from the wall, and they gathered before the door. Without hesitation, Vorden yanked it open and stepped inside. The others quickly followed, pulling the door shut behind them.

Before the Squires, a stone stairway descended into the darkness. A musty smell arose from below, and even here at the very gateway to Old Keep the gloom had a sinister feel to it. The dark was deep and heavy over the cold stone that had lain undisturbed for centuries. The Birlote torch could not shine far enough down the steps to penetrate the blackness below.

"Let's not do this!" Timlin whispered shakily. The boy was trembling from head to foot. "I don't want to go down there, Vorden."

Vorden turned and glared at him. "We're still in Taris' keep, Timlin. We haven't even entered Old Keep yet, let alone the mines! What's left of the Old Keep is pretty much underground, from what

I've heard, and so we have to go down a ways. Do you really think
something lurks right down there? If so, it must be pretty weak, or
a simple wooden door wouldn't stop it. Now quit being a coward.
We've come this far, and we have to finish this!"

Vorden seized Timlin's cloak. "Dremlock Kingdom is in
trouble. We all know it. It might even fall to the Goblins, or worse-
-the Deep Shadow. I dreamt of the Divine Essence, and it has all
the answers. This quest could be incredibly important. I may
discover something to help save the kingdom."

Timlin nodded sheepishly.

Lannon said nothing about his dream, but secretly he
wondered if Vorden was lying about his own.

With that, Vorden draped his battle axe over his shoulder and
started down the stairs. Lannon held his sword ready, and Timlin
unsheathed his preferred weapon--a long, curved dagger called a
Flayer. Then they followed him below, struggling to keep pace so
the shadows wouldn't engulf them.

The stairway led down to a circular chamber. The stone walls
were made of uneven, crudely cut blocks that hadn't been fitted
together well. Two iron doors stood here, and another stairway
descended into darkness.

"Which way should we go?" said Lannon.

Vorden pointed to the stairs. "We need to keep going down.
From what everyone seems to think, the Divine Essence dwells in
the mines somewhere. This is just the keep the old Knights built
above those mines, and hopefully the entrance leading down there
isn't sealed off with bars of Glaetherin like Cordus Landsaver said.
If it is, then I guess all this is going to be for nothing."

The stairs led them down to another round chamber--this one
with four doors. Iron torch holders hung from the walls, and the
broken remains of several tables and chairs lay scattered about the
room, as well as chunks of pottery. The Squires checked behind all
the doors, and found the remains of a kitchen, a forge with a
blackened stone furnace, and a large room with wooden bunks
lining the walls.

Behind the last door they checked, they found what they were
looking for.

The square room behind this door was cut from the stone of
the mountain. Steps led down from the doorway to the chamber

floor. Directly opposite the stairs, on the other side of the room, was the dark mouth of a tunnel that was blocked by a gate of silver bars. A wheel lock stood at the center of the bars.

"No!" muttered Vorden, leaping down the steps. He lowered his axe in defeat. "Bars of Glaetherin, just like Cordus said. Indestructible." He turned back to the others, who were right behind him. "That's it. We can't go any farther."

Vorden gave the wheel a hard spin. It twirled for a couple moments and then slowly came to a stop. No click could be heard.

"Is there a way to pick it?" asked Timlin.

Vorden glared at him. "Are you stupid, Timlin? This is a wheel lock like those ones on the gates of Darkender Tunnel. Only a Wheel Master is able to open a lock like this--and only if he has been trained to open a specific one. And the pattern that opens this particular lock has probably been long forgotten. That means no one alive could open this, most likely. From what I've heard from Cartlan, wheel locks are so tough that you could spin one all day for the rest of your life and still never open it. It has to be spun at a certain speed, while an extremely precise amount of pressure is applied--and then the wheel must spin for a certain length of time. Trust me, it's practically impossible. It's an Olrog creation, and the Grey Dwarves are masters at making such devices."

"Then I guess we go back," said Lannon, feeling both tremendously relieved and somewhat disappointed. Maybe Lannon's dream had meant nothing after all. Now if only they could get back to their quarters without getting caught!

"Let's go," said Timlin. "I don't like it down here, anyway." The lad continued to shiver, his flesh covered in large goose bumps.

"Not even sorcerers can open a wheel lock," said Aldreya, "without knowing the process for a specific lock. It just cannot be done."

"But there has to be way!" said Vorden, turning back to the bars.

Lannon found Vorden's refusal to give up bizarre and a bit frightening. What was driving Vorden on like this? Clearly they weren't meant to go farther.

Suddenly Vorden turned back to them, his eyes blazing with excitement. "We can do this. We can use the Eye of Divinity to open the lock!"

"The Eye of *what*?" said Aldreya.

Lannon felt a surge of excitement at the prospect, but then it gave way to darker feelings. "Maybe we could, Vorden. But the bars were placed here for a reason--to keep something from coming through. And it must be something powerful, or they would have just used steel or iron. Glaetherin is probably pretty rare. "

"I don't believe those fairy tales," said Vorden. "They used Glaetherin because they wanted to keep people from seeing the Divine Essence. Look at it this way, Lannon. Something down here killed Kuran Darkender, right? Well, his armor was made of Glaetherin. So that metal couldn't stop the evil creatures, anyway. The Knights must have destroyed the beasts and put the bars here to keep people out!"

Lannon thought it over, and could not find fault with Vorden's logic. But at the moment his thinking wasn't perfectly clear, either. "Maybe you're right," he said. "I'll try the Eye. If it works, we'll keep going. But any sign of danger, Vorden--"

"And we turn back of course," Vorden finished. "I'm not a fool, Lannon. I don't want to die down here anymore than you do."

"Let's just leave," Timlin said again, peering into the stone cavern beyond the bars. "I don't like this at all."

Vorden glowered at him. "At least help Lannon call out the Eye. Then, if you want to be a coward, you can go back. But don't you dare get us caught, Timlin! Just wait in the shadows somewhere by the door."

"I can't go back in the dark!" said Timlin, shivering.

Vorden shrugged. "Looks like we go on together, then."

"How can we go on?" said Aldreya. "I just told you--no one can open a wheel lock without knowing the combination. It is impossible."

The boys took position on either side of Lannon. It took several tries to get their words and taps to synchronize, but eventually Lannon's mind split in two and the Eye of Divinity came out. He directed it on the lock and the answer was revealed-- and much more. He glimpsed a mind-numbing process of mathematical calculations, trial and error, and sorcery behind it all. He knew exactly what to do.

Lannon stepped forward, applied a slight pressure to the wheel, and gave it a hard spin. When the wheel stopped, a click could be heard--very loud and intrusive in the stillness of the stone chamber. The gate split, coming partly open.

A moment of silence followed, interrupted only by tense breathing.

Then Vorden whispered, "You actually did it!"

"Goodness!" Aldreya gasped. "How did you do that?"

Lannon shrugged, unsure if he should tell her.

Vorden stepped through the open gate, leaving the others in the shadows. Hurriedly they swallowed their fears and followed. The Eye of Divinity probed the darkness of the cavern, revealing the echoes of centuries. It gave glimpses far into the past--of dark and bloody affairs in vague yet horrifying detail, mingling with the moans of the dying in the deep places of the mountain. Olrog pickaxes clanged fiercely against the stone, driven by powerful grey-skinned bodies, as dark things crept through the caverns and up the mineshafts in search of flesh.

It might have showed Lannon more, but he frantically drew it back inside himself and decided it was time to get out of here. The images had been too horrible to be ignored. He turned away, pushing Timlin and Aldreya aside, and started back towards the gate. But as he left the torchlight behind, the darkness closed around him, gripping him to the soul and leaving him helpless. Down here, the dark seemed alive and hostile.

With a violent shudder, Lannon turned and raced back to the torchlight.

"What was that all about?" Aldreya said.

"I was just checking behind us for danger," mumbled Lannon, blushing.

He lacked the courage to face the dark, and so there was no turning back now, until Vorden decided it.

The cavern widened some and then split into three tunnels. Vorden gazed at the tunnel mouths for several moments, scratching his head, while Lannon, Timlin, and Aldreya fidgeted about impatiently. Finally he shrugged helplessly.

"I guess we take the left one."

No one questioned his decision, and they found themselves moving down a long, sloping course that eventually leveled off again. They passed the remains of some mining tools, including a broken cart and a rusted pickaxe, and piles of rotten rope. They also encountered yellowed bones and even a couple of oddly shaped skulls with wide teeth.

"Olrog skulls, I'll bet," said Vorden, nodding towards them.

Furlus Goblincrusher's kinfolk, Lannon thought.

At the sight of the skulls, Timlin almost lost his nerve, and stood paralyzed for a time while Vorden chastised him.

"Quit being such a coward, Timlin!" Vorden whispered harshly, "and act like a Blue Squire for a change. Those skulls are obviously ancient, and who knows how they got here? And remember, if you go back--you do it in the dark."

But Vorden's words seemed hollow, and the lad from Gravendar suddenly didn't look so confident anymore. His eyes darted back and forth into the shadows, and his knuckles were white as he gripped the handle of his axe.

Suddenly the cavern widened into a chamber so large the torchlight could not reveal the walls or ceiling of it. The Squires instantly felt exposed in the open space around them that was swallowed in darkness. Anything could be watching them from the shadows beyond the torchlight--yet they would not be able to see it. Their own light source gave them away, making them easy targets.

And at this point Vorden halted, and Lannon could tell by the expression on his face he was considering turning back. But then that expression faded into one of determination, and he trudged forward into the unknown.

After about a hundred feet they came to a stone wall, and the torchlight revealed the very edge of a tunnel mouth to their left. Vorden led them into it. This was a crudely hewn tunnel, the walls and floor uneven. The Squires had to be careful not to trip. A gloomy, desolate feeling hung in this particular cavern--different somehow, more dreadful, than what they had encountered thus far. This tunnel seemed old and cramped, leading them into a place where only fools would dare go.

"Vorden, this is crazy!" Lannon whispered. "We can't go on anymore. It's too big down here, and the Divine Essence could be anywhere."

"But we must be close," said Vorden. "I think I can feel it somehow. Are we just going to leave now, with the Essence somewhere nearby? This might be our only chance to ever catch a glimpse of it."

Lannon sighed. "I really don't care anymore. I just want to get out of here. We can come back later, when we have more torches and we're better trained. Listen--we need to go back right now, before we get ourselves lost or killed! And maybe they've already discovered we're missing. We could lose our chance at Knighthood!"

Lannon felt sickened by the whole affair, his mind overridden with gloomy thoughts and terror. And yet Vorden seemed so foolishly stubborn. Lannon deeply regretted his decision to come down here, and if he could have taken it back and lost Vorden's friendship forever, he would have. None of this seemed worth it in the least--despite his dream of the Divine Essence. And still Vorden trudged onward, holding the only torch. Vaguely Lannon considered making a grab for that torch and running. But Vorden held it in a death grip, perhaps anticipating such a maneuver.

Timlin remained silent at this point, obviously overcome by fear. He pressed close to Lannon, keeping his eyes fixed on the floor, and he was trembling all over. Through all his dismay, Lannon felt extreme irritation over Vorden's selfishness. Timlin looked ready to fall apart at any moment, and still Vorden refused to give in.

Aldreya stopped. "I don't think I can go on," she said. "I feel horrible, like I'm being smothered down here. Lannon is right, Vorden. We need to get out of this place and never come back."

"Get going then," said Vorden, "or stand there and wait. But I'm moving on, and that's the way it is."

With a glance into the shadows, Aldreya started moving again. "You're being ridiculous, Vorden. What kind of Squire are you? You don't care about anyone but yourself. I knew it from the moment I saw you. You think you're superior to everyone else!"

Vorden stopped, turning towards her. His mouth hung agape in an exaggerated expression. "That's the silliest thing I've ever heard. Have you looked in the mirror lately? You're the biggest snob in Dremlock!" With that, he turned and started walking again.

"That's not true, Vorden," said Aldreya, in a hurt voice. " I've just been too busy to make friends. But what are we even talking about? We need to get out of these mines before we get killed!"

The tunnel finally gave way to another round chamber, this one much smaller than the last. Six cavern mouths were cut into the walls. Two of them had the remains of heavy iron bars across them, which had been bent and ripped in two, leaving large holes. Amidst some mining tools, more skulls and bones lay scattered.

"We can't go any farther," Lannon whispered. "We'll get lost. There are too many tunnels, Vorden."

"We can't turn back now," Vorden muttered. "One of these tunnels has to lead to the Divine Essence. You need to use the Eye again."

Lannon shook his head. "There's no way I'm going to do that." His words could not express the horror he felt at that prospect.

"So you're a coward like Timlin," snapped Vorden, raising his voice. He turned and stepped close to Lannon, his eyes narrowed with an accusing glare.

"Quiet!" hissed Lannon, backing up a step. "You're being too loud. And I'm not a coward. You're just being selfish. I thought you were my friend. If you are, then take us back now."

"Look at the bars." Timlin's words were a choked whisper. "Something must have..."

"I thought you were brave," said Vorden, still talking above a whisper. He pushed closer to Lannon. "But now I know you're just a weakling. You and Timlin are both the same. Well, I'm going on with or without you two. And if you try to stop me or tell on me..."

Vorden glowered at them, his face red with rage. Then, from the tunnel mouth directly behind him something emerged. Lannon caught a glimpse of grey, bumpy skin, an enormous pumpkin-shaped head, and oversized hands and feet. Great claws scraped the stone floor, and a wide mouth hung open to reveal rows of lumpy teeth that looked like bone fragments. A chilling darkness filled the cavern, plunging their minds into despair.

Aldreya screamed, while Lannon and Timlin stood in stunned

silence. Vorden whirled around.

Lannon managed to find his voice, and he cried, "It's an Ogre!" He remembered the monstrous breed of Goblin from his book, *The Truth about Goblins.* Ogres were intelligent by Goblin standards and had poisonous claws. They were night stalkers who preferred to strike quickly from the shadows. They could feed until they swelled up to twice their normal size.

The creature lunged towards Vorden. Vorden recovered from his surprise and tried to swing his axe, but the creature's shovel-sized hand batted the weapon aside and it clanged to the floor. Vorden was lifted into the air and wrapped in a bear hug, pulled fiercely against the giant's barrel chest.

Vorden's bones started to crack and he screamed, dropping the torch--which continued to provide light for a scene Lannon didn't want to view but couldn't rip his gaze away from. Vorden would be crushed to death in a matter of seconds.

Lannon stood paralyzed, watching Vorden's life end in this those gnarled grey arms. He couldn't bring himself to even breathe--let alone fight or flee. Months of rigid training suddenly seemed meaningless. His sword dangled uselessly from his hand, and vaguely, somewhere in the back of his mind, he thought he wasn't Knightly material and should never have been chosen as a Squire.

But help for Vorden came from a most unlikely source. A swift shadow darted past Lannon and then a long, curved dagger sliced deep into the Ogre's arm. It was Timlin--the smallest and (seemingly) least courageous of all the Squires.

"Let him go!" Timlin howled, ripping the Flayer along the Ogre's arm and laying bare some of the flesh within.

With a roar, the Ogre dropped Vorden to the floor and swiped at Timlin. The Ogre's hand lashed out in a blur, and Lannon cringed, certain Timlin's head would be smashed from his shoulders. But the lad somehow managed to duck the blow and dove between the monster's legs. The Ogre turned to attack him, but Timlin scrambled up and ran around it towards Lannon. His eyes were blazing with a wild mix of terror and determination.

The Ogre ignored Timlin--save for a roar of irritation in his direction--and it knelt over Vorden, licking its lips hungrily. It bent down, its teeth ready to tear into Vorden's throat. Vorden tried to move, but the Ogre pinned him with one hand.

"It's going to kill him!" Aldreya screamed.

Timlin grabbed Lannon's cloak, nearly yanking him off balance. "He's going to eat him!" Timlin yelled. "Help me save him, Lannon!"

Timlin's words jarred Lannon into action, and he raised his sword, struggling to remember his training. Yet there was little time for recollections. In an instant, Vorden's throat would be ripped open by those fragmented teeth.

The two Squires charged the Ogre. It glanced up at them with its round black eyes and snarled. Timlin reached it first and tried to stab the beast in the chest, but the Ogre caught the lad with a lazy blow to his side that knocked him halfway across the room. Lannon drove his Dragon-bone sword at the creature's head, but it was a poor thrust and the weapon merely glanced away from the thick skull, leaving only a small gash.

The force of his thrust threw Lannon forward--nearly into the Ogre's lap. The beast caught his shoulder with one hand and shoved him away. Lannon tumbled across the stone floor, striking his head and almost blacking out.

Again the Ogre bent down to feed. Then a searing ball of green fire struck its chest, knocking the beast over. Calmly Aldreya walked into the room. She was holding forth her stone dagger, which was engulfed in flames. She drew it back again and flung another green fireball at the Ogre--this time striking its shoulder where the beast lay. The Ogre growled in pain and clawed at its blackened wounds, but then it leapt up from the floor, preparing to crush the foolish Birlote girl who had dared burn its flesh so painfully.

Then a clanking sound arose. Something or someone was moving down one of the tunnels. The Ogre paused, listening. Then it lifted Vorden's axe from the floor. The double-bladed battle axe looked like a small hatchet in its hand. Due to the length of its claws, it grasped the weapon in a clumsy manner, and it held the axe more like a club than an edged weapon.

Out into the torchlight emerged a stocky Olrog in dark plate armor. A horned helm protected his head, with only a small portion of his bearded face, including two fierce grey eyes, visible. In one hand he held a broadsword, and slung across his other arm was a dark shield engraved with runes. He carried a burning torch, which he cast down upon entering. Like a walking fortress, this Dark Knight strode into the chamber and charged the Ogre.

With a roar, the monster met the Knight's charge with one of its own. It swung Vorden's axe at the Knight's head. But the Knight defected the blow with his shield, and his broadsword caught the Ogre's shoulder, staggering the beast and finally taking it down. The Ogre tried to get up again, but the Knight drove the rune-covered shield into its chest, knocking it backwards. Then his broadsword hurtled down against the Ogre's skull, splitting it open. The Ogre still sought to regain its footing, while one long and crooked arm snaked out. The Ogre seized the Knight's leg and gave a yank. The Knight fell backwards to the floor with a clatter of plate mail.

Lannon and Timlin sat up and watched the battle, throbbing with pain from their blows, and from where he lay on the floor, Vorden was also watching. As they saw the Knight go down, their hopes sank.

The Ogre leapt towards the fallen Knight, swinging the axe. But again the Knight defected the blow with his shield, lashing out with his broadsword at the same time and striking the monster's leg, ripping flesh from bone. The Ogre twisted sideways from the impact and then fell forward. The Knight just managed to roll out of the way as the monster slumped to the cavern floor. The Knight staggered up and drove his broadsword down against the Ogre's head again, and this time its skull was shattered. The beast stopped moving.

The Knight stood still for a moment, panting hard from exertion, watching the dead Ogre. At last he turned to the others and spoke in a gruff voice. "Well, look what trouble you've brought upon yourselves, young Squires."

The Knight bent over Vorden and studied him carefully. "You look somewhat pale. Take a good knock, did you? How's your breathing?"

"I'm okay," said Vorden. "My ribs hurt, and my back. I think I can walk, though. I just need to get back to my room."

The Knight turned to the others. "And what about you three?"

Timlin groaned and stood up shakily. "I don't care if we get in trouble. I just want to get out of here. Can you take us out of this place?"

The Knight nodded. "I can and I will."

Blood ran down Lannon's forehead from the gash where he'd struck the floor, and he wiped it away before it got in his eyes. He stared at the fallen Ogre, his mind swallowed in dark thoughts. His soul seemed frozen within him.

"Take us out of here," he said quietly.

"In moment, I will," said the Knight. "But I want to make sure you've learned your lessons. I'm not going to report you to the High Council, because I think you're brave Squires--though certainly foolish--and that you're a credit to my kingdom in some ways. But before I let you go, I'm going to show you a few things about the Mines--and then you'll understand why you should never venture down here. First, though, we've got to close that gate you opened." He gave them a hard stare.

"We've seen enough," said Lannon. "We'll never come back here."

"We just want to leave!" said Timlin.

"Please take us to the East Tower," said Aldreya, and her soft green eyes made the Knight hesitate for a moment.

Vorden kept quiet, holding his ribs and watching the Knight.

The Knight shook his head. "You're not getting off that easily, Squires. Now get up and follow me, if you know what's good for you!"

After going back and closing the gate, the Squires followed the Knight into the tunnel from which he'd first come. The Dark Knight strode along at a swift pace, and the others had to struggle to keep up. Vorden especially had difficulty due to his damaged ribs. But the Knight showed him no mercy and marched on through the stone cavern without slowing.

"My name is Garndon Steelbreaker," he said. "I am a Guardian of the East Tower, put here to defend it against the creatures that would rise against Dremlock."

"What Color are you?" said Vorden.

"I belong to no color class," said Garndon. "Once I was Red, but now I bear no color. I am a Guardian, and I seldom leave these tunnels to see the light of day. That's the way it will be until I retire from Knighthood. What are your names, by the way? Yes--I can read. But I want to hear you speak them."

They gave them in full.

Garndon chuckled in amusement. "I like Flameblade, Sunshield, and Silverhawk, but Woodmaster is a little odd. Sounds more like someone who fells trees for a living instead of the last name of a Divine Squire!"

He stopped and turned to them, raising an eyebrow. "How were you able to get past the gate? No one should have been able to pass through, with that old wheel lock defending it. Even I can't open that gate."

"Lannon did it," Timlin said, pointing. "He used the Eye of Divinity to solve the lock. I just followed him."

Lannon glared at Timlin.

"The Eye of Divinity..." The Knight spoke the words slowly. "Then it is very fortunate indeed that I happened along and heard the sounds of battle. Few Knights in the long history of Dremlock have ever possessed that great gift. And yet you waste it on foolhardy pursuits!" He turned away and began walking again.

Lannon's face burned hot, so overcome with shame was he. He felt deep annoyance at Timlin for telling on him so quickly, and it led him to wonder if Timlin would tell Garrin about what they'd done.

Suddenly the tunnel widened and two more branched off--to the right and left, while up ahead stood a large iron door. The door had a small, barred window in it. Garndon produced a ring of keys and unlocked the door.

"We go now into the Dark Dungeon," he said grimly. "Prepare yourselves for the sights I will soon show you."

Timlin froze and would not move.

"Come on," Vorden said, pulling on Timlin's cloak.

"We need to follow him, Timlin," Lannon said. "It's for our own good."

"Just do as Garndon says," Aldreya whispered to him. "We'll be okay."

The Knight pointed at Timlin. "Show courage, little Squire.

Follow me now, or face the loss of your future Knighthood." With that, he turned and passed through the doorway.

Lannon followed without looking back. All he cared about now was saving his career at Dremlock, of doing things the right way from now on and becoming a great Knight. Timlin would have to make his own choice.

But Timlin didn't get to choose, because Vorden--though he winced in pain from the effort--dragged Timlin through the doorway.

Garndon closed it behind them.

Dungeon cells lined a stone hall before them. Dark waves of despair washed over the Squires immediately, choking their minds. The presence of the Deep Shadow was strong here. Growls, hideous feasting sounds, and a quiet hiss like water sizzling on a hot stovetop could be head coming from the cells. Another Knight stood near a door at the far end, and like Garndon, he was a stout looking Grey Dwarf adorned in dark plate mail. He carried a battle axe and a round shield.

"Brought us a few sneaks, Garndon?" said the Knight at the hall's end. "I can't believe my eyes!"

Garndon nodded. "They solved the wheel lock. It's the Eye of Divinity at work, believe it or not. Anyway, I'm going to show them a few things, Saferus. Teach them a lesson or two about why they need to stay out here."

"Smart lads to beat that old lock," said Saferus, shaking his head. "Even with the Eye of Divinity. I've never heard the like of it. But now we'll see what they're actually made of."

The Squires didn't like the sound of that, and they hesitated.

"One of the reasons you should never come here," said Garndon, "is because the Iracus Trees grow down here--Black Mothers in the mountain that spawn powerful Goblins like that Ogre. These mines are infested with them. But something else lurks down here as well--a thing that possesses the bodies of other creatures. It may have been what slew Kuran Darkender so long ago. Who can say? There are too many hidden caverns and deep places we cannot get to. There's an ongoing war down here. There has been ever since the Old Keep was built. And now I'm going to show you a few prisoners of that war, which we keep locked up to study their weaknesses."

With that, Garndon walked to the first of the cells on the right. "Come have a look, Squires, at my little friend that I named Graxnul."

Fearfully the Squires approached, with Vorden still dragging Timlin along. They stood well clear of the bars and peered through.

A huge Cave Troll--much bigger than the Ogre they had faced--sat within, gnawing a bone. It glanced up at them and growled, then went back to its feast. Like the Ogre, it had grey, bumpy skin and a massive round head, but its shoulders were much broader and its body far more heavily muscled. Unlike the more human-looking Ogre, the Troll had a nose like a pig snout and a mouth full of crooked fangs.

"Graxnul is a mighty Troll," said Garndon, with a touch of pride in his voice. "I keep him well fed. The more a Troll eats, the stronger he becomes, and the harder his flesh and bones grow, until they become almost impenetrable by ordinary weapons. You're lucky you ran into a half-starved Ogre. Graxnul here would've killed all four of you without blinking an eye--if Troll's had eyelids to blink!" He motioned to the Troll, calling him over.

Immediately the Troll stood up and walked forward, clutching the bone like a weapon. His arms and chest were massive, his skin deep grey in hue and almost scaly. He gazed at the Squires with his black eyes, and raised the bone menacingly. But Garndon stopped him with a motion of his hand.

"Not too close, Graxnul."

The Troll continued to stand there motionless. Then slowly he lifted the bone to his fang-filled mouth and started gnawing again.

"He's like your pet!" Timlin remarked. The skinny lad was still shaking, but he managed a smile.

"Old Graxnul isn't so bad," said Garndon. "He won't attack me, because I keep him fed and I'm good to him. I'd get him to fight for me if the Sacred Laws didn't forbid it. But come, now. I have other sights to show you."

Garndon moved down to the third cell on the right.

"See, Timlin, that wasn't so bad," whispered Vorden. "Now come on."

The Squires followed him to the cell, and what they saw within made their hearts freeze. Timlin tried to flee, but this time Garndon grabbed him.

"None of that, boy," the Dark Knight said gruffly.

Inside the cell was a vaguely humanoid shape. It had crooked arms twice as long as a man's legs that ended in clusters of barbed claws. Its flesh was brown and slimy, and wormy things seemed to crawl upon the surface of it. Its head was rodent-like in shape, with bat-like ears and two huge, curved yellow fangs that hung down from its mouth. Its nose was a wolf-like, wrinkled snout that dripped fluid. Hanging from its arms were folds of bony skin like half-developed bat wings.

When it saw the Squires, it went insane, hurling itself against the bars of Glaetherin and trying to rip them apart. Its mouth opened wide and pressed against the bars, its fangs seeking fruitlessly to dig into the metal. Its stench was unbearable--not its physical stench (which was quite bad in its own right) but the stench of evil and despair that radiated from it. The monster had no eyes, just leathery skin where the eyes should have been.

The four Squires shrank back. The other Knight, Saferus, ran over and helped hold them in place.

"Get a good look!" muttered Garndon. "And be thankful you met a starving Ogre and not one of these Bloodfangs. They'd tear the flesh from your bones before you knew what hit you, and leave you drained of blood. It took five Knights to get a net over this thing and hold it, and one lost his arm in the process!"

Garndon and Saferus yanked the Squires away and herded them to the last cell on the left. Inside this one was a dark shape with sickly yellow eyes. It was a black serpent-like thing that slithered around inside the cell and hissed, yet its head was disturbingly humanoid in shape. It pressed that head against the bars, trying to squeeze through, revealing two stark-white fangs and a pink, forked tongue.

"A Pit Crawler," said Garndon, shaking his head. "If it were up to me, I'd put my sword to its skull and be done with it. These horrors lurk in the dark places, and their bite is deadly poison. I've seen good men--stout Knights of Dremlock--die in unbelievable agony from a single bite because they blundered into the wrong places. We're trying to find an antidote to that poison, but we're not having much luck."

Tears rolled down Timlin's cheeks. "Get us out of here, Garndon. We've learned our lesson. I promise!"

"And have you learned yours?" said Garndon, gazing sternly at Vorden from beneath his helm. "I can tell you're a hard one--like I was at your age."

"I have," said Vorden. "But tell me one thing--where is the Divine Essence? That's the only reason we came down here. I have to see it!"

"I suspected as much," said Garndon. "But the Divine Essence can't be reached from here anymore. It's been sealed off permanently. There is another way to get to it, but I won't tell you how. Now it's time to be going."

Garndon led them back through the tunnels to the door with the wheel lock. "Do your thing, boy," he said to Lannon.

With his nerves so badly on edge and the Knight looking on, it took Lannon a lot of effort to summon the Eye of Divinity, but with the help of his friends he finally managed it. Once Lannon had unlocked the door, Garndon motioned them onward. "Now get going and don't come back here--ever. And keep your mouths shut about what you saw down here. If word gets out--and goodness knows there are enough rumors floating around up there from what I hear--I'll have you all banished from Dremlock forever."

The Squires nodded and hurried through.

"And that especially goes for you!" He pointed a finger at Timlin. "I know your kind. Keep your mouth shut, or it will be the worse for you!"

Meekly, Timlin avoided the Knight's gaze, keeping his sight fixed on the floor. "I promise I'll never say a word to anyone."

Garndon slammed the bars shut behind them. "Good riddance!"

Lannon licked his fingers and cleaned dried blood from his forehead. Surely they were going to get caught, he thought to himself. They'd been gone too long, and they still had to sneak back to their quarters without being seen. Yet if they could just make it out of Old Keep and lock the door, no one might ever suspect they'd gone this way. That, at least, could save them from being banished.

The horror of what they'd experienced clung to them like icy fingers. It seemed to reach forth from the mines beneath Old Keep, desiring to yank them back into the dark places below. They trembled--even Vorden--as they raced ahead, determined never to return here as long as they lived.

They locked the door to Old Keep again, and placed the Birlote torch back in its holder on the wall. Then they crept upstairs.

Aldreya assured the boys that she often returned this late from her training and the other girls she bunked with would think nothing of it. "Grey Squires have lots of freedom," she whispered. "And we train at odd hours. Sometimes I stay up later than this in the Library or the Dark Rooms."

"What are the Dark Rooms?" the boys questioned.

"Never mind," she said. "There are many secrets in this tower--like the Watcher. Even now I wonder if he saw us. It seems unlikely he could have missed us--or at least missed *you three.* Actually, I guess I shouldn't have mentioned him, either. But what's done is done, I suppose."

"Who is the Watcher?" the boys asked.

"Goodnight!" said Aldreya. "That was wretched, and I hope I never go anywhere with you three again." With that, she entered her quarters.

Chapter 10: Child of Winter

On the following day, the Squires said little to each other, with Lannon and Vorden spending most of their time meditating on healing their minor injuries inflicted by the Ogre. By using that Knightly healing technique, which was drawn from the power locked within their own minds rather than from any type of sorcery, they were able to make the injuries fade very quickly.

Later, Garrin joined them for dinner in the Hall, and they had to struggle to act natural around him--something Vorden excelled at, while Lannon and Timlin seemed rigid and quiet. But Garrin appeared to take little notice of them, as he was busy chatting with some of the other Squires--except at one point when he looked up, gave them a strange, piercing stare that made their hearts lurch, and then resumed his conversations. They gulped down dinner and headed back to their room.

When training began the next day, Lannon and Timlin felt fine, but Vorden was still a bit sore in the ribs--indicating the damage had been more severe than he'd thought. But he was able to compensate for it and give a fair effort. At one point Cartlan asked about the small bump and cut on Lannon's head (barely noticeable though it was) and Lannon replied that he'd suffered an accident and left it at that. Cartlan didn't press the issue, and by the end of the day, things looked like they would turn out fine.

But Lannon had another issue to deal with. He'd unlocked the Eye of Divinity and was supposed to tell Garrin immediately. Yet because their ordeal in Old Keep was so fresh in his mind, he decided to wait until he was sure he could trust himself to look Garrin in the eye and not blurt out what had happened in the mines. Also, it had taken him this long to accomplish the task, and so what would another few days matter? Besides, he hadn't actually done it on his own. He thought maybe he should wait until he could call it forth by himself before telling Garrin.

But after only a week, to Lannon's disbelief, Vorden again began pressuring him to break the rules. It was evening, their training done for the day, and they were in the Library seated at a table. The Library was a round chamber that was modeled, according to a plaque on the wall, after the famous Round Library of the North Tower. The bookshelves completely covered the walls, all the way up to the ceiling. Statues of Knights, Dragons, and Goblins stood within, big and small--with some holding books or leering down from the shelves. There was a stone fireplace with wood stacked next to it, and four Birlote torches on the walls. The only other door (besides the main entrance) bore a wooden sign that said:

OLD EAST LIBRARY.
NO ONE MAY ENTER WITHOUT PERMISSION FROM
THE EAST TOWER MASTER

Timlin was humming to himself in his annoying fashion, and looking at a book of artwork depicting Lord Knights throughout the ages. Lannon was reading a book from the library called *Fairy Goblins--Do They Exist?* written by a former Lord Knight named Eldrich Hawkshield. Vorden had an ancient, leather-bound book in front of him called *The Dragons of Tharnin*, which he had not yet opened.

"I have an idea," Vorden said suddenly. He looked around, making sure the library was empty of eavesdroppers, and then continued. "I think I know how we could see the Divine Essence." He spoke casually, as if talking about the day's weather.

Lannon's mouth hung open for a moment. Then he shook his head, his face flushing crimson with anger. "Vorden, what are you talking about? After what I went through in those mines, you think I'd be stupid enough to follow you anywhere again?" He closed his book and laid it on the table.

"I'm sorry about that," said Vorden. "And I take all the blame, Lannon. I could have gotten us killed, or ruined our chance at Knighthood. It was a really stupid thing to do. And do you know why it was stupid? Because I should have asked around first, researched the issue a bit. Well, I've done that, and guess what? I think I know an easy way to get to the Divine Essence."

"I don't care!" Lannon said. "Whatever you have in mind, forget it. After what I saw in those mines..."

"We don't have to go into the mines," said Vorden. "I've learned that the way to the Essence is through the Temple itself. There's a passage right under the altar that leads down to a wheel lock. Beyond that locked door is the crystal chamber."

"Well, go ahead and find out," said Lannon. "But I'm not going." He stared back at Vorden with determination. This was a moment he had dreaded--having to say no to his friend. But he'd decided never to back down from anyone again if his future Knighthood was at stake. He imagined Cordus Landsaver nodding with approval at his decision, and he held fast to that image, drawing strength from it.

Vorden sighed. "You know I can't open a wheel lock, Lannon. If you don't go with me, I have to give up."

"Maybe you should give up," said Lannon. "You're good at a lot of things, Vorden. You could be a great Knight. Don't waste it chasing a foolish dream."

Vorden's face burned with anger. "So the Divine Essence is just a foolish dream? Maybe to you it is. But to me it means everything."

Lannon gulped, and glanced towards the door. "Don't talk so loud. Someone might be coming. Anyways, I didn't mean it that way. I just meant that there's a reason we're not allowed to see the Essence. Even Master Garrin has never seen it. We shouldn't break rules we don't understand."

"But others besides Lord Knights have seen it," said Vorden. "And I can prove it right here and now."

"It's getting late," said Lannon. "We should head to our quarters. I'm supposed to be doing my Eye of Divinity training."

"Hold on" Vorden said. "This will just take a moment. Timlin, go stand by the doorway and watch for anyone in the hall."

Timlin rose and did as he was told, peeking around the doorway. "It's all clear, Vorden," he said.

Vorden opened the book in front of him and leafed through the pages. Then he began to read aloud.

So it was that I, Logan Firehand, broke the Sacred Laws and ventured forth to that chamber that holds the Divine One. I bear the Eye of Dreams, and I have become the seeker of lost relics. In one shining moment, I solved the wheel lock below the Temple's altar and made it to the chamber of crystal.

The Divine One was more beautiful than the light that warms our world each morning, and my heart was seemingly cleansed of all shadow--save for my deep desire to obtain the ultimate source of power that lies within those cursed hills. I was shown how to use my gift, how to reach my true potential. And I was warned to make use of that gift for noble purposes or pay a dreadful price.

Am I then a selfish man? An ignorer of gods? Will I eventually pay dearly for my folly? I cannot truly say if I am on the proper path. It is said that to meddle with the Deep Shadow is to invite doom into the heart and madness into the mind. Yet I have done so, and my sanity appears to remain intact.

The real question is whether or not I am using my gift in a noble fashion.

I believe the seeking of facts is indeed a noble task, for all of humanity benefits from the results in one form or another. However, shadows of doubt remain.

Here, in the first of seven books, I shall attempt to reveal the workings of the Dark Realm of Tharnin (that hated place called the Deep Shadow) beginning with the Dragons, for they, widely considered the most powerful of all Goblins, represent the Hand of Tharnin, which crushes life...

Vorden stopped reading and closed the book. "Okay, so you get the point. This Knight broke the rules and visited the Essence. And it helped him. So it could probably help you, too, Lannon. It might even teach you about the Eye of Divinity."

Lannon sat in silence. Had the Divine Essence actually spoken to that Knight and given him assistance? Was it simply a matter of sneaking down through the Temple to the crystal chamber? He glanced about. The Goblin statues seemed to leer at him in accusation, as if they were judging him--as if the books they held were tomes of law. He suddenly felt like he was being watched, and goose bumps flooded his back. He quickly turned his attention back to Vorden.

"Where did you get that book?" Lannon asked. "It doesn't seem like the Knights would want anyone to know about that."

"I borrowed it from in there," said Vorden, pointing toward the door marked Old East Library. "I picked the lock yesterday and poked around in there. Its full of old, dusty books that look pretty boring. This one mentioned Dragons, so I glanced through it and found that part I just read to you."

Lannon glanced around nervously. "Put it back," he said. "If someone comes along and sees it..."

"That's what Timlin is watching for," said Vorden "But even if I'm caught with this, I'll just say I found it on the shelves in here. Who can prove otherwise? How would they know I'm the one that moved it from the Old Library?"

"What has happened to you?" said Lannon. "When I first got here, you talked about wanting to be like Kuran Darkender and live honorably. But now look at the things you're doing, Vorden. You're going to end up getting tossed out."

Vorden sighed. "It's the Divine Essence, Lannon. I just can't stop thinking about it. And I'm not the only one. Aldreya told me she dreamt of it too. She wanted to know when I was going to try to find it again, so she could come with me. She told me she believes the Essence is calling to her, that it will teach her to unlock her full potential. She practically begged me to accompany her on a quest to find it!"

Lannon's eyes widened. "You must be kidding."

Vorden shook his head. "I can't believe it either. I thought she'd never want to hang around with us again."

"But what if she's setting us up?" said Lannon.

"She isn't," said Vorden. "I'm certain of it. She might be a bit of a snob, but right now she's pretty desperate. You should have seen the look in her eyes! There's no way she would tell on us. I think she's afraid of what's happening here at Dremlock, Lannon."

"So am I," Lannon admitted. "Every day I hear something new about how bad off Dremlock is--usually from you."

"Sorry," said Vorden. "I just like to keep you informed."

"I know," said Lannon. "And I'm glad you do. I just never expected this. I grew up believing Dremlock was the best place in all the land. It's still kind of like that, but there are a lot of problems here, I guess. It's hard to explain."

"I know exactly what you're talking about," said Vorden. "I expected shining towers and honorable Knights--white horses and good deeds, that sort of thing. I visited Bellis when I was younger, before my parents died. We were passing through on our way to Silverland. And you know what? That's exactly how Bellis is--like the grand kingdom you would always imagine. So I thought Dremlock would be even better. But it has a dark side to it, and I can't help but wonder if this place has seen better days."

"Yeah, it's definitely going sour," said a boy.

Lannon and Vorden jumped up, looking around. Someone was hiding behind a Goblin statue, with just the edge of his brown cloak visible.

"Who's there?" Vorden said. The lad from Gravendar had gone pale.

Out from behind the statue stepped a tall boy with bright blond hair, fair skin, and blue eyes. It was Jerret Dragonsbane, the Red Squire Lannon and Timlin had met very briefly outside the Temple on the first day they'd visited there with Garrin.

From behind another statue stepped a big, dark-haired lad. He had a pointy chin and a hook nose, and also wore a red sash. They recognized him as Clayith Ironback, a quiet Squire who was usually somewhat of a loner.

"What are you two doing here?" Vorden said. "Shouldn't you be in the West Tower this time of the evening?"

"We came to look at some books," said Jerret. "It was Clayith's idea, actually. He wanted to read about potions or poisons or something. Anyways, we heard you guys coming, so we ducked behind those statues to eavesdrop on you."

Clayith gave a crooked grin. "Yeah, we wanted to eavesdrop."

"Well, what of it?" said Vorden. "Now I guess you know we're up to something. So what are you going to do about it?"

Jerret shook his head and smiled. "Nothing, Vorden. I couldn't care less what you do--except that I'd like to get in on it. If you're actually going try to get a look at the Divine Essence, count me in."

"And me, too," said Clayith, still giving an odd grin.

Vorden was thoughtful for a moment. "You're a good friend,

Jerret. And Clayith's alright, I guess."

"I wouldn't tell on you," said Clayith, with a chuckle. His grin broadened. "I like you, Vorden."

Vorden laughed. "I'll think it over, and let you know later."

"Vorden, I already told you..." said Lannon. His words sounded weak, and he knew his resolve had crumbled some. But if he ended up agreeing to go, the thought of taking two more Squires along did not please him at all. He could trust Vorden and Timlin, and possibly even Aldreya, yet he knew little about these two Squires--especially Jerret, who seemed somewhat cocky and was hard to figure out. Clayith, however, had always struck Lannon as being exceptionally polite, kind-hearted, and shy. Lannon had liked him from the first moment he'd met him at the training grounds. Yet could he be trusted? There was no way of knowing at this time.

"At least consider it, Lannon," said Vorden. "You know we can't do this without you--if there is actually a wheel lock down there. So if you don't go, the whole thing is done with. I want to go, and so do Jerret, Clayith, and Aldreya."

"And me!" whispered Timlin, from the doorway. "From what you said, it doesn't sound very dangerous--if it's just beneath the Temple."

"We'll see," Lannon said reluctantly. Again he glanced about, still feeling like they were being watched. Here they were, in the Library, discussing a plan to violate the Sacred Laws--with two more Squires eager to jump in on the action. The whole situation seemed very risky and ready to blow up in their faces. Couldn't Vorden see that, or had his desire to visit the Divine Essence become so strong it had clouded his judgment?

"We can talk about it tomorrow," mumbled Lannon, experiencing a deep urge to get away from this scene. "But don't get your hopes up, Vorden."

With that, Lannon left the library and headed upstairs. As he passed through the shadowy halls, a deep sadness and anxiety filled him. What had happened to his dreams of being a valiant Knight in a grand kingdom? Where was the nobility and the glory? He'd been here less than a year, and already he'd become a lawbreaker in a kingdom where things seemed to be falling apart (if one could believe the countless rumors). He felt isolated and detached, floating free and lacking direction. He had always imagined Dremlock would be a place where everything was in solid order, where everyone knew where they stood and laws and rules were set in stone. Now he was seeing a place where the darkness and light seemed melded together, where devious plots were hatched while Knights were too busy or too reluctant to take notice. It disturbed him to think of what they had gotten away with so easily already. What else was going on here that went unnoticed by the Tower Masters? Just how deeply had Dremlock decayed?

The answer seemed to come to him later that night in a dream. He dreamt of the kingdom, and it appeared Dremlock was balanced on the edge of a dagger, with the flames of doom burning on either side. The wind howled down the mountainside, bringing winter's breath and blowing it into his soul. The snow became as thick as the Northern Hills, and shards of ice the size of continents shifted about, changing the face of the land. The ice became unstable, cracking and lurching, creating pockets deep within the stone, earth, snow, and mossy ruin. From out of that ice came a shadowy hand, reaching out over the land and growing ever larger.

"I am the Child of Winter," a voice said. "I lived even before the world was warmed, when nothing existed but the timeless ice."

For a moment Lannon was helpless within that grasp. All the struggles of life seemed pointless, and he longed for things to return to the purity and timelessness of before which the voice spoke of. Then the infinite darkness swallowed him and he realized the Shadow was indeed *deeper* than he could have ever imagined, even deeper than despair itself. There could be no return from such a void.

Eyes appeared in the darkness, crazed and piercing, burning into his soul. The eyes seemed all too familiar, and then he remembered the statue upon the hilltop, amid the ruins of Serenlock Castle. They were the eyes of Tenneth Bard, the Black Knight. A hand, bound in a steel gauntlet, reached forth to claim Lannon's soul.

"I've come for you, Lannon," Tenneth Bard whispered. "Soon you will wish you had died down there in Old Keep."

***

Lannon awoke from the nightmare, chilled yet sweating, with one clear realization in mind. Only the Divine Essence could exist beyond the grasp of the evil. Lannon could trust no one else, for the Deep Shadow was a clever foe, and could seize a person's soul before they realized what was happening.

When he fell asleep again, much later, he dreamt of the wondrous light in the crystal chamber. Again the Essence spoke to him, demanding he come to it, telling him it would share its secrets with him.

"Come to me swiftly!" it urged, "or all will be lost."

When Lannon awoke in the morning, that sense of urgency remained with him. He considered telling Garrin or Taris everything, but then decided that would undoubtedly ruin any chance he had of ever visiting the Divine Essence. They were great Knights, who had worked hard to gain their positions, and they would be very reluctant to break the Sacred Laws over a mere dream.

Yet Lannon knew he must go. His fears, however dark, must be put aside forever, until he attained his goal. The Deep Shadow thrived within Dremlock. No one doubted that. And Lannon had grown paranoid during the winter months, wondering if a simple stare in his direction was sinister in nature or if a shadowy figure on the wooded trail at dusk would mean his doom. His friends felt it too. The rumors had gotten to them as well, and like Lannon, they too looked to Dremlock's god-king for help.

He needed to know more about the Eye of Divinity and how it could combat the evil. He needed to know if there was anyone left in Dremlock he could trust. And he needed to know just what his destiny was.

Kuran Darkender had dreamt of the Divine Essence. He had acted on that dream, and Dremlock Kingdom had been born.

Only the Divine Essence could give Lannon the answers he sought.

Chapter 11: The Fire and the Shadow

Four days passed after Lannon's dream, and still Vorden made no specific plans to visit the Divine Essence. The tables had turned, and now Lannon was the one trying to persuade Vorden to go. Yet Vorden seemed detached and uninterested in anything but his training. Meanwhile, Lannon grew ever more impatient. The dream stayed fresh in his mind, and each night in his sleep he believed he could feel the Divine Essence calling to him, demanding he come to it. His need to visit the god-king became overwhelming, crushing any lingering doubts or fears.

"Why are we waiting so long?" Lannon finally asked Vorden one evening. "We should get this over with."

Vorden shook his head. "Something's wrong, Lannon. Why would Jerret and Clayith want to go with us? They can't really sneak out of their quarters like we can, because they bunk with the other Squires. Jerret might be brash enough to try it, but Clayith-- that's just not like him. I have a bad feeling about this."

"So we're not going?" Lannon shook his head. "This is ridiculous, Vorden. Now that I'm all ready and everything, you change your mind."

"What are you talking about?" said Vorden. "You're the one who didn't want to do this. What changed *your* mind?"

Lannon shrugged. "It's not important." He didn't know if he should tell Vorden of his dream or not, but he doubted it would make any difference either way. Vorden did things to suite his own needs.

"Why not go without them?" said Timlin. "We could go tonight, and they'd never know about it." He seemed strangely eager to try this adventure, considering how terrified he'd been down in the mines.

"That's a great idea!" said Lannon.

"No, it isn't," said Vorden. "They might have already told on us, and then someone might be waiting at the Temple to catch us sneaking in. I want to see the Divine Essence as bad as you do, Lannon. Maybe more so, since I came up with the idea. But I think we need to wait a while--maybe even a month or two."

"A month?" said Lannon. "I can't wait a month!"

Vorden gave him a piercing stare. "What's wrong with you, Lannon? You don't seem like yourself lately."

Lannon thought about it. He certainly didn't feel like himself. He felt scared and isolated, overflowing with anxiety. He needed to talk to someone he could trust, and the only one he could think of was the Divine Essence, which he felt was the answer to all his problems. He had seen nothing of Taris or Furlus lately, and Garrin seemed distant, as if he had much on his mind.

"Alright," Lannon said, swallowing hard. "I guess we wait."

Vorden nodded. "What else can we do?"

Even as Vorden finished that statement, the door to their room was yanked open and in stepped Jerret and Clayith. They wore armor and weapons (which was perfectly acceptable in Dremlock-- and even encouraged, since the Knights wanted the Squires to get used to such adornments). It was snowing hard outside, and they were covered in heavy flakes and panting hard.

Jerret nodded to them, grinning.

For a moment there was total silence in the room, and nobody moved. Then Jerret fixed his gaze on Vorden.

"So are we doing this or not, Vorden? I'm tired of waiting."

"I don't think so," said Vorden, choosing his words carefully. Casually he signaled to Timlin--a hand sign the Squires had just recently learned that meant *passage check*. Timlin hopped up and went to the door, peering out. He gave a quick signal back indicating the hallway was clear.

This bit of silent communication had not gone unnoticed by Jerret. "So you don't trust us," he said, with a humorless smile. "I thought that was it. Why didn't you tell us that from the start, instead of wasting our time?"

"It's not that," said Vorden. "I'm just wondering how you two can pull this off. Won't the other Squires notice you're missing?"

Jerret smiled. "Probably. But what's the big deal? We'll just get in trouble, and have to do cleaning chores and the like for a while. But I think it's worth it. You three aren't the only ones sneaking around--Squires do it a lot. I think the Knights are really distracted right now and don't notice what's going on right under their noses. Cartlan's supposed to do a count on us each evening, but he usually doesn't bother."

"What if they search for you?" said Vorden.

"They won't," said Jerret. "I can guarantee it. They're not going to waste time looking for us." He laughed. "You really have been living in a cave! Do you think they'll awaken the High Council and send a legion of Knights to find us? If they even find out we're gone, they'll just wait until we come back to punish us."

Vorden's face burned red with embarrassment. "I was just trying to cover everything, Jerret. It doesn't hurt to be cautious."

"Sure," said Jerret. "So are we in, or not?"

"One more question," said Vorden. "The West Tower has door guards. How'd you get past them?"

Jerret chuckled. "We never went back after training. We've been hiding out in the woods all evening, freezing our skin off."

Vorden sighed. "This doesn't look good, Jerret."

"We took a risk," said Jerret, "and we're probably going to be in trouble. But that's our problem, not yours. So at least make it worth our while."

"Yeah," said Clayith. "Make it worth our while, Vorden."

Vorden fell silent for a time. Then he said, "Alright, we'll do it--but only if Lannon and Timlin agree. I'm not their boss or anything."

"I want to go," said Timlin. "I don't care what happened last time. This time it's going to be better. We're going to see the Divine Essence!"

"Let's just get going," said Lannon. He pulled his weapons and armor from beneath his bed and started putting them on.

"I guess it's decided then," said Vorden, nodding with approval at Lannon. "Looks like you're leading this adventure."

Lannon shrugged. "I don't care who leads. I just have to see the Divine Essence, and I'm not turning back until I do."

Clayith was staring intently at Lannon. He smiled, and Lannon thought Clayith looked like a bird of prey, with his hooknose and pointy chin. Clayith was the largest and strongest of all the Squires. But accompanying that physical strength was a gentleness that ran as deep as any Lannon had ever seen. Clayith saved drowning moths from water pools, and he defended any small creatures (even bugs) the other Squires sought to maim or squash. He always spoke in a soft voice, and never seemed to think very highly of himself but always gave praise to others.

Lannon had often wondered how, when the time came, Clayith would be able to kill. For wasn't that what Knights always did--*kill Goblins?* What were the Knights thinking when they chose Clayith Ironback, who would not hurt a bee that stung him? Had they somehow missed seeing that huge part of his personality, or had Clayith disguised it from them?

"Just tell me what to do, Lannon," said Clayith.

Lannon laughed, and marveled at his own progress. Less than a year before he had been an isolated lad with no friends. Now he had someone looking up to him, thinking of him as a leader.

"That's okay, Clayith," he said. "I'm not actually in charge here."

"A skull-and-bones formation, then," Clayith said, chuckling.

"Huh?" said Lannon.

Clayith frowned. "Its...leaderless. That's what I meant. A dead unit, so to speak." Clayith shook his head, as if to clear it. "I don't care!" he muttered, half under his breath, and then turned away.

"Are you okay?" said Lannon.

Clayith turned back, smiling in his kindly way. "I'm sorry, Lannon. Sometimes my thoughts get mixed up. Its...the dark."

"The dark?" said Lannon.

Clayith cleared his throat. "I mean--that's what I call it when I blank out."

"Clayith's crazy," said Jerret, with a laugh. "He talks to himself sometimes, like an old man. Don't worry about it, Lannon. He's totally harmless."

Lannon nodded, suddenly feeling uncomfortable. "It's alright. I don't mind if you do that, Clayith."

Clayith's mouth formed the words *dead unit* one more time, and then he clamped his lips together for a moment, before adding,

"I'm watching your back, Lannon. Let's go!"

"What's our plan?" said Jerret.

Vorden thought for a moment. Then he looked to Lannon and said, "It's your call this time. What should we do?"

Lannon hesitated, thinking carefully. He tried hard to come up with something brilliant, while the others fidgeted impatiently, but at last he gave up and settled for something simple. "We should split up, at first," he said. "Jerret and Clayith can go on to the Temple and wait for us. Then, after a bit, we'll follow them. Once we're all at the Temple, Timlin can sneak in and check the place over. If it's clear, we'll all go in and...I guess just go on from there together."

"Why split up at first?" said Jerret, with a look of distrust.

"We won't get in as much trouble if we're caught," said Lannon. "It would look very suspicious if Blue and Red Squires were all sneaking around in one group. And our best chance to be seen is when we're journeying to the Temple."

Jerret nodded. "I guess that's true."

"Good plan," Vorden said. "But what about Aldreya?"

"She's in the Library," said Jerret. "We saw her on the way up. Should we have her go with us, or should we just forget about her?"

"She can go with us," said Vorden.

"She's pretty," said Jerret, smiling. "She can go with me and Clayith."

"She's from the East Tower," said Vorden, giving him a hard stare. "If you two got caught with her, the Knights would know something's up."

"Is that your real reason?" said Jerret. "Or are you afraid I'll ruin your chance to get close to her?"

Vorden's face was stony. "What are you talking about, Jerret? Have you ever heard of the Sacred Laws?"

"Sure," said Jerret. "But they don't mean much, apparently. We're going to be breaking them anyways."

"Show some manners," Vorden said coldly, straightening his clothes. "I have no interest in Aldreya other than...for the sake of this mission, I guess."

"You're a tough one to figure out, Vorden," said Jerret, "Sometimes you seem cut from rough cloth, and other times you seem like some well-to-do snob with your neat hair and talk of manners. I can't understand you."

"Why?" said Vorden. "Because I believe in what Dremlock stands for, even if I'm forced to break the Sacred Laws when I know it's the right thing to do? I just don't like what you're hinting at."

"Fine," said Jerret, with a shrug. "I guess I won't mention it again." Then he mumbled, "I must have touched a sore spot or something."

Vorden glared, his hands knotted into fists.

"Anyways," said Lannon, in an effort to change the subject before the situation turned ugly, "I just hope the hidden passage to the Divine Essence isn't guarded by those Dark Knights like that Garndon fellow."

"Dark Knights?" said Jerret, with wide eyes.

Clayith stepped forward, staring at Lannon with an odd, troubled expression--as if Lannon had said something confusing or appalling.

"Don't say such things!" Clayith hissed.

"Never mind," said Lannon, feeling his body recoil. Something about Clayith's expression, or way of standing, made Lannon feel almost physically ill. Did Clayith hold some hidden, important knowledge?

"I guess I wasn't supposed to mention that," Lannon added. "So forget I said anything about Dark--"

"Quiet!" Clayith put his finger to his lips.

"You're better off not knowing," said Timlin to Jerret, with a giggle. "That's our secret. Right, Lannon? Right, Vorden?"

"Not anymore," said Vorden, sighing.

After Jerret and Clayith left, the Blue Squires sat around for a while talking things over. The wind howled fiercely outside the tower, and now and then puffs of glittering snow would blow in from beneath the window shutters. They agreed that the Red Squires seemed trustworthy--though all three boys noted that Clayith seemed to be acting a bit strangely. But Clayith always had been somewhat quiet, and they reasoned that this was probably just a side to him they had never seen before. He was, after all, the kindest Squire any of them knew.

At last they crept from their chamber and headed downstairs. They went down two floors and then encountered a Red Squire-- his sash well decorated with gold ribbons--standing outside his quarters in the hallway. He was an Olrog, about eighteen years old, and already his beard was as wide as his chest. They had seen this Squire before many times, but didn't know his name. (They barely knew any of the older Squires in the East Tower, though they had lived so near to them for almost a year.) He regarded them with suspicion in his grey eyes.

"What are you boys up to?" he said. "Shouldn't you be in bed? If Taris catches you wandering about it will spell bad business for you."

"We heard a noise outside the tower," Vorden said quickly. "It sounded like a crash or something."

"You sure it wasn't ice breaking off from the ledges?" said the Grey Dwarf. "I hear that a lot. Sometimes it wakes me up in the night."

"Could have been," said Vorden, "now that you mention it. Why didn't we think of that? Well, I guess we'll get back to sleep."

"Alright," the Olrog said. "Just watch yourselves. I don't know what you're up to, but Taris knows everything that goes on in this tower. Nothing escapes his eye. He has spies that lurk in the shadows. You can't see them, but they can see you. They're always watching. He won't always act right away, either, if he catches you breaking the rules. Sometimes he'll wait for a while and see what you're up to. He knows you're down here, Squires. Make no mistake about that!"

"Then I guess we better hurry back to bed," said Vorden. With that, he started back towards the stairs. The others followed.

Glancing back, they saw the Olrog enter his quarters and close the door. Vorden stopped them with a motion of his hand.

"It's okay," he said. "He's gone to bed."

"I wonder what he was up to," said Lannon.

"I'm also wondering that," said Vorden. "He questioned us, but maybe we should have questioned him. Of course, he was well decorated--almost a Knight by the looks of him. I guess we handled it well."

"His hands were dirty," said Timlin.

The other two stared at him for a moment.

"What do you mean?" said Vorden.

"Black dirt," said Timlin. "Like he'd been digging. It was under his nails. And his weapon was missing. He was wearing his sheath, but no sword. Oh, and one of his boots didn't match the other one--it was old and cracked and didn't have any laces. And the name on his sash was Golath Stonesplitter."

"You noticed all that?" said Vorden.

Timlin smiled, nodding. "I just looked him over the way we were trained to. Remember how Master Garrin said never to ignore anyone's appearance, to always study them carefully?"

Vorden nodded. "You make a good Blue, Timlin. Well, let's get moving. That Squire was obviously up to no good. He won't tell on us. I think he was just hoping we wouldn't tell on him."

"Right," said Lannon. "But do you think it's true what he said about Taris knowing all that goes on here?"

"If it was," said Vorden, "do you think that Golath fellow would have been out sneaking around? I don't think so. He just told us that to scare us, so we'd forget to question what he was doing running around with dirty hands and a missing boot. I think that if Taris knew what we were doing, he'd stop us."

As Vorden spoke those words, deep feelings of guilt swelled within Lannon. He remembered Taris' kindness during their journey to Dremlock. He thought of his father. What would the old man think of this? This was not Knightly behavior. But then he remembered his dream and his fears returned, along with his overwhelming need to visit the Divine Essence. Shutting his guilt away, he started back down the hallway with the others.

They made it to the library without encountering anyone else. Yet Aldreya was nowhere to be seen.

"Maybe she went with the other two," whispered Vorden, and the look in his dark eyes said he wasn't happy about that.

"I guess we should just keep going," said Lannon. "We can't afford to go looking about the tower for her. It's too risky."

They continued down to the first floor. Lannon (again having to swallow his guilt) swiped a Birlote torch from the wall, which-- because it generated only light and no heat--he hid under his cloak.

As they started towards the door, a form materialized out of the shadows.

The Squires' hearts lurched, and Timlin nearly cried out, clamping his hand over his mouth at the last instant.

"Leaving without me?" said Aldreya, her green eyes twinkling.

"We wouldn't dream of it," said Vorden, smiling.

When they stepped outside, the snows were blowing fiercely. The night sky was black with storm clouds, and the wind howled down the mountainside, chilling the Squires to the bone. The snow was drifting up around the tower.

"Great!" said Lannon, practically yelling to be heard over the wind. "I can't see a thing in this storm. I'm going to have to use the torch. I just hope no one's out and about tonight."

"Not likely," said Vorden. "Who'd be out in this? Except us and those other two fools, that is."

Vorden's words did not inspire confidence in Lannon.

The torch provided enough glow to see a few feet around them, but it was hardly adequate. As they headed towards the forest, they struggled to stay on the path, which was swiftly disappearing beneath the snows.

"What about Jerret and Clayith?" said Vorden. "You think they could find their way to the Temple in this blizzard? Did they even have a torch?"

"Who knows?" said Lannon. "If they're not at the Temple, I guess we go on without them. We can't wait all night."

Aldreya pressed her hand against her forehead, struggling to keep her silver curls from getting in her eyes. "I don't know about this," she said. "Maybe we should try this some other time."

No one replied, and as they entered the forest, the wind continued to whip snow into their faces, with the Knightwood trees offering only a little protection against its wrath. The treetops swayed back and forth, creaking giants. They paused behind one of the cabin-sized tree trunks to get out of the wind and driving snow for a moment and catch their breath, brushing melting flakes from their faces.

"I've never seen it this bad!" Vorden said.

The others could only shake their heads, and they started moving again. At some point, they strayed from the trail and didn't realize it, as the snow had become too thick. Suddenly they were wandering randomly through the Knightwood pines, going in circles for all they knew, until at last they came up against an iron fence.

"What is this?" said Lannon. "Where in the world are we?"

Vorden shook his head disgustedly. "This could be the Cemetery fence. If it is, we have to find the main trail, which is somewhere by this fence, and follow it straight to the Temple."

"It's no good," said Lannon. "We can't see anything, Vorden. We can't stick to any trail. We need to try to get back to the tower, before they find out we're missing. What do you think, Timlin?"

Timlin wiped snow from his eyes. "I can't see where to go. I'm sorry." The lad hung his head, as if he expected the others to be upset with him.

"I can't do anything, either," said Aldreya. She took out her stone dagger and made it burn with green fire, but its light was too small to make any difference in the raging snowstorm. She put it away again. "See, it's no use."

Lannon struggled hard to think. All he could see was the dark and the swirling snow. Yet he could feel the Divine Essence calling to him.

"I can use the Eye," he said, suddenly inspired. His words were smashed apart by the howling wind.

"What did you say?" said Vorden.

"The Eye!" Lannon yelled. "Help me unlock it."

Aldreya leaned close to him. "What is the Eye, Lannon? I still have no idea what you're talking about! Taris has never taught me any sorcery like that, and when I asked him about it, he smiled and said I shouldn't concern myself with it. So I really don't know..." Her words slipped away in the storm.

The two Squires flanked Lannon, and spoke their opposing words directly into his ears while tapping his shoulders. It took many tries this time, for the storm was distracting to Lannon. But at last, when he began to doubt it was going to work, his mind suddenly split, and the power surged forth.

The Eye of Divinity reached into the storm, and Lannon could feel a strange and hidden strength there. He probed deeper, and the

Eye showed him glimpses of things he would have never pondered on his own. He saw that the storm struck fear in the hearts of the living, causing people to huddle away beneath blankets and sit next to comforting flames. But it also removed the pettiness from the world and made all things equal. Beneath the storm's fury, social status became insignificant, and people strove simply to weather it out--until the sun's warmth came again, exposing flaws and dividing humankind. Inside the storm was a hidden power, a freedom from the chains of life that could allow one to open doorways ordinarily never glimpsed.

Lannon turned the Eye away from that vision, for he did not understand its true meaning and it did nothing to help his current situation. He directed the Eye on finding a path, and it passed beyond the iron fence and into Dremlock Cemetery, touching lightly upon the tombs of the dead. Lannon kept the Eye moving, for he did not like the bits and pieces of mortality he was shown there. The tombs were built not out of respect for the dead--but out of fear. Fear of death ruled this place. Yet something frightful lurked amid the tombs as well, something that had succumbed to its fear and had crafted its own reality--its own prison. It watched Lannon with a deep hunger, desiring his existence while disbelieving its own. Piece by piece the centuries had worn its prison away, until the illusion itself had become thin and lacking in substance. Yet still it stubbornly remained.

"Go away," Lannon whispered, as he directed the Eye past that wretched being. "You must know by now there's nothing for you here!" He shuddered, shocked by his own unexpected words and overflowing with dark anxieties.

For an instant, the Eye touched on something even more horrible--a smug, vain thing that believed itself superior to all others. This monstrosity could reach forth and crush Lannon into pudding--a massively powerful hand that was hunched beneath the soil, bearing a tension like a coiled spring.

For a moment Lannon faltered at that last hideous image, and the Eye wandered this way and that, displaying confused sights. Then he managed to steady himself and bring it under control. He knew one thing for sure, now. The Cemetery was a place he would never go--not in daylight or darkness.

He located the path beyond the Cemetery. He motioned to the

others and they followed, keeping close to him, as he wandered the fence line. When they reached the trail, he sent the Eye out farther, seeking to know what had become of Jerret and Clayith. But the Eye could reveal nothing about their whereabouts. And so, from that point on, he kept it focused on the trail. (He carefully avoided turning it on the others, not wanting to see their deeper truths after what he'd been shown the last time.)

As they left the Cemetery behind, the Eye suddenly lurched off to one side on its own, revealing a figure wandering through the woods. It was Jerret.

The Eye probed the Red Squire, showing an honorable, courageous heart that could be easily corrupted. Jerret Dragonsbane would follow the lead of whoever got to him first, whoever pleased him the most. He walked the knife edge between light and dark. But right now he was trustworthy, and that was all that mattered.

"Jerret!" Lannon called out over the wind.

"Lannon?" came the reply. A moment later Jerret lurched out of the drifting snow and bumped into them. He looked half frozen.

"Am I glad to see you people!" Jerret said. "I got separated from Clayith, and I don't know where he went. I've just been feeling my way around, trying to get back to the West Tower. It was bad enough earlier, when there was still a little daylight. But now that it's dark out, you can't see anything at all!"

"We've noticed," said Vorden. "Lannon's leading the way. He knows how to get there. Just stay close to us and follow along."

"We're still doing this?" said Jerret. "Well, okay. But I don't see how we're going to find our way there. This storm is crazy."

Huddling around Lannon, they trudged straight to the Temple. When they finally stood before it, unable to see it save for the front entrance, which was barely visible in the torchlight, the Eye of Divinity probed the structure. This Temple was erected in honor of the Divine Essence, and it had been built with tremendous care. Each stone had been placed flawlessly and purposefully. But it was an uncertain structure nonetheless--because the god of Dremlock was an uncertain deity. This god did not exist in the heavens in a shimmering palace--instead it lay underground in a cavern--and the

Temple reflected that. It was a sacred place, yet something was wrong here. It had been built for a god that had known great suffering.

Lannon shook the vision away, feeling strangely empty. The Eye seemed to be leaping about too quickly, revealing the truths behind truths, teaching him things he wasn't ready for. He didn't want to know such things, for he felt unworthy. Why should he, of all people, be shown such knowledge? And was it even trustworthy? Perhaps the Eye was showing only possibilities, speculation. Or perhaps that's just what he hoped. He realized he would have to learn to control the Eye better, or it might eventually put a strain on his sanity.

Lannon focused on the Temple door. It bore a stout lock, but nothing Timlin couldn't handle. Lannon nodded to the little fellow, then stepped aside and let him go to work. It took Timlin several moments, but at last he got it unlocked.

"I don't want to go in by myself," said Timlin. "I know that was our plan--to have me check the place over--but I guess I'm still thinking about what happened before. Let's all go in there together."

"You don't have to," Aldreya said gently. "I'll go with you." She glared at the others. "Even if they won't."

"Don't worry about it, Timlin," said Lannon, feeling guilty beneath Aldreya's stare. "I wouldn't want to go in alone, either, even though this is a good place--not like the mines. We'll all go in."

Lannon was growing weary of receiving so much knowledge so quickly, and as he stepped inside, he drew the Eye partially within himself. There would be time for studying the true nature of things when he felt ready. The Eye was a powerful force, and already it had awakened deep fears within him. Perhaps the Divine Essence could help him understand it better.

They closed the door behind them, leaving it unlocked in case they needed a swift exit, and hurried down the short hallway, which still smelled of incense even though none was lit. The door at the end bore no lock. Lannon pulled it open and started through. Glancing back, he saw that Jerret hadn't moved.

"I don't think I can do this," Jerret said, looking grim. "It feels wrong. This is the Temple of the Divine Essence. What right have

I to sneak in here?"

Lannon searched his own feelings. Surprisingly, he felt no guilt now that he had reached the Temple. He could feel the Divine Essence somewhere below. It wanted him to come here, to break the Laws.

"It's okay," said Lannon. "You can wait here if you want to."

"What?" said Vorden, with a disgusted look. "Come on, Jerret. Don't be a fool. You risked a lot to come here, and now you're going to turn away at the last moment? If you ask me, that's just plain stupid."

Jerret swallowed. "I just... Alright, Vorden, let's keep moving." Still looking grim, and a bit sheepish as he glanced at Aldreya, the Red Squire started forward.

They entered the sanctuary and hurried up the steps to the altar. The torchlight fell on it, revealing the runes of the Sacred Text.

"I guess we should push on it or something," said Lannon.

Vorden snickered. "Use the Eye, Lannon."

"Oh, that's right," said Lannon, his face reddening. He let the Eye extend out and probe the altar. At first a jumble of thoughts ran through his mind, revealing tiny glimpses of religion and worship throughout the ages, but Lannon ignored that fragmented knowledge and focused on finding the hidden entrance. He saw that the top of the altar simply lifted off, with a stairway leading down underneath. Lannon explained it to the others.

"We can't lift that," said Timlin. "It's solid stone. We need Clayith."

"We can do it," said Vorden. "Right, Jerret?"

"Sure," Jerret said reluctantly.

The four Squires grabbed the edges of the stone slab and strained to lift it. Putting forth a tremendous struggle, they still couldn't manage it. Months of rigorous strength training still had not given them enough power to move the great slab.

"Forgetting someone?" said Aldreya.

"It won't make any difference," said Vorden. "It's too heavy."

She placed her hands on the slab and concentrated. Her lips muttered silent words. The stone slab shuddered and shifted, suddenly filled with energy. "Lift it," she said, her voice strained.

The Squires pulled with all their might, but it wasn't necessary. The slab had grown much lighter, and they lifted it off the altar with ease and sat it aside.

Aldreya wiped sweat from her forehead and smiled. "Well, that drained me quite a bit. But I'll be okay. Let's get going, then."

A stone stairway descended from the very top of the altar down into the darkness. A dank, musty smell arose from below--a cold and wet smell.

Lannon suddenly felt afraid. Was he expected to go first? He drew the Eye back into him a ways, dreading what it might show him.

Vorden smiled at Lannon and leapt up onto the stairs. He started down, as if he needed no torchlight to find his way.

Lannon and the others quickly followed.

At the bottom of the stairs were two doors of Glaetherin--one on the right and one on the left, with a wheel lock at the center of each. Lannon let the Eye probe the door on the right, peering beyond it into the passage. He glimpsed a powerful force up ahead, though from this distance he couldn't make out anything about it except that it was not an evil power. Beyond the left door, he sensed something dark and powerful--and quite evil--that he didn't dwell on for more than an instant.

"We should go right," he said, his body trembling.

Vorden nodded. "Whatever you say, Lannon. Lead the way."

Lannon focused the Eye on the wheel lock, and it took him only a moment to solve it. Then the door stood open.

Jerret gasped in amazement. "Lannon, how did you do that? Those things are supposed to be impossible to solve."

"He does that all the time," said Aldreya, shaking her head. "Don't bother asking, because apparently he likes to keep it to himself."

Lannon felt a surge of pride, but could think of nothing to say for a moment. At last he shrugged and said, "I guess I just have the gift."

Lannon suddenly began to feel ill and weary. His stomach felt heavy. It seemed the Eye had been out too long and had revealed too much. He needed a break from it. Having accomplished this major task in solving the wheel lock, he drew the Eye all the way into himself, and the halves of his mind merged into one.

As the Squires started through the doorway, a noise behind them made them jump. Someone was coming down the steps-- heavy footsteps and panting. They froze in horror, not even able to ready their weapons, while the figure descended.

"Hey!" a familiar voice called out. "Don't forget about me."

A tall, burly form stepped into the torchlight. It was Clayith Ironback.

The others breathed sighs of relief.

"You scared the wits out of us!" whispered Jerret. "But I'm glad to see you. How did you find this place in the storm?"

Clayith shrugged. "I just got lucky, I suppose." His skin was pale, his hair and eyebrows frosted with snow and ice. He licked his lips. "It wasn't so bad, you know. Just follow the east wind, like winter's breath..."

"What?" said Jerret. "Are you alright? You look like a snowman."

Clayith laughed. "No, I'm just fine. Hey, that purple thing's up ahead, you know. We should go deal with it." He cleared his throat, looking confused.

"Purple thing?" said Lannon. "Oh, you mean the Divine Essence. Right, let's get going. I think we're past the hard part now."

They passed through the doorway and found themselves moving down a short hallway. The hallway ended at a trapdoor, which bore a huge iron padlock.

"It's all yours, Timlin," said Lannon.

Timlin knelt down, and a moment later the lock was open. "I'm getting faster," he said, grinning, while the others looked on in admiration.

Vorden lifted the trap door, revealing an iron ladder that stretched down beyond the torchlight. The sound of running water came from below.

The ladder looked sturdy, and they immediately started down, with Vorden in the lead. They descended about thirty feet and ended up in a round stone chamber. Four tunnels lad away from the chamber, but three of them had been sealed permanently with solid barriers of Glaetherin that bore no locks. Flowing through the middle of the cavern was a little stream that came out of a hole in one wall and disappeared through a hole in the opposite wall. The chamber, and the stream, looked like natural formations.

"I guess we've got one choice," said Vorden.

His heart pounding with anxiety and growing excitement, Lannon hurried towards the open cavern. As they passed along it, they could see shards of multi-colored crystal protruding from the rock.

"We're getting close!" Lannon breathed excitedly.

"Ugly things!" muttered Clayith. "Those crystals hurt my head."

The others heard him, but paid little heed. They were bent on seeing the Divine Essence and nothing could distract them. The cavern curved up ahead, and the crystals became the walls, replacing the stone. The Squires could feel optimism building in their minds. As the light of truth fell upon them, they felt like anything was possible, that all would work out for a greater purpose. Behind them, Clayith began to whimper.

As they rounded the curve, the light became radiant, and then before them, in the chamber of fantastically colored crystal, stood the three purple Flamestones that made up the Mind of the White Guardian. Tall, pointy gems rising from a flat base, they were narrow at the bottom and widened out at the top. They were spaced unevenly apart, forming a triangle. The gems were rugged, a bit misshapen--far from the perfection the Squires had been imagining. Yet the Divine Essence was revealed at last, and the Squires were swept away with emotions, bathed in a wondrous glow of truth. Vorden and Timlin stood transfixed, while Jerret dropped to his knees.

"The King of Dremlock!" Aldreya breathed. Then she knelt next to Jerret.

Instantly Lannon's mind split of its own accord, and the Eye of Divinity came forth--as if being pulled out of him. It surged straight into the Divine Essence. It showed him things about the Essence that astounded him. Despite everything the Knights of Dremlock seemed to believe, this was not some all-knowing god. This was a lonely child with an uncertain future, a child partially destroyed yet still clinging to life. It was a lone candle burning in the darkness, struggling to give hope, yet threatened from all sides by the swarming shadows.

Lannon was overcome with a desire to help this child, to make it whole again and allow it to grow. But that was beyond his power. The White Guardian was no more--just shattered fragments that still pulsed with life.

Lannon was deeply saddened, and in his despair, the Eye of Divinity drew back inside him. Yet even as it retracted it revealed images, and he glimpsed a dark danger just behind him. Someone else in this chamber, like the Essence, was lonely and suffering--a puppet controlled by rage and hatred. In his mind he saw the poison blade slice the air towards his back, but he saw it too late to take action.

Lannon screamed as the cold steel pierced his shoulder. His body went numb and his legs gave out. He collapsed, but for a moment he remained coherent and was able to lift his head long enough to glimpse what was happening around him. He heard shouts, and he saw Vorden leap across the floor towards Clayith. Clayith was holding a black dagger, and his eyes gleamed with insanity. Vorden's axe bore down upon the burly Squire. Then Lannon's mind went black.

Chapter 12: Squires on Trial

When Lannon awoke, he was lying on a bed in a huge rectangular room. The room was lined with beds, and had much greenery in it, with tall plants in the corners and flowered vines growing on the walls and twined around some of the bedposts. A stone fountain stood at the center of the chamber, with statues of tiny, mythical Fairy Goblins in dancing poses around the water flow. Some of the beds were occupied by wounded Knights, who were being tended to by White Knights. Lannon recognized none of the wounded by name, but he had seen a few of them before.

Standing over Lannon was Vesselin Hopebringer, the ancient Lord of the White Knights. Firelight gave a red tint to his flowing silver hair and beard as he leaned forward with his gnarled hand clutching one of the bedposts. Vesselin smiled. "It is good that you have awakened, Lannon. I was very concerned. Yet it appears that you shall fully recover."

Recent memories flooded Lannon's mind, and he groaned, wondering where he was and how much time had passed. His throat felt as dry as dust, the flesh feeling ready to crack apart. He couldn't feel any pain his shoulder where Clayith's blade had struck, but he couldn't bring himself to probe the injury to see if it was healed. He simply waited for Vesselin to explain things.

"You went through a horrible ordeal, young one," said Vesselin. "I shall try to answer any questions you might have."

Lannon tried to speak, but nothing came out. He pointed to his throat. "I need some water," he managed to croak.

Vesselin called to one of the healers, who brought a mug of water to Lannon. The boy slurped it down, spilling much of it on his chest. When he could manage to talk, he blurted out, "Where are my friends?"

"They're all fine," said Vesselin. "Except for Clayith Ironback, who unfortunately is dead."

Lannon sighed and looked away. Clayith was dead, and Vorden had slain him. Lannon had seen it with his own eyes.

"How long was I asleep?"

"Two nights. But we need not speak of these things right now, if you wish. You can get more rest before we talk."

"Tell me everything. I need to know what happened."

"Very well." Vesselin lowered his voice to just above a whisper. "Clayith Ironback was possessed by the Deep Shadow. He was being controlled by someone unknown to us. He attempted to murder you with a poison dagger. It was a deadly poison, needing only to prick your skin to bring instant death. In fact, the dagger wound was quite shallow, as just the tip managed to pierce your armor. But that's all that was needed. We believe Clayith learned how to concoct this poison after studying one of the books in the East Tower Library--a book which has since been removed. After Clayith attacked you, your friend Vorden Flameblade slew Clayith, which is understandable but very unfortunate, because we might have been able to free his mind and learn who his master was. Yet it is too late to dwell on such things. We must now look to the future."

"How did I survive?" Lannon asked.

"We believe the Divine Essence saved you," said Vesselin. "It cast a healing light upon you that neutralized the poison. Yet you remained unconscious, leading us to fear that too much damage had been done for even the Divine Essence to heal."

"It saved me?" Lannon whispered in awe.

"Yes, it did," said Vesselin. "You know there is something different about you. You know the Knights have special plans for you, that the fate Dremlock may depend upon the Eye of Divinity. The fact that the Divine Essence brought you back from certain death confirms that your gift is of great importance, I believe."

"What happened after that?" said Lannon.

"Two of your friends waited in the Temple with you, while Vorden Flameblade and Jerret Dragonsbane went out seeking help. The boys got lost and nearly froze to death in the woods. Finally they made it to the North Tower and reported what had happened. We expected to find you dead."

Lannon didn't know what to say, and so he stayed silent.

"You Squires brought much trouble upon yourselves," said Vesselin. "The High Council is up in arms. A trial has been set for tomorrow evening, to determine the fate of you and your friends."

Lannon grimaced. "You mean...we could be banished?"

Vesselin nodded sadly. "Unfortunately, yes. This is a very serious matter. Not even the East and West Tower Masters are permitted to see the Divine Essence. Only a Lord Knight is allowed to do so. The Scriptures clearly state that."

Lannon closed his eyes, his thoughts twisting like a whirlpool. How had this all happened? Was it his fault? He thought of Clayith, and to his horror, he realized the lad might have been specifically targeting him.

"Why did he try to kill me?" Lannon asked.

Vesselin's face was grim. "That's a good question, Lannon. Perhaps he was just striking out at someone randomly."

Lannon searched Vesselin's face. "But you don't believe that, do you?"

"No, I do not."

Lannon glanced about nervously. "Then am I in any danger?"

"You will be watched closely from this point on. Always someone will look after you, though you may be unaware of their presence. Yet I would advise using all the knowledge you have learned--your skills as a Blue Squire and the Eye of Divinity. Trust no one fully--not even those who seemingly have earned your trust--and keep your eyes open. Be alert for signs, Lannon. That's the only advice I can give."

His heart racing, Lannon gave a quick nod.

"We made a grave mistake," said Vesselin. "We should have watched you from the start. We felt secure in the knowledge that no Squire can access the truly forbidden areas. We didn't count on you using the Eye of Divinity to solve the wheel locks. Yet there are other reasons you should have been looked after more closely, and I think what happened last night has opened our eyes to that. But as far as the trial goes, the High Council is made up of several stubborn men, who may not take into account your importance to the kingdom when deciding your fate."

Vesselin sighed. "This all should have been handled very differently, right from the moment you first entered Dremlock. We brought this trouble upon ourselves."

Lannon said nothing, knowing Vesselin was wrong. It was Lannon's fault this had occurred, for without use of the Eye, the journey below the Temple would never have taken place--and Clayith might still be alive.

"I must leave you now," said Vesselin. "I'll be back later on to check on your progress. Until then, try to get some rest."

Vesselin left the Hall. Lannon closed his eyes, knowing he could not simply rest as Vesselin had suggested. Far too much was on his mind. But after a while, he did begin to doze a bit, and he knew he was still suffering the after effects of the poison, which felt like hands trying to drag him back down into the blackness.

Lannon heard soft footsteps approaching and snapped awake. Garrin Daggerblood stood before him, a disappointed look on his face.

"I'm sorry for the trouble I've caused, Master Garrin," Lannon said. "It won't ever happen again." His words sounded weak and pitiful.

"You should have come to me," said Garrin. "You should have told me you had unlocked the Eye of Divinity. I would have helped you. Now I fear you are beyond my help. I am not part of the High Council, and my words shall go unheeded. I feel betrayed by you, Lannon Sunshield. I expected better of you." With that, the Blue Knight turned and walked away.

"Wait!" Lannon called out, but Garrin left the hall without looking back.

Lannon closed his eyes, almost wishing he had died down there instead of Clayith. Clayith's mind had been possessed by darkness. What was Lannon's excuse? He had knowingly violated the Sacred Laws, and his dreams of being a great Knight were crumbling apart. He sighed, longing for home, for as unhappy his old life had been, it seemed preferable to this in some ways.

From that point on, Lannon lay awake all day long and late into the night, deeply troubled, wishing he had someone to talk to about his anxieties. He avoided thinking of his father, for such thoughts were like daggers of pain in his heart. If Lannon were cast out of Dremlock, what would Doanan think of him? How could he ever go home and face his father? Also, he felt partially responsible for Clayith's death.

Lannon turned his thoughts towards the Divine Essence, but no help existed there. The Essence, in spite of its great power, was a scared and lonely child, not a god that could answer prayers and change the future. A deep emptiness swelled within Lannon--the realization that things might indeed be hopeless. Dremlock was in grave danger, and it appeared no one could stop it. If the rumors were true, not many Knights were left to defend the kingdom, and Goblins were on the move. He had believed the Divine Essence would give him answers, but instead it had left him feeling that all hope was lost.

***

The next day, Lannon remained in the Hall of Healing, bored and anxious, hoping someone of importance would come along to speak to him. But no one did--not even Vesselin Hopebringer. Yet he noted that White Knights were always watching him from close by, and he was not allowed to leave the Hall, or even his bed, most of the time. The day crept by very slowly towards the trial that would decide his fate.

Trenton Shadowbane, the Investigator, at last came to escort him to the trial. He entered the Hall and approached Lannon with a grim look on his face, while taking quick puffs of a small wooden pipe. "The trial is set to begin," he said, "so hurry up now. We can't keep the Council waiting. Your things are under the bed."

Lannon grabbed his pack and donned his winter cloak, but noticed that his weapons and armor were missing. He never went anywhere without his armor and sword these days, and he felt naked without them. He glanced questioningly at Trenton.

"Where is my sword and armor?"

"You are a possible threat to this kingdom," Trenton said, frowning. "Your weapons will be returned to you if you are found innocent." He smiled--a predatory grin that showed perfect teeth. "But if found guilty, you won't be needing them anyway, of course."

Lannon nodded, gazing at the floor. "Where are my friends?"

"I escorted them to the North Tower earlier," said Trenton.

"They are in Dremlock Hall, where all trials are conducted. Now let us be off."

Lannon followed Trenton from the Hall of Healing. It was another cold day, with a grey sky from which sprinkled snow. The path to the North Tower had been shoveled out after the blizzard, leaving snow banks taller than Lannon on either side. The Investigator made great strides as his boots crunched along the path, puffs of smoke from his lips blowing a sweet tobacco scent back towards Lannon, who had to struggle to keep pace with him. The lad was shaking from the cold and his anxieties as he stumbled along, and he was weary from lack of sleep. His stomach felt like he'd swallowed a lump of lead. Lannon could not see the Temple, which lay upon the opposite side of the North Tower, and he was glad of that. He had no desire to look upon it this day.

"You and your friends have caused quite a turmoil," said Trenton. "Some Council members are calling for your heads...not literally, of course. Well, actually, maybe some are being literal, but that's not my point. You need to be punished, and punished severely. Dremlock doesn't need this foolishness right now!"

Lannon kept silent, knowing if he said the wrong thing, it could make his position worse--if that were possible.

But Trenton would not let it be. He stopped and turned towards Lannon. "Don't think you're going to get away with this, boy. Tell me, what motivates you, Lannon Sunshield? Do you like things as they are?" His grey eyes shone with accusation as he glared at Lannon. He reminded Lannon very much of a wolf studying its prey, and out of sheer nervousness, Lannon was forced to speak.

"I regret what I did," he said.

The grey eyes narrowed. "How pathetic, child. You lack conviction in your words. There can only be one fate for the likes of you."

Lannon sighed, already knowing what Trenton's vote would be. If there were more people like this Investigator on the High Council, his career at Dremlock was definitely finished.

"I get your point," Lannon said, losing his temper. "You don't like me. But there is no use in beating me over the head with it!"

Trenton raised his eyebrows. "It has nothing to do with my personal feelings toward you. The Sacred Laws must always be obeyed!"

Trenton started walking again at an even faster pace. Lannon had to practically run to keep up. The North Tower was nearly the width of the East and West towers combined, and at least thirty feet taller than either, with six balconies encircling it. The black and silver Crest of Dremlock was emblazoned upon a giant flag that stood atop the peak. Six Red Knights, heavily armed, stood guard atop stone steps that led up to a towering iron door. They didn't move a muscle as the two approached, and their bearded faces were stern. They were part of the elite force of Knights that would defend the North Tower to their last breaths.

As the two ascended the steps, the guards pulled the door open. They nodded to Trenton, but the Investigator ignored them and strode on through. Lannon glanced at them, and saw pity in their eyes directed his way. He wished he hadn't looked at them. The door was pushed shut behind them.

They stood in Dremlock Hall. It resembled the Great Hall in the West Tower, except everything within was larger and grander. The floor was covered in a rich silver carpet, upon which sat five long tables bearing fancy adornments, such as candy dishes, wine jugs, and jars of tobacco. Fifteen foot tall paintings of Knights lined the walls, with one twenty foot masterpiece depicting Kuran Darkender that hung above a huge iron fireplace. On either side of the fireplace stood a door, one labeled Green Hall and another labeled Main Hall. Ten large Knights--bearing full plate mail, crossbows, battle axes, and shields--lined the chamber, with five on either side. A Grey Knight stood near the fireplace, holding a green crystal rod in her hands that she slowly turned this way and that while her gaze wandered the room.

The High Council was gathered at one of the tables, along with Lannon's friends. Timlin, Jerret, and Aldreya were pale and anxious-looking, but Vorden appeared relaxed, leaning back with his arms folded across his chest. Taris and Furlus flanked the four Squires, with a chair beside the Squires left open for Lannon.

Trenton pointed to the empty chair. "Go sit by your friends and keep still. Speak only if you are granted permission."

Lannon went and sat down. At first he avoided looking at

anyone, but then his gaze began to wander about, searching the faces of the Council members for any sign of hope. But he could tell nothing from their expressions.

Clearing his throat, Cordus said, "We are here to discuss the fate of these five Squires. I must remind you all that this is a closed trial, and anything spoken here should not be discussed once this meeting has ended."

"What is there to discuss?" said a Green Knight named Kealin Lightsword. "The Squires have admitted their guilt, and now a vote must be taken." Kealin was a tall, broad-shouldered man with a thin beard and mustache. Deep lines cut through the flesh of his cheeks and forehead, and his mouth was always set in a cold, cynical line.

"Not all of them have admitted wrongdoing," said Taris. "Lannon Sunshield has admitted nothing, as far as I know. He may have been a prisoner, dragged along against his will." The sorcerer's hood was thrown back, revealing his silver hair, pointed ears, and bright green eyes. He seemed very human to Lannon all of a sudden, lacking the mysterious aura he usually possessed.

"This is ridiculous," muttered Kealin. "Guilt has already been established beyond a reasonable doubt. This trial is about punishment alone. I suggest we get on with our vote, so we may then proceed with more important matters."

"Well said, Kealin," spoke another Green Knight. This one was an Olrog named Moten Goblinsbane, a short, bald, and heavyset Grey Dwarf with a peculiar feature--his beard had been trimmed short, while his sideburns remained extremely bushy.

"These Squires have violated our Sacred Laws," said Kealin. "And there can only be one punishment for that--banishment from the kingdom."

"Let me remind you all," said Cordus, "of Lannon Sunshield's importance to this kingdom. He alone possesses the Eye of Divinity, which has the potential to solve the Goblin Puzzle that has caused us so much trouble."

Lannon's heart leapt with hope. If Cordus Landsaver was on his side, surely he would not be banished. Lannon couldn't believe the others would dare go against the Lord Knight. Cordus seemed too commanding and powerful to be challenged.

But Lannon was wrong, and if he held any illusions after several months of being at Dremlock about how the kingdom was run, they were shattered an instant later.

Kealin slapped the tabletop with his hand. "Nonsense, I say! This is just another way of pushing the burden off our own shoulders. It's time we stop pointing fingers at fate, or the Deep Shadow, or riddles. We are the Knights of Dremlock, the ones who must defend this kingdom--not a mere boy who lacks honor. This Eye of Divinity--this ancient magic that few know anything about--is not the answer. We must bear the responsibility for what has happened to Dremlock and our Knights."

"What do you know of responsibility, Kealin?" said Taris. "If Lannon is banished, I cannot train him, correct?"

Kealin nodded. "Yes, the Scriptures state that."

"Yet he must be trained to use the Eye," said Taris. "Now that he has unlocked it, he must learn to control it. Only I am knowledgeable enough in the ancient magical arts to administer that kind of training. If he is not shown how to properly use his gift, the Goblin Puzzle will remain unsolved, and Dremlock will fall."

"We cannot violate the Laws for any reason," said Kealin. "It is as simple as that. If we do, then Dremlock has already fallen and is not worthy of defending. And again, I say this Eye of Divinity is not the answer."

Furlus shook his head. His skin had reddened, his breath growing raspy. "I've heard enough of this, Kealin! The Divine Essence healed that boy, saving him from certain death. Doesn't that mean anything to you?"

"Yes, it does," said Kealin, calmly. "It means our god is merciful, even to the unjust. And that is all it means. This is not an excuse to violate the Sacred Laws, which must be adhered to at all costs. *At all costs!*"

Moten nodded, his grey eyes fixed on Furlus. "What kind of Olrog are you, Furlus Goblincrusher? You would go against everything that we stand for as Knights and side with criminals? What happened to your honor? Grey Dwarves don't act in such a manner as this. I am ashamed to belong to the same race as you."

Furlus shook with rage. "How dare you speak to me of honor,

Moten. I know what you've been up to, having dealings with the dark--"

"Furlus!" Cordus growled. "Hold your tongue."

Reluctantly, Furlus fell silent, but did not take his eyes off Moten. Furlus' face was like stone, his hands clenched into meaty fists.

"The rest of you watch what you say as well," said Cordus. "We shall maintain order at this trial and not forget our purpose here."

Moten stared back at Furlus, a smug look on his face. A hint of a smile was at the corners of his mouth.

Lannon and the other Squires couldn't believe what they were seeing. Furlus had just all but accused Moten of having dealings with the Deep Shadow, and Moten's only response was to stare smugly back. Lannon wanted badly to say something, but Vorden beat him to it.

"Who should be on trial here?" said Vorden. "Us, or those--"

"Be quiet!" Cordus interrupted him. "Do not speak without permission. I better not have to tell you this again, Vorden Flameblade."

"The lad is arrogant to speak out thus," said Moten. "Dremlock doesn't need such brazenness, such blatant defiance of our Laws. I think we can see what kind of Squires we're dealing with here."

"I understand his desire to speak," said Taris. "Why should he not be allowed to state his case? The rule is not fair."

"Regardless," said Moten, "it is a rule and should be obeyed."

"This discussion is pointless," said Kealin. "The trial has just begun, yet already it has degenerated into a verbal brawl. And to what end? I say the final vote is all that matters. So let us waste no more time with this foolishness."

Cordus glanced around the table. "And the rest of you? How do you feel about this matter? Should the Squires--including Lannon--be banished?"

The Squires glanced at each other. Among them, only Vorden continued to show confidence, leading Lannon to wonder if he held some knowledge that might get them out of this mess. If anyone could think of a way to save their careers at Dremlock, Vorden was the one.

"I do not think Lannon should be banished," said Vesselin Hopebringer, "regardless of what happens to the other Squires." He folded his wrinkled, trembling hands before him. "I've been Lord of the White Knights for over one hundred and twenty years, and I've always longed for peace. Yet I know that peace can never exist in Silverland until the Goblins are completely vanquished. The other kingdoms won't help us. We must defend Silverland on our own. My dream is to see peace come to our land before my passing, yet my time in this realm grows short. Lannon Sunshield, and his Eye of Divinity, could make that dream a reality."

"I think they should all be banished," said Carn Pureheart, Lord of the Blue Knights. "I believe the Divine Essence does not want us to break its Laws. I believe this is a test, and if we fail it and take the easy route, Dremlock will fall."

"Beautifully said!" exclaimed Kealin. "I fully agree with you."

"As do I," said Moten. "This is indeed a test of our Knightly virtues."

The remaining Council member, a Birlote woman named Krissana Windsword, spoke up. "I have to agree with those in favor of banishment. This does appear to be a divine test, which we cannot afford to fail."

"I think all but Lannon and Aldreya should be banished," said Taris.

"I agree with Taris," said Furlus, "concerning Lannon."

"Then everyone has spoken," said Kealin. "It is time to vote."

"And none of you will change your minds?" said Cordus, his eyes searching theirs for any hint of doubt. "About Lannon, I mean."

They shook their heads.

"Our minds shall not be changed so easily!" said Kealin. "We are firm in our moral convictions, Lord Knight."

"Very well," said Cordus, sighing.

Lannon's heart went into a flutter. Jerret and Timlin were staring at the tabletop, obviously unable to watch at this point. Aldreya's eyes were closed, her hands clasped before her as if in prayer. Vorden, however, still maintained his relaxed pose, only now there seemed something fake about it--as if it were all show and no substance. He seemed frozen in that position.

Cordus spoke sternly: "Anyone in favor of banishing Vorden Flameblade forever from Dremlock Kingdom, raise your hand."

All of the Council members raised hands. Vorden's confident look disintegrated into one of shock, his mouth dropping open. "You can't do this!" he cried. "This kingdom needs us."

"Vorden Flameblade," Cordus continued coldly, "you are hereby cast out of Dremlock until the end of your days. And if you speak again, you shall spend some time in the dungeon."

The Lord Knight then went on, "Anyone in favor of banishing Timlin Woodmaster, raise your hand."

Again, all the Council members agreed that Timlin should be banished forever. The scrawny lad began to weep.

Cordus ignored him and continued. "Anyone in favor of banishing Jerret Dragonsbane, raise your hand."

Again, there was the same result. Jerret put his head in his hands, his eyes sullen. He mumbled something no one could quite understand.

Aldreya's turn was next. And when the vote called for her banishment, she leapt up. "You can't do this!" she cried, glowering at those who had spoken against her. "I was sent here from Borenthia. My father will very displeased with this decision. You're making a big mistake."

"We stand by our decision," said Kealin. "Whether or not we lose favor with the Birlotes is something we cannot be held responsible for."

"Nevertheless," said Taris. "She is right. As I've already officially stated, this could potentially ruin our ancient relationship with the Elder Family. Dremlock will suffer greatly because of this decision to banish the girl."

"She deserves no special treatment," said Carn. "She violated the Laws and must be punished like the others. The Elder Family, I hope, will understand why we had to take this course of action."

Her face red with fury, Aldreya slumped back in her chair. "You're all going to regret this!" she muttered one last time.

"And now," said Cordus, "anyone in favor of banishing Lannon Sunshield--anyone who would ignore the potential of the

Eye of Divinity to save our kingdom--think carefully and make your decision."

Kealin, Moten, Krissana, Carn, and Trenton all raised their hands. Cordus, Taris, Furlus, and Vesselin stood opposed, hands at their sides.

"The Council has decided then," said Cordus, grimly.

"And decided well!" said Kealin. "Truth and justice have triumphed this day." He turned and shook hands with Moten, and they clapped each other on the back. Krissana and Carn sat in thoughtful silence. Trenton Shadowbane looked thoughtful as well, his eyes distant.

"Now," said Kealin, "if these ex-Squires may be escorted from here, we can get on to other matters--such as the *important* affairs of this kingdom."

"Wait," said Cordus, raising a hand. "This is not over yet."

Kealin's eyes widened. "What is this outrage? The High Council has made its decision, Cordus, harsh as it may seem."

"Indeed it has," said Cordus. "But now I must make a harsh decision of my own. This is a time of war! Goblins have taken over the forestlands of Hethos. They are near the borders of Kalamede, and if not stopped, will soon overrun the city. And even now they are advancing on Dremlock Kingdom. During a time such as this, a Lord Knight may assume full command of the affairs of Dremlock. Well, I am *officially* declaring us at war! The Black Torches shall be raised in the towers, and the Three Chambers of Law shall be sealed. This decision gives me the right to overrule any decision made by the Council."

Moten jumped up, his bushy jowls shaking with fury. "How...how dare you? You are just abusing this privilege to get your way!"

Kealin grabbed the Dwarf's arm. "Relax, Moten. I anticipated this lowly move on the part of our Lord Knight, and I have an answer for it. You made your decision, Cordus Landsaver, and now I make mine. I have the right to call for a vote on your removal from power at any time and upon any grounds. Even during a time of war, an incompetent Lord Knight can be demoted."

"That's nonsense!" said Taris. "I would strongly question your motives concerning this matter, Kealin. You would have one of the greatest Lord Knights since Kuran Darkender lose his position because of a few Squires?"

"We must stick by our principals," said Krissana, the Birlote. "We cast our vote, and we cannot back down now. I stand with Kealin on this matter, and call for Cordus' immediate removal from power."

"Agreed," said Moten and Carn.

Taris shook his head in disbelief. "I never thought I would see the day when the High Council of Dremlock would sink to such a level."

Furlus stood up, hand on his battle axe. His eyes had turned light grey, almost white, and his skin was deep red--the signs of an Olrog about to engage in warfare to the death. "We shall see who is cast out and who isn't!"

"Furlus," sighed the Lord Knight. "Sit down and compose yourself. These Council members are exercising a legal right. The vote must be cast."

"And cast now!" said Kealin.

"You dare take a threatening stance against us?" Moten said to Furlus. "Perhaps we should call for another vote--to remove Furlus Goblincrusher from his seat as Tower Master on the grounds that he cannot control his temper."

Reluctantly, Furlus sat back down and folded his arms across his chest. "The time will come, Moten, when the vote is cast against *you*--when the truth about you is revealed. I await that day with fire in my blood."

Moten scowled, but for the first time, he appeared less than confident for a moment as he gazed into Furlus' eyes.

"Cordus Landsaver," said Kealin, "has sided with lawbreakers. He has gone against everything Dremlock stands for, and he has gone against the will of the Divine Essence. Anyone in favor of his removal from power, raise your hand."

Kealin, Moten, Carn, and Krissana all raised hands. Trenton Shadowbane stared into the distance, his hands at his sides.

"Trenton?" questioned Kealin, his eyes reflecting uncertainty. "What are you doing?"

"What would you have me do?" said Trenton. "Cast out our

great leader, Cordus Landsaver, over a few Squires? I think not. Do you take me for a fool? Do you think I want any of you to end up as Lord Knight? Anyone on the Council could pass that silly Divine Test and end up leading Dremlock. Yet I prefer the one who is in power now--even over myself. There is none better fit to lead us than Cordus."

"Then you back away from your principals," snapped Kealin, his voice shrill. "You are a coward, Trenton!"

Suddenly, Trenton Shadowbane growled like an animal, startling the Squires and some of the Council members. "Enough! My vote is cast, and I'll hear no more of it. I know of the darkness that lurks behind these walls. I know of the creeping disease that rots away all that is wholesome. Even the rains that bred life, before the great darkness, cannot wash away the stench of it."

"You're insane!" hissed Moten.

"Nevertheless," said Cordus. "Trenton has spoken. Whether you understand his words or not--you certainly understand his vote. This matter has been decided. Lannon Sunshield will remain a Squire, and I will remain Lord Knight."

Lannon nearly leapt out of his seat in excitement, but then he glanced towards the other Squires, and his heart sank. How could he go on without his friends?

"So be it," said Kealin, his face gone crimson. "But at least I can now have these other former Squires removed from my sight. Guards--come escort these youths to their rooms and keep watch over them until they can be sent home."

Two of the Red Knights came forward, looking uncertain.

"Hold on a moment!" said Vorden, standing up. The lad from Gravendar seemed to have quickly recovered his composure.

Cordus glowered. "You better have something important to say, Vorden Flameblade, or banishment may be the least of your worries."

"Lannon cannot use the Eye without us!" Vorden blurted out. "We helped him unlock it. If you banish us, you can forget about the Eye."

"Is this true, Lannon?" asked Cordus.

Lannon nodded quickly. "That's right. I just can't do it on my own. I've tried lots of times, but it doesn't work."

"I see," said Cordus, a slight smile appearing on his lips. He gazed at Kealin, daring the Green Knight to oppose him. Then he focused again on Vorden. "Well, it seems you Squires have me over a barrel. And so for now, you shall all be escorted to the East Tower, where you will be placed under guard while I decide what to do about all this. If any one of you cause the slightest bit of trouble, I will personally take you down to Dremlock Dungeons and give you a new home."

"You won't get away with this, Cordus," Kealin said. "Justice will inevitably prevail, one way or another."

"I believe it already has," said Cordus. "Though there is certainly more justice that needs doing...when the time is right."

Elated, the Squires jumped up and followed the two guards. As Lannon walked away from the table, Kealin made a quick sign to the lad--pulling his fingers across his throat in an unmistakable gesture.

"It's your day, Lannon," he whispered, smiling. "Enjoy it while you can."

Chapter 13: Whispers of Flame

When the Squires arrived at the East Tower, Aldreya was taken to her room and the boys were led to the Blue Squires' quarters. The two Red Knights warned the boys not to try to leave their rooms without permission and that they would be watched at all times. "You dodged an arrow, Squires," they said. "Anyone else would have been banished for what you did. But don't go trying to pull anything on us. The East Tower is on full alert, and which means that *you-know-who* is creeping around somewhere right outside your door."

"The Watcher?" said Vorden.

The guards glanced at each other. "Let's just say nothing you do will be a secret from this point on, so just do as you're told. If you need anything, or if you observe anything unusual, give a holler."

The boys were herded into their room and the door was closed and locked behind them. They suspected at least one of the guards was posted just outside, though no one checked. They sat close to each other on the beds, and kept their voices at a whisper, though at this point they had little to hide.

"I guess I should feel happy about remaining a Squire," said Vorden. "But I can't stop thinking about Clayith. Clayith was a good person deep inside, and I'm not proud of what I did. It was just an instinctive thing, I guess." Vorden gave a troubled sigh, running his fingers through his black hair.

Lannon nodded. "I just wish there had been another way."

"I've thought of that, too," said Vorden. "It's not like Clayith knew what he was doing. But how was I supposed to know that? All I knew what that he was trying to kill you, and I just reacted. I keep seeing it in my mind, and I don't like it. I don't like the thought that I killed an innocent person."

"There's nothing to be done about it now," said Jerret. "It's just a bad way things worked out. But hopefully we've learned our lesson."

Timlin just sat watching, offering no opinion. For an instant, Lannon wondered what motivated the little fellow, if Timlin ever really cared about who lived or died. In some ways he was very likable, even sympathetic, yet in other ways he seemed strangely unfeeling towards others.

Timlin seemed to notice Lannon's scrutiny of him, and he lowered his gaze, looking uncomfortable. But he still said nothing.

"I guess I just need to put it out of my mind," said Vorden. "If I can, that is. It's not going to do me any good to dwell on it."

"But what's going on with that Kealin fellow?" said Jerret. "He didn't look too happy with you, Lannon."

"Not at all," Lannon agreed.

"It's obvious," said Vorden, "that Kealin and Moten, and maybe one or two other High Council members are corrupt. Kealin might even be involved with the Deep Shadow, like some of the rumors suggest. I don't think I'd want to be in your shoes, Lannon. They must see you as a threat, because you have the Eye of Divinity, and they probably sent Clayith to kill you."

"I just can't believe any of this," said Jerret. "What has Dremlock come to? The Knights should just round up anyone they suspect of having dealings with the Deep Shadow and imprison them."

"They can't do that," said Vorden. "They need evidence. Otherwise they would be just as bad as the guilty ones."

"That's stupid," muttered Jerret. "If they know who's evil, they should take them down--with or without evidence."

"They should kill them," said Timlin. "Before they kill Lannon."

"Not without evidence," Vorden insisted. "People have rights. Laws are important. I don't think either of you understand how it all works."

"I understand someone wants me dead," said Lannon. "I understand that Clayith was used against his will as my assassin.

I'd rather see Kealin imprisoned on weak evidence than have him plotting to kill me. If he's the one, that is."

Vorden frowned. "I'm surprised at you, Lannon. You always seemed like you had a solid grasp on right and wrong."

"You're pretty righteous all of a sudden, Vorden," said Jerret, rolling his eyes. "What's got into you?"

"It's not that," said Vorden, looking away. "Like I said, I feel bad about what happened to Clayith. Maybe I'm just trying to get things in order, to figure out where I stand. Is there anything wrong with that?" He moved off to his bed and lay down, a troubled expression on his face.

"No, there's nothing wrong with that," Jerret said. "Clayith was my friend, but I know you did what you had to do. I don't hold it against you--at least not on the surface, I guess. Deep inside, who knows what I feel?"

The Squires fell silent. Lannon glanced about the room, where the shadows were deepening. "We should light a lantern," he said.

They did so, and then lay down on their beds to sleep. For a long time no one spoke, as there was much on their minds, until Timlin finally broke the silence. "I'm just glad we're still Squires," he said. "Because before I was..." Timlin let his words trail off, and looked away sheepishly.

"Finish what you were saying," said Lannon.

"I guess I never really had anything," said Timlin, turning onto his side to face Lannon. "Now I feel like I belong, like I have something worthwhile. And I'm just glad I didn't lose it and end up back where I was."

"I feel the same way," said Lannon. "When I lived with my parents, things were a lot less interesting. They argued a lot, and my father was sick most of the time. Now I feel like I have some kind of future."

"I'd rather die than go back to my parents," said Timlin. "They were never nice to me, no matter what I did. My aunt was okay--a little strict, but not too bad. But living with her was really boring. We never did much, and I spent a lot of time just sitting home doing nothing, wishing I had someplace fun to go."

"I know the feeling," said Lannon. "It's like sometimes you think the rest of the world is moving on without you--like you have no place in it."

"Exactly," said Timlin. "But now that's all changed. I could be a Knight someday, and have anything I want. Even now, it all seems too good to be true."

Timlin turned away, and not long after that, he was asleep. Lannon rolled onto his back and adjusted his quilt. He thought back to the gesture Kealin had made--the fingers across the throat--and wondered if he should make sure the guards were still there. But then he decided they must be. After all, the Knights were not stupid, and Vesselin Hopebringer had said he would be watched closely.

As he drifted towards sleep, his thoughts focused on his parents. If Goblins were threatening Kalamede and other places, were they in any danger? Their little valley was a long way off, but still it worried him, making him wish the Knights would take some sort of action to turn the tide, though he suspected they were doing all they could.

And then he slipped into a surprisingly deep sleep.

***

When Lannon awoke, he could barely move because of the Whispers. He had been dreaming of the Whispers. He had watched them in his mind as they materialized out of the shadows, taking physical form and becoming talons of flame that burrowed into his soul and froze him. His eyelids could move (they popped open as he awoke) and he could wiggle his toes and fingers, but that was about it. It was as if he were buried up to his head in sand. He panicked, and his heart beat furiously, yet he still couldn't move his arms or legs.

The Whispers were some form of dark sorcery unlike anything Lannon had ever imagined. They were alive--writhing serpents of flame and evil that sought only to stop a living being from moving. They fed off paralysis and grew stronger. Each surge of panic, and each failed attempt at movement, caused the Whispers to constrict ever tighter. They were of flame, yet they seared like ice.

Lannon knew what was happening, with a bloodcurdling dread that flooded his mind, and he realized both he and the Knights had made a terrible mistake. They had underestimated their enemies.

The lantern had gone out, and someone was moving towards

him in the darkness, quiet footsteps that he could hear only because his training had sharpened his senses. Then a figure leaned over him. He knew this because the rustling of fabric was just above him. A moment later he saw a cold blue knife blade appear, and in its glow he saw a face that was a mask of shifting shadows. Glowering down at him were crazed eyes of a violet hue that burned into Lannon and invoked a haunting memory.

There was no mistaking it. These were the eyes of Tenneth Bard, a man believed long dead. These were the eyes of the Black Knight, the founder of the Blood Legion, and the sworn enemy of Dremlock Kingdom. Lannon knew this beyond a doubt, because he had seen those same eyes on that stone statue in the ruins of Serenlock Castle. Only now, in reality, they were far more powerful and evil.

But Lannon could do nothing. The Whispers still held him frozen, and his vocal cords would not work, his scream lost in silence.

"Lannon Sunshield," came a quiet hiss. "At last I have you. You won't be causing me any trouble, boy. This is my time, and you must die!"

The knife blade glowed brighter, charged with some magical energy--soon to swipe down and piece Lannon's heart. He closed his eyes, hoping for a quick end if nothing else, and in desperation, he struggled to call forth the Eye. He did not believe he would succeed, but he knew he had to somehow or all was lost. He imagined Timlin and Vorden assisting him, and his body started to tingle.

Then, perhaps out of sheer desperation, his mind split, and the Eye of Divinity reached out, probing the figure before him. The things Lannon glimpsed might have driven him mad, for he observed the fringe of some terrible darkness that sought to drag him in. But then the Whispers became intertwined with the Eye of Divinity, and the Eye rebelled against them. The Eye suddenly shifted and became a physical power that seized the figure and held it motionless.

The evil eyes widened in shock. Then the figure fought back furiously, striving to break the force that held its blade in check. "I'll slay you yet, Lannon Sunshield!" the dark form grunted, and slowly the blade began to descend. Lannon struggled with all his might, commanding the Eye to stop his assailant, yet it was a losing effort. In a moment the blade would come down into his chest.

In a last effort to save himself, Lannon diverted a small portion of his power to a bed next to his, flipping it over and knocking Timlin to the floor. "Hey!" Timlin yelled. "What's happening?"

Moments later the door opened, spilling torchlight into the room. A cloaked figure entered, holding a stone dagger that burned with green fire. A tongue of flame hurtled out from the dagger and burned into Lannon's attacker.

An explosion of sparks erupted, and the figure staggered to one side, its shoulder on fire. More tongues of flame shot out at him at him from the stone dagger, only this time the figure somehow eluded them and they burst against the stone wall, sending green sparks bouncing about the room.

"You'll die yet," the figure muttered at Lannon, and then, still partially on fire, it leapt out the open window and was gone.

The Whispers departed from Lannon, the burning fingers releasing his soul and vanishing, and he could move again. He sat up, feeling lightheaded and dizzy. The Eye of Divinity drew back inside him completely. Vorden, Timlin, and Jerret had all gotten up, and were staring on with wide eyes. Vorden held his axe at ready (*the axe that had slain Clayith*, Lannon thought numbly, as random emotions swirled through his mind). He directed his gaze on the one who had entered the room.

It was Taris Warhawk. Behind him were two Red Knights, their weapons drawn. One of them was holding a lantern. The two Knights ran to the window and peered out, muttering in disbelief.

Taris calmly walked over to Lannon. "Are you alright?"

Lannon wasn't sure, but he nodded. He felt sick to his stomach, and still in the clutches of the darkness. He didn't even try to speak.

Taris turned to the guards. "Go to Cordus immediately. Organize a search of the Kingdom grounds. This would-be assassin must be caught!"

Bowing, the guards hurried off to do as ordered.

Taris walked to the window and peered out. "It's a long way down," he said. "The fall should have killed him instantly, even if he landed in a heap of snow. Yet there is no sign of his crushed body below--no blood even! It's as if he simply got up and walked away after falling hundreds of feet. Who could have done this? No one I know possesses that kind of power. It is very fortunate that I happened to be here talking to the guards when you were attacked. Did you get a look at him?"

Lannon nodded. He tried to steady himself enough to speak. "I know who it was, I think. He's supposed to be dead."

Taris went and knelt beside the boy, his green eyes narrowing. "Who was he, Lannon?"

"Tenneth Bard," Lannon whispered.

"Tenneth Bard, the Black Knight," Taris said. "Yes, I think this is starting to make sense, now. When the search is ended, we must call a meeting at once. I would like to involve the Ranger as well. In fact, I would like to involve her in the search. Who better to track a man than a Ranger?"

Lannon and the other boys watched Taris in silence.

"If this is indeed Tenneth Bard," Taris said, turning to stare at Vorden, "we will not find him right away. His powers must have grown drastically. On the other hand, he wasn't expecting to get caught, so perhaps there is a chance. Well, am I right?"

Vorden nodded, obviously unsure of how to respond. "I think so."

Taris stood up. "These are grim events, my young friends. And yet the veil of mystery has, perhaps, been partially lifted. The answers to the riddles that have haunted Dremlock may at last be within our reach."

Taris motioned to Timlin. "Come here."

Trembling, Timlin hurried over and stood before him.

"Did you see anything?" Taris asked.

Timlin nodded. "Just a glimpse." He closed his eyes for a moment. "Wait--I remember something. He carried something in his hand--not the knife, but in his other hand. Something dark and round. He pulled it against his chest as he jumped out the window. And his face was strange, like shifting shadows."

Taris looked beyond the lad, gazing into apparent nothingness. A light of understanding was in his eyes. "I must say, Squires, that

I think there may be hope for this old kingdom yet--something I wasn't quite sure of just a short time ago."

The others could only stare at him in confusion. Lannon clutched his stomach. He could still feel the Whispers inside him-- just a memory now, but still potent enough to make him ill. In the back of his mind he realized the Eye of Divinity had saved him, that he had called it forth on his own and it had changed form and become a different type of force. But at the moment, it didn't seem to matter. Tenneth Bard was alive, perhaps more powerful than ever, and he wanted Lannon dead. In his shocked state of mind, Lannon felt that surely the Black Knight would eventually get his way, that no one could stop him.

The Whispers would make sure Lannon met his doom.

Chapter 14: The Secret Meeting

For the rest of that night, and the following day, Taris personally guarded Lannon. Mostly Taris was a silent companion who spoke only when necessary, and he refused to discuss the current situation at Dremlock. As the day progressed, Furlus dropped by now and then, and each time he and Taris went into the corner and talked quietly. The Squires assumed they were discussing the search for Lannon's would-be assassin and wished they could hear what was being said.

At one point, Taris took Lannon to the Library to talk privately with the lad about what had happened the night before. Lannon explained how he had called forth the Eye, and how it had changed form, slowing Tenneth Bard's attack.

"Much about the Eye of Divinity is mysterious," said Taris. "Even the most powerful of the Dark Watchmen did not know all of its secrets. Yet it appears you've already made slight use of the Body stage of the Eye, which is very remarkable for someone as inexperienced as you."

"What more can you tell me about the Eye," asked Lannon, "that will help me use it more effectively."

"We have one book at Dremlock," said Taris, "that specifically deals with the topic. It is a collection of the Dark Watchmens' writings. Long ago, the Eye of Divinity was more common, and the Knights who possessed it organized themselves into a special group whose goal was to unlock the mysteries of the Deep Shadow. These Dark Watchmen were successful in their task, as many secrets about our enemy were revealed, giving us an advantage. However, they probed too deeply into the affairs of the Deep Shadow, and some became possessed by it or went insane. After that, the group was disbanded.

"Yet the Dark Watchmen--for all they learned about the Deep Shadow--knew little about the workings of their own mysterious power. Yet that is the nature of the Eye of Divinity--it is very unpredictable. Once it is unlocked, there are no established rules for using it. What works for some may not work for others. It can be very frustrating at times to try to understand it. However, as I mentioned, they left notes and letters--different techniques that can be attempted."

"Can I see the book?" Lannon asked excitedly.

Taris sat in thoughtful silence for a while before answering. "I don't feel you are ready yet for such knowledge. It might only make things harder for you. You will learn on your own for now-- as you have done so, impressively, already. But there may come a time when you can go no further and have need of the book. The power you possess is what led the Dark Watchmen to a bad end. Always bear that in mind. We must watch you closely as your training progresses and make sure you don't meet the same fate as the others before you, that you take things slow and don't delve too deeply into the workings of the Deep Shadow. The book could be dangerous for you to read right now."

Lannon gave a disappointed nod.

"You're afraid," said Taris. "You think we cannot protect you, that Tenneth Bard will somehow get to you again and destroy you. Am I right?"

"I am afraid," Lannon admitted. "Those Whispers were powerful. I couldn't even move. If the Eye hadn't come out... "

"But it did," said Taris. "And it could do so again."

"But it wasn't strong enough," said Lannon. "If you hadn't come along, I would have been killed."

Taris was thoughtful. At last he said, "The Eye is a powerful force. The question is whether or not your own will is strong enough for you to wield it properly. It appears that at this time the answer is no. But that could change."

"How?" said Lannon.

"Age and experience is one way," said Taris. "There may come a time when you can stand against Tenneth Bard, yet I cannot guarantee it. If he actually still lives, his powers are unknown to me. But at least, with a stronger will, you would have a better chance of defeating him."

"If I live that long," Lannon said gloomily.

Taris nodded. "Yes, if you live that long. The Knights will do their best to protect you, but nothing is certain."

"Kealin Lightsword didn't seem to like me much," said Lannon. "So that's someone else I apparently have to watch out for."

Taris nodded. "I saw the gesture he made to you--as if he wanted you dead. But there is nothing to be done about it at this time. Kealin is a Green Knight, protected by our laws, and right now we lack evidence against him. Moten, the Grey Dwarf, is another suspicious character. We've been investigating those two for some time, but they are sly. If they dwelt in the East Tower rather than the North, I might have exposed them long ago for the corrupt men they are, for very little of what happens here is not known to me."

"If that's true," said Lannon, "why didn't you know we snuck out the other night, when we went below the Temple?"

"I did know," said Taris. "I also knew of your journey beneath Old Keep, and I got word to the Dark Knights below, which is why you were saved from that Ogre. Did you think one of the Knights just happened along?"

Lannon stared in speechless shock for a moment. Then he said, "If you knew, why didn't you punish us?"

"I did," said Taris. "Forcing you to view the horrors in the Dungeon was my punishment to dissuade you from ever going back into Old Keep. Nothing exists down there but the shadows of doom."

"Then you knew I had use of the Eye," said Lannon.

"Yes," said Taris. "But I didn't report it to the other Knights. I wanted to learn just what you were up to, Lannon. And now I know that you were acting honorably, and for a good cause-- though a Squire has met his end in the process."

"You mean..." Lannon began.

Taris nodded. "I believe you were meant to see the Divine Essence. Therefore, I did not try to stop you when you left the tower. I wanted you to reach the Temple and see the Essence."

"You wanted me to break the Sacred Laws?"

"Of course not," said Taris. "But the Divine Essence must never be ignored. After all, it made the Laws in the first place. Don't try to understand what motivates me, Lannon Sunshield. I have my reasons."

Lannon said nothing, staring at the tabletop.

Taris chuckled. "You look stricken. But fear not, I'm on your side at the moment. I just wanted to tell you this so you would realize that the Tower of Sorcery is not ignorant of what takes place within it. There is no safer place for you in all of Dremlock than the East Tower. But no place in this world is entirely safe, and unfortunately that assassin was somehow able to get to you unseen."

"If you know so much," Lannon said, "then why didn't you know about Clayith?"

"I knew he had come here," said Taris. "But I did not know why. Some things even I cannot know without further examination. Had I been able to talk with the boy, I might have realized he was possessed."

Taris sighed. "The Deep Shadow is a tricky foe."

"Did you really know about everything we were doing?" said Lannon. For some reason, he doubted Taris' words.

Taris' face hardened for a moment, but then he smiled. "You don't believe me? I have spies all over this tower, including the Watcher, who cannot be seen when he doesn't wish himself to be."

Lannon shrugged. "I'm just not sure."

Taris grinned. "You're a smart lad. I will admit that you are right in your suspicion--but only to a point. You and your friends were trained well as Blue Squires, and with many of our Knights out on important missions, this tower is not as secure as it used to be."

"Then I'm not as safe as you suggested," said Lannon.

"This is the safest place for you in Dremlock," said Taris, "which is why you are here. Will it be enough to protect you from an assassin who can climb icy walls and survive a fall from the top of this tower? Sadly, I cannot say for sure."

"I have something more to tell you," said Lannon. "It's about the Divine Essence." He explained what he'd learned to Taris--

about how their god was actually just a lonesome, scared child.

Taris smiled. "This is not unknown to me. The White Guardian was very young when it was shattered. But it still possesses wisdom beyond us mortals. It revealed that knowledge to you for a reason--one that is difficult to understand at this time. A great puzzle lies before us, Lannon, and it may take a long time before all the pieces fit together and we can see beyond the haze of the Deep Shadow that shrouds our vision."

***

Once evening arrived, Taris told the Squires to put on their cloaks. "We must get Aldreya and travel to the Temple," he told them. "A secret meeting has been arranged there, and none must know of it but the ones invited."

As they left the tower and started along the trail, a full moon hung in the sky, its pale light glistening off the snow and ice. The night air was frigid. At one point a Midnight Crow soared overhead, and Taris pulled the Squires into the shadows until it passed by. Midnight Crows were rumored to be servants of the Deep Shadow, and Taris' attempt to hide them from this one gave that rumor much credibility in the Squires' minds. As usual, wolf howls echoed about the woods.

When they arrived, the sorcerer led them into the sanctuary, to the round room where the altar was. The stone slab that covered the altar lay at the bottom of the steps, cracked into pieces. A message was burned into the floor:

DEATH HERE SOON

Several lanterns were alight that cast flickering shadows upon the walls and domed ceiling. Cordus and Furlus were already seated, as well as the Ranger woman Saranna that Lannon had met along the North Road on his way to Dremlock. Her black wolf lay by her, his head resting between his paws.

Also present were a Blue Knight and a Red one. The Blue Knight was a Birlote, tall and lanky and bearing two short swords at his waist. His green eyes glittered dangerously in the torchlight and he had a hard, weathered face. The Red Knight was a handsome black-haired man, probably in his late thirties, with a thick mustache and blue eyes. His arms and neck bulged with muscle, but his waist was noticeably lean, giving him a powerful yet athletic appearance. He wore a silver breastplate and carried both sword and longbow.

Once everyone was seated, Cordus spoke. "This is not an official meeting, so we'll avoid any formalities. You are all free to speak. The reason this gathering has been conducted in secrecy is because, as I'm sure all of you know, some of the High Council members cannot be trusted. This is a critical moment for Dremlock, as Goblins are advancing upon us. Several Goblin Lords have been spotted amongst them. For now we are safe, as it is highly doubtful they can get through Darkender Tunnel. Yet it is our duty to protect the towns and dwellings that exist close to our kingdom.

"We continue to be haunted by the Goblin Puzzle. It is a complicated affair, but the basic riddle that we need solved is how to permanently defeat a Goblin Lord. They seem to be invincible. Since they began appearing over a year ago--from a place that remains a mystery to us--we've not found a way to kill a single one! It does no good even to hack them to bits, for they will just become whole again. The flesh binds itself together instantly and full health is restored. This is a seemingly impossible power the likes of which has never been witnessed by the servants of Dremlock Kingdom.

"That's why we need you, Lannon Sunshield, to use the Eye of Divinity upon a Goblin Lord to try to find a weakness. But first we must confront one. Dremlock is bordering on ruin. Many of our Knights are dead, and many have abandoned us. A sizable force is defending Kalamede but swiftly losing ground, while another force is attempting to head off the Goblins advancing toward Dremlock. Neither force is impressively large. Yet enough Knights remain that we could prevail--but only if we can kill the Goblin Lords. We know where your would-be assassin went, Lannon. We tracked him right here to the Temple. We intend to take a small party below and try to find him. He appears to have gone through the left door below, which has a wheel lock that we no longer know how to open. Yet somehow, as far as we can tell, he managed to solve it."

"He went through that door," said Saranna. "Darius is never wrong." She patted her wolf on the head.

"What about the Divine Essence?" said Lannon, his heartbeat racing. "Has it been harmed?"

"I've checked on it," said Cordus, "and it's fine. It's doubtful that anyone could harm our god. Its power is the very opposite of the Deep Shadow, and dark sorcery would undoubtedly only falter against it."

"We must not underestimate the Deep Shadow," said Taris. "Even the Divine Essence may not be safe from it's evil."

"Will you be leading the search party?" said Furlus.

"It would be better if I didn't," said Cordus. "I should remain here to make sure Dremlock has a worthy leader and to be ready in case of an attack. The party shall be made up of you, Taris, Caldrek, Shennen, and the four Squires. It must be kept small and rely on stealth. I chose Caldrek and Shennen because they are the best at what they do. I could not have picked two better, or more trustworthy, men for this task. I don't like the idea of sending Squires into the mines, but apparently I have no choice." He sighed. "It's a shame, Lannon, that you depend on the others to help you summon the Eye of Divinity. I can only hope you're being truthful, as their lives will be at risk."

"He's telling the truth," said Vorden. "He needs us."

Jerret fidgeted uncomfortably and glanced at Aldreya.

Lannon stayed quiet, taking comfort in the fact that it was at least partially true. As far as he knew, he still needed Vorden and Timlin to summon the Eye.

"We believe," said Cordus, "there are other wheel locks down there which we cannot open. Otherwise, the Squires wouldn't be needed."

The Red Knight, Caldrek, shook his head in disgust. "I find it absurd that the Lord Knight and his Tower Masters should encounter places in our kingdom we cannot access. What were we thinking in designing such locks?"

"The locks are necessary," said Furlus. "They have protected Dremlock from invasion both above ground and below for centuries. If their secrets have been forgotten in some cases, whose fault is that? Not the Olrogs who forged them."

"The search party," said Cordus, "shall depart this very

evening. Time grows short and we can wait no longer. Once this task is complete, we must take Lannon to confront a Goblin Lord. But right now it is necessary to learn what kind of threat exists down in the mines."

"Do you know who the assassin is?" Caldrek asked.

"We have no clue," said Cordus.

"Actually," said Taris, "Lannon thinks he knows. Why don't you tell the others what you believe, Lannon?"

Lannon hesitated, his eyes fixed on the floor. He could imagine how they might react to what Taris wanted him to say. Finally he said, "I think it was Tenneth Bard, the Black Knight."

The Knights exchanged surprised glances. Saranna looked confused.

"But that's impossible," said Cordus. "Were that true, he would have to be hundreds of years old. No Norack man can live that long."

"On the contrary," said Taris. "The aging process can be slowed dramatically, even stopped in some cases. Throughout history elite sorcerers have managed it--only to end up dying of other causes."

"Yet I can scarcely bring myself to believe it could actually be Tenneth Bard," said Cordus, "whose statue still stands in the ruins of Serenlock."

"I, too, find this hard to believe," said Caldrek.

"It's ridiculous," said Furlus.

"It was him!" said Lannon, surprised at his own insistence. "I recognized his eyes."

"Just his eyes?" scoffed Furlus. "Who can recognize a man by his eyes alone? Further proof is needed to back such a claim."

"I believe what you say, Lannon," said Taris. "And bear in mind," he said to the others, "that the Eye of Divinity reveals many truths."

A moment of silence followed. Then Cordus said, "Regardless, we know our enemy is powerful, and so we must proceed with great caution." He pointed to where the top of the altar lay shattered in pieces. "We're dealing with a foe that even fully trained Knights might not be a match for--which is why I must send my best fighters. Now I believe Saranna has something important to tell us."

"Despite the weapons and other supplies Dremlock sent to us," Saranna said, with bitterness in her voice, "the North Road has fallen to the Goblins. The Rangers that managed to escape have vowed never to return there. I myself share that vow. Yet I have come here not just to bring the bad news, but also to see if I can somehow help in your war against the Goblins. They killed many of my good friends. I want to play a part in their downfall."

As Lannon watched her speak, he admired her courage and beauty. Her auburn hair was pulled back in a ponytail, just as it had been the first time he had seen her, but now her green eyes held a hurt, defiant look. Her rugged chain mail bore unmistakable claw marks. Just gazing at her caused his own courage to swell, and he sat a little taller and straighter.

"So you want revenge?" said Cordus.

"If that's what you wish to call it," said Saranna. "Goblins are my sworn enemy, and I'll see them all destroyed, if I'm able."

"Whatever your reason," said Cordus, "we gladly accept your help. We can use your tracking skills to hunt down our enemies below ground. Though you are not a Knight, it would please me to have you join the party I'm sending into the mines."

"I'll go," Saranna said quickly.

Cordus nodded, and then his gaze on fell on Taris. "So you actually believe Tenneth Bard yet lives. But what would he have been doing all this time? Hiding out somewhere, dreaming of revenge?"

"Not merely hiding," said Taris. "The Blood Legion has been around throughout the centuries, making mischief. I believe he may have continued to lead it in secrecy. Or perhaps he went away for a while and has recently returned. It is a grand mystery, and we're not close to solving it."

"I'll speak to the other High Council members," said Cordus. "We'll finish preparing Dremlock for war and send some of our Knights down the mountainside to protect Hollow Deep and the surrounding dwellings. Yet our kingdom needs a strong final defense, since it is possible, though very unlikely, they could find a way through Darkender Tunnel. Or they may try to scale the walls or mountainside--a very difficult but certainly not impossible feat, especially for Goblins."

"I would place many defenders at Darkender Tunnel," said Taris. "If the assassin went below, he must know how to solve a wheel lock. The wheel locks might all be worthless now, if their ultimate secret has been discovered. I would gather half of your forces near the Tunnel mouth, and the other half here at the Temple, in case of an attack from below. Also, I would have some of the more highly trained Squires prepared for battle as well. And put our *special* Knights on alert, if they haven't been already."

Cordus sat quietly for a moment, and then nodded. "Your advice is sound, Taris. I'll certainly consider it."

"Won't the rest of the High Council question our absence?" said Taris. "Maybe Furlus should remain above ground, to draw away suspicion."

"What do you think of that idea, Furlus?" said Cordus.

"I'm going with the search party," Furlus said. "I haven't had a chance to wield my axe in quite some time. Taris, why don't you stay behind?"

"I need to remain with Lannon," said Taris.

"The party needs an Olrog," said Cordus, "to help navigate the mines. I have chosen Furlus to lead the party because of his navigational abilities and knowledge of the mines--both of which are unmatched in Dremlock. (Furlus beamed at these words, looking smugly at Taris.) Yet we also need sharp Birlote instincts to warn of danger, as well as your vast knowledge of sorcery, Taris, in dealing with a foe who obviously uses magic. Both of you will go on this quest. I'll deal with the High Council myself, if they grow suspicious. I have authority here, and they must obey me."

"What if another vote for your removal is called?" said Taris.

"They can call another vote," said Cordus, "but the entire High Council must be present for it to be carried out. If it isn't, new Council members must be temporarily appointed in place of the missing ones. By then, you should be back from your journey."

"And if we are not?" said Taris.

"This must be done," said Cordus.

Caldrek nodded in agreement. Shennen, the Birlote, continued to sit in silence, his hard face empty of expression. He appeared relaxed, yet watchful--his eyes taking in everything around him. His hands were never far from his short swords.

"Now unless there is anything else," said Cordus, "we should get our plan underway."

"Agreed," said Furlus, standing up. "We should gather food and water, extra torches or lanterns, blankets, and matches. We don't know how long we're going to be down there. We also will need plenty of rope, grapple hooks, iron spikes, and hammers, as well as medical supplies."

"I could send a White Knight," said Cordus.

Furlus shook his head. "The going may be rough, and a healer might only slow us down. We'll just have to take our chances."

"Then let us begin," said Cordus.

The others waited at the Temple while Taris and Furlus went to gather supplies. Soon they returned. Some muttered words were exchanged between them as they entered the chamber bearing sacks stuffed with the items. The supplies were quickly distributed among the Knights and the Squires.

"If the danger below becomes too extreme," said Cordus, "or if there is evidence of a trap, turn back at once. Dremlock cannot afford to lose its Tower Masters or the one who possesses the Eye of Divinity. Your goal is not so much to hunt down an assassin as it is to see what might be going on down there in this area of the mines. We need to know if a significant threat lurks below."

"We'll do our spy work," said Furlus, "*and* bring back the assassin."

"He won't escape us," Caldrek said confidently.

"I believe the fate of our kingdom will be decided below," said Cordus. "Good luck to you all." With that, the Lord Knight left the Temple, leaving Dremlock's fate in the hands of his Tower Masters, two specialists, and five uncertain youths.

Chapter 15: The Goblin Puzzle

With Furlus leading the way, they readied their weapons and descended the steps that led below the altar. Saranna stayed at the rear to guard the Squires' backs, her saber in hand and her wolf at her side. The Squires all carried lanterns, leaving the adults free to more easily wield their weapons. On the way down, Vorden whispered something to Jerret and Aldreya that no one else could catch a word of.

As they stood before the wheel lock, Vorden and Timlin got on either side of Lannon, while Jerret, looking uncomfortable, took a position behind him and placed his hand on Lannon's back. For a moment, Aldreya stood next to Taris, looking uncertain. Then she stepped forward and also placed her hand on Lannon's back.

Lannon could feel the Tower Masters gazing at him, and he wasn't immediately able to summon the Eye due to his nervousness. Also, the two hands pressed into his back were distracting, though Lannon realized Jerret and Aldreya were simply pretending to be helping with the process.

After several failed attempts, the Knights began to grow restless. "Is there anything we can do to help?" asked Furlus.

"Are we distracting you?" asked Taris.

Lannon shook his head. "Sometimes it takes awhile."

"What are these Squires up to?" said Caldrek, to Taris.

Taris did not reply, and they all waited in silence.

At last the Eye emerged, and a moment later Lannon had solved the wheel lock. As the wheel stopped spinning and the click arose, Caldrek whispered in awe, "The Eye of Divinity," to Shennen.

Shennen nodded. "Only the Eye could do this."

Furlus clapped Lannon on the back. "Good work, boy!"

All of Lannon's attention had been focused on the lock, but now, acting on a whim, Lannon turned and directed the Eye upon Taris Warhawk. And he saw nothing. The Eye of Divinity reached forth, probing the Birlote sorcerer from head to toe, but the only thing that came to Lannon's mind was an image of darkness. Then he realized that Taris was smiling at him from beneath his hood.

"You wish to learn my secrets?" Taris mused. "Yet you have not mastered your powers well enough for that task. I do not wield the power of Tharnin, if that is what you're wondering. My mind and body are shielded from you for another reason. You should beware of what you gaze upon, young Lannon, until you're able to deal with the things you are shown. You still have much to learn."

Embarrassed, Lannon turned away. As he did so, Darius, who was sniffing around by the door, suddenly let out a warning growl. Before the others could react, the door of Glaetherin burst open, knocking Darius aside, and something dark leapt through, long talons swiping at Lannon. Lannon caught a glimpse of half-developed bat wings, a rodent-shaped head that had no eyes and tapered into a wolf-snout, and long, crooked arms that ended in clusters of deadly claws. A sickening stench--both physical and of evil itself--flooded the passageway. The will of the Deep Shadow gripped their souls.

It was a Bloodfang, like the one the Squires had glimpsed in the dungeons below Old Keep. Only this one was not caged.

Screeching insanely, the Bloodfang hurtled at Lannon with a blur of wings, teeth, and claws. But Furlus grabbed Lannon with one meaty hand before the beast could maul him and tossed him out of harm's way. The Blood Fang's claws ripped into Furlus' plate armor, and the Grey Dwarf was born backwards to the floor, locked in a death struggle. The claws tore at his chest, while the teeth sought to pierce his throat. Furlus fought furiously, protecting himself with his hands and knees. His great beard helped to defend his throat, for the creature's claws became momentarily tangled in it.

The others recovered from their surprise. Caldrek leapt at the beast, and Taris raised his burning stone dagger. But Shennen got there first. His shimmering short swords moved with blinding speed, cleaving deep wounds in the Bloodfang, yet he failed to dislodge it from Furlus.

Caldrek plunged his own gleaming blade into the monster's back an instant later, which caused a shudder to run through the Bloodfang but again could not drive it off of Furlus. Cursing, the Red Knight twisted the blade around inside the beast--but to no avail. The Goblin still refused to give up on the Grey Dwarf.

Saranna reacted slower than the other two, but made the most effective move, slicing her saber deep into the Bloodfang's neck in an effort to behead it. But as good a stroke as it was, the razor-sharp blade still could not cleave all the way through the knotty flesh and bone. The Bloodfang screeched and loosened its grip some, swiping at Saranna with one claw that shredded her chain mail and drew blood. Meanwhile, Darius lunged at the monster and bit into one of its legs.

The Squires stared on helplessly, their faces gone pale. In Lannon's shock, the Eye of Divinity retreated partially back into him, and he could only lie on the floor where Furlus had thrown him and watch as the frantic struggle took place.

Then Taris hurled a blinding fireball from his dagger and it exploded into a shower of sparks against the Bloodfang's skull. The Goblin collapsed on top of Furlus and went limp, green smoke rising from its head and dark blood pouring from its jaws.

Furlus lay coughing and sputtering for a moment, and then he shoved the creature off of him. He wiped the foul Goblin blood from his beard. Then he clambered up from the floor. "One less filthy Goblin," he remarked.

They studied the fallen monster. A steel chain was fastened to its leg, leading beyond the door to an iron ring embedded in the tunnel floor.

"Placed here to guard the passageway," said Caldrek. "Not a bad choice, I must say. I've never seen a Goblin quite like it."

"There are worse ones down here," Furlus said grimly.

Shennen knelt by the creature, his cold eyes glittering in the lantern light. "Who could have captured one of these in such a manner? A simple chain on its leg? Surely the beast would have torn its captor apart."

The others had no answer.

They gathered by the doorway. As the watched in tense silence, a figure stepped from the shadows and began walking towards them down the tunnel. It was a Goblin Lord--a Foul Brother dressed in a black robe and carrying a dark, twisted scepter that seemed to radiate a purple glow. Black runes were painted on its bald head and face, making its cunning, evil eyes stand out. It grinned at them, showing yellow, lumpy teeth. "Greetings, Knights of the Divine Order," it hissed.

Taris pulled Lannon near to him, and called forth the fire into his dagger.

The others readied their weapons.

None among the party had imagined such an event would occur. A Goblin Lord in the mines beneath Dremlock was strange enough. Yet for it to walk casually towards them, its staff held loosely in its hand, was a sight no one was prepared for. For several moments no one said a word. The Goblin stopped just a few yards away from them, its grin broadening into sheer malicious glee.

Then Taris Warhawk spoke. "What game have you come to play, showing yourself so boldly?"

The Goblin Lord gave a choked-sounding laugh. "I want the same thing you want. I've come to give you what you seek."

The others stood silent, confused.

"The Eye of Divinity," said the Goblin Lord, its black eyes growing wide. "You wish to use it on me? Well, isn't that correct? You want to find my weakness. The boy..." It pointed a bony finger at Lannon. "Go on, lad, use your power upon me. I will not resist."

Trembling, Lannon glanced towards Taris.

"Do nothing, Lannon," said Taris, "until I tell you to."

"Why hesitate?" said the Goblin Lord. "Now is your chance, while I give it freely."

"This is a trap of some sort," said Furlus. "Obviously."

"No trap," said the Goblin Lord. "Just an offer."

"We don't want your filthy offer," said Furlus.

Caldrek stroked his mustache, shaking his head. His blue eyes were narrowed into slits. "How dare you show your face like this? So many friends of mine perished trying to rid Silverland of your evil..."

"And more will perish, feeble Knight," said the Goblin Lord.

"That is--if Dremlock does not surrender. You know what is taking place. You know that I serve a master who seeks your downfall. And you know that Goblins are no longer mindless animals hunted down by the Knights of Dremlock for their amusement. We have a voice now and a purpose. You speak of *your* companions who were killed? What of my brothers, who have been hunted mercilessly by the so-called Divine Knights for centuries?"

"That's different!" growled Caldrek. "Everyone knows Goblins are the filthy spawn of the Deep Shadow. None of you are fit to live."

"And I say the same of your race," said the Goblin Lord.

"Your race was hunted by us Knights," said Taris, "because of your aggressions against Birlotes, Noracks, and Olrogs. Had you lived peacefully, Dremlock would have had no need to make war on you. But time and again, you have risen against us. Time and again, you have killed unjustly. That is why we seek to banish you from Silverland."

The Goblin's grin twisted into a sneer. "I have not come to beg mercy for Goblins, Tower Master. We neither need it nor desire it. It is the Divine Knights who will beg for mercy from us, soon enough. Now, will you accept my offer?"

Shennen stepped towards the Goblin Lord. "You have a weakness. Now it is my turn to search for it. And I do not fail so easily!"

"Wait a moment, Shennen," said Taris. "Maybe we do want his offer. Let the Goblin first tell us exactly what it entails. If the offer proves unworthy, you may then put your skills to the test. All of us will--and I very much doubt even a Goblin Lord could survive an attack by all of us combined."

The Goblin Lord went into a laughing fit, snorting and drooling. "No need for that, I assure you. My offer is simple. I will allow the Eye of Divinity to be used on me because I have no weakness. I will prove to you beyond a doubt that Goblin Lords are invincible, that Dremlock's fate is sealed. And then you will have no choice but to surrender."

"Surrender?" rumbled Furlus. "We shall see about that. I've heard enough of this nonsense. Let's see if you can put yourself back together again when Furlus Goblincrusher gets done with you!"

Taris stepped towards the Goblin Lord. "You think we are fools? Taris Warhawk is no fool. I have seen through your plan. Somehow, you know Lannon isn't ready to see the things you would show him, that he might find your weakness but not be able to speak of it because he would be driven mad."

The Goblin Lord glanced about with uncertainty and backed up a step. It held its gnarled staff before it in a defensive posture. Whether invincible or not, fear was clearly reflected in its dark eyes as its gaze passed over the party. It backed up another step, its muscled tensed as if in preparation to flee.

"But nevertheless," Taris said, "we will accept your offer."

Its eyes widening in surprise, the Goblin Lord hissed, "You will use the Eye on me?"

Taris nodded. "Lannon, release the Eye of Divinity upon the Goblin."

"What are you doing?" said Furlus. "If this is a trap, why are we going along with it? I say let's settle this the way an Olrog would! As you said, the boy could lose his sanity. We should not risk this, Taris."

"Leave this to me," said Taris, placing his hand on Lannon's shoulder. "I have prepared myself well for this situation."

Lannon stared at the Goblin Lord, hesitating. The Eye was still unlocked, waiting to either be sent forth or be sealed away. But what was this talk of him being driven mad? What would he see when he probed the Goblin?

"Do not be afraid," said Taris. "You can do this, Lannon."

Taris' words eased Lannon's mind somewhat, and he slowly reached out with the Eye, probing the outer surface of the Goblin Lord. He intended to proceed with caution, but the Eye was suddenly sucked into the Goblin Lord, revealing its secrets in a rush of feelings and images. Lannon saw and felt something abhorrent to nature, a mutating of life that had come to resemble a sort of living death. A dark power bound this creature together-- one that radiated from its heart, which was protected by a thick shell of bone and existed in the lower back. As long as this heart was intact, it could bind the creature back together again under most any circumstances. To kill the Goblin Lord, the heart would have to be utterly destroyed--burned completely into ashes by magical fire.

But the Eye of Divinity probed deeper, revealing that the Goblin Lord did not actually possess the power that it appeared to possess. It was only a powerful illusion placed in the minds of those who confronted it. Goblin Lords did not regenerate after being cut into pieces, because it only *appeared* that they were cut into pieces. The blades actually hacked through empty air. The Knights would have to see through that illusion and destroy the Goblin Lord's heart that was the source of all its power. It would not be an easy task, but it could be done.

Lannon had seen enough, and he tried to draw the Eye back inside him. But this Goblin was a puppet controlled by the Deep Shadow, and Lannon could not stop himself from delving into it. The Eye groped about, finding the threads that bound the Goblin to its master, and then it followed them to the source.

Lannon found himself drawn into a realm from which he could not escape. He felt a sense of coldness and loss beyond reason. It was as if his flesh had been stripped away, and all that remained of him was a ghostlike entity trapped in the Shadow Realm. Ages seemed to pass in the black silence, and Lannon's life of before became vague and shadowy, dreamlike. Lannon suspected that once he had dwelt in another world outside the Shadow Realm, but that it had been so long ago that the gateway to that world no longer existed. Regardless, he certainly could not find it in this endless void. Lannon felt that he would dwell in the Shadow Realm for infinity.

But then came Taris' whisper, faint and distant, telling him to abandon that place and come back to the world of the living. The whisper inspired hope, making Lannon wonder if indeed there was something beyond the great darkness, and he willed himself towards the sound of it. The whisper sought to lure him on, but Lannon lost his grasp on it. He thought he would never regain it.

Yet the whisper suddenly called to him again, much fainter than before. Lannon followed it, and this time it grew louder, until it became a command to wake him. Green eyes gleamed in the darkness, and burning fingers reached into his soul.

"Wake up!" Taris commanded.

Lannon's eyes sprang open and he sat up, his body trembling. The others stood over him looking relieved. The Eye of Divinity had drawn all the way inside him, and the Goblin Lord was gone from the passageway.

"We need to burn their hearts," said Lannon.

Chapter 16: Dark Evidence

Everyone was gathered around Lannon, exchanging anxious and concerned glances. Lannon stood up. He felt strangely refreshed, as if he had just awakened from a long slumber. His body felt light, his mind bubbling over with enthusiasm. In an excited voice, he told them exactly what he had seen--where the Goblin Lord's heart was located in its body, how it was encased in a protective shell of bone, and how the heart must be thoroughly destroyed.

"It's just an illusion," said Lannon. "Whenever Knights attack the Goblin Lords, they aren't actually making contact with them. So the Goblin Lords only appear to be invincible. But they're still very powerful, which is why it's necessary to destroy their hearts."

Taris smiled. "Sometimes, one only needs to *appear* invincible to actually *be* invincible. Their plan worked perfectly. Until now, that is."

"That was easy enough," said Furlus. "But we're not through yet. That Goblin Lord has escaped, and we still have the assassin to deal with."

"As soon as you blacked out," said Taris, "the Goblin fled down the tunnel. It must have realized it had overstayed its welcome."

"What happened to me?" asked Lannon.

"The Deep Shadow drew you in," said Taris. "When the Eye of Divinity looked upon it, it bound you tightly in its web and would not let you go. You could have been lost to us forever in the phantom mists, but I managed to call you back by means of my sorcery. It was a risky gamble, but a necessary one. However, our foes made just as large of a gamble--and they lost."

Lannon shuddered. "I might never have come back?"

"It was a possibility," said Taris. "One does not escape the Deep Shadow's clutches easily. It takes an incredibly strong will to do so. But take heart, Lannon, in your accomplishments. You are alive, and the Goblin Puzzle is solved."

"We need to get word to Cordus at once," said Furlus, "so that he can send a messenger to our Knights. At last, we know how to kill the Goblin Lords!"

"How will the Knights do it?" said Lannon.

"The fire of sorcery," said Taris. "They will use their burning blades. It will be difficult, for the heart is obviously well protected on these creatures--but it is certainly possible now that we know exactly where to focus our attacks. The main difficulty will be seeing through the illusion and actually making contact with the creatures, but I feel that too can be accomplished. The upper hand will now be ours!"

"Let all Goblins fear!" said Furlus. "The tide is about to turn. We will avenge our fallen Knights and rid Silverland once and for all of the evil."

"Jerret Dragonsbane," said Taris. "You should go back to North Tower to tell Cordus what we've discovered."

"But we need him," said Vorden, "in case Lannon has to call out the Eye."

Taris smiled knowingly. "I think Lannon has gone a step beyond that. From now on, he'll only need *two* of you to help him with the task."

"What about me?" said Aldreya.

"You shall stay with us," said Taris. "And learn."

Jerret looked both disappointed and a bit relieved. "Okay, I'll go. I guess someone has to." With that, he departed, stepping around the Bloodfang's corpse with a shudder. He did not look back.

"It is not wise to send him alone," said Furlus. "The knowledge he bears is too important."

"I can trail him," said Shennen. "I will keep myself hidden. If any harm befalls Jerret, I will make sure Cordus gets the message. Also, if I do not return soon, you will know there has been trouble."

Furlus nodded. "Have at it, then. We will wait for you here."

Shennen slipped off into the shadows.

"What now?" said Lannon, glancing down the tunnel. "Shouldn't we go after the Goblin Lord before it gets away?"

Taris studied him piercingly. "Relax yourself, Lannon. You've just gone through a terrible experience. It is strange how quickly you seem to have recovered, and I don't trust what my eyes show me. Just try to stay calm and focused."

Lannon nodded, but he could not do as Taris asked. He was too excited over his accomplishment, and he wanted to take some sort of action.

"I feel fine," he said.

"That is good to hear," said Taris, "but bear in mind that there are still some who would like to see you dead."

Taris' words had their intended effect. Lannon's excitement slipped away, and his gaze started searching the shadows of the tunnel. He stepped close to Taris, grateful for the sorcerers' presence.

"When Shennen returns," said Furlus, "we will continue on. There are still questions that need answering, and our mission remains unchanged."

After a while, Shennen's lean, shadowy form suddenly stepped into the lantern light, startling the others. He regarded them with emotionless, glittering eyes. "The message has been delivered," he said quietly. "Young Jerret is fine."

For a moment Taris gazed solemnly at the Blue Knight, as if searching for something hidden. Then the sorcerer nodded. "Let us move on, then."

No more enemies came out to greet them, and so they started along the tunnel. Unlike the passageway that led to the Divine Essence, no glowing crystals shone in these walls. This looked like, and had the feel of, the tunnels below Old Keep. The same musty smell was there, the lingering gloom hanging in the shadows. Now and then dark Iracus roots poked out of the stone.

"This tunnel connects to the mines," said Furlus. "It is the only one that hasn't been permanently sealed off. It was left as an escape route, and now our assassin has made good use of it, apparently."

The tunnel sloped downward some and then leveled off. Pillars were hewn from the stone near the walls, lining the passageway. Rusted pieces of chain hung from some of the pillars, and Olrog bones lay scattered here and there. A skeleton, still partially intact, was chained to one of the pillars, its skull lying grinning at its feet.

Furlus paused for a moment and bowed his head, a troubled look on his face. "I am not proud of this sight," he said. "Olrog punishments can be all too harsh at times. These are the bones of miners who were chained here to die, probably for petty crimes. My people have a dark and glorious past, and like all the races, we've done our share of evil."

The others kept quiet, knowing it was best not to agree or disagree, lest they unwittingly provoke the Olrog's quick temper.

They went a little farther and discovered an iron door up ahead. The Knights checked the door and found it unlocked and not trapped. They pulled it open and stepped through into a short, wide hallway that ended at another iron door. At the center of the hallway was a wooden trapdoor with a brass ring at the center.

The Knights gathered before the trapdoor and examined it. Then Taris motioned Lannon forward and placed his hand on the boy's shoulder. "Very carefully," he said, "turn the Eye below this door. Once you learn what lies down there, do not linger."

Lannon did as he was told, slowly pushing the Eye down past the trapdoor and into the depths below. At first he glimpsed only cold stone leading down about twenty feet, but then a flood of dark images struck him. He saw ancient, sealed tombs, where the restless dead had lain hidden for centuries. He felt crushing strife, countered by fierce pride and determination--the will of the Olrogs. Something terrible had occurred below their feet, represented to Lannon by a creeping shadow that smothered all in its path. Some final battle had been fought amid the tombs below, and a curse laid forth upon that area. Yet something else existed down there as well--a shining scroll bearing some important knowledge that needed to be discovered.

Lannon wanted to probe the scroll further, but he remembered Taris' warning not to linger and drew away from it. Lannon pulled the Eye back to the surface and then partially within him. The others stared at him anxiously.

"It's a bad place," Lannon said. He hesitated, knowing if he told the Knights about the scroll, they would want to go below to retrieve it. But he had to tell them, for that item was very important somehow. "There is a scroll down there," he added. "Something that could be helpful."

"Then we need to go down there and get it," said Furlus.

"It's protected by something evil," said Lannon. "I don't know what it is, but it's very powerful." He realized he was breathing heavily and that his heart was aflutter. The fear was nearly too much to bear, and for an instant, he thought he was going to demand they head back to the surface and let Tenneth Bard escape.

But Lannon never got a chance to say anything. Furlus threw open the trapdoor and said, "So who's going down there with me?" An iron ladder descended along the stone into the blackness.

Taris glanced about. "I am tempted to leave the Squires up here, but that could be just as dangerous, if not more so, considering what we've faced so far. We shall all go down, that I may keep the Squires near me and protect them. Also, Lannon must use his power to guide us to the scroll."

The ladder led them down twenty feet to another tunnel. Shennen went first, slipping quietly below to make sure all was well. After Shennen gave his signal, Caldrek went next, and then Furlus. The Squires were sent below after that, followed by Taris and Saranna. Darius was left above to guard the trapdoor opening. They knew the wolf would fight to the death before allowing an enemy to pass that way.

When everyone had gathered below, they started along the tunnel. Almost immediately, a stone door was revealed, blocking their way. Strange writings were engraved in the door, beneath a symbol of a crimson battle axe.

Furlus nodded. "As I suspected, the tombs of my ancestors lie beyond this door. That battle axe is the ancient symbol of my race. This is sacred ground and we must treat it as such. Take nothing and disturb nothing."

"We shall tread carefully here," said Taris.

"What does the writing say?" asked Caldrek.

"It reflects my words," Furlus said. Then he read it aloud. "Within this chamber lie the sacred tombs of the honored dead. May the Axe of Tharnin smite whoever disturbs the peace of the dead, and scatter their blood before the altar of Graylius."

Furlus bowed his head. "Graylius was our god in olden times. He was believed to exist in the realm of Tharnin. As you may know, the Olrogs gained power from Tharnin long ago in our war against the Noracks and Birlotes."

"A pagan god, then," whispered Caldrek, shuddering. "Not fit to be worshiped."

"Graylius was the God of the Forge," said Furlus. "He taught my ancestors wondrous knowledge. For that, we remain ever indebted to him. As for our dealings with Tharnin--we have paid for our mistakes."

"Graylius was a servant of Tharnin," said Taris. "A beast similar to the Great Dragons, yet more humanoid in form. There is some evidence to suggest that Graylius was not altogether evil, that he may have dwelt apart from his master. Which, if true, is indeed surprising, considering that Tharnin itself is believed to be purely evil. But the true workings of the Shadow Realm remain mostly a mystery. All of our knowledge comes from ancient and sketchy Olrog accounts and the sometimes vague and twisted insights of our own Dark Watchmen."

"Well, we can't stand around and chat," said Caldrek. "Not down in these wretched tunnels, anyway." With that, the Red Knight stepped forward and reached for the door handle.

Furlus grabbed his wrist, his eyes blazing. "You have much to learn about Olrogs, Caldrek. I will lead the way."

Caldrek pulled his hand back, raising his dark eyebrows. "Alright, then," he said calmly. "I guess you better do it."

"What if it's locked?" Timlin said anxiously, his meek voice sounding strange and forgotten in the stillness of the tunnel.

"I'll take care of that," said Furlus. "I'm not much for lock picking--which is work more suited to thieves and not a fit occupation for an Olrog--but I know Dwarven locks inside and out. If Shennen will pass me some tools, I'll get it open."

The Blue Knight handed his lock picks to Furlus. The Grey Dwarf mumbled something that sounded almost like a short prayer and then tried the door. It came open. "The lock has been broken," Furlus said, examining the other side of the door. "Something or someone of unnatural strength has passed this way, for Olrog locks are very stout." His grey eyes smoldered with rage, and he tossed the lock picks back to Shennen. "The peace of the dead has been disturbed."

Furlus shone his lantern through the doorway. Then he muttered a curse and stepped within. The others followed. Twelve rectangular stone coffins lay side by side in the chamber beyond, each one bearing the symbol of the crimson axe. The lids had been smashed or tossed aside, and bones and skulls now lay scattered here and there. A couple of the skulls had been smashed into pieces, as if from being stomped on by a heavy foot. If there had been any treasure in the coffins, it was undoubtedly missing. Tracks in the dust led around the room and then to another stone door.

"Who would dare commit such an outrage?" growled Furlus.

"It was done long ago," said Saranna. "For the dust lies undisturbed for the most part. Whoever recently came through here simply examined the coffins, and then exited the room. They did not commit this act of vandalism."

"Lannon," said Taris, "I need you to search for the scroll again."

"It isn't in this room," said Lannon. He felt that it lay beyond the door--along with the creeping darkness. He pointed. "I think it's in there."

As they approached the door, Furlus motioned everyone to halt. He pointed to some yellow, odd-looking bones beside the door. A silver pike lay amid the bones. "A trap in the wall did that," he said. "Let me make sure it is disarmed."

Furlus poked at the wall on both sides of the chamber with a dagger, before grunting in satisfaction. "The trap has already been disarmed," he said. "And that, at least, is a good sign for us. It might mean any other traps--and I'll guarantee you these tombs will be full of them--are disarmed as well."

"But by whom or what?" said Taris.

No one had an answer.

The Grey Dwarf pulled open the door. Like the entrance door, this one bore a shattered lock. The lantern light revealed a much larger chamber, the edges of which were lost in darkness. The coffins in here were bigger and engraved with elaborate runes, and they were positioned around an altar at the center of the room. Barrels, crates, and rusted mining tools lay scattered everywhere, as well as bones strewn around from the coffins. It seemed that everything the Olrog miners had possessed had been dragged into this chamber. They had made their final stand amid their dead, protecting the tombs with their last breaths.

Stone steps led up to the altar, where stood a large statue of a horned, man-like beast holding a crimson battle axe. The beast's skin was scaly, and it had claws, a tail, and a fanged snout. Its body was massively muscled, and something in the way it stood spoke of a confidence and sturdiness of will that matched its physical might. Despite its savage appearance, its eyes were calm and wise, and it held its head high with pride.

"Graylius, our ancient god," whispered Furlus, nodding towards the statue. "The Olrogs of Grayforge Kingdom still worship him to this day, while all other Grey Dwarves have sought to sever any connection to Tharnin and the Deep Shadow."

"Lannon," whispered Taris, "locate the scroll and any dangers that might be lurking in the shadows close by."

Lannon hesitated, his throat tightening. He felt there was no way he could bear the burden of what the Eye would show him in this chamber. The glimpse from above had been bad enough, but now that he was right in it....

"What's wrong?" said Taris.

"I'm afraid," Lannon admitted, "of what I might see."

"I understand," said Taris. "And so what you must do is stay focused on your tasks. Ignore anything not related to the two objectives I have laid out for you. Do not let your curiosity dictate your will. You command the Eye. Bear that in mind."

Lannon nodded. Slowly he reached out with the Eye, commanding it to find the scroll. It instantly located it, on the other side of the altar. A dead body lay there as well, which Lannon did not examine. The Eye seemed to act on its own, seeking to read the scroll as if it were curious, but Lannon shifted it away, searching for any nearby danger. Frightful images sought to draw the Eye's attention, but Lannon did as Taris had instructed and ignored them, staying focused on his task. He discovered no dangers, but he knew something evil lurked down here. Somehow the thing was hiding from his gaze.

"The scroll is beyond the altar," Lannon whispered. "I didn't sense any danger, but I know something is down here. Something very powerful."

"You have done well," said Taris.

"Allow me to go," said Shennen. "I can sneak through the shadows and retrieve the scroll. The rest of you can stay and protect the Squires. I will move swiftly and silently, that we may exit this chamber without incident."

Taris nodded. "Good luck, my friend."

"Can I go with him?" Timlin said.

Everyone stared at Timlin in surprise. Furlus patted the boy on the shoulder, and nodded approvingly. The scrawny lad was clearly shaking from head to toe, but he held a determined look in his eyes. And he gazed at Shennen with deep admiration.

"Timlin, are you crazy?" whispered Vorden. "I cannot figure you out!"

Shennen smiled. "I admire your courage, Timlin. But I must do this task alone. Your time will come. For now, wait and keep watch for danger."

With that, the Blue Knight vanished into the shadows.

Several moments passed, while the others waited impatiently, but still Shennen did not return. Furlus began to mumble under his breath.

Several more moments went by, and then the Olrog muttered, "Shouldn't take this long to grab a scroll, now should it?"

"No, it should not," said Taris. "Yet we will wait a bit longer."

When, after another period of waiting, Shennen still did not show, Taris sighed. "Furlus, guard the Squires. I'm going to find out what became of Shennen."

"If anyone goes over there," said Furlus, "it should be me. You need to stay with Lannon and the other young ones."

"My power will be needed to defeat this foe," said Taris.

"Then we all go," said Furlus. "We can't turn back now and leave Shennen to his fate. I think we have made a mistake. We should have stayed on the trail of the assassin, and returned later-- with more numbers--for the scroll."

"It is too late to dwell on that," said Taris. "Squires, huddle close to each other. Sneaking will not avail us here, for this enemy already knows of our presence." Taris made his stone dagger burn with a white-hot glow that extended beyond the lantern light, yet their enemy had many places to hide amid the coffins, crates, barrels, buckets, and mining equipment that filled the room. And the altar still blocked their vision. In the new light, another stone door was revealed. This one stood partially open.

As they cautiously moved around the altar, Furlus, who was in the lead, let out a gasp. "What in Tharnin is this evil?" he said.

Two human-shaped figures were encased in some slimy, green substance and stuck to the stone wall. Just the edge of a blue cloak was visible, poking out of the slime near one figure's feet. Neither figure was moving. Lying on the floor near them was a golden cylinder.

"Shennen!" cried Caldrek, his eyes narrowing. "What could have done this?" Caldrek raced over to the figure whose blue cloak was partially visible. He pulled away handfuls of slime that sought to stick to his skin. Meanwhile, Furlus swiped up the golden cylinder and stuck it in his backpack.

Saranna rushed to Caldrek's side to help. They managed to free Shennen's face, but his eyes were closed and his head hung limp. He did not appear to be breathing. Timlin let out a snarl, his face twisting with disbelief and anger. He held forth his flayer, turning about, seeking the enemy.

Then a silent shadow rose up from amid some barrels, reaching a height of over ten feet--a monstrous bulk of furry green flesh and massive fangs. Long, thick legs reached out over the barrels, and a half squealing, half hissing noise erupted from the creature. Then it spit a big glob of slime at Taris.

The sorcerer burned through the slime with his dagger, and flung fire back at the creature, burning into its head. It screeched, but otherwise did not appear to be harmed.

Lannon recognized the creature as a Goblin Worm, but his book *The Truth about Goblins* had insisted that such a creature was only a myth.

With a roar, Furlus charged the Worm, driving his axe at the creature's legs. But where the blade struck, it did minimal damage. It was like striking something made of tough rubber, and the blade seemed almost to bounce away from the monster's flesh, leaving it virtually unscathed. The creature had eight legs that were fastened to a long, slime covered body made of sections like a caterpillar. Its head was also worm-like, but had the multiple eyes of a spider. Its face was shockingly evil in appearance--bearing features that seemed almost like those of a spiteful human female. It moved with astounding speed and agility.

The Worm spit slime into Furlus' face, blinding him, and the Grey Dwarf stumbled and fell. Two of the legs reached out and the beast quickly spun Furlus into a thick coating of slime, then lifted him and stuck him to the wall. The Dwarf had dropped his axe, but he continued to struggle beneath the slime.

Saranna leapt over and grabbed the Squires, holding them in a bunch to protect them and keep them from trying anything heroic.

"We may have to flee," she whispered to them.

"Let me help the others!" Aldreya pleaded. But the Ranger only tightened her grip on the Squires.

Overcome with rage, Caldrek attacked the Worm with a flurry of blows. His sword burned with blue fire. A natural warrior of unsurpassed talent, he dodged globs of slime while seeking to find a weakness in the beast. But each stroke, no matter how sure, merely glanced away from the rubbery surface.

"You'll pay for Shennen's life!" he grunted.

But the Worm apparently grew tired of this game, and used four of its legs to trap Caldrek. Then it buried its fangs into the Red Knight's shoulder, piercing his armor. Caldrek's mouth gaped open. He tried to say something, but the words were lost as his body went limp from the poison.

The Squires cried out in shock.

Taris struck the Worm with several blazing fireballs that burned into its flesh. The beast, obviously sensing danger, suddenly leapt up and clung to the ceiling in a move that was so quick the eye could not follow it. Seeking to escape or perhaps gain a better vantage point, it scuttled across the ceiling. But the hissing fireball caught up with it and exploded with a deafening roar that shook the chamber. Streaming jets of flame dropped to the floor and lay burning.

For an instant, they thought the Worm had been disintegrated.

But then some barrels tipped over and the monster leapt out into the open, clumps of molten green fire falling from its body. It raced towards a dark hole in the stone wall. It screeched in rage at them, then crawled into the hole and was lost from sight.

With Saranna still guarding the dismayed Squires, Taris raced over to his trapped companions. Furlus had managed to free one of his arms, and he was pulling slime from his beard and sputtering in fury. Taris helped finish freeing him, and then set to work on Shennen. A moment later the Blue Knight lay on his back on the floor, released of his prison.

Shennen opened his eyes and started breathing, as if coming out of a deep trance. His face was grim. "It was too fast, too silent. I got caught off guard."

"Are you okay?" said Taris.

In answer, Shennen stood up.

Caldrek was not dead, either. The poison had left him weak, yet he was conscious. Shennen lifted him, while Furlus quickly freed the head of the remaining figure. They discovered it was a dead Jackal Goblin.

"Apparently," said Taris, as they fled the chamber, "that creature does not play favorites with other Goblins. All races are equal food in its eyes."

When they reached the surface and closed the trapdoor, Caldrek shifted about, and whispered, "That felt wretched. But I think it's starting to wear off. I should be able to move around soon enough."

"Perhaps we should take you back to Dremlock," said Furlus. "We haven't come that far."

"No!" Caldrek sputtered, coughing. "Just give me a moment. The poison obviously isn't deadly. At least I hope not."

"It's not supposed to be deadly," said Lannon. "According to my book *The Truth about Goblins,* that is. The poison was just meant to weaken you. Of course, that Worm wasn't supposed to exist, either."

Taris chuckled. "You must know every word of that book, Lannon. How many times have you read it?"

Caldrek stumbled to his feet. The Red Knight did not seem to have fully recovered, as he staggered a bit, but he insisted he was okay. "I can make it!" he insisted. "I'll be fine."

"We'll see," Furlus said. "If you're anything less than perfect, you go back. I'll not have your death on my conscience."

Caldrek nodded, then doubled over and went into a coughing fit. When he stood up, his eyes were watering, but he looked steadier.

Furlus unscrewed one end of the cylinder and read the scroll aloud:

Master,

This message is extremely urgent. A lad named Lannon Sunshield has come to Dremlock, and apparently he bears the rare power known as the Eye of Divinity, which could eventually be a threat to our plans. It would be difficult to have him cast out, and even if we were able to, he could remain an outside threat. And so we have opted for the easier and more sturdy route. We shall have one of our servants kill Lannon. Don't worry, Master, the boy shall meet his end one way or another. I have trusted this letter to Creglin, so that he may get it to you with all speed. However, you need do nothing. I have the matter well in hand. Lannon Sunshield will die!

Your Loyal Servant

"There you have it!" growled Furlus. "The evidence we sought! Justice shall come of this, my friends."

"And yet it fails to mention Kealin or Moten," said Taris.

"It is Moten's writing," said Furlus. "I can tell Olrog handwriting, and Moten has a very unique style. And we can have this examined by a Scribe and a comparison made. Moten shall be found guilty. I have no doubt of it. We may find evidence down here against Kealin too."

"Hopefully not as well guarded," said Shennen. "How could that scroll have ended up down there?"

"The Jackal must have taken a wrong turn or something," said Taris. "Regardless, it is very fortunate for us that it met its doom. Now at least one corrupt member of the High Council will earn his rightful place in Dremlock Dungeon."

"I want to go confront him myself," said Furlus. "But first we need to finish our mission down here. Yet I can hardly wait to face him! And though he will undoubtedly spend his years in the dungeon, being treated humanely, I have a better punishment in mind."

"And what is that?" said Taris.

"We should toss him down there," said Furlus, nodding to the trapdoor. "Let one fiend prey upon another. That would be true justice."

Taris frowned. "And yet you should bear in mind how your people once administered punishments like that."

Furlus sighed and nodded. "It is true. But nevertheless, if anyone deserves to be fed to an oversized Worm, it is Moten."

"The Worm..." Taris pondered. "That was a creature of extraordinary power, and I hope never to encounter it again."

"It may have been leftover from the Great War," said Furlus. "It probably fled into these mines to escape Olzet Ka and the Crimson Flamestone."

"As for that scroll," said Taris, "perhaps we should take it to Cordus before we continue on. If we meet a bad end down here, the scroll might vanish with us, and justice would not be served."

Furlus put the scroll back in its case and stowed it away in his backpack. "Like I said, I want to confront Moten myself. And we can afford no more delays. The Goblin Lord and the assassin are escaping even as we speak."

Taris said nothing, seeing the determined look on Furlus' face and perhaps knowing it was useless to argue with a stubborn Dwarf.

Chapter 17: Into the Depths

They cautiously proceeded past the iron door and along another tunnel. It turned a corner and began to slope downward, and they soon encountered a tangle of black roots that had been chopped through. The roots grew out of cracks in the stone walls, and ceiling, and the tunnel floor was stained dark with blood from them.

"The Iracus roots grow thick here," said Furlus. "There is a huge den of Black Mothers down this way. The Mothers have been sealed off, but their roots still creep all over through the stone, splitting it and sometimes causing cave-ins."

"You know this area?" said Taris, in amazement.

"Of course I do," said Furlus. "I've never been here in person, but there are stacks of old books down by the Deep Forge, some of which have these areas mapped out in great detail. I've studied them thoroughly."

"Yet haven't you claimed on many occasions," mused Taris, "that I spend too much time with my books?"

Furlus ignored this, and concentrated on leading the company down the long, sloping course. Eventually it leveled off and they emerged into a round chamber. At the center of the room was the opening of a mineshaft, about fifteen-feet wide, with old wooden planks partially covering it. Lying off to one side were old mining tools, piles of rotten rope, buckets, and some sort of badly rusted device that stood about nine feet tall and displayed many gears, levers, and wheels, with piles of thick chain at the foot of it. Furlus gazed at that last device with pride shining in his grey eyes.

"What is that thing?" said Taris.

"It was called a God Arm," said Furlus. "It helped pull Glaetherin ore up the mineshaft. It could drag tons of it up with no difficulty. If that doesn't represent Olrog ingenuity, I don't know what does."

Taris nodded. "The Olrogs are amazing inventors."

Furlus went to the edge of the shaft and knelt, holding his lantern over the hole. "It looks like someone carved a ladder right into the stone, but we'll use our ropes just to be on the safe side. Now, who wants to get lowered down first?"

Caldrek stepped forward. Furlus tied his rope around Caldrek and lowered him over the edge. Shennen and Saranna held the rope's end, adding extra support, while the wolf stayed alert to danger. Caldrek said nothing as he was being lowered. But at last the rope went slack, and his whisper arose from the pit.

"As far as I can tell, it's safe to come down."

"How deep is it?" Furlus asked.

"At least forty feet," said Caldrek. "But that is merely a crude guess. Regardless, a fall could be fatal, so be careful!"

"I better go next," said Furlus, "since I'm the heaviest and it will probably take all of you to lower me down."

One by one the others (including Darius) were lowered in, until all of them except Shennen stood on the stone floor below. They were in a large chamber with a low ceiling, its walls hidden in shadow beyond their lantern light. From where the mineshaft (and the stone ladder) ended eight feet above them, an iron ladder hung down to the floor.

Aldreya glanced upward. "What about Shennen?"

"Stand aside," came Shennen's whisper. "I'm climbing down. I don't want anyone under me in case I slip."

Moments later, Shennen's lean form descended into the light. He was moving swiftly down the rope. When he reached the chamber floor, he readied his weapon. Shennen had fastened the rope to something above, and it continued to hang down, offering a second means of climbing up in case a swift escape was needed.

Shennen nodded. "Let the wolf lead the way."

"Darius is already on it," said Saranna, pointing to where the wolf was crouched at the edge of the lantern light, his nose pressed to the floor.

They followed Darius, passing huge mining carts and buckets, piles of ore that glittered silver, and heaps of rusted pickaxes. The gloom hung thick in the air here, the feeling of doom and despair and of being closed in. They could feel the countless tons of rock bearing down on them, and they could only imagine what the miners must have dealt with spending endless days and nights in this place. Yet the miners had been Olrogs, stout of heart like Furlus. They had chosen to devote their lives to the mines, and in grim proof of that, Olrog bones and skulls were strewn here and there.

Furlus bowed his head in respect. "They fought to the last to defend what was theirs," he said. "But the Deep Shadow was too strong."

Suddenly Timlin stopped. He was breathing heavily, his eyes darting into the shadows. He avoided looking at the others.

"What's wrong, Timlin?" said Lannon.

"I'm afraid," Timlin said, his face reddening. "This reminds me of the last time we were down here. I don't want to go any farther."

"Timlin!" Vorden sighed disgustedly. "What's the matter with you? We have Knights with us this time, and a Ranger. It's not like before, when it was just us. Now quit being such a weakling and get moving."

Aldreya shook her head in confusion. "Look at what we just went through down in those tombs. You were brave enough then. I can't understand you, Timlin."

"It's different now," Timlin whispered. "We're closer to..." He closed his mouth, and shook his head.

Shennen placed his hand on Timlin's shoulder. "Fear is not always a bad thing. It can help keep you alert. But it is important to stay focused. Do you really want to go back, and leave Lannon with no means to summon his Eye of Divinity?"

Timlin shook his head. "I just feel afraid."

"We will protect you," said Shennen.

"If you *can*," said Timlin, looking at the floor.

"The boy has a point," said Furlus. "We may not be able to protect him. In fact, that Worm was nearly too much for us, and that certainly might not be the worst creature lurking in the mines. He could die down here."

"Furlus, what are you trying to do?" said Caldrek, raising his eyebrows. "We should be trying to comfort the lad."

"I'm just being truthful," said Furlus. "If he goes any farther, he could be killed. After all, we don't know what's down here. So if you want to turn back, Timlin, you can, and the rest of us will too. And then we won't know what's in these mines, or whether Dremlock could be attacked from below. The choice is yours. Furlus Goblincrusher is no slave driver. If you want to go back, say so now."

Timlin was quiet for a moment. Then he whispered, "I'll keep going, I guess. I don't want to ruin things for everyone."

Saranna stepped next to Timlin and smiled at him. "I'll stay close to you, Timlin. If anything attacks us, we'll face it together."

"Don't worry about me," said Timlin. "I just don't like the mines, because they remind me of something."

"What do they remind you of?" Saranna asked, touching his shoulder. Timlin flinched away from her.

Timlin's voice grew bitter. "Never mind. Just something that happened once when I was younger. It's not important." He held up his flayer, a gleam in his eyes. "But I feel better now, and I'm ready to find that Tenneth Bard fellow. He tried to kill Lannon, and he needs to pay. So let's get going."

Saranna gazed at Timlin with uncertainty. She seemed about to ask him something more, but Timlin had already started forward, a small and silent shadow, his flayer held ready.

Lannon watched Saranna, impressed with her kindness and courage (and even more impressed with her beauty). Despite his fears, and his need to stay alert, he found himself glancing her way more often than he should have.

After a time, the chamber floor became covered in silver dust, and they could make out boot prints in it. The tracks led them into a tunnel blocked by an iron door that was locked. The Knights studied the lock, and came to the conclusion that Lannon would have to use the Eye. But Timlin begged to be allowed to try picking it, and so he was given a set of tools.

"Give it a quick try," said Furlus. "But this lock is very stout."

"You can do this, Timlin," said Shennen. "If you stay focused and let nothing distract your mind, the lock will succumb to your will."

Timlin went to work, his tiny fingers moving skillfully, his face set in a determined look. Just when the others were beginning to grow impatient, a click arose. Timlin backed away, grinning. "I got it!" he said.

"Well done," said Shennen, patting him on the back. "Amazing, really. I myself would have struggled with it. Your Knightly essence must be very strong. And those tiny, quick fingers you have are a bonus."

The Squires were instructed to stand behind the four men, with Saranna and Darius guarding the rear. While Taris and Furlus readied their weapons, Caldrek yanked the door open--to reveal a short hallway that ended at another door. The floor of this hallway was strewn with loose boards and rusty spikes.

Caldrek and Taris started forward, but Furlus ordered them to stop. "Hold on, now. Don't be wandering off without knowing what you're getting into."

"What's wrong?" said Taris.

Furlus pointed to the debris in the passageway. "Doesn't that look a little out of place to you?"

"It looks like loose boards and spikes," said Taris. "There is a lot of debris down here. What's different about this?"

Caldrek shook his head. "Even I cannot glimpse what Furlus sees."

"I see it," said Shennen. "Those boards may have been put there deliberately. They look a bit *too* randomly placed. See how none of them overlap? This could be a trap of some sort."

Furlus held forth a lantern, studying the tunnel. "The walls and ceiling look okay. The trap, if it exists, must be under the boards themselves." He frowned. "I guess I'll go first. You others wait for me. I have a suspicion..."

The Olrog carefully stepped along the tunnel, avoiding the loose boards. When he drew close to two of them lying side by side, near the tunnel's end, he sat his lantern down and raised his axe. The others could hear his raspy breathing as he cautiously stepped towards the two planks.

Then the planks exploded into the air and a dark, serpent-like shape surged out of a hole in the stone floor. The others caught a glimpse of a humanoid head, its reddish mouth split wide to reveal dripping fangs. Yet the instant that head popped up from the hole, Furlus' swung his axe and severed it from its body. The head rolled away, while the body writhed about, oozing dark fluid, until it lay still.

Furlus tore a piece off his clothing and cleaned his axe with it. "Alright," he said, wiping sweat from his brow. "It's safe now."

Exchanging glances, the others started forward. When they reached the edge of the hole, they could see that the Pit Crawler had been chained down there, leaving just enough slack so it could rise up and bite anyone it smelled approaching its lair. Animal bones (and human ones) lay in the pit, gnawed clean of flesh--food to insure the creature's poison stayed potent.

"Whoever set these traps," said Furlus, "wields some kind of power over Goblins. Otherwise his own snares would doom him. And he must be thoroughly evil to use a Pit Crawler to do his dirty work."

"I think we'd already guessed he's evil," said Taris

Lannon glanced at the severed head. It bore a human expression, its eyes widened in shock. He turned away, wishing he hadn't looked.

They examined the door at the tunnel's end. It was made of iron, had a lock similar to the one Timlin had just picked, and runes were engraved in it. Taris studied the runes, while Furlus examined the lock.

"Writings of the Deep Shadow," Taris concluded.

"But what does it mean?" said Furlus.

Taris shook his head. "Only a sorcerer who gains his power from Tharnin could perhaps understand this."

With Shennen's encouragement, Timlin eagerly set to work and soon had the door unlocked. Taris pulled it open, and another hallway was revealed, ending this time in a lighted chamber up ahead.

They crept forward with extra caution, Taris and Furlus in the lead. Soon they emerged into a round chamber lit by Birlote torches. Another tunnel mouth stood on the opposite side of this room. Wooden tables and chairs stood in the chamber, and shelves lined the walls. Jugs and bottles, some broken and some intact, sat upon the shelves, along with other items such as candles, writing utensils, books, and so forth. Also, on one of the tables lay a

Goblin Lord's corpse. It was chained down, and it had been sliced open to reveal the innards of its chest and stomach. Its eyes were open wide in death.

"Well, look at that!" said Furlus.

Taris examined the Goblin. "It looks like surgery of some sort was performed here. Do you see that cavity in the lower back? It appears the Goblin Lord's heart has been removed."

"Could this be where the Goblin Lords are created?" said Furlus.

"Not likely," said Taris. "This is a small room for such a grand accomplishment as creating Goblin Lords. This chamber probably served another purpose. But what is the meaning of this? Why is the heart missing? And look--there is fresh blood on the table, which means this was done recently."

"Perhaps this Goblin Lord was punished," said Furlus. "Look at the face and head--those black runes. This could easily be the one that escaped us earlier."

"Yes," said Taris. "I think it is. He must have been punished for his failure to destroy Lannon."

"He was simply spared my axe!" growled Furlus.

"I want to take a moment," said Taris, "to examine the contents of some of these jugs and bottles."

"We have no time for this, sorcerer," said Furlus. "While you poke your nose in those bottles, the assassin could be escaping us."

"Very well!" muttered Taris. "I'll check them later."

But Shennen ignored both of them, and uncorked a couple of the containers to sniff at them. He brought one to Taris, and let the Birlote sniff it.

Taris wrinkled his nose in disgust. "This is water tainted by the Deep Shadow. It is found in pools north of these mountains--in that place called the Desolation. It has been known to cause bizarre mutations among those who drink it. It can even mutate plants, from what I've learned, causing them to behave like animals."

"So what does this mean?" said Furlus.

"It could play a role in the creation of these Goblin Lords," said Taris. "But I suppose we are just grasping at straws here. We need to find the actual place where the Goblin Lords are created, before we can know what is really going on."

"Regardless," said Furlus, "one thing seems certain. These tunnels are soon to be used as an attack route. Otherwise, why would this be down here?"

"I agree that it is likely," said Taris.

"This is strong evidence," said Caldrek. "Shouldn't we send someone back to report it, while the rest of us search for the assassin?"

Taris was thoughtful for a moment. At last he said, "Who should be sent back? We have need of everyone, it seems. I suggest we go a bit farther and poke around a little more, before we have Cordus commit any Knights to these mines. This could be a mere diversion, while the true attack takes place above."

"Then let's get moving," said Furlus.

The company entered the tunnel, which led them a short distance before giving way to a round chasm spanned by a stone bridge. At its center, the bridge widened out briefly and displayed what appeared to be a pool of water. On the other side, another tunnel mouth could just barely be seen in the flickering light. The sound of rushing water came from the depths of the chasm below.

Furlus waved a lantern over the bridge. "Looks sturdy enough. But that's an odd place for a pool of water--in the middle of a bridge. We better go on ahead and check it out. Squires, you stay here. Saranna, you and your wolf stay with them and guard the rear."

The four Knights walked halfway across the bridge to the pool and gathered around it. The water was green and slimy looking.

"What do you make of this?" said Taris.

Furlus shook his head. "My knowledge of this area isn't good. I don't remember reading about any bridge over a chasm, or a water pool, but I do know there's a big river that flows through the mines. That could be the river down in the chasm."

Caldrek shrugged. "This pool looks harmless."

Shennen knelt by it. "Perhaps, but there is something more."

"It could be another trap," said Taris.

Even as he spoke, a dark arm arose from the pool, vine-like and dripping with algae, displaying a hand with ten fingers. The fingers, which had little green sprouts on the ends of them, wiggled about for a moment, while the others gazed on as if hypnotized.

Then, with blinding speed, the hand swatted Caldrek off the bridge. It struck him with such force that his breastplate split. Only his startled cry was left to mark his passing, as he plunged into the blackness below. A moment later a splash could be heard.

The others stared in shock, trying to gather their wits. Then Furlus dropped his lantern and swung his axe at the arm, but it was like chopping into a twisted root. The axe did little damage to the wood-like flesh, and the arm shot out and coiled about Furlus, lifting him into the air and striving to crush the life from him. His axe clattered to the stone, just on the pool's edge where flaming oil from his fallen lantern lay burning.

Then another arm rose from the pool, and this one batted Taris towards the chasm. He caught hold of the edge of the bridge as he went over and hung there, while the shovel-sized hand groped for him, its fingers wiggling and probing. He struggled fiercely to avoid the hand and pull himself up.

Shennen leapt over to help him, but the hand lurched over and bumped the Blue Knight's leg. Shennen fought for balance and then the hand bumped him again from behind. He toppled forward off the bridge. With spectacular agility, he twisted about and grabbed for the edge, but his hands fell just short of their goal, his fingertips scraping the stone. He fell silently into the chasm.

"Stay here!" Saranna ordered the Squires. She and Darius bounded out onto the bridge. When she reached Taris, she hacked at the arm that was threatening him, but her saber could not sever it. The hand batted at her several times, but each time, despite its terrible swiftness, she somehow managed to dodge it, continuing to hack away. Finally she was able to sever it and the arm slipped back into the water.

Saranna looked to Furlus. The Olrog was being squeezed viciously, but he was holding his own, his muscles bulging from the strain. His face was deep crimson, his eyes crazed with fury.

She turned to Taris and knelt, extending her hand.

"Watch your back!" Taris cried, but it was too late.

Another hand shot out of the pool and swatted Saranna's backside, knocking her headfirst into Taris and sending them both tumbling into the darkness.

With a snarl, Darius bit at the hand, but it managed to get a hold of him. It lifted the wolf into the air and tossed him from the bridge.

"We have to help them!" exclaimed Aldreya, starting forward. Her stone dagger began to burn with the green fire.

"Stay back!" Furlus bellowed at the Squires.

Aldreya paused, a desperate look in her eyes.

Vorden grabbed her shoulder. "We can't fight that thing!"

With a grunt, Furlus suddenly snapped the arm that held him in two, and the Olrog dropped into the pool. He grabbed the edge and hauled himself out, retrieving his axe. He drove it against the remaining arm and somehow lopped through it in one fierce stroke. The waters went still for a moment. He held his axe ready.

"Get away from there," Aldreya cried to him.

But Furlus would not retreat. He held his ground, his face twisted in a grimace of rage over what had happened to his companions.

Then a huge hand shot out of the slimy water--twice as large as the others. It seized Furlus before he could react. It lifted the Olrog high into the air, shook him furiously, and then flung him into the chasm.

The huge hand then wiggled its fingers before sinking below the surface of the pool again. Everything went deathly still, save for rushing of water deep in the chasm below. The Squires glanced at each other, pale and horrified.

But they had little time to mourn, for they suddenly heard something approaching from behind. They could hear groans and heavy, dragging footsteps. There was a sound like something metallic scraping the stone.

Chapter 18: The Black Knight

As the Squires watched, a huge form dragged itself into the lantern light. It was a Cave Troll--but certainly not one that was full of vigor. Its grey flesh was wrinkled and cracked with age, its face was mapped with countless lines, and long white hair grew on its body. It was somewhat thin, with its ribs standing out under its withered skin. In one hand it carried a dark sword, holding it by the blade. One of its feet had somehow become lodged in a metal bucket, and unable to free the foot, the Troll simply dragged the bucket along with it. It was a bizarre and pathetic sight.

The Troll caught sight of them and snarled, showing only a few remaining teeth. It raised the sword handle up high like a club.

"What should we do?" cried Lannon, glancing first at the Troll and then at the bridge where the dark pool stood. The Troll blocked their path back.

"Run for it," said Vorden. "We can make it."

"But those big hands!" cried Timlin, pointing at the pool. "What if they come out and grab us?"

Aldreya glanced back and forth from the Troll to the bridge, her burning dagger held out at arm's length. "We can't beat a Troll," she said.

"But the hands!" Timlin insisted.

"They won't catch us," said Vorden. "Now come on. All at once!"

As the Troll drew close, the Squires raced across the bridge. They tried to run as swiftly and silently as they could. Somehow, they made it around the pool and to the other side of the bridge without provoking the hands in the water. They stood panting, watching in fascination as the Troll staggered slowly after them.

When the Troll reached the pool and started around it (making its thumping, scraping racket in the process), the remaining giant hand groped up out of the water, wiggled its fingers, and swatted the Troll. The Troll stumbled backwards, the sword falling from its fist and clattering to the stone. Snarling, the Troll tried to grab for the wiggling hand, but it swatted the Troll again and this time knocked it off the bridge. A big splash arose from below. The hand then slipped back beneath the pool.

The Squires breathed sighs of relief.

"Come on," said Lannon. "Let's see if we can find the others."

"What if they're dead?" said Timlin. "What will we do?"

"Taris..." whispered Aldreya. "He can't be dead."

Lannon nodded in agreement. "They can't all be finished. I just can't imagine it." It was just too horrible for Lannon to accept. A repeating image ran through his mind of them being flung into the chasm. It had happened so swiftly and shockingly.

"I'd like to fix those hands," muttered Vorden, "after what they did."

"Don't go near the pool, Vorden" said Aldreya. "Or you might end up going over, too. If the Knights couldn't beat that monster, we definitely cannot."

Vorden's gaze fell on the black sword that lay by the pool. "Look at that sword! I've never seen anything like it. I'm going after it."

"Don't go, Vorden!" cried Timlin. "You don't even use a sword."

"Just leave it," said Aldreya. "What's wrong with you? The others need our help, and all you can think of is yourself."

Vorden glared at her. "Whatever you think, Aldreya, doesn't concern me, so just shut your mouth. That sword could come in handy."

"You're so incredibly selfish!" she said. "I've never met anyone so self-centered as you in my entire life."

She grabbed his arm. "We're going to help the others."

Vorden shoved her away. "Don't touch me."

Her green eyes burning with anger, Aldreya raised her stone dagger. "I can stop you from going out there, if I want to."

Vorden turned away, ignoring her. He handed his lantern to Lannon and started back across the bridge, his axe held ready.

"Vorden!" Aldreya whispered pleadingly. "Come back here."

While the others watched with pounding hearts, Vorden crept to the edge of the pool and laid hands on the sword hilt. He lifted the weapon silently off the stone, grinning, and held it up for the others to see.

Then he rose and started back. As he did so, the great hand reached forth and hovered menacingly above him.

"Watch out!" the others cried.

Yet even as the hand grabbed for Vorden, the black sword slashed around in an arc and sliced through the tree-trunk sized arm. The hand dropped to the bridge, its fingers still wiggling--like a giant insect lying on its back.

Vorden ran to where the others stood, his eyes blazing in triumph. "There," he said. "I got the sword, and killed the hand."

Lannon nodded. "Let's just hope that's the last hand."

Timlin's eyes were wide with awe. "That sword must be pretty sharp to cut through that thing so easily."

Vorden examined it. It was a straight, double-edged sword of black hue with a hilt that displayed four silver claw-like protrusions on either side. At the center of the hilt was a silver symbol that looked vaguely like a spider, while smaller runes of equal color ran the length of the blade.

"It must be," he agreed. "It kind of felt like..."

"Like what?" said Lannon.

"Like the sword moved on its own," said Vorden.

Aldreya shuddered. "Maybe you shouldn't keep it."

"What are you talking about?" said Vorden. "Of course I'm going to keep it. And you better not tell anyone I found it!"

"But it might be cursed," said Aldreya. "Just be careful, okay?"

"I will," said Vorden. "But it's a good weapon, and right now we need one, since we're on our own. I'll just leave my axe here for now."

"We could go back now and get help," said Aldreya.

Even as she spoke, the pool began to boil. Something was twisting around in the water, perhaps in agony.

"I think it's dying," said Lannon.

"Or healing itself," said Vorden. "Who knows? I'd like to keep going and see if we can locate the others. You could use the Eye of Divinity to help find them. Maybe when we come back later, that thing will be dead."

Lannon nodded. "I don't really want to go past it right now. And the others might need our help right away."

"Let's find our friends," said Timlin. "We can't leave them

behind."

***

In the chasm below the bridge, much farther down from where they had first fallen in--though it was impossible to tell exactly how far--Caldrek, Shennen, Taris, Saranna, and Darius dragged themselves out of the water and lay dripping on the riverbank. In the utter darkness of the chasm, they were forced to call out each other's names. Only Furlus failed to answer the call. Taris pulled a Birlote torch from his pack, and the crimson light revealed the swiftly flowing river, from which pointed rocks protruded.

As they watched in tense silence, a thick hand suddenly reached up out of the water and grabbed one of the rocks. Then another hand came up, and Furlus Goblincrusher pulled himself above the surface, gasping for breath. He hung there, in the middle of the river, his chest heaving beneath his plate mail.

"Don't just gawk at me," he muttered to the others. "Help me out. I can't fight the current anymore. This armor is too heavy."

"Can you remove your armor?" said Taris.

Furlus shook his head. "Not while I'm hanging from this rock."

Suddenly, a big shape drifted past in the torchlight. It was an old Cave Troll. Oddly enough, it was almost in a standing position, as if something were weighing down its feet. It bobbed along down the river, its round eyes gazing at them, and disappeared into the dark.

"Did you see that?" said Saranna. "It looked like a Troll!"

No one answered. They just shrugged and shook their heads.

"Was that a Cave Troll that just floated past?" Saranna asked again, her eyes wide in disbelief. "Or am I seeing things?"

Shennen readied his rope. "Tie this around yourself, if you can, Furlus, and we will pull you onto the bank."

"If I let go of this rock," said Furlus, "I'll sink like lead."

"I guess I can swim out and tie it around you," said Taris. "If I must..."

"I'd rather drown," said Furlus.

"I can do it," said Saranna.

"Hurry now!" said Furlus. "I'm losing my grip."

Shennen handed Saranna one end of the rope, and she dove into the river a bit upstream from where Furlus was. The current pulled her along, but she managed to fight her way over to the struggling Dwarf.

"If you weren't so thick in the belly," mocked Taris, "she might actually be able to get that rope around your waist."

Furlus was clinging to the rock with his last bit of strength, but he managed to grunt out a response. "When I get...to shore...watch out...sorcerer!"

"It's done," said Saranna. "You can pull us in."

Shennen, Caldrek, and Taris tugged on the rope. "You can let go now," said Taris, "unless you want us to try to pull that rock along with you."

Furlus let his hands slip from the rock, while Saranna held onto him and the rope. The others dragged them up onto land. Furlus lay coughing and hacking. Then he sat up, his beard dripping, still panting from his exertion.

"Let us hope the Squires returned to Dremlock," sputtered Furlus.

"I doubt they did," said Taris, shaking his head.

Furlus looked surprised. "What makes you say that? Do you actually think they would try to continue on without us?"

"Perhaps," said Taris. "They might try to find us, believing we need their help. And that Vorden fellow... Well, let's just say that I understand his nature."

"They would be fools to try to cross that bridge," said Saranna, wringing out her hair, "after what happened to us."

"Could Squires possess such courage?" said Caldrek.

"Why not?" said Shennen. "When we were young, Caldrek, we might easily have tried it. When it comes down to it, age has less to do with courage than people might think, my friend."

"I think Taris has a good point, for once," said Furlus. "Look at what those Squires have done already--sneaking down to visit the Divine Essence."

"Where Vorden goes," said Taris, "trouble shall follow."

*　*　*

In full agreement to continue on, the Squires entered the tunnel. It led them downward at a steep incline and then leveled off. Stone pillars lined the passageway here, grey and smooth in the lantern light, hewn from the mountain's rock. Hanging from the pillars were rusted chains. Still caught in some of these chains was evidence of their grim purpose--a skeletal arm here, a thighbone there. Skulls and other bones lay scattered at the base of the pillars. This was another Olrog punishment hall. The Squires wondered how many such grisly places existed down here.

They left the pillars behind and journeyed for what seemed like hours along the stone passageway, occasionally encountering thick black roots that split the rock here and there (having caused small cave-ins in some areas).

The tunnel gradually began to widen, revealing even more roots, and they had to push their way through fierce tangles of them at times. The gloomy feeling thickened, smothering them, while a sickening stench--reminding Lannon of the Bloodlands-- had begun to assail their nostrils. Despair built in their hearts.

"Maybe we should go back," said Lannon.

"Let's go just a little farther," said Vorden.

"I think the others are dead," said Timlin, shivering.

"I feel that way now, too," said Aldreya.

"It has something to do with this area," said Vorden. "It's like the Bloodlands, making us feel as if things are hopeless."

"I feel like everything is crazy," said Aldreya "What are we doing here? What's happening to Dremlock? I never thought it would be this way."

"I didn't either," said Lannon. "It seems like ever since we snuck into Old Keep, things have gotten strange. Now someone wants me dead."

"I know what you mean," said Vorden, stopping and turning to them. "I always imagined the life of a Squire would be somewhat exciting--but nothing like this. I wanted adventure, but not necessarily this much, this soon."

"When I first came to Dremlock," said Aldreya, "I had no idea things were this bad here. I grew up in Borenthia, the great Birlote tree city to the west, and all my life all I ever heard was how wonderful Dremlock was. I dreamt of being a Knight from the time I was a little girl." She giggled, and then sighed. "I finally got my wish, for my parents had it planned for me all along. It is a tradition among my family."

Aldreya bowed her head. "I've worked really hard, but lately

I've been starting to wonder what it's all worth. Is Dremlock just going to fall apart soon? I miss Borenthia very much, and lately Dremlock leaves me feeling empty inside."

The others had nothing to say. They wondered the same thing. Would all their training end up being for nothing, if the Goblins prevailed?

Vorden put his hand on Aldreya's shoulder. "It's not really that bad. Somehow, the Divine Essence will make things right. I know it will."

Aldreya blushed. "I hope so."

They started off again. Soon afterward, the tunnel narrowed into a crawl space. The rocks bruised their knees. This didn't last long, and they soon emerged onto a ledge. They stood up, choking on the foul stench, striving to see beyond the lantern light. The ledge was narrow, and a sheer cliff dropped away into the darkness, spider-webbed with black Iracus roots. Down below they could hear hideous sucking and feasting noises, along with swaying and creaking sounds, and an occasional hiss or screech that sounded like Goblins.

Timlin huddled close to Vorden and Lannon.

"What's down there?" whispered Lannon.

"Probably Iracus Trees," said Vorden. "Look at all those roots on the side of the cliff. There must be a lot of those trees down there!"

Suddenly it dawned on Lannon. "That must be the Mother Nest that Furlus mentioned. The Goblins must be feeding. Who knows how many are down there? Vorden, let's get out of here now!"

"Let's just see where this ledge leads," Vorden said. "Then we'll turn back."

"Not this again!" whispered Lannon. Grim memories of Old Keep flooded back, and he silently cursed Vorden. Why did Vorden have to be like this?

"Turn back!" Timlin begged.

"Vorden--you are not putting me through this again," said Aldreya. "This time, we will just leave you behind. I swear we will."

But onward Vorden went, ignoring their pleas. Unwilling to abandon him at this point, the others followed. The ledge ended at another tunnel.

"Come on," he said. " I think I hear water."

They listened carefully, faintly hearing what sounded like a river up ahead. Yet it was hard to tell from this distance exactly what the noise was.

"Let's see if the others are by that river," said Vorden. "When we get close enough, you can use the Eye to help find them."

"I guess we can go a little farther," said Lannon, "now that we're past those Iracus Trees. But I'm starting to feel wretched."

"I feel so bad inside," said Aldreya, "and that smell..."

They could walk upright in the next tunnel, and it led them along for a short distance and then into a large chamber. They walked around the edge of this room and saw many tunnels, all of which looked the same.

Finally Vorden paused, fear in his eyes. For several moments no one said a word, while Lannon, Timlin, and Aldreya waited in dread for him to tell them what was wrong. Finally he said, "I made a big mistake. I'm not sure which tunnel is the one we came in here through. Have any of you kept count?"

They shook their heads.

"It looks like we'll have to go back and try them all," said Vorden. "I have no idea which way we should go, and the river sounds like it's coming from all around us now, only still far away. This isn't going to work. I've come to realize we need to go back to Dremlock and get help."

"Good idea!" the others quickly agreed.

"A little late in coming, though," Aldreya grumbled.

Yet before they got a chance to start back, the lantern suddenly died, plunging the chamber into utter blackness. In an instinctive panic, Lannon tried to flee in any direction he could, but cold fingers suddenly gripped his throat, and the whispers of flame burned into his soul, paralyzing him. A quiet laugh reached his ears from mere inches away, and hot breath was on his cheek. Two insane eyes burned in the dark.

"Tenneth Bard!" Lannon thought, his legs going weak.

"Greetings, Squires of Dremlock," came a quiet voice. "Are you surprised to meet me here? Did you think I would be hiding away somewhere, protected by my Goblins? Well, if you want something done right... Anyway, so here I am. We've found each other. Now what do you intend to do?"

"Nnn...nothing," Timlin stammered. "We just want to leave."

"I'm afraid that won't be possible," said the Black Knight. "You came here seeking me. And we must see this through."

"What do you want?" Vorden said. "Why are you doing this?"

Tenneth Bard sighed. "My boy, it's not about what I want. I simply desire the downfall of Dremlock, and if I my wish were to come true, I would be content to live out my life in peace. But my master has greater plans, and I owe him so much. Now before you die, I shall allow you to look upon your slayer."

The lantern suddenly began to shine again, only now it was blue--a cold and bitter glow. Tenneth Bard wore a ragged black cloak that seemed to merge with the darkness beyond the lantern light. His face was a mask of shifting shadows. Yet his violet eyes remained the same--crazed and inhuman.

"See how I planned everything out?" said the Black Knight. "Soon Dremlock will be invaded from below--yet not in the manner you might believe. I've created a diversion in these mines. Cordus shall send his Knights down here to battle a few sorry Goblins, while the bulk of my forces emerge from another point--a hidden one. And this army is made up mostly of Knights of the Blood Legion rather than Goblins. Victory will come easily.

"And now I will choke the life from you, boy. Go ahead--try to summon your powers. I assure you that your efforts will be in vain. Beneath my touch, your Eye of Divinity is rendered useless. Goodbye, Lannon Sunshield!"

"Wait!" said Vorden, his voice surprisingly calm. "While you're killing Lannon, I'll flee and tell Cordus what you said. Your plans will be ruined."

"Flee if you wish," said the Black Knight. "You won't even escape this chamber before you're destroyed."

"Then maybe we can make a bargain," said Vorden.

"I like you," said Tenneth Bard. "You're a thinker, I can tell--much like I was in my youth. But there will be no deals this night, only death."

"Don't do this!" Aldreya cried. "Let us help you somehow. If you're cursed by the Deep Shadow, the Knights can cure you. I know it is possible."

"I don't need your help," said Tenneth Bard. "Nor do I desire it. I have everything I need. Perhaps if that help had come long ago, it might have saved me. But now I'm quite set in my ways. And now I must finish my task."

"No, you won't!" Timlin suddenly howled, and he flung himself upon Tenneth Bard, ripping his Flayer against the Black Knight's throat. But the Flayer only glanced away, as if striking stone. Chuckling, Tenneth Bard batted Timlin aside.

Timlin struck the floor and rolled, rising up again. But he made no move to attack, and simply stood there in defeat. "Please don't kill Lannon."

Aldreya raised her dagger and cast a ball of green fire at the Black Knight. But the fire deflected away from him, doing no damage.

"See there, boy?" Tenneth Bard said to Lannon. "Your friends cannot harm me. No mortal weapon can damage me. Even those that burn with the flames of Knightly enchantment cannot. I have evolved beyond such weaknesses. Soon there will be nothing in this realm that can bring me harm."

Desperately Lannon struggled to call forth the Eye, even praying to the Divine Essence. But the Eye felt completely closed off to him--blocked by a coldness that spread from Tenneth Bard's fingertips all throughout Lannon's being. Nor could he manage to move, for the whispers held him fast, speaking to his body and freezing it. And slowly the fingers were squeezing tighter on his throat.

Lannon's mind began to go black from the choking, and he felt the end was at hand. Is this what the Divine Essence had intended for him? But the Essence was just a scared, lonely child, and he knew it had not planned his destiny. It may have granted him a divine gift, but it certainly had not written the book of his life.

"Let me tell you a story as you die," Tenneth Bard said. "Once I was a young, hopeful Squire like you, Lannon. I had talent the likes of which few had ever witnessed--not the Eye of Divinity, mind you. But for sheer talent, I was unmatched. I became a great Knight, and brought much glory to Dremlock. But that wasn't enough for them. I fell in love with a woman, thus violating the Sacred Laws, and was banished from the kingdom forever. It ruined my life, and I became a worthless drunkard. My woman left me, and then I had nothing. It seemed the Knights had taken everything from me. Of course I grew bitter towards Dremlock, and eventually sought revenge.

"But you know what? I am bitter no longer. Now I fight against Dremlock for another reason--because my master demands it. If you think I'm still angry about losing my Knighthood so long ago, you're sadly mistaken. I care nothing about the past. A new and glorious age is soon to be upon us. Unfortunately, you won't live to see it."

I guess I won't, Lannon thought dimly.

Then Vorden's words penetrated Lannon's foggy mind--a sudden whisper in the dark. "I've got something for you, Tenneth Bard. I hope you enjoy it!"

A screech arose, and the fingers loosened on Lannon's throat, dropping the lad to the floor where he lay struggling for breath. His vision was a tad blurry, but he saw Vorden leap away from the Black Knight, his dark sword dripping blood. Tenneth Bard staggered, clutching his ribs, in obvious agony.

And then an image of the Divine Essence sprang into Lannon's thoughts. He realized it was a memory he was seeing. The Essence had taught him things about the Eye of Divinity during his encounter with it, but he couldn't remember what he had learned-- save for one thing. He now understood how to unlock the Eye on his own.

He envisioned hands reaching into his mind, pulling it in two. The hands were the force of his will, and they effortlessly split his being into separate halves. The Eye of Divinity sprang out through the gap. With Tenneth Bard's concentration disrupted, the whispers departed from Lannon, leaving him able to move. Yet no movement was needed. As the Eye sprang out towards Tenneth Bard, it underwent a change, becoming a physical force that seized the Black Knight in a crushing grasp.

Tenneth Bard howled in pain and fury, but then slowly he began to break out of the clutches that held him. But Vorden sensed his opportunity, and he drove the dark sword unmercifully into the Black Knight's chest. Tenneth Bard convulsed in pain, falling to his knees, blood soaking the floor at his feet.

"Cut off his head!" Timlin cried.

Vorden withdrew his dark blade and raised it up for the kill. But Tenneth Bard suddenly broke free of Lannon's hold and lunged up, staggering away. He turned towards Lannon and hissed, "Not over yet... Just beginning..."

But Vorden flung the sword like a spear, and it lodged in the Black Knight's side. He clawed at the blade, then toppled over and lay still.

Vorden leapt over and retrieved his sword. Tenneth Bard's eyes were open wide, glazed over in death. Blood pooled out around him.

The lantern light changed back to normal.

"That's the end of him," whispered Vorden.

Lannon grabbed the lantern. He used the Eye to locate the tunnel they had come through, and then he drew his power partially inside him.

"Come on," he said. "Let's get out of here!"

The Squires raced through the tunnel and out onto the ledge. They could hear the slurping, sucking noises coming from the Mother Nest below. As they ran across the ledge, a clawed hand reached up and grabbed Aldreya's leg, nearly tripping her. She screamed, kicking furiously in an effort to escape.

A small Goblin clung to the roots on the cliff face, snarling. It wasn't much bigger than a Tree Goblin, but already it had clusters of deadly claws. Aldreya kicked its arm, and the Goblin lost its grip on the roots and tumbled back down into the darkness. Bleeding wounds were left in Aldreya's leg.

Vorden searched his pack for cloth to bandage it, but Aldreya grabbed his arm. "I'm okay for now," she said. "Let's just get away from here!"

They continued on and entered the small tunnel where they were forced to crawl upon aching knees. When the tunnel widened enough to stand, Vorden took the time to bandage Aldreya's leg. After that they pushed their way through tangles of Iracus roots. The Squires hurried as fast as they were able. Their backs felt exposed as they raced along, and often they found themselves glancing behind them.

At one point, Vorden again asked the others not to mention his new sword. "I could be cast out for using this blade," he said. "This is obviously no ordinary weapon. It must be magical."

"Then maybe you should leave it here," said Lannon. "Otherwise, you might get caught with it, and get banished anyway."

"I'll take my chances for now," said Vorden, tucking his sword away beneath his cloak. "I just can't leave it behind! It's extraordinary--better than your Dragon sword, Lannon."

"I'm happy with my Dragon sword," Lannon replied, shuddering at the thought of Vorden's dark blade which had done so much damage to Tenneth Bard.

At last the Squires reached the stone bridge, and to their delight, they encountered the Knights and Saranna. The adults were on the other side, about to start across. When they saw the Squires, Taris ordered them to halt.

"Come no closer," he said. "The creature yet lives."

"We can make it," Vorden said to Taris. "We did it once already."

Taris nodded. "One at a time, then. And be swift!"

Vorden raced across without incident, swiping up his axe on the way. (He kept his other arm pressed to his body, holding the sword in place beneath his cloak.) Timlin and Aldreya managed to make it, and then it was Lannon's turn.

Lannon suddenly found he had lost his nerve. The last thing he wanted was to be flung into that dark chasm and end up alone-- with all the Iracus Trees and Goblins down in these mines.

Then Lannon's gaze fell on Saranna, and he blushed. Not wanting to appear cowardly in her eyes, he pushed his fears aside and bounded across the bridge. Yet when he neared the pool, a wooden hand suddenly rose up, wiggling its leafy fingers. Lannon froze, watching in horror.

Then Lannon remembered the Eye of Divinity, which was still at the ready, and he directed it at the creature in the pool, hoping it would do more than just reveal things about the monstrosity. Lannon willed the Eye to grasp the beast, and it responded to his command, squeezing the bulky thing motionless. The creature fought fiercely but could not break the invisible force that held it. The hand stayed fixed in the air above the pool.

Still holding the monster in check, Lannon drew his Dragon sword and slashed through the wooden arm. The light, ultra sharp blade easily severed it, and the leafy hand dropped into the pool with a splash.

Calmly, Lannon walked the rest of the way across the bridge, while the others watched him with open mouths and raised eyebrows. When he reached the other side, a sick feeling overcame him, and he released the creature and drew the Eye all the way inside him. He held his stomach for a moment, feeling the urge to vomit.

"Are you okay?" Taris asked.

Lannon nodded. "I just need to clear my head."

"What happened to you Squires?" the sorcerer asked.

Lannon explained how they had encountered Tenneth Bard, and how the Black Knight had tried to kill him. "I used my power to overcome him," Lannon said, with a sharp glance at Vorden. "Tenneth Bard is dead."

"So your power has grown," said Taris. "And an old enemy has met his end. This has been a great night for our kingdom thus far. Now, if only we knew what Tenneth Bard was planning exactly."

"I do know," Lannon said excitedly. "He was planning a diversion. The actual attack on Dremlock won't come from under the Temple. It will come from somewhere else--maybe another entrance to the mines."

"Old Keep is well defended," said Furlus. "As is the Deep Forge. There must be another passage into the mines--one we've forgotten about."

"We must make haste," said Taris.

As they entered the tunnels, three figures suddenly stepped into the lantern light. One was a giant, bearded man dressed in black plate armor, bearing a battle axe that glowed with crimson fire. Two Goblin Lords stood side-by-side behind him, holding twisted staffs. The staffs smoldered with black flames. Though they seemed outnumbered, they regarded the party with calm, focused expressions.

"Your master lies dead," Taris said. "Stand aside, or join him."

The giant spoke in a gruff voice. "No matter. The Blood Legion has functioned without him for a thousand years. We shall endure. And we have other masters who are unknown to you. We have come to destroy you and the Squires. Then Dremlock will follow."

"Looks to me like you're outnumbered," said Caldrek. "And in case you haven't heard, we know how to defeat the Goblin Lords."

The giant smiled. "Yes, but the Goblin Lords have turned the odds in my favor. Or haven't you noticed?"

"I can't move," Shennen whispered.

"I can't, either!" Timlin cried. "What's happening?"

Lannon tried to call the Eye, but it wouldn't work. Nor could he move. A force similar to Tenneth Bard's Whispers was at work within him.

Even Darius was rendered motionless.

"Just some foul magic," said the giant, sighing. "It will hold you fast while I cleave off your heads." He spoke matter-of-factly.

Furlus bellowed with rage, but he too was held immobile by the invisible force. All his strength would not avail him against these bonds.

"I should have been alert to this," Taris said quietly. "I have failed us all." Then he closed his eyes and fell silent.

The Squires could scarcely believe their ears, for never had they heard Taris speak in such a grim tone. Lannon fought to unleash the Eye, yet it seemed to lie just beyond his grasp. He knew in his heart there was a way to reach it, but he couldn't seem to summon the will to do it. His helplessness frustrated him to the point where he felt like he was going to explode, and he begged the Divine Essence to give him even the slightest assistance. But still the Eye of Divinity remained just out of reach.

The giant shook his head. "Don't blame yourself, sorcerer. These are Priests of Tharnin, and their magic is a match even for yours."

"If I could only move!" Caldrek muttered. "I'd show you three. At least finish me first, so I can die with honor."

The giant nodded. "It shall be done." He stepped forward and raised his axe for the kill, a passive look in his eyes.

And then Caldrek struck. The Red Knight lashed out with his blade and cleaved into the giant's armor. For an instant, the Squires' hearts lurched with glee, for they were certain Caldrek would prevail and all would be well. But the giant somehow reacted swiftly enough to twist sideways and avoid serious injury. Bringing his axe down, he knocked Caldrek's blade aside and then stepped back.

Caldrek cursed. "Almost had you--you lucky devil!"

The giant glanced questioningly at the Goblin Lords, but their eyes were narrowed with focus as they struggled to maintain the sorcery they had cast over the party. With a shrug, he calmly waited for Caldrek to make another move.

"Guess your priests couldn't hold us all," said Caldrek. "And now it's just you and me, big fellow."

The giant nodded. "As it should be. A fair fight."

The two men moved in on each other, looking for an opening. Caldrek's blade burned blue as he brought his own sorcery into play. The giant stood guard before the two Goblin Lords, always staying close to them should Caldrek try to disrupt their focus.

Their blades finally met with a clatter and a burst of sparks. Back and forth they went, slashing furiously at each other with their weapons. Then Caldrek caught a glancing blow to the shoulder that staggered him. He retreated a bit.

"Not bad," Caldrek said. "But it will take more than that."

Lannon gave up on trying to call the Eye, and he simply stood and watched, hoping Caldrek was skilled enough to beat this foe. The fact that Caldrek seemed highly regarded by Cordus and his Tower Masters gave Lannon confidence he would find a way to defeat this servant of the Blood Legion. It was the two Goblin Lords that worried Lannon the most, for if they could hold Taris in check, and the Eye of Divinity, who knew what they were capable of?

Caldrek leapt in and they traded another flurry of blows, and this time the Red Knight took a partial slash to the ribs that drew blood. Again Caldrek retreated, and this time a shocked look appeared on his face. Sweat dripped from his brow and mustache, and he used his sleeve to wipe it from his eyes. He was panting hard.

"I can't believe it!" he said, with a sideways glance at Shennen. "This fellow is faster than anyone I've ever sparred with."

"Stay focused," Shennen urged him. "You can defeat this foe. If you fail, all of us will die. Do not let that happen."

"Fail?" Caldrek gave a little laugh. "You know me better than that, Shennen. I'll get him for you. Don't worry."

The giant did not speak, and his face remained passive. Again he waited for Caldrek to strike, preferring to stay on the defensive.

Caldrek moved in on him and again they clashed, and this time Caldrek ripped a small wound in the giant's arm. For an instant the Red Knight seemed to gain the upper hand, as the giant retreated, wincing in pain. Caldrek lunged after him, determined to finish him while the giant was off balance.

Yet the giant quickly recovered his composure, and in response, he drove his axe at Caldrek with a slew of vicious strokes. The Red Knight blocked all but one of them--and that one caught him in the throat.

Caldrek gazed in disbelief as he staggered back, clutching his throat. "Can't...believe...you..." His words disintegrated and he collapsed, his sword clattering to the stone floor. The fire died in his blade.

The Squires cried out in dismay, and again Lannon strove to summon the Eye, realizing if he did not, his head would end up separated from his neck. Panic gripped him and he gave everything he had, yet still it was not enough. It was like groping unsuccessfully for something only an inch away from his fingertips.

The giant bowed his head with respect to Caldrek, and then started forward. "Time to get this over with," he muttered. "I'm not fond of killing men in this fashion, but it must be done in a time of war." He raised his axe, going for Taris first.

"You must break free now," Taris grunted. "Do it, Furlus!"

Apparently, Taris had been using his own power, working on freeing the strongest member of the party, and now Furlus, his face gone purple with strain, suddenly managed to break the invisible bonds with the sorcerer's help. A flash of blue erupted, momentarily blinding everyone, and Furlus Goblincrusher was free. The others, however, still remained locked in place by the spell.

His bearded face bearing a scowl, the Grey Dwarf leapt towards the giant, and their axes clanged together deafeningly. The glowing crimson axe met Olrog Glaetherin, and a shower of sparks erupted. Growling like a bear, the Dwarf drove the giant backwards with maddened strokes. The giant's passive look disintegrated into one of surprise, so taken aback was he by the Olrog's fury. Furlus shook with rage, and his axe blows were delivered with the legendary vigor of a battle-crazed Dwarf.

The giant was on the defensive, struggling to regain his composure. In a fatal move, he saw a brief opening and tried to take Furlus' legs out from under him. The Olrog leapt over the blade, and in the same motion, Furlus drove his axe into the giant's chest, crunching through armor. The force of the blow sent the giant tumbling into the two Goblin Lords, breaking their spell in a fizzling flash of light. The giant crumpled to the ground and lay still.

The Goblin Lords turned to flee, for even two Priests of Tharnin were no match for the entire party. Still on the attack, Furlus caught one of them even as the Goblin turned, his axe cleaving the creature in two. The other one made it a little farther before Shennen's blade cut him down.

Taris stepped in and destroyed their hearts with his burning dagger.

Furlus quickly searched the corpses, and stuck a couple items in his pack without commenting on what they were.

Shennen lifted Caldrek's body. "It must have been that Goblin Worm's poison," the Blue Knight said. "He was still weak from it, or Caldrek would have beaten that big fellow. I know it in my heart. He saved us all, and we must honor him well. We survived many perilous missions together. He was my friend."

Furlus bowed his head.

"He shall receive the highest honor," said Taris. "The White Blood will adorn his body, and he shall be promoted to Green. I'll see to it, my friend."

Then the party hurried onward, bearing their slain companion.

***

They made it back up to the Temple without further incident, sealing all the doors they passed through. When they at last reached the top of the stairs, they felt as if a great burden had been lifted off their shoulders, though Caldrek's death left them very disheartened. Twelve Knights of varying color classes stood guard in the Temple, and when they saw the group emerge, they quickly gathered around, some expressing cries of dismay when they beheld Caldrek's corpse.

"We encountered Goblin Lords below," said Furlus, "and members of the Blood Legion. Cordus was wise to send you here."

"Spread the word," said Taris, "that Caldrek died saving us."

"We shall!" the Knights swore. Their faces were pale over what they saw, and dismayed to the point where some had tears in their eyes. Caldrek had been a legend to many of them, a warrior no one wanted to spar with, who was used only for the most important and dangerous missions. He had seemed almost like an immortal presence, someone who inspired hope and who never lost his sense of humor, whatever the situation. It would be some time before these Knights could put this behind them, and talk of his days would linger on for weeks.

A sorrowful feeling gripped Lannon, and he did not glance at the body. Not long ago, Caldrek had been a powerful, living Knight, yet now he was nothing more than a part of history. Lannon could feel strongly his own fragile mortality, and he realized how easily he could be removed from the world. And when that happened, like Caldrek he would be just a piece of history, and like all history, he would eventually be forgotten. It had come close to happening in the mines (more than once), and he wasn't even yet a Knight. He took some comfort in knowing he possessed the Eye of Divinity, which could protect him, but that was balanced by the knowledge that it also had made him a target.

They laid Caldrek before the altar, and held a moment of silence in his honor. Then the Tower Masters discussed their plans.

"Shennen and Saranna," said Taris, "you should guide the Squires to the East Tower, while Furlus and I take our evidence to Cordus. Lannon should come with us, for we may need him to locate the place where the attack will come from."

"Lannon might need our help," said Vorden, obviously not

wanting to miss out on the action. "What if he has to summon the Eye?"

"He will not need your help," said Taris, "and so there is no use putting you other Squires at risk. You will do as I say, and be thankful."

"Once the Squires are safely in their quarters," said Furlus, "have them placed under guard. Then both of you should come to the North Tower. We will probably have need of your skills before this night is through."

"What about Caldrek?" said Shennen.

"We shall leave his body here," said Taris, "and return later for it. Let him rest peacefully by the altar of the Divine One for the time being."

"We will look after him," the guards said. "And if anyone dares come forth, we will be waiting! We shall fight in his name."

Cries of agreement arose among the other guards. "Let no foul Goblin or failed Knight dare set foot in this Sacred Temple," one of them said. "For to our last breaths, we shall fight to honor Caldrek!"

"Caldrek will be avenged!" another cried, tears flowing freely.

Furlus nodded. "Your words ring true. I see that the Temple is left in worthy hands, and know it will be well defended."

Taris turned to Shennen and took him aside, whispering so no one else could hear. The Blue Knight nodded several times.

With that, the company parted ways.

Chapter 19: The Blood Legion

As Lannon, Taris, and Furlus stepped out into the frozen, moonlit night, they encountered four Squires, who were wandering past. These were older boys, nearing Knightly age, and their faces were tense and excited. With shaky voices, they greeted the Tower Masters.

"What are you Squires up to?" said Furlus, studying their sashes. "I see you bear the Silver Axe." Furlus was referring to a small symbol stitched onto their sashes. It was a special promotion given to some Squires on rare occasions allowing them to carry out limited Knightly duties. "Does Cordus have you on a mission of some sort?"

"Yes, Master Furlus," said one of the boys. "We're supposed to watch for any suspicious activity around Dremlock and report it at once."

"And have you noticed any?" said Furlus.

"None," they replied.

"Then carry on with your duties," Furlus said. He whispered something to Taris, and the sorcerer nodded.

With that, the Tower Masters and Lannon continued on. They met more groups of Squires on their way to the North Tower, all bearing the Silver Axe insignia on their sashes. Like the first bunch, these ones too were wandering around Dremlock watching for anything suspicious. Furlus questioned each of them briefly, and hearing nothing of value, waved them on with their task.

At last the North Tower loomed over them in the moonlight, and they found Cordus Landsaver standing at the top of the steps talking to four of his Red Knights. When Cordus saw the others, he hurried down to greet them.

Taris and Furlus explained all that had happened to them.

When Cordus heard about the evidence they had uncovered, and the death of Tenneth Bard, he was ecstatic, but his mood took a downturn when he learned of Caldrek's death.

"That is very sad news," Cordus said quietly, shaking his head. "Caldrek was the most talented fighter Dremlock has seen in ages, and he was one of my most trusted Knights. It is only fitting that he died a great hero, and we shall give him the highest honors allowed. For three days, this kingdom will lie beneath a veil of silence and prayer."

"What has happened while we were gone?" said Taris.

"Dremlock has been put on full alert," Cordus said. "However, it may not be enough, if the attack comes suddenly and in great numbers. We have to find their entry point into the kingdom, if indeed one exists, and then perhaps we can strike first. Obviously, we'd do better to fight this out in the tunnels below rather than right in the midst of our kingdom. I wonder if the Blood Legion knows that you've learned of their plans. If they do know, the attack will undoubtedly come very soon, for any sort of diversion on their part will no longer be necessary."

Taris shook his head. "There is much guesswork involved. We know very little about our enemy, and I did not recognize the man who slew Caldrek. Could this be the original Blood Legion we're dealing with? Or is this an entirely different group bearing the same name? And what was Tenneth Bard's connection to them?"

"After years of spying on our foes," said Cordus, "we could not learn the truth. The Blood Legion appeared to pose only a minimal threat at best, at least compared to the Goblins. They apparently managed to keep their dealings below Dremlock a secret, and it seems possible they are connected to the Goblins somehow."

"I don't know about the other Black Knights," said Taris, "but I believe Tenneth Bard had something to do with the new, intelligent Goblins. I'm fairly certain he played a hand in creating the Lords--if that truly was him down there." The sorcerer glanced apologetically at Lannon. "We cannot know for sure, until we retrieve his body. And even that might not be enough to identify him."

"At least the Goblin Puzzle is solved," said Furlus. "That alone was the burden that nearly proved Dremlock's undoing.

"Indeed," said Cordus. "And I've already sent out the messengers. Let us pray they arrive in time to save Kalamede. As far as Dremlock goes, I've put all our Knights and many of our Squires on full watch, so at least we cannot be caught entirely by surprise. The High Council is assembled in the Hall, demanding answers. But I have been too busy thus far to provide any. You can imagine Moten and Kealin's reaction to this. They seem to think I'm the one that's plotting Dremlock's downfall."

"We won't be worrying about what Moten thinks much longer," mumbled Furlus. "His days of glory are soon to end."

"Why don't you tend to the High Council?" said Taris. "Furlus and I will take Lannon and scout around for the attack point."

"I should check all the books and maps," said Furlus. "I might be able to locate any forgotten entrances to the mines."

"We have no time for that," said Taris. "The Eye of Divinity can do what needs to be done." He placed his hand on Lannon's shoulder.

"I will put someone else on the task of searching the books," said Cordus. "Meanwhile, Furlus, you should go along with Taris and the boy and see what you can find. Your knowledge of the mines might be needed."

As they watched Cordus enter the North Tower, they did not envy his task of having to pacify the Council. At Taris' bidding, Lannon summoned the Eye of Divinity and held it at the ready. He was surprised and delighted at how easily he could call it forth now, and his confidence soared. He felt ready to undertake this mission.

"So where should we begin?" said Taris.

Furlus thought in silence for a time. At last he said, "What about the Cemetery? Could the opening lie amid the tombs?"

Lannon's confidence took a dive and his face went pale. He remembered the horrors he had glimpsed in that place, and their encounter in the Olrog tombs was still fresh in his mind. Dremlock Cemetery was the last place he had expected or wanted to go, and he wished Taris would suggest something else.

His wish was not granted.

"That is a good idea," said Taris. "Some of the crypts run

deep, with tunnels and sealed doors. Could it be that one of them leads to the mines? And what better place to begin their attack than in a place no one dares venture into at night? While Knights and Squires patrol the borders, our enemies could easily sneak out from the tombs and quickly spread throughout Knightwood."

Lannon wished his friends were with them, for if he had to face going into that area, he could have used their company. They had defeated Tenneth Bard together, and he felt a unique bond with them that he did not share with these Tower Masters. Taris and Furlus were wise and powerful, and could probably protect him better than anyone else, but it wasn't the same somehow.

"I'd rather not go in there," Lannon said. "Maybe I could stand outside the Cemetery and use the Eye. I think that place is haunted."

Taris nodded. "It is very much haunted, Lannon. Dremlock Cemetery holds numerous restless spirits who, for differing reasons, have not found peace. But the main curse upon that place is caused by sixteen Dark Watchmen who reside in the crypts. Their souls, tainted by the Deep Shadow, never sleep."

"But there is something else," said Lannon. "A huge hand."

Taris and Furlus exchanged a puzzled glance.

"Like the ones that knocked us off that bridge?" said Furlus.

Lannon shook his head. "No, more like a ghost or something. It doesn't feel like a living thing, but something else. I guess I can't explain it."

"A giant spectral hand?" said Taris. "I am not familiar with such a ghost. I have met and spoken with nineteen of them--the Watchmen, a former Lord Knight, a former Green Knight and sorcerer, and a former Tower Master. I did not know there was a twentieth Ghost in there!"

"But you don't have Lannon's power, either," said Furlus. "He sees things even a sorcerer like yourself cannot."

"Indeed," said Taris. "Regardless, the ghosts appear rarely and are mostly harmless. They can cause a nasty feeling or two, brought on by the aura of the Deep Shadow, or they can cause tremendous fear, but that is about all."

Lannon nodded uncertainly. That giant hand had seemed different, ready to crush anyone who got too close--worse than those wooden hands down in the mines. Can't I just try the Eye from outside first?" he said. "Or maybe we could just put guards around the Cemetery."

"You can try searching from beyond the fence first," said Taris. "But if the range is too far for you, we shall have to go inside. This is something we need to investigate. Our Knights and Squires are spread around the kingdom. We cannot afford to concentrate them all in a single area, for if the attack came from elsewhere, it could be disastrous. We have no time to stand here and debate this issue."

Furlus had already turned and was walking in the direction of the Cemetery. Taris motioned Lannon along and then started walking. Having no choice, Lannon reluctantly followed.

As they entered the woods, Taris patted Lannon on the back. "I know you're afraid of the Cemetery. Most in Dremlock are. And I know you feel we should be trying something different. But that's because you do not yet know me. I work best when I'm alone or with just a few others. Mark my words--while Knights, Squires, and High Council members argue and scurry about, we will find the forgotten entrance to the mines, if indeed it exists."

"Listen to Taris," said Furlus. "For once he knows what he's talking about. He has sound intuition concerning such matters."

Taris raised his eyebrows. "Praise for me? From Furlus Goblincrusher? What strange times I find myself in."

"Enjoy it, sorcerer," said Furlus. "Because you probably won't hear it again anytime soon."

Their boots crunched loudly in the frosty stillness. Off in the distance, they could hear faint voices, as Knights and Squires went about their tasks. Then a wolf howl erupted close by. Taris paused and raised his hand, bringing the others to a halt. A moment later, another howl came from a little farther away.

"Why can't I try the Eye from here?" said Lannon. The Cemetery lay just ahead through the moonlit woods, and he found, despite all he had been through recently, that he was shaking with fear. He kept seeing the giant hand in his mind, reaching forth to crush his bones into fragments.

"The distance is too far," said Taris. "You dare not stretch yourself so thin, for the danger becomes magnified, I believe."

"What danger?" said Lannon.

"You might see too many sights," said Taris. "And there are other concerns. A servant of the Deep Shadow could use your power against you, and you would not realize it until too late. The farther you stretch out the Eye, the less accurate your viewings will be, and the easier it would be for a foe to threaten you. Remember what happened when you gazed upon that Goblin Lord? There are methods that a clever adversary could use to destroy your sanity, if not your life. Always get as close to your target as possible before using the Eye, for your control will be greater and the risks much less."

Lannon said nothing and just gave a slight nod. He knew there was no sense in arguing with the sorcerer at this point, for Taris had made up his mind and clearly was intent upon journeying to the dreaded place.

When they reached the iron fence that surrounded Dremlock Cemetery, Lannon gazed in at the tombs of the dead. The crypts glittered with frost in the moonlight, and the pine boughs that hung over them were heavy with snow and bent down. Lannon couldn't help but notice how some of those boughs looked like giant, groping hands. He was tired of giant hands trying to crush him-- Ogre hands, Troll hands, giant wooden hands, and now something that seemed worse than all the others combined.

"Well, here we are," said Furlus. "So what happens now?"

"Lannon will try the Eye from here," said Taris. "Not only may it save us time, but he could also discover any dangers lurking within."

"Then get on with it, Lannon," said Furlus.

Lannon nodded, but he dared not speak because he had doubts about whether or not he could utter a sound, so dry was his throat. He swallowed and fought to steady himself, trying to stop the trembling of his body. Taris spoke a few soothing, encouraging words, and Lannon slowly released the Eye into the graveyard.

Lannon tried to block out any images that did not pertain to his goal, but it wasn't easy. Phantom visions tried to force their way in, disrupting his focus, and he felt a deep revulsion that almost made him physically ill when he thought of that giant hand hunched somewhere in the hollow spaces below. He probed much of the Cemetery, and then extended the Eye beneath it as far as he was able, searching for an entrance to the mines. He ignored Taris' warning about stretching his gaze too thin, for he was desperate to complete his goal from beyond the fence. But his gaze could only go a short distance below ground once it neared the middle of the graveyard--certainly not deep enough to prove anything.

Before he drew the Eye back completely, Lannon summoned all his remaining courage and searched for the giant hand. It took all the will he possessed to bring himself to look for that horror, and he was grateful, in many ways, when he failed to find it. Much uncertainty remained, since he could not cover all the areas below ground from here, but now it wasn't difficult to persuade himself that the hand might have been a product of his imagination. After all, Taris claimed to know the ghosts that lurked within. Perhaps Lannon had misinterpreted one of them, or perhaps one of the ghosts had used its power to scare him with an illusion. Taris had said they sometimes tried to frighten people.

"I can't find an entrance," Lannon said. "But I don't see any dangers, either."

"Were you able to view all the crypts?" Taris asked.

Slowly Lannon shook his head, knowing what this would mean.

Immediately, Taris pulled out a ring of keys and unlocked the gate. "We shall begin near the center," the sorcerer said, "and then work our way out towards the edges. I have a strong suspicion a lost entrance lies in here somewhere, and so we must be thorough, Lannon. The fate of Dremlock may depend on it."

Lannon nodded, and with wobbly legs, he followed the Tower Masters into the Cemetery. The snow was deep here, having piled up over the course of the winter, but it was frozen into a crust that they were able to walk atop it. Some of the tombstones were just barely visible as they poked out of the snow, while other, more splendid ones towered overhead. With each step, Lannon imagined huge fingers exploding up through the crust and latching onto him, and he held the Eye of Divinity in a defensive posture, imagining that it was a shield protecting him from harm.

When they reached the middle of the Cemetery, they stood in the shadow of a stone tomb dedicated to a Lord Knight named

Harswald Greatsword. In spite of an inscription that told of Harswald's nobility and heroics, the tomb had a strange and ugly look, decorated with depictions of leering Goblin heads and grinning skulls at the base. Lannon was confused.

Taris smiled, as he watched the boy study the tomb. "Old Garthane," he said. "That is what we call this style. Garthane Goldenaxe did the design work on some of the tombs of this Cemetery, and several other places, including the East Library in my tower. He was an eccentric Olrog Knight, and fiercely stubborn--even by Dwarven standards. He had an exuberant personality, which contrasted his fantastic and grim sculptures. Throughout the ages, many have declared his work unfit for a holy kingdom like Dremlock. However, I very much like his work, and find it quite unique."

"Always time for a bit of history and philosophy," said Furlus, rolling his eyes, "when Taris Warhawk is present. Now are we going to stand here and freeze, or get on with our task? Last I knew, we were facing a possible invasion."

Taris nodded. "Begin your search, Lannon."

Lannon sent his gaze straight down, and about thirty feet below discovered a tunnel with a door of Glaetherin--protected by a wheel lock. The passageway had the unmistakable feel of the mines. The stone had been tunneled through around the door of Glaetherin, and in that tunnel was a man in his final stages of life. He wore stout black armor, yet he had been partially crushed, and he had crawled into that tunnel, where he lay bleeding away his life. Shocked at this sight, Lannon momentarily lost his control, and the Eye veered off in a random direction, going past the tunnel and into a large chamber--where an even more dastardly sight awaited Lannon.

The floor of the room was littered with corpses--black-armored men and women who had all been crushed and battered. Echoes remained of screams, pain, and terror. Some had escaped, fleeing off down the tunnels, vowing never to return. Other echoes crowded in, ancient and reeking of evil, and he grew sick to his stomach, doubling over. Too late, he realized he had stretched himself too thin, and for an instant, he found he could not draw his power back. He realized Taris was clutching his arm, mumbling strange words in his ear. The Eye suddenly retreated all the way into him.

"They're all dead!" Lannon panted, struggling to catch his breath. "Killed by something... Wait, one man is alive. He crawled into a tunnel, but he won't last long." For an instant, Lannon thought he was going to pass out. But then the sickness slipped away and he managed to stand up straight.

"Wait here," Taris said sternly, to Furlus. "I am going to go down and speak with the dying man. We need to know what caused this."

Furlus scowled, but knowing he needed to stay and protect Lannon, he did as Taris commanded. "Just hurry up!" he muttered.

Taris unlocked the tomb and entered, closing the door behind him. The lock clicked from inside.

The two waited in silence. Only Furlus' raspy breathing could be heard, as the Olrog's barrel chest rose and fell. He fidgeted restlessly, switching his battle axe from hand to hand.

Moments later, the lock clicked and Taris stepped out, carrying the dying man over his shoulder. Gently, Taris laid him in the snow, and then locked the tomb again. The sorcerer knelt over the wounded man.

The Black Knight was big fellow, as wide as Furlus and a foot taller, and his face was covered in a bushy red beard. His plate armor had been caved in, his bones broken beneath. The snow turned crimson around him.

The Black Knight smiled as he gazed at the heavens. "Open sky," he rasped. "Thank you, Birlote, for granting my last wish. "In return, I will answer your questions. Know this, however--I shall never betray my brothers."

"I understand," said Taris. "Was Tenneth Bard your leader?"

"Tenneth Bard?" said the Black Knight. "You speak a name I haven't heard since I was a Squire of your kingdom."

"A Squire?" said Taris. Then his eyes opened wide. "Thadin?"

The Black Knight nodded. "You should have recognized me sooner, sorcerer. I dwelt in your tower, until the High Council cast me out for a single incident of daring to enter a forbidden area. No second chances, just banishment."

"So you joined the Blood Legion?" Taris said quietly. "You

traded your honor because you felt wronged."

"No," said Thadin. "I wanted to be a Knight, and that is all. Most who join the Blood Legion are not as vengeful as you think-- they simply want the glory of Knighthood, and the Blood Legion offers that if Dremlock will not." He made choking noises for a moment, and coughed up blood. "Speak swiftly, sorcerer."

"Who is your leader?"

"Arnin Deathbringer, a powerful sorcerer."

"With eyes of violet?" Taris said.

Thadin nodded. "That is him. Does he yet live?"

Taris didn't answer. "Who slew your brothers, Thadin?"

"A fiend that Arnin raised from the depths," said Thadin. "We were supposed to be able to control it and use it to bring down Dremlock, but it went insane and attacked us. Now it is loose in the tunnels, seeking the blood of whoever it comes across."

"Describe it, Thadin," said Taris.

"Terrible beauty," Thadin said. "I know of no other way to tell of it. And now I say this... We are the Blood Legion, and we are mighty. Dremlock's time is nearing an end. Your victory will be a brief one, and soon enough, you'll come to understand why you cannot prevail against us. All is not as it appears to be. I have long suspected the truth, and I have feared it. But now, as I pass from this world, I have no fear. Let the future come swiftly, and let all so-called Divine Knights tremble in the face of--"

Thadin's eyes rolled back in death.

Chapter 20: Spiders, Honors, and Promotions

For nearly two weeks following what had occurred in Dremlock Cemetery, Lannon was confined with Vorden and Timlin to the East Tower, and they didn't see Aldreya at all during that period. They were permitted to leave their quarters only when absolutely necessary. (The same was true for all the less advanced Squires.) They didn't know what was happening around the kingdom--only catching bits of pieces of rumor that could not be substantiated.

Each evening, Lannon would lie awake for hours wondering if Dremlock had finished off the Blood Legion and the Goblin Lords, and the powerful fiend that had killed all those Black Knights, or if things had taken a turn for the worse. Many times he thought of his parents, so far away in Knights Valley and undoubtedly knowing nothing of what was happing at Dremlock. He believed his father would have been proud of how he had helped the Knights--even if their victory turned out to be short-lived.

And what of Kalamede? Had the city fallen, or were the Goblins driven back? Lannon could get no answers from the Knights, and the Eye of Divinity lay dormant, for he had no desire to call it forth at this point. He felt he needed to relax his mind, to recuperate from the great toll his use of the power had taken on his body. After each day of rest, he felt a little stronger and a little more energized.

Yet Vorden had begun to act strangely. When Lannon tried to talk about the questions that haunted his mind, Vorden acted as if he couldn't care less, brushing Lannon aside with a statement such as, "You worry too much, Lannon." Each night Vorden would take out his new sword and just stare at it--sometimes for hours. He seemed distant and irritable, and his once hearty appetite had diminished. He had lost weight and his skin looked pale.

When Lannon at last questioned him about it, Vorden insisted nothing was wrong, but Lannon wasn't fooled. Something else was wrong with Vorden, and there was no doubt in Lannon' mind it had to do with that dark blade.

Finally Lannon confronted him about it one night, demanding to know why he hadn't been himself lately.

"I told you," Vorden replied, rolling his eyes. "You worry too much. Why can't you just go find something to do?"

"You should get rid of that sword," Lannon said. "It came from the mines, and it can't be a good thing. And it's ugly looking, too."

Vorden glowered at him, placing his hands protectively over the sword. Lannon suddenly felt like he was staring at the face of total stranger. "Mind your own business, Lannon!" Vorden snapped. "This sword saved your life. It hurt Tenneth Bard when nothing else could. So quit complaining about it."

"I'm just saying--"

"Well, don't!" Vorden interrupted. He went back to staring at the sword. Suddenly, spiders seemed to be crawling on his face-- little shadowy ones. They appeared there for an instant, and then Lannon blinked his eyes and they were gone.

Had the spiders actually existed?

Vorden looked up. "I'm sick of having you stare at me like I'm a freak. So you want to know the truth? Fine! There is a shadow under this thing, Lannon. It interests me because it seems so full of depth. I don't know what it is. Sometimes when I watch it, it changes form. It's not really good, but I know it's not evil, either. It's not the Deep Shadow if that's what you're thinking. It's some kind of new thing--like no one has ever thought of. And I'm going to learn its secrets!"

"Just be careful," Lannon said, chilled to the bone.

***

Thirteen days after Tenneth Bard's death, the Squires were at last permitted to leave their quarters but not the East Tower. Lannon met in the Library with Aldreya and Timlin to talk things over. Lannon was grateful for this bit of freedom, for he knew it meant the Knights must be faring well in their war--yet always he felt like he was being watched by someone or something whenever he left his room.

"I think Vorden is becoming possessed," Lannon whispered. "All he does is lie around and stare at that stupid sword. I can't reason with him."

"Can you use your power to find out?" said Aldreya. "Also, you could take a look at the sword and learn if it's evil."

Lannon shook his head. "I haven't used the Eye of Divinity since we were down in the mines. I don't think I should right now."

"Why not?" said Aldreya. "If I had a power like that, I would use it. What is stopping you, Lannon?"

Lannon shrugged. In the back of his mind, he knew he should be practicing with the Eye now that he was rested, learning its secrets. But something was thwarting him--a deep fear he could not explain. He reasoned that although he felt better overall, he was still worn out mentally and required more rest.

"Maybe we should tell Master Garrin about Vorden," said Timlin. "Before Vorden ends up possessed like Clayith was."

"We should tell Taris instead," said Aldreya. "He would probably be more understanding than anyone else."

"I don't know," said Lannon. "I don't want Vorden to get banished. Maybe we should just steal the sword and get rid of it. He keeps it under his bed, wrapped in cloth. It wouldn't be hard to swipe it, except that he always stays near it. We'd have to get it while he's asleep--take it right out from under him."

"I can do it," said Aldreya. "No one will see me."

Lannon nodded. "Just be careful. Vorden is really obsessed with that sword. If he catches you stealing it, who knows what he might do?"

Aldreya smiled. "I can protect myself, Lannon."

"That's true enough," said Lannon, remembering Aldreya was a talented Birlote sorceress. "I guess I don't have to worry about that."

"I'll get the sword," she said, smoothing her silver hair away from her pointed ears. She smiled devilishly, and for the first time, Lannon saw the Tree Dweller in her very strongly. He did not doubt she would complete her goal.

But Aldreya never got a chance to prove her words, for soon

after their discussion, Vorden stepped into the Library. His color looked better, and he seemed like his normal self. "Talking about me?" he said, smiling.

The others said nothing, and exchanged glances. The tension was thick between them.

Vorden chuckled. "I got rid of that sword, you know--in case you were wondering. I tossed it down a well. I do think it was evil. I know I'm better off without it. I snuck outside late last night and dumped it. Hopefully, it sank deep into the mud and no one will ever find it down there."

Aldreya smiled "I'm glad you got rid of it. I was worried about you, Vorden. You have not seemed yourself, lately."

He shook his head in amusement. "Of course you were worried, Aldreya. You always worry about silly things, just like Lannon. But it's taken care of. The well swallowed it up...forever. It took a lot of strength to part with it, but I did it. Now I think everything's going to be okay."

The Squires glanced uncertainly at each other. Something about Vorden's expression seemed haunted and afraid for just an instant.

Then Vorden smiled, looking even more like his usual self. He smoothed his hair and adjusted his cloak. "Anyway, it's all done with. Believe me."

The Squires smiled back, and did believe.

***

Two days later, Lannon and his friends, including Jerret Dragonsbane, were summoned to the Temple to honor Caldrek. The smell of spring was in the air, and the snows were melting swiftly, as Taris came and led them to their destination. They were the only Squires called to attend--the rest of the people present were Knights. Taris explained that traditionally Squires were not allowed to participate in honoring ceremonies for Knights, but Cordus gave them special permission this time due to their recent heroics and because Caldrek had died protecting them. Lannon got up the nerve to question Taris, but the Tower Master refused to speak of anything concerning their war against the Goblins and the Blood Legion, saying that it would all be revealed at a feast that would take place a few days later.

Cordus, Furlus, and Taris were at the Temple, along with the rest of the High Council--save for Moten Goblinsbane. The broken lid of the altar had been replaced, and Caldrek's body lay atop it, bearing armor and sword. Cordus stood before the altar, and spoke to the crowd, telling of Caldrek's heroic deeds. Several others spoke as well, and by the time everyone was finished, Lannon and his friends were in awe of Caldrek and knew a great Knight had passed from the world. Caldrek was promoted to Green, with a unanimous vote from the High Council, and a sash bearing that Color was laid across his body.

Then the final ceremony began, in which Cordus took a bottle of white fluid and poured it over Caldrek's body. For a moment, nothing seemed to happen, but then the torches in the Temple all suddenly burned with white fire. A gasp of amazement arose from the Knights, and they bowed their heads as one.

Confused, the Squires did the same.

The torches returned to normal, and Cordus once again stood before the altar and spoke. "Behold!" he cried. "The Divine Essence has called upon Caldrek and blessed him, in an act not seen in more than a hundred years! His body shall be preserved for time untold for others to look upon."

Upon the altar, Caldrek's body had become encased in crystal.

***

For the next three days, almost all activity in Dremlock ceased, and people stayed indoors. This was a further gesture to honor Caldrek--along with all the other Knights who had died fighting for Dremlock.

On the fourth night, most of Dremlock was called to a huge feast in the Great Hall. It had been a warm day, with a light spring rain falling, and everyone seemed in good spirits as they gathered at tables. Though its warmth was hardly needed on this night, the huge fireplace was ablaze. Cordus Landsaver, dressed in his silver cloak, alone spoke at this gathering, before the food was served and the great celebration began.

"I have things to inform you of, Squires," the Lord Knight said. "I know that by now all of you are wondering just what is taking place in our war against the Goblins. I also know that all of you must have learned through rumor much of what we once sought to keep secret. But now the truth shall be known, so that afterwards, you may all focus on your training and put everything else out of your minds.

"First of all, the city of Kalamede was successfully defended by our Knights, and the Goblins driven deep into the Bloodlands."

Cheers erupted amongst the crowd, and Cordus smiled. "Secondly," he continued, "the evil below Dremlock has fled deep into the mines, and new doors of Glaetherin have been forged to replace the old ones. These doors bear more complicated wheel locks that require two wheel masters to solve, so Dremlock should be well protected from below. Also, we have taken other means, which I shall not mention, to protect our kingdom from any threat that might exist beneath us.

"The rumors that Tenneth Bard is alive," said Cordus, "or *was* alive, have turned out to be completely false. The Blood Legion was led by a sorcerer named Arnin, who was not even pretending to be Tenneth Bard, as a member of the Blood Legion informed us. As far as we can tell, Arnin had no connection to that long-dead Black Knight whatsoever. Arnin was slain some time ago in the mines. While it is true that all we could find was a pool of blood where his corpse once lay, the signs indicated he was dragged off by a Cave Troll and undoubtedly devoured. We certainly have nothing more to fear from him.

"And I have one more thing to add, before we begin a special promotion ceremony. Moten Goblinsbane is no longer on the High Council, and he will not be returning. Shennen Silverarrow has been promoted to Green and will replace him." Cordus motioned to Shennen, who stood up and bowed. The Birlote now wore a green cloak rather than a blue one. "And I believe," Cordus added, "Shennen will bring much honor to the High Council.

"Now, before we eat, I want Lannon Sunshield, Aldreya Silverhawk, Timlin Woodmaster, Vorden Flameblade, and Jerret Dragonsbane to come forward and stand before me." The Lord Knight spoke sternly, and the Squires hurried over to him, their hearts pounding anxiously.

"I have called you up here, Squires," said Cordus, "to commend you for your bravery in the mines. You did Dremlock a great service, and now you will be appropriately rewarded." Cordus smiled and winked at them. "Your sashes are looking rather dirty, Squires. Why don't you give them to me?"

Confused, the Squires removed their sashes and handed them to Cordus, while the other Squires grinned and whispered amongst themselves. The younger ones looked baffled, while the older ones exchanged knowing looks. The Lord Knight carried the sashes to the fireplace and, one by one, tossed them into the flames, while Lannon and his friends glanced at each other in uncertainty. Was the Lord Knight being sarcastic? Were they actually here to be punished rather than praised?

Turning back to them, an amused smile on his lips, Cordus said, "Fear not, Squires. We call this the Burning of the Sashes--an ancient ritual here at Dremlock. I have new sashes for you. Better ones."

Cordus nodded to an Orange Squire, who brought him a wooden box containing five new sashes. He handed one to each of the five Squires, while the spectators applauded loudly and vigorously. Each new sash had a single silver ribbon stitched onto it, as well as the Silver Axe insignia.

With trembling, excited hands, the Squires put on their new sashes. An Orange servant brought them a pitcher of water, and the Squires wetted the fabric, watching while their names appeared out of nowhere.

"The Silver Axe," said Cordus, "will allow you to perform limited Knightly duties. As to you other Squires who may be feeling a bit envious, you should know that Promotion Day is coming soon, when the rest of you shall have a chance to earn your silver ribbons. Now let our feast begin!"

As the Squires helped themselves to an abundance of delicious foods, Vorden glanced at Lannon and said, "Do you believe that, Lannon? Do you think it was actually someone other than Tenneth Bard?"

Lannon studied his friends' faces. Aldreya, Vorden, and Timlin watched him intently, and he knew they already believed it had been the Black Knight. Jerret, who hadn't actually confronted Tenneth Bard, watched with simple curiosity. Lannon thought back to the insane, violet eyes and then pictured the statue amid the ruins of Serenlock Castle in his mind, and he nodded. Even if the man hadn't spoken as if he were Tenneth Bard, the eyes alone were a giveaway.

"It was him," Lannon said. "I don't care what anyone says."

The others looked relieved. "I'm glad you think that," said Vorden, "because I know in my heart it was."

Timlin kept running his tiny hands over his sash.

"You're going to wear that thing out," laughed Vorden, "if you keep rubbing it that way. You'll make it unreadable."

"We're almost Knights now!" Timlin said excitedly.

"Not quite," said Jerret, grinning. "We still have a lot to learn, Timlin."

"But it is a step in the right direction," said Aldreya. "Now, if we do well during Promotion Day, we'll already have two ribbons."

"Why only two?" said Vorden. "I'm going for three altogether, at least. What about you, Lannon?"

"I'm happy I got this one," said Lannon. "That way if I don't get one on Promotion Day, at least I'll still have made progress."

Vorden shook his head. "I see not much has changed with you since the Color Trials, Lannon. You still lack confidence in yourself."

Lannon considered Vorden's words, and then dismissed them. Truthfully, a lot had changed--including some things deep within that he was perhaps barely aware of. Things had changed faster, and more thoroughly, than he had ever believed they would. Tenneth Bard's words echoed through his mind: *"Not over yet... Just beginning..."*

End.

Printed in Great Britain
by Amazon